MW00855917

FOUR RUBBINGS

JENNIFER L. HOTES

Booktrope Editions
Seattle WA 2013

Copyright 2013 Jennifer L. Hotes

This work is licensed under a Creative Commons Attribution-Noncommercial-No
Derivative Works 3.0 Unported License.

Attribution — You must attribute the work in the manner specified by the author or
licensor (but not in any way that suggests that they endorse you or your use of the
work).

Noncommercial — You may not use this work for commercial purposes.

No Derivative Works — You may not alter, transform, or build upon this work.

Inquiries about additional permissions should be directed to: info@booktrope.com

Cover Design by Jennifer L. Hotes

Edited by Toddie Downs

*This is a work of fiction. Names, characters, places, brands, media, and
incidents are either the product of the author's imagination or are used
fictitiously. Any resemblance to similarly named places or to persons living
or deceased is unintentional.*

PRINT ISBN 978-1-62015-163-1
EPUB ISBN 978-1-62015-259-1

For further information regarding permissions, please contact
info@booktrope.com.

Library of Congress Control Number: 2013947204

This book wouldn't have been realized without the unfettered enthusiasm and support of the three people I love most in the world; my husband, Doug and daughters, Ellie and Bryn. You are my mirror, and when I look at myself through you I see something better. Thank you.

Thanks to my team at Booktrope Publishing with a fierce shout-out to my editor, Toddie Downs. You employed sharp eyes and gut-busting humor to keep me combing the words to make them better.

Thank you to my brave beta-readers. Next time, don't be so kind. And Dad, you did good.

And finally, to the invisible scaffolding around my life, my friends and family. Thanks for cheering me on and enduring the frayed version of me as I learned to be a writer.

GRACE TOPPLES
THE FIRST DOMINO

WHY DO PEOPLE have to mess with the dead on Halloween anyway? They're dead. Respect the dead. Didn't their folks teach them any better? I squint into the distance at a cluster of folks standing inside the cemetery gates.

"I'll scare them good and give them a piece of my mind along the way," I mumble as I stomp the three hundred or so yards it takes to reach the cemetery entrance from my caretaker's cottage. Can't help but think if I had just done my job in the first place, I wouldn't be standing knee-deep in a pile of trouble right now.

Not five minutes ago I'd stood staring out the kitchen window watching a dull, dreary day change into something better. Leafless gray trees framed an orange and white fireball sky, framed it like iron gates, and that is when I'd remembered. Damn, Grace.

Ten years of watching over Lakefront Cemetery and tonight of all nights I'd forgotten to lock the gates. My forty-year-old bones felt soggy from a day of rain-chilled grave tending. Clearly, I was thinking more about a hot bath and a cup of warm cider than doing my job. Ah, well. With an hour before sunset, I'd figured I had plenty of time to put things right.

I'd found my mud-caked work boots and damp flannel coat piled on the back porch where I'd shed them an hour ago. As I shoehorned my boots onto bare feet, I'd spotted a group gathering at the cemetery entrance. I checked my watch. Five o'clock seemed awful early to start Halloween trouble, but there they were. I made out four bodies, four or five. Couldn't tell for certain without my glasses, and I wasn't willing to trudge back through the cottage with muddy boots to collect them up. I'd know soon enough.

As I stomp across the grounds, I rehearse what I will say. I'll give them a lecture about respecting the dead, then shoo them off speedy quick. All worked up, I don't pay no mind to the noise my boots make as I dodge headstones and thunder through wet leaves and mud. I want them to hear me coming and be afraid. Too bad I don't have time to go back for my hefty flashlight, or better yet, a rusty shovel, to shake at them. Boy, the stories they could tell their friends tomorrow about the crazy cemetery lady and her wicked shovel.

"You'll all think twice about coming around here again after I get through with you," I spit into the wind.

As I near, I see they're decked out in costumes. I count four of them, teenagers, of course. It's mostly the teens that make trouble around here. I duck behind the Yessir's family tomb to get a better look. "Sorry if I'm blocking your view, folks," I whisper.

I steal quick peeks around the white marble structure and make out an oversized superhero, a football player, Pocahontas and some kind of dapper fella.

Pocahontas, a tiny copper-headed girl, is giving them instructions. I can't hear everything she says, but catch phrases like, "Let a stone call you…. open your heart…. connect with the person buried underneath…"

She doesn't sound like my typical vandal rat; I give her that much credit. I rub my chest where a knot has formed and lean in closer to catch the gist of her words.

The girl reaches into a tan leather pouch and hands around oversized pieces of paper and chunks of black chalk, not the toilet paper and spray paint I expect to see. Art supplies. My knees give out as the truth dawns on me. They've come to rub the stones. They've come to remember the dead, not hurt 'em.

The breath I didn't know I'd been holding bursts from my mouth. My eyes cloud over. My calloused hands ball into sweaty fists and shake. My cheeks burn with shame. I've been wrong about these kids, pegged them as vandals when they are bent on doing something good. I fall apart, but gather it all up again quick. I am wrong and have to atone. Good thing I'm already down on my knees.

It's been so long since I've said any kind of prayer. Too long. I'm clumsy about how best to place my hands, how far to bow my head, and how to muster the words. But I close my eyes, and feel warm tears roll down my cheeks. I send a prayer up to the God I've been cursing for the past decade.

"Let them have a journey, Lord, a journey that begins with remembering the dead and rubbing a stone. Amen."

JOSIE LEADS THE
TRICKS AND TREATS

IT IS HALLOWEEN, the night the dead speak, and as I walk with my three best friends to Lakefront Cemetery, my overactive imagination has me convinced that the whistle of the wind is not wind at all. It is the graves five blocks away whispering to be rubbed. Imagination is my blessing and my curse, I suppose. It's the magic ingredient that helps me sketch interesting pictures, and the poison granules that nurture my wild, vivid nightmares.

Nightmares like the one I had last night; in it, my friends and I stumbled into Lakefront. I got separated from them and had to walk alone to find a grave to rub, my mother's grave. As I cut across the dark grounds I fell, nearly tumbling into a wide, open grave. I gawked into the hole and as my eyes adjusted to the darkness, a silhouette formed in the shadows.

Goosebumps erupt down my arms at the memory. Imagination, meh.

"Bye, Josie!" shouts my little seven-year-old brother, Owen, from half a block away. "Watch out for zombies tonight. They prowl cemeteries looking for brains to eat, you know!" With dramatic flair, he hops away on one foot, his yellow alien antennae bobbing above a crown of red curls. His neon green costume hurts my eyes and I huff with relief as he grabs our father's hand and skips off to beg the neighbors for candy. Owen is a great kid, but tonight his happy energy makes me want to shrink into the background. I am worried the evening will not go as planned.

My father sends the group of us off with a hearty, "Good luck!" and jogs away with the boy.

My friends do what I don't think to; they wave goodbye and make spooky noises at Owen's back. His high, soprano giggles burst through the muggy air and sprinkle around our feet like confetti.

I brush off the tops of my moccasins and give the suede pouch at my side a quick pat to make sure the tube that sticks out of the top is still tucked safely inside. The rubbing kit feels too heavy for something made up of paper, charcoal, and tape. Maybe the weight is due to the heavy load of desperation I slipped in at the last minute and the cracked rubber band of hope that binds everything together.

"You sure your father's up for trick-or-treat duty, Josie?" asks Blaze, a six-foot boy/man dressed in a tight blue shirt, crimson cape, and knee-high white boots. The light blue shirt makes his bronze skin glow. He is really working the superhero vibe tonight. I grin as I think how close he came to having his own Mini-Me. Owen's runner-up costume–a red cape, blue unitard, glossy white boots and all–lie across his bedroom floor back home.

"Yeah, he'll be fine. I made them a map of the route so Dad won't get lost. Even wrote down some of the rules he might not know, like 'Check candy before eating,' that sort of thing."

"Jeez! Who do you think took you trick-or-treating when you were little? They'll be fine," scolds Casey. Worry lines ripple across her porcelain forehead. Her tiny form is swallowed up by the gigantic football jersey and oversized white pants she wears.

"Actually, my mother always took us trick-or-treating. Well, technically, she was only able to bring Owen out once before she died," I whisper, trying to cap any conversation about my mother that might make me cry. But more gushes out before I can put a cork in it. "And then after that it was always me, you know, that took Owen."

Casey drops her gaze to her cleats and lets a curtain of black hair fall over her pretty face. She hides behind her hair when she feels bad, easy to do when you are growing out your bangs. With a tight laugh, she stuffs a battered gold helmet on her head. And I feel guilty because it should be okay to bring up my mother, but for some reason it never goes well.

If I should be able to bring up my mother with anyone, it is these three people. We've been friends since we were first born. They've seen me through teething, potty training, first days of school and my mother's illness. And this same group of friends didn't even laugh when I suggested we rub tombstones for Halloween. But at fourteen, our options are limited. Trick-or-treating is out of the question. So are high school parties. And who wants to stay at home and give out candy?

Last night, instead of finishing my Spanish assignment, I called and texted the others to set a plan for Halloween: meet at my house for dinner, walk ten blocks to Lakefront, rub graves, and then hit the coffeehouse. They said it sounded like fun. Sure. Fun. To me, though, tonight means more than that. I'm losing her. My mother has been dead six years now and my memories of her are blurring into nothing. And her voice, I can't even remember it anymore. Why couldn't I have inherited her voice?

That is why the dream I had last night bothers me. The bit about the body in the grave is just par for the course when it comes to my nightmares. I close my eyes and give in, letting the dream play back in my mind.

* * *

Razor-thin scratches crisscross my pale hands as i struggle to unroll a long, stiff tube of paper across the craggy stone face of the grave. My hands burn and itch as I tape the gossamer-thin sheet onto the rough granite. The wind flares and animates the paper, making it dance and flutter, and erases my progress in a moment. Determined, I clutch the paper against the stone with a white fist and rub the surface with a chunk of damp charcoal. My mother's name, Sarah Jameson, emerges in white voids between black strokes.

The granite angel that stands vigil over my mother's tombstone stares down at me. The hint of a smile curls the corners of her lips like she is holding in a secret. Raindrops collect on her face and spill from her eyes like human tears. They fall onto the rubbing and transform into soupy gray pools. I try to erase the moisture with my sleeve and instead drop the charcoal, which disappears into the plush mossy grass below. A fierce gust rips the paper off the tombstone and sends it spiraling into the sky. I run to

*catch up with the paper but trip on the lumpy ground and must cling to
wet grass to keep from falling into a wide, dark hole.*

*Heart pounding, I kneel over the open grave and hold my breath in to
avoid inhaling the sulfur that steams up from the earth. My eyes adjust to
the shadows in the hole and I make out a figure. Someone lies face down in
the dirt! I stumble back to get away and look up in time to see the white
rubbing shrink into the night sky, soon disappearing entirely. Hot tears
slide down my cheeks, and as I wipe them away, the cuts across my hand
burst with pain.*

* * *

Losing my rubbing cannot happen. I need to leave with a piece
of my mother tucked away in my leather satchel tonight. I desperately
need a fresh memory I can cling to for the next six years.

As we approach the rusty wrought-iron gate that stands guard over
Lakefront Cemetery, the knot in my jaw loosens. To my great relief, the
gate stands wide open. In spite of all my planning, the one thing out of
my control was the lock. I've been saved from the embarrassment of
pushing three people over a slippery six-foot obstacle.

What's that saying? Thank heaven for little favors? *I got mine*, I
think, as I stare into the sky. Casey lays a hand on my shoulder. The
warmth seeps into the thin suede fabric of my costume and I smile.

They are my three favorite people in the world, the Baby Group.
We call ourselves that not to be cute, but because it is where we first
met. We were four screaming babies in a hospital parenting group
attended by our mothers, who had the same tendency to run late and
have to grab the last scrap of open carpet available. We have grown
up together and I love them.

A ray of sunshine cuts through a mass of charcoal clouds and
shines down on us. The sky is streaked with an orange and grey that
reminds me of a smoldering campfire without the smoky odor. The
air is wet and the wind is gusty. We'll need to work fast. I rub my
hands together, more from excitement than cold, and then I stop. I've
picked up this little hand rubbing quirk from Seth. We are morphing
into one person, the Baby Group and me.

Seth cocks his head and notices me shivering. "Take this, Josie! You must be freezing," he says as he offers a soft, weatherworn pilot's jacket.

I shrug off the gesture. Seth is looking old-school dapper in pinstripe charcoal pants, button-down white shirt, black bolo tie and gray top hat. His ever-changing hair color is currently a bleached blonde. Before I can stop myself, I reach out and wrap a stray curl around my finger.

"So, how's your dad liking the new dye-job?" I ask, letting the curl spring free.

A gust of wind pushes through the cemetery gates and slaps my naked legs. The brisk air cuts through my skimpy costume and leggings. Too late, I wish I had taken Seth's jacket.

I need the comfort of his coat around my shoulders. I need the warmth, the kindness behind his gesture to keep me strong for the evening's activity. I brought the four of us here tonight to try and communicate with the dead: to rub a tombstone, remember someone long forgotten, and wait for a sign, a sign that says, "I'm still here, just not as flesh and bone."

Last night it seemed so possible, like something remarkable could happen. Now though, my feet are cemented in reality, well reality and doubt. When did everything change? It was that damn dream that did it!

I choke in fresh air and feel the hair rise on the back of my neck. The world seems like it is starting to spin around me and I bend over, not sure if I am about to faint. Casey asks if I am all right and I feel her hand stroke my back. As always, she is here for me. The warmth, like the time Dad snuck me rum-laced eggnog, begins in my cheeks and spreads down the length of my body until my mind clears again.

Blaze bounces from leg to leg. "When are we going to do this thing?"

If he were Owen, I would remind him to hit the potty. Instead, I blink to rearrange myself into the person my friends expect to see, the leader of the Baby Group. After all these years, it comes as easy as breathing. Roll the shoulders. Review the plan. Take a breath. Teach.

"We'll start now. Everyone gets a roll of tape, a piece of paper, and a chunk of graphite. After we split up, find a grave. When you find one, tape the paper over the face of the tombstone. Then, use the side of the graphite to rub the surface. Make sure to go over the whole tombstone, top to bottom. The paper I'm giving you is super thin, so be careful not to rip it as you rub. When you finish, we'll all meet back here. Then we'll head to the coffeehouse to warm up and talk."

I scan the group to make sure everyone's clear, and I see that Blaze has Seth in a headlock and I grit my teeth. Seth's ears poke out from beneath Blaze's elbow.

"Come on guys! This is serious!" *Damn.* I know this night does not hold the same importance for them as it does for me, but I feel my resolve to be patient crumble around my feet.

"Relax, Josie. Have some fun, man. I'm a superhero tonight! It's my job to rid the planet of evil scum like this blood-sucking vampire!" Blaze shouts. His scarlet cape ripples out from behind his broad shoulders like a cartoon character. He flings Seth's felt hat to the side and rubs his knuckles into Seth's two-toned hair and chuckles.

Seth, still in a headlock, grimaces up at me with "Help" written all over his tortured face. He chokes out, "I don't ..," but stops as a foam ball pops out of his copper-colored Nerf gun, bounces off a white obelisk, and rolls into the shadows. Seth wriggles free and chases after his ball, flashing me a sheepish glance. "Sorry."

"Man, Seth! This isn't a joke. And for God's sake, control your props," I bark.

When he smiles, I see the hint of a fang glint from behind plump pink lips. A gold pocket watch falls free from his trousers as he joins the group. He tucks the watch away, reloads his gun and glances down at me with bright green eyes filled with contrition. He tucks his gun back inside the holster and tucks his curls under the brim of his hat.

"Why does a vampire need a gun anyway?" Casey asks, touching a finger to the bumpy copper details. "Isn't that a little redundant? Fangs *and* a gun?"

"Nice use of those PSAT words!" Blaze jokes.

Seth pushes Casey's hands off the copper gun. "It is not redundant. First, I stun my victim with this, and then I suck their blood with these babies." Seth smiles wide and his pointed teeth shine. "Mmwaahaahaa." He stares into my puckered face and quiets.

"Sorry, Josie. You were saying something about choosing a grave, right?" Seth asks. "How will I know which grave to rub?"

I grumble under my breath and bite my tongue to keep from spewing something mean and parental. I clear my throat and finish the instructions in the sweetest voice I can muster. "Choosing the right grave is the most important part of tonight's activity." My mind flits to my mother's grave up the hill. "So, after you get your supplies, walk around the grounds. As you walk, try to shut everything else out of your mind and let a stone call you. I'm hoping everyone will be drawn to a grave. Before you do your rubbing, I want you to try and connect with the person buried there.

"Stroke your hands over the headstone. Lie across the grave. Pray. Meditate. Do whatever seems right at the time. Make an effort to open your heart to that person, and see if they find a way to speak back to you. Then, you'll be ready to rub the stone."

Like ripping a Band-Aid off a fresh wound, saying my secret graveside ritual aloud leaves me sore and breathless. Tweaked and honed over six years of visits with my mother, this is the first time I have shared this side of my life, the Josie that lies across a grave and prays for some tiny indication that Sarah Jameson still exists in some form.

I rub my neck to erase the blotches that erupt across my throat when I am upset and finger my mother's ring through my dress. Hidden under a layer of cheap brown suede, the ring hangs from a chain and acts as my lucky talisman. It does the trick and my hands settle. I dole out supplies to the group.

Blaze scans the grounds with alert, sparkling gold eyes. He stuffs his supplies into his pockets and tucks the roll of paper into a scarlet cape. "Do you guys feel that? It's like the air around us is filled with electricity!" He brushes a hand across his skin-tight shirt and touches a finger to the thunderbolt taped to his chest. Of course, the bolt is made of gold duct tape; Blaze is obsessed with the stuff.

"Yeah, electricity," I mumble. I am anxious to get on with the activity, but something about Blaze's eager puppy dog expression makes me laugh. "So, Blaze, I've got to ask. Why the jeans? Aren't superheroes supposed to wear tights?"

Without warning, Blaze grabs me and lifts me high over my head, and I shriek and flail in the air like a fool. I should be pissed, but I am not. The only thing that worries me is losing my stuff, especially Owen's old teddy bear. "Watch it, Blaze! Baby Sacagawea is going to fall!" I squirm and kick, but he keeps me high above the ground and I laugh, letting myself act fourteen.

Still holding me over his head, Blaze smiles. "Josie, I was being merciful when I picked jeans," he grunts. "You ladies couldn't handle this beautiful form in tights."

He sets me back down to earth and does a little chest flexing while I tuck the chain with my mother's ring safely away again.

"Tonight, I am the invincible Captain Blaze!"

A gust of wind blows past and twists his cape around his throat. The rest of us chuckle as he fumbles to unknot the fabric from around his throat. I double-check that Baby Sacagawea is still inside Owen's backpack and then collect the pieces of charcoal that fell free during the superhero melee.

"Mother Nature – one, Captain Blaze – zero," says Casey. "I expected more from a superhero!"

"Yeah, well. What you see is what you get, a cheap knockoff," Blaze answers.

The last of the happy feeling I felt as I hung in the air above Blaze's head slips away. I glance into the cemetery and cross my fingers in my sleeve. Give me something to remember tonight, Mom.

Since the cancer took my mother from me six years ago, I've fought to remember her. But now, after all this time, I'm left with next to nothing, traces of memories held together by a web of fiction, things I make up to fill in the gaps. When my aunt gave me a rubbing kit for Halloween, I knew it was a chance to make a new memory with my mother. I let myself make one last childish wish, take one last puff on a dandelion that's gone to seed. I let myself hope.

"*Close your eyes and wish, Josie,*" I imagine her whispering.

"You didn't mention all this 'Let a stone choose you,' stuff last night," Casey says as she chews the inside of her lip. She takes a nervous peek behind her before tossing a battered football in the air.

"You sure seem jumpy, girl," Seth says.

She fidgets with the football. "It's just that I've never been to a cemetery before. My parents thought I was too young to go to your mother's funeral." The ball flies at my face and I bat it away as it grazes my cheek. Casey holds me by the shoulders and checks to see if I am fine.

"Jeez, I'm so sorry!" she says. "Are you okay? Dang, it's not even safe for me to dress as an athlete! I still manage to hurt people." She gives a sheepish grin behind the helmet and casts her eyes to the ground.

Seth says, "Maybe you should leave the sports to your brother, huh?" The famous Drew Starbaugh, older brother of largely ignored, mostly forgotten Casey, is on every sports highlight reel these days, thanks to his stellar college quarterbacking skills.

"Yeah, probably," Casey answers. "Speaking of brother, I hope mine doesn't take a trip down memory lane any time soon. He'll get a head full of graphite dust if he puts this sucker on," she giggles as she stuffs the art supplies inside the helmet.

"Oh, don't worry. His head's too big to fit into that thing anymore." Seth says.

"True enough," says Casey. She quickly readjusts her crimson jersey and touches a finger to the black grease paint beneath her eyes leaving a smear down her cheek like a smudge of ash.

"Well, I think we better head out," I command.

I feel reckless, ready to take my chances. My heart races as my thoughts flicker back to the dream. I picture a dandelion puff before me and mentally blow the seeds into the wind.

As we go separate ways into the cemetery, a slick black crow glides past us at eye level and sings, "Caw! Caw!" The bird takes me by surprise and I stumble.

"What was that?" Casey shouts.

"Just a crow, that's all," Blaze answers.

We give a collective giggle and fracture four ways onto the cemetery grounds.

JOSIE AND THE FLUFFY DISTRACTION

MY MOCCASINS TRAVEL ON AUTOPILOT to the grave of Sarah Jameson. As the others shrink into the landscape, I wait for a sweet blast of relief to hit me–the old, familiar one that comes after everyone is taken care of, and I get to focus on me. But nothing happens.

A stone sits in the pit of my stomach and acid bubbles around it. I am worried. Last night I looked up YouTube videos on séances. I lit candles around my room and propped up a picture of my mother in the center of them, a photo from back when she had hair. I asked her to make the candles flicker if she was near. Nothing. My inane experiment confirmed six years of epic failures. I try to reach out to her, I wait for signs, I use the ghost app on my phone to collect evidence that might confirm she still hovers around my life, but I have gotten nothing. No whiffs of her perfume when I visit her grave, no quiet whisperings as I paint in her art shack, no feelings of closeness when I struggle to fall back asleep after a bad dream. Nothing.

I am hoping tonight will be different. The date on the calendar says Halloween. A rubbing kit given to me by my mom's sister, a group of friends, and a heart-felt prayer might come together to make some kind of magic thing happen. But, only thirty minutes in and I already feel the hope leaking out of me like a balloon with a pinhole. I'm a leaky, suede-fringed balloon. Curse this stupid costume. Curse Halloween. Curse hope.

When I called and texted the others to set the plan, Seth gave me a quick rundown of the history of Halloween, because that is what he does. He memorizes facts about everything. The part that stuck with me is that October 31st was once thought to be the day when the barrier between the living and the dead became paper-thin; in fact, people originally dressed as spirits to blend in with all the ghostly visitors. Seth's facts gave me hope. I crossed my fingers and hoped that tonight would turn out differently.

"Is the barrier thin enough? Can you come through tonight, Mom?" I ask the wind. "Please meet me at your grave."

As I near the gnarled, ancient cedar that stands guard over her remains, I watch my step to keep from breaking my neck on the exposed roots and rocks that riddle the surface of her grave. Every time I visit, they seem to have bubbled closer to the surface and threaten to break an ankle.

Sarah Jameson rests midway up a central hill that separates the haves from the have-nots. Realtors might describe her plot as boasting a peekaboo view of Lake Washington, but a dense growth of pines along the shore leave most of that view to the imagination.

I study my mother's grave. A granite angel kneels on the headstone and weeps, her face buried in her hands. There is no trace of the smile I saw in my dream last night. Feather wings spread out behind the angel's slight shoulders. Before my head can catch up with my heart, I run a finger across the feathers etched into the stone. The bumpy chevrons flow from one to the next and tickle my fingertips. I love the wings, always have.

The angel stoops over a smooth, black stone heart that reads:

> *Sarah Jameson.*
> *1968-2006*
> *Heaven rejoice!*
> *Our angel walks with you now.*

As I kneel down, I notice the brown, withered flowers that slump over the sides of the vase. The vibrant sunflowers we brought for her birthday only a few weeks ago have exploded with rotting gray seeds. I dig my nails into my palms to keep from tossing the dead bouquet behind a bush. The leaves crawl with gnats and tiny worms that feast on the fetid offering. "You guys are glad I forgot fresh flowers, aren't you?" I say, content to leave the rotten bouquet in place.

I stretch out across the grave, tossing my satchel and backpack to the side. Goosebumps erupt down my naked arms and legs as the back of my head sinks into the damp, yielding grass that forms a mossy pillow. I suck in the air that hangs thick around my face, a mix of rotting leaves and smoky sweet mulch that tickles my nose and makes me sneeze.

After blessing myself, I cross my legs at the ankles. I close my eyes and picture the porcelain white vault below that encases the last of my mother's earthly remains. I imagine the cedar roots that have wrapped around her coffin by now, blotting out the delicate gold leaf details entirely. I think about my mom the gardener, tucked inside the roots of a tree, and smile.

"Most of my memories of you are tied to our garden." My voice comes out scratchy and weird. "You bought me miniature tools, so I could work alongside you, remember? A lot of help I turned out to be! I was a little weed factory, that's all I was."

A wet, rib-wracking laugh bursts out, and I cover my mouth. I wipe away a happy tear and take a quick look around to make sure no one is within earshot. Fortunately, tombstones wouldn't know crazy if it came up and bit them.

"Of course, I *had* to love dandelions more than any other flower, so you let them grow. And when they turned into puffballs, you let me make wishes and scatter the seeds across your pristine garden. You always said, 'I hope you wished for more dandelions.'" I smile at the memory, one of only a handful that has its roots in reality. There are so few of them left now.

"All right. Let's get started," I whisper.

Desperate to make the ritual work, I concentrate on opening my heart. I paint a vivid mental picture of my mother, plucked from fuzzy memories and fading photographs. In this particular time capsule, I'm seven years old and she snuggles next to me as we lie in a pink canopy bed. Her lush copper hair drapes over her shoulders still. It was before the days when she hid her chemo-ravaged head with scarves.

She wears a soft white t-shirt with a giant grinning cheeseburger emblazoned across the front and a pair of fuzzy plaid pajama pants. Her eyes glint with mischief as she looks down at me to ask which book I want first.

My tiny hands reach for *The Runaway Bunny*. Her arms, tan and muscled from a summer of tending a community pea patch, wrap around my body and open the worn board book. The thick spine creaks as she turns to the first page and I nestle deeper into her.

My small hands nest inside hers as we hold the book open together. *Team Jameson.* Resting her chin gently on the top of my head, she begins to read a book we both know by heart. Her voice vibrates down my back, and her warm breath washes over me like a blessing as she whispers, "Once there was a little bunny who wanted to run away. So he said to his mother, 'I am running away.' 'If you run away,' said his mother, 'I will run after you. For you are my little bunny.'"

These are the words I need to hear most. "If you become a crocus in a hidden garden... I will be a gardener. And I will find you.... If you become a bird and fly away.... I will be a tree that you come home to."

The day we shared this book also brought the news of my mother's cancer, and her dire prognosis. So today, my favorite baby book brings me a special comfort. She won't die. Mothers don't die. She will be here to watch my whole life, because I need her. That's what mothers do.

As she closes the book, I lean into her chest and soak in the scent of her so I will never forget: baby powder, sunshine, and coffee. She kisses the top of my head and tucks a curl behind my ear. "I will always find you, Josie. Before you were born, our hearts were stitched together in heaven. I'll always be this close." She lays her hand across my bony rib cage.

Lying on her grave, I bite the inside of my cheek to keep from crying and taste blood. I hold a hand over my ribs and ache to feel a trace of the string that ties our hearts together, but all I feel is cheap fringe and fake beads. The cold, wet grass beneath my body sets a chill down the length of me. My fingers tingle to hold her hand again. Our hands would be the same size now.

Tears flood my eyes before I can stop them, spill onto freckled cheeks, and slip to the grass below my head. It takes effort to make my voice come out. "I try to keep you alive for Owen, but I don't think it's working. And Dad... he's still so incredibly sad. He's sleepwalking through life and there's nothing I can do about it. I try, but you did everything so much better than I can. I try my best, Mom, but I'm not enough."

My whole body shakes as I weep. I cover my face with my hands and let it all come up to the surface, like the roots under my back. "I miss you."

I hear movement behind me, and before I can sit upright, something big lands squarely on my gut. Without a thought, I jump to my feet and scream. A furry gray ball catapults off of me onto the ground, landing on top of the satchel. I see a pair of giant, black eyes gleaming on a smoky gray cat. My heart pounds as I watch him wiggle his bottom and pounce on the rotting sunflowers in one smooth motion. Seeds fly every which way. Laughing and crying all at once, I reach down to stroke his shiny gray fur, fur so gray it appears blue. My pulse slows with every stroke across his bunny-soft back.

"Where'd you come from, little guy? Are you lost?" The cat pushes his head against the palm of my hand in answer. "Oh! I love your curly blue fur. I've never seen a cat with curls before."

I scratch him under the chin and he lifts it higher to permit better access. A deep purr vibrates under my hand.

"You're a sweetheart," I coo.

He takes me in with shimmering yellow eyes and I stare back. Something tight and hard under my ribs breaks free and I smile, and then laugh. The cat tilts his head sideways and his batty ears flick backward.

"I know! I'm crazy," I confess.

"Caw! Caw! Caw!" A loud clamor comes from the branches above us. Out of instinct, I crouch over the cat to protect him from a greasy black crow that dives at our heads. The cat shoots out from beneath me and sprints away into deeper parts of the cemetery as I try not to fall on my face. The crow races off to hunt him down, and I clap my hands and shout, "Leave him alone!"

The crow spins in the air and circles back toward me. The bird swoops past my head, his glassy black eyes stay fixed on mine. He turns in a graceful spiral and lands on the cedar branch that dangles over my mother's grave. His whole body arches as he caws, over and over. I cover my ears to block out the shrill noise.

A black feather falls and spirals through the air and lands across my moccasins. I pick up the feather and tuck it behind my ear; all the while his caws and shrieks continue. I scan the grounds for the cat and catch a quick movement in the distance. The silhouette of a cat darts to the outer edge of the cemetery. Determined to find my new friend, I scoop up my leather pouch and race toward the smoky blur while I wave a hand over my head to shoo away the crow that follows me from the air.

CASEY THE PRETENDER AND A PINT-SIZED GRAVE

TYPICAL OF ANY OCTOBER in the Pacific Northwest, the weather tonight is soggy and blah. A steady spray of mist silently soaks my football jersey, an irritating rain we locals call spit. Not worth the trouble of opening an umbrella. Not worth spit. Kind of like me.

It was the perky Mylar balloons that drew me to the far corner of the graveyard after we split up, not some psychic mumbo jumbo like Josie predicted. My English teacher would have called the balloons "garish," a good college-prep word. Bobbing above the graves, the balloons put a tacky coating on what had to be the children's cemetery. That's right. I didn't need a sign to tell me; pint-sized plots, lamb-adorned headstones, and stuffed animals were a dead giveaway. No pun intended.

As I struggle to remember why I agreed to spend the night in a cemetery, my cleats sink another half inch into the soft, muddy earth. I hope I'm not stepping on anyone. But then I remember. Josie talked me into this. Truth be told, she didn't have to try very hard. As our unofficial entertainment director, Josie notoriously plans the perfect activities for the Baby Group—well, usually. This one is not so fabulous. But, with my folks off at some benefit for a new pet charity, I had nothing else to do tonight. Actually, my parents probably assumed I would hand out candy at the house. No way I was doing that, so I agreed to come on Josie's little adventure.

I didn't ask permission, I didn't leave a note. If I'm lucky, they will notice I am gone and get pissed. Doubtful, though. I'm the invisible woman in my own family. Take my birthday, for example; between my brother's all-important football schedule and Thanksgiving, my birthday is mostly celebrated with a candle stuck in the middle of a leftover pumpkin pie. Don't even get me started on the presents. I usually receive something impersonal, like a gift card wrapped inside a new sweatshirt from my brother's university bookstore. Are they hinting I should go there? As if. The point is, I'm an afterthought, not a special event.

So, when Josie's arty aunt gave her a tombstone rubbing kit to celebrate Halloween, I admit I was a little jealous. Yes, I envy my friend who receives gifts on random holidays. I hate her a little, too.

Still, she's my best friend, which is why I was the first one she called last night to toss around the idea.

"Casey, what do you think about rubbing tombstones? Do you think the gang will go for it?" she asked.

"A cemetery on Halloween? Are you crazy?" I said. "I'm not so sure about that. You know what my parents would say? We will bring home spirits with us. Disturbing the dead for no good reason brings massive bad luck."

"Yeah, well. So, you're going to let your mother's Chinese superstitions keep you home? I can't believe you, Casey!"

"Well, if you knew about the hungry ghosts, you would listen to me. I don't want to go," I said.

Josie tapped on the cell phone. *Tap, tap, tap.* "So what are you going to do instead? Stay home. Alone?"

"Nice."

"I'm sorry, Casey but, I really want to do this. I have a good feeling about it. We'll have fun, I promise. And you can sleep over after," she coaxed.

"Fine," I answered. It wasn't worth fighting about.

Josie picked Lakefront as the venue, said it was the closest cemetery to her house or something. We would meet at her place around three, finish our costumes and then head to Lakefront. I wasn't completely sold, but the thought of being left behind was enough to convince me.

At present, I stand under a knotty apple tree, helpless as my brother's old football jersey gets slowly drenched by the spit. I am such a chump. My brother's stiff white pants from sixth grade football (when his epic career began) keep sliding down my skinny legs, even with the laces cinched as tight as humanly possible across my waist. And by now, I'm sure the grease paint beneath my eyes is smeared, making me look like a benchwarmer for the losing team. Perfect.

His ancient uniform doesn't fit, but it is the only one I could find without our last name plastered across the back. I don't want other people to know I'm the lackluster little sister of the nation's premier college quarterback, Drew Starbaugh. It's best to fly under the radar when I can.

This dwarf apple tree I stand under knows a thing or two about pretending to be something it's not. Spindly, misshapen branches reach out every which way but make a horrible umbrella for the pint-sized graves below. Dotted with buds that might bring a little cheer in April, I know the branches will be stripped clean in the next good downpour. The cursed blossoms remind me of all the bones buried under my feet, tiny bones that never got the chance to grow. I swear I can feel tiny bones poking into the soles of my shoes.

If this was my cemetery, I'd chainsaw the apple tree to the ground or, better yet, take an axe to its trunk. Then I'd hire a chainsaw artist to carve a chubby bear out of the stump. Now that would be an improvement. This place is depressing, and reading the tombstones makes me feel worse.

Born: February 2003; Died: July 2003.
Born: October 2010; Died: December 2011.

The tombstones go on and on. My mouth dries up like I have been sucking the Mr. Thirsty straw at the dentist's office too long, and as I squat down I see stuffed animals, baby rattles, Matchbox cars, and teething rings. Toys that were bought and never used rest on graves in various states of decay. Some are sun bleached, others are black with mold, and a few are brand-spanking new. The new ones make me feel the worst.

A couple feet to my right is a rectangle of rust-colored mud. Grass hasn't had time to grow on this newest grave in the children's cemetery. No tombstone has been carved and placed yet to mark this life. But the air is thick with the scent of yellow and white roses that cover the grave.

They must have buried their little one in the last day or two, because the carefully placed sympathy cards are sagging but not completely defeated by the damp weather. A line of perfect tiny toys sits upright across the dirt patch as if standing guard over the new resident. Stuffed sentinels. Now I understand what Josie said about letting a grave pick you. But this one has nothing to rub; it's a patch of mud.

Feeling completely deflated, I sit, resting my head in my hands. Then, through my hair, I see him: a marble carving of a beautiful little boy decorates a nearby tombstone. His pudgy hand grasps a stone tree trunk. Itsy bitsy fingers clutch a white bouquet that appears so lifelike I can almost smell the blossoms. His smooth face is frozen in a timeless half smile. Swirly curls frame his face. Dimpled knees peek out of old-fashioned trousers. At his feet rests a white vase filled to bursting with a holiday bouquet. Underneath, a carved plaque reads:

In memory of Ettore Versino
Born: December 20, 2000, Died: October 5, 2002.

Across the bottom of the tombstone lies a fuzzy yellow and black bumblebee outfit. Dead more than a decade, his parents have left a Halloween costume for their son. Do they do this every year?

I shove the costume to the side so I can start my rubbing, but the plush, fluffy fabric makes my fingers itch. I must be allergic to kind gestures. Tears prick at the back of my eyes. Sadness, and something else, something ugly, eats at my stomach as I yank the paper, tape, and graphite free from the helmet. Hot tears and snot crisscross my face and drip onto the paper. My chin quivers as I smooth the warped paper. The paper rips in the middle.

"God, I've already ruined it."

I wipe my wet face with my sleeve, take a breath, and try to tape the paper to the white marble. The paper fumbles out of my worthless fingers, and I lose my grip on everything. Down goes the tape, out slips the graphite, and off sloughs the last of my composure.

I force myself to breathe, and I close my eyes. I can't show up without a rubbing. I clench my teeth and tape the paper to the plaque. I try to draw out some tender thought about the parents Ettore left behind, but all that comes is a quick glimpse of a little green monster named Envy. Before I let myself wad up the paper and slink back to the entry gates, I begin to rub.

The wet graphite leaves sloppy kindergarten smears across the white sheet. By the middle of the rubbing, my touch improves. A shiver ripples down my spine as I reach the bottom of the words. I mangle the deceased date, but I steady myself and try again, making it worse. Of course. The graphite jumps out of my fingers and lands among the baby toys. Fine. Stay there!

I pull the tape free of the tombstone and roll up the paper, desperate to be done and find a friendly face. I jam the supplies inside my wet helmet, which slips out of my hands and rolls away, stopping at the foot of the dwarf apple tree. As I duck down to get it, I spot a shadowy movement through the bushes that surround Ettore's grave. What I first mistake for a brown squirrel turns out to be someone, I can't make out who. The person's hands dart out from the leaves, swift and silent and tidy the fallen toys and straighten the yellow and black costume. I hold my breath and stare. As I stand, I smack my head on the bottom branch of the tree.

"Ugh!" Wet blossoms and dead leaves rain down on me and I shake them off my jersey and pull bits from my hair. I turn back to Ettore's grave, but the person is gone. If there was someone behind the bushes, they are long gone. I shiver, thinking of the Chinese hungry ghosts and wish I had one of my mother's blasted joss sticks handy to burn, to ward off bad spirits.

I take one last glance over my shoulder and then run as fast as I can from the children's cemetery, grateful for the plastic cleats that make me faster than usual. As I near the entrance gates, I make out the faint outline of a figure. I cross my fingers. God, I hope that's a friend.

Seth Finds
an Unknown

WHILE TALKING WITH JOSIE on my cell last night, I did a quick web search of Lakefront Cemetery. The oldest boneyard in the Pacific Northwest, it is a popular tourist destination. Housing the graves of people from city founders to dead musicians, how I could live so close to this property and be oblivious to its rich history? I scanned the cemetery map on my monitor for names I might recognize as Josie explained our Halloween plans in my right ear. She was going to rub her mother's grave, but I wanted to find the grave of someone that shared my love of inventions and history.

"Have you ever heard of someone named Harvey Yessir?" I asked Josie.

"Sounds familiar, but I can't peg why. Was he a professor at the U?" she asked.

"Naw, his name's on half the buildings downtown. He was a founding father, big lumber guy. Now do you know him?"

"I think so. Is he buried in Lakefront? Wait! Are you doing research while you are on the phone with me?" she asked. I pictured her cute, freckled cheeks colored with an angry, pink tinge.

"Busted. But, where would you be without my research? I found that bit about Halloween for you didn't I? I'm your guy, right?"

"Yeah, you're a keeper. So, are you going to rub Yessir's grave? Is he historically significant enough for you?" she asked.

I roll down a couple screens and scan the man's history. He made a lot of money selling dead trees, built the original city and all, but I'm not intrigued. "No, he's interesting, but he's not the one. I want someone less known. I want to find someone that made a contribution to the world, but isn't what you would call famous. Seems like that would be more fun. I could rub someone and then unearth their life story afterward." I shut down my computer.

"Do you have your costume figured out yet? Want to go as Lewis or Clark?" Josie asked. She is going as Sacagawea, Lewis and Clark's guide.

I grunted. "No way. I don't want to be a matchy-match with you. I was thinking about being a vampire, a stylish, steampunk blood sucker." I finger the Nerf gun I retrofitted last weekend for the big Nerf gun tournament at Marymoor Park. The details turned out great. I glued on metal gears, attached a leather belt for a shoulder strap, and painted the whole gun copper, two coats. It is epic cool. "I think I'll wear my gun."

"No kidding, but what else are you going to wear? Do you still have that monkey suit from the wedding last year?"

I rifled through my closet, shoved hangers out of the way and found the grey pinstriped suit she was referring to. "The pants look too small. The shirt will work though." The white button-down shirt appeared relatively clean. "If I wear my Doc Martens, maybe no one will be able to tell the pants are high-waters."

She giggled. "Well, now I know. What about your bolo tie? I love that thing. Is a bolo steampunk?"

"Not so much. Steampunk is when you mix vintage stuff with high-tech sci-fi, think monocles and robot parts. But yeah, I can wear the bolo. I need something vintage."

"How about a pocket watch? I've got an old pocket watch that was my grandfather's from World War II. The glass is cracked on the face, but otherwise it is fine," she offered.

"Perfect. Thanks, Josie. Do you think it'd be too much to put blotches of red ink down the front of my shirt?"

"You do that and your mom will make sure there are some real bloodstains to go with them," she joked.

"I'll put the shirt on at your house. She'll never know."

"And that makes me an accomplice....awesome." I heard a beep on the other end of the line. "Hey, Seth. That's Casey, I've got to try and convince her to come. Bye."

Now, a day later, I wander the paths of Lakefront in search of an unknown to rub. I find Yessir's tomb immediately. It is right next to the entrance gates and I nod hello. I keep moving toward the center of the grounds where the flags whip and dance over the military graveyard. This property isn't technically part of Lakefront. I found that out doing research last night. Once upon a time the different branches of the military had small cemeteries spread out over the Seattle area until one group got a chunk of federal funding to buy this area from Lakefront. They spent the next five years relocating bodies and headstones into a new united military cemetery.

I unlatch the white picket fence that defines the military section and wander inside. The clang and clatter of chains against the flagpole draw my attention. I look up and admire the United States and Washington State flags that flutter and wave in the wind. I put my hand over my heart and recite the Pledge of Allegiance.

The grave markers in this area are simple, humble things. Most lie flat on the ground and are no bigger than a computer keyboard. A few are decorated with fresh flowers and potted plants, a couple have bouquets of fake flowers stuffed into metal urns. All of them sport a thin layer of dead leaves. The huge tree that looms above must be the culprit. I continue to wander until I stop at a marker coated entirely in wet leaves. I kneel and wipe away the leaves and read the name:

Sergeant Isaac Paxton
1925-2013
Let freedom ring

I remove the supplies from my briefcase and rub the simple stone. I don't lie across the grave, don't utter a prayer–heck, I don't even introduce myself. My relationship with Sergeant Paxton will commence behind the screen of a computer later tonight. I make quick work of the rubbing and fold the results into the briefcase and rise.

As I walk to the cemetery entrance to meet the others, I see Casey and smile. She doesn't see me yet. I unstrap my Nerf gun and duck behind a thick tree trunk. I stuff a foam ball into the gun and laugh under my breath. *She is going to be so surprised*, I think as I wait for her to come closer.

BLAZE STIRS
THE GIANT

"BLAZE, DON'T DO ANYTHING STUPID!"

My mother's last words rattle through my mind, the words tossed at me as I exited the car at the Josie's house hours ago. Hard to imagine doing something smart dressed in this get up!

"And don't ruin those boots either!" she shouted as she peeled out of the driveway.

Yeah. Do you mean the boots I found buried in the back of the garage, you hoarder? I thought. No, way I'd say that out loud.

In the cemetery, I let Josie's voice erase my mother's harsh words like a giant broom. She gives us instructions for the night but rubs at her throat, so I know she is nervous. I take a quick peek at my stolen white boots and kick off a clump of mossy mud from the toe. Casey dodges the flying muck, giving me a sour face with big surprised eyes. I laugh. The others pivot my way, and I cover my mouth to stuff the noise back inside. Josie stares down her nose at me, and then picks up her explanation without missing a beat.

In spite of touchy girls, bossy mothers, tight clothes, and fussy capes, I buzz with anticipation. Something big is going to happen tonight; I can feel it.

I do a slow, panoramic scan of the surroundings to put my superpowers to good use. My three favorite people in the world gather beside me. Dressed in a crazy assortment of costumes, Seth and Casey seem wrapped up in what Josie is saying unaware of our incredible surroundings. We are standing in a cemetery on Halloween! How cool is that?

Something wet plops on my head. I look up to the sign that reads, "Lakefront Cemetery" and a second raindrop plunks into my eye. I take the supplies Josie doles out with greedy hands and a wink. She frowns at me, staring at my legs, which bounce up and down, up and down with energy. I bite back another obnoxious laugh.

I breathe deeply. The air smells like apples, fresh-cut apples. And like an overcharged toy, I bounce and twitch and wiggle. I stretch my arms out to the side and give in to the electricity pulsing through me. *You're in charge. Make it happen!* I think, smiling ear to ear. When Josie texted last night, I knew she was onto something big. After years of lame parties and junk candy, the big adventure was finally upon us! And now that we are here, it doesn't take superpowers to sense something bigger than all of us is in the driver's seat tonight. Call it karma, call it fate, but please don't call it God. You call it God and my mother, the proud atheist, will kill you. And being a chef, she has the knives to back up that promise. Something buzzes in my pocket and I take out my phone to read the text that crosses the screen.

"B. Stop bouncing. UR making me motion sick."

The text is from Casey. I send back an emoticon that sums up my thoughts, a puking smiley face. She checks her phone and scrunches her little nose at me. I caress the thunderbolt she helped craft and she shakes her head. She's so cute when she gets all pouty.

Somehow I end up two steps behind the others as they head into the cemetery. I take slow steps and watch them walk away. Casey veers toward a grove of apple trees, her white football pants nearly falling off her skinny body. See! I knew I smelled apples! Seth aims for the center of the property where a massive flagpole whips and clatters, and Josie takes a quick glance behind her before walking to her mother's grave. As if we didn't know...

I take the gravel path that cuts through a series of dirty white tombs to wait until a grave "calls me." But so far, I've got nothing. My spiritual divining rod needs an adjustment.

Past the tombs where a line of pines meets the sky, a cottage comes into focus. A swirl of wet wind blows my cape over my shoulders and tugs me toward the house. In seconds, I reach the corner of the garden. Employing my superpowers once again, I scan the house and surroundings.

Hulking yellow sunflowers scrape the top of a single-story rambler. More pretty flowers and greenery gush out of the planter boxes that hang underneath shuttered windows and graves. Graves–lots of them–stand where other yards sport trees.

I walk a slow circle around the house to try and put my finger on what makes this place so perfect. Smooth round river rocks make up the walls of the house, and I run a hand across the cool, bumpy surface. As I turn the corner, I catch the noise of the lake waters that lap onto an unseen shore. The faint stink of fish and algae hangs in the air. If I squint, I can see the slimmest slice of choppy gray water through a dense stand of trees.

Someone takes good care of this place. A thick layer of shiny white paint around the windows and roofline testifies to regular touchups. The solid window frames hold imperfect, distorted panes of glass. Gold light shines from the warped glass. Someone is home. I tiptoe around the corner and wonder if I should leave.

Something about that old glass keeps me there. I snap a picture and text it to Seth, my friend who loves old things. I tuck the phone away and decide I better go before someone rushes out of the cottage pointing a gun at my head.

I jog through the yard toward the cemetery boundary and halt at a lush herb garden full of things my parents grow for the restaurants. The smell of rosemary fills my nose, and my stomach growls. In front of the rosemary bush stand purple, green, and white cabbages, their leaves alive with busy ladybugs. As I crouch down to study the red ladies, I spy a grave marker buried inside a clump of mint.

I brush the greenery to the side and uncover a stocky cross. The black and white marker reads:

Father Daniel Kujala
January 10, 1942 - April 17, 2007
All thanks to Him that saved me.

A priest? Really? I cringe as I make a quick sweep of the garden, hoping beyond hope I will discover a different grave to rub. But all I see are flowers and craft store scarecrows. No tombstones.

I consider going back to the gravel trail. But like riding backward on a train, finding a new grave doesn't feel right. This grave picked me. No. This is my grave. My heart pounds and I gulp in air, dizzy at the thought of rebellion. And now that I've decided, I am determined to get it done fast before my resolve evaporates!

"Hey, Father Kujala. I'm Blaze. Nice grave." I feel stupid talking to a grave, so I drop my voice to a whisper. "Your grave is really cool. "

As I reach for the roll of paper tucked into my cape, I remember what I am wearing. I look down at my Halloween clothes, then back to the black and white monument. My cheeks burn. I laugh and bow to Father Kujala's tombstone. "I don't usually dress like this!"

I scrabble deep inside a pocket and dig out the tape and charcoal. It takes some work to get the paper taped down right. I want to capture the cross and the Father's inscription on my rubbing. With the paper in place, I rub and surprise myself with the results. Somehow, I manage to copy the stone. Josie will be so proud.

The rubbing looks good and I want to keep it that way, so I pull gently on the tape so the thin paper does not rip. But halfway through, a scream cuts across the graveyard and startles me. It sounds like one of the girls. In a hurry to get the heck to the noise, I tug at the paper, tearing the top third clean off. I cringe, trying not to cuss in front of the good Father. I pick off what I can from Kujala's tombstone and roll the pieces of the rubbing into a loose tube. I shove all of it into the back of my cape and run toward the shriek.

Josie Discovers Her Grave

BETWEEN HIS SMOKY FUR and the shadows, I lose track of the cat as he darts away from my mother's grave at breakneck speed. The crow that scared away the poor fellow caws and shrieks from his high perch in the cedar.

"Why couldn't Sacagawea carry a slingshot?" I shout into the tree.

The crow cocks his head to the side and quiets. I stick a finger in my ringing ear and he jumps off the branch, landing on the stone angel. He studies me from her wing with a glassy black eye, and I wonder... but the distant sound of the cat startles me into action. His throaty caterwaul cuts across the property and I search for him again.

Desperate to find my new friend, I scan the grounds and spot a blur of motion near a knot of berry brambles a good hundred yards away. I slip and slide to close the gap between us, mentally cursing my choice of rubber-soled moccasins with each precarious step. He makes escape look so easy; a few swift bounds and he reaches the far edge of Lakefront Cemetery. He jumps on top of a three-foot wall of brambles and meows. His gray head cocks to the side and I am taken in by his cuteness. I have to catch him. I eye the wall and creep closer to the cat. I get within an arm's length and the cat leaps to the other side of the wall.

"Great! I can't do that!"

Beneath the thorns and ivy stands a three-foot high gate held closed with a rusty latch. I reach through the sharp brambles and push away the pain to grip the lock. I wrench the stubborn latch up, and it releases with a crusty click.

I can imagine Seth reciting tetanus statistics as I shove the gate in with a hip, but the rotting boards are too riddled with ivy and thorns to give. Determined to catch the cat, I kick at the gate with my foot once, then twice, until I hear the wood groan and crack. The gap I make isn't much, but it's wide enough, and I squeeze past the splintered boards. The fringe of my dress catches, so I tug the fabric free and stumble inside, falling face first onto a carpet of moss and flowers. Should've worn kneepads tonight, Josie.

I look up; where I expect to find a rocky shoreline lies an eerie, forgotten garden. "What is this place?" I whisper.

A canopy of thick, steeple-high oaks runs in a straight flank from the gate to the lake, naked of all but a handful of crimson red leaves. Silky puffs of mint green lichen drape across the lowest branches as if the fog was caught on its great escape to the sky. A thin, gravel path cuts through the center of the grove and dead ends at a rose-covered archway that frames the steely gray lake beyond. My arms ripple with goosebumps as my eyes lock on the jade eyes of the cat. I spring to attention and freeze, afraid of scaring the poor thing. He rests on his fluffy haunches halfway down the gravel path and looks past where I stand.

"Waiting for me to catch up? How polite of you," I say.

A flank of gnarled, low creeping bougainvillea bursting with out-of-season fuchsia flowers stretches behind the cat. Lush, lime green moss carpets the underside of the floral shrubs, a stark contrast to the fluorescent blooms that seem to glow in the shady space.

A worn wooden sign pokes out from within the shrubs. Elaborate black lettering scrolled across the damp wood reads "Non-Endowment Care Section." I touch a finger to the painted letters and black chips crumble from the ancient sign. Non-endowment? What does that mean?

I have no time to think about the sign, as the cat zips further down the path in a noisy burst. He stops near a pile of rubble and stares at me while he grooms his charcoal face with a bubble gum pink tongue and swift white paw.

"Well, now. Nice of you to hold still for a minute."

As my eyes adjust to the shadows, the tombstones that surround us come into focus. Gravestones are scattered here and there. No two are alike, except for their age and state of neglect. Some are no larger than a brick, while others are over two-feet high. The tombstones look like they were colored with the gray row in a 96 pack of crayons; Slick Nickel, Fuzzy Wuzzy, Silver Swirl, Manatee. A few of the tombstones remain whole and upright. Most are cracked near their bases and lie in fractured pieces across the ground.

"I'm in a cemetery within a cemetery." Less organized, but no less beautiful, this place seems older than the one beyond the brambles. Who's buried here?

Suddenly tired, I take a seat on the flat stone at my feet. The cat jumps up and curls into a cozy ball by my side. If I could, I would purr. I stroke his fur, and the nagging feeling that I've forgotten something important recedes. I prop myself up with my hands and touch the warm stone beneath me. Why is the stone warm? It is October in Seattle, for God's sake. Fascinated, I stroke the stone and sharp pain erupts from my hand. I inspect my skin in the weak light and find bloody scratches and bits of green glass. The sweet iron-laced smell makes me gag. I gingerly remove the glass pieces and dig a tissue out of my satchel to wrap a crude bandage.

I look down at the stone that serves as my bench and see the letter 'E' etched into the surface, splatter-painted with my blood and large shards of glass, the remnants of a beer bottle.

"Oh, my Lord! I'm so sorry!"

I spring up to get away from the piece of tombstone I have defiled with my blood, and ram my leg into something hard. Pain blasts across my rump and the leather pouch slips off my shoulder. The contents scatter across the neglected plot and disappear into the knee-high grass. I fumble in the grass to collect my things and wonder why this plot isn't mowed short like the rest.

As I scramble to repack my bag, I understand. "Oh! This is the grave I am supposed to rub, isn't it?" I say.

The cat rises and stretches in a wide arch, wipes his cheek against the edge of the tombstone, and purrs.

"You led me here didn't you, little guy?"

I pick the roll of paper off the ground and stall. I was going to rub my mom's grave, make a new memory. How did I end up here? The cat comes to my side and rubs his lean body against my calf. I reach down and scratch his head and feel his affectionate vibrations with my fingertips. "No, this is the grave for me, right?" I ask the cat.

He squirms between my feet, falls to the ground and rolls onto his back showing off the curly white fur across his belly. He rolls to his feet and saunters to the tombstone. He stands on his back legs and stretches his front paws up, curling his claws over the top of the tall marker and scratching them across the face of the stone.

I take it as a sign. The cat is the sign that I was supposed to rub this tombstone. "If it wasn't for you, I would've missed out on all this. Thanks, buddy."

Without hesitation, I stand back to appraise the stone. Shaped like a pointy surfboard, the monument is thicker than its modern cousins. The lettering and symbols carved into the matte blue material appear ancient and cryptic. A pattern of recessed circles decorates the top part of the unusual stone. Standing almost three-feet high, it is the lone survivor of some faraway time. Tombstones on all sides of this mysterious plot have been knocked over, cracked, reduced to rubble. That this one has survived is nothing short of a miracle.

I pull graphite, paper, and tape out of my pouch and start a one-sided conversation with the person buried below. Pushing back the tall grass, I tape the paper to the stone face.

"I can't read this, so I don't know your name. I can't even tell when you died. Your grave seems old to me, old and forgotten. What's with the long grass? Don't they have people around here to take care of that sort of thing?" My voice shakes with emotion.

Using the side of the graphite, I recreate the tombstone on my own paper. Careful to go the whole surface, I take a step back and assess the results. Satisfied, I pull off the tape and roll up the artwork, stowing it inside my leather satchel.

The cat stretches and gives my leg another affectionate rub. He chomps down a mouthful of the weedy grass, chews, and then coughs it back up in a moist, yellow pile. He bursts from the plot and runs toward the bramble boundary.

Ready to find my friends, I follow the cat down the gravel path to the main cemetery. I hear the loud squawks first. I cover my ears and duck down to keep from being hit by the black crow that swoops from the trees. I fall to my knees and watch the bird dart toward the pouch at my hip. The greasy crow jabs its beak into the pouch and tears at the paper tucked inside.

"You can't have this!" I pull back on the bottom of my bag, but the crow persists.

"Arrrrrr." I hear an unearthly growl and do a quick scan of the trees, but I can't find a source. When the cat pushes against my leg, I understand. The cat's lean body stands taut, ready to take down the crow with his claws and teeth. Deciphering the unspoken language between predator and prey, the crow knows what the cat plans to do and instantly releases the paper. He flies into the evening sky, leaving with a cacophony of caws.

"Ha! I beat you!" I yell and shake a fist at the sky. "You didn't take my rubbing!"

Triumphant, I run toward the gate to find the others, cat at my heels, and the rubbing buried safely inside my pouch.

BLAZE AND WHY CAPES ARE NOT AWESOME

SUPERHEROES NEVER PANIC, so why am I still standing here? The scream came from the front of the cemetery and it was definitely a girl. Maybe Casey thought she saw a ghost or something. She was scared to come tonight. Or what if some weirdo grabbed Josie? Don't bad people, like devil worshippers or something, hang out in cemeteries on Halloween? Oh, man!

I race in the direction of the sound with a fresh dose of determination pounding beneath this duct-tape lightning bolt. I round the corner of the cottage full throttle, when something grabs my cape and slams me back hard against the cottage. I choke as the cape cuts into my windpipe.

"Ack!" I wheeze. Sweat pours down my face and neck as I struggle with the slippery knot at my throat, but it will not budge. I try to pull the cape over my head, but the ties are too tight to get past my big ears. I squeeze in thin gulps of air through my constricted windpipe and use my hands to follow the cape fabric to the sharp thorns that hold it fast to a trellis trailing up the cottage wall. I pull the slightest bit of fabric free and suck in air.

I twist the fabric around both hands and tug, but the woody black thorns dig in deeper as I pull. Beads of sweat trickle down my neck and I blink my stinging eyes. I yank the cape one more time but lose my grip on the sweat-soaked cape. I'm losing a one-sided tug of war.

"Help! Can someone help me? Anyone?" I sputter.

From behind, I hear a warm voice. "I'm comin.' I'm comin.'" A caramel brown face catches up to the strong voice. The woman is tiny and lean, dressed in overalls that hang off her lean frame like she borrowed clothes from a giant. Her skin is slightly darker than mine and her face is kind. Lots of long black curls tangle into a bun at the back of her head.

She says, "Well, you got yourself into a pickle! Wrapped up good in my roses. I'd shake your hand, but I better help you first!"

My savior smiles up at me with bright eyes and then gets down to business. She unties the cape with deft fingers and I draw in a long breath. With a quick shake and snap, as if folding clean sheets, she frees the cape from the trellis.

"Yeah, well, even superheroes need help every now and again," she says.

And with those simple words, we laugh.

"My name's Grace, by the way. I take care of this place." She hands me the folded cape and I tuck it under my armpit; no way I'm tying that sucker around my neck again. I introduce myself to Grace.

"Boy, am I glad to meet you," I say.

"Is this yours?" Grace asks, bending down to retrieve a roll of paper at her feet.

"Oh, yeah, it is. I forgot I'd put it in my cape. Thanks."

"So, are you guys art students or something?" she asks, squinting into the distance.

"No. My friend had a rubbing kit. Is it okay that we're here?"

"It's fine. Actually, Blaze, it's nice. I saw you all by the front gates earlier, about the same time I remembered I didn't lock them," she says, grinning. A black curl falls free from her bun and hangs down the side of her face. It is a pretty face in a mom kind of way; she looks around forty, so I guess she could be a mom. She certainly doesn't look like a cemetery caretaker.

She continues. "It's usually vandals that come around here on Halloween. It took me by surprise when your little friend pulled out art supplies. And I'm a tough lady to surprise."

We both laugh at that. A pig snort escapes from me, but Grace doesn't seem to notice.

"Who'd you rub?" Grace asks. "Can I take a gander?"

"Yeah, sure. It's a guy named Father Kujala." I pass her the paper and massage my windpipe, feeling grateful for each gulp of cool air.

She unrolls the artwork and studies the image. Her hands are tiny, smooth, and brown. Her fingernails are trimmed and short, tidy and practical for a person who works with her hands for a living.

"He's my neighbor, Father Kujala," says Grace. "Been nearly five years since he died. But the church folks still come regularly to spiff up his plot. Makes my yard look downright plain, that plot does," Grace says, shaking her head. She absently tucks the loose curl into her bun and looks up at me.

"Plain? You must be crazy. This place is amazing. In fact, I don't really know if I was so much drawn to his grave or drawn to all this." I sweep my hands outward to indicate the cottage and surrounding yard.

"Well, thanks for the compliment. But he's tough competition. They buried him in the Russian Orthodox tradition, from what I gather. Do you know anything about that religion?" she asks.

I shrug and she continues.

"Sometimes they build brightly colored spirit houses above the graves, and sometimes they plant a garden," Grace says, letting her voice trail off. She glances at me and looks away quickly, her lips pinching up as if she's trying to hold something inside.

"You doing okay?" I ask. Grace nods and I remember that someone else wasn't so fine just a minute ago.

"Oh my gosh! Grace, I just remembered. I've got to go. I think one of my friends may be in trouble. I heard a scream and then I got caught on your house. Sorry, I've got to find them." I turn to leave, but halt as I see my friends approach.

Casey waves. "Hey! We found you. Now the only person we're missing is Josie. Have you seen her?" She glances over at Grace and gives me a questioning look.

I shrug, ignoring her for the time being. "No Josie yet. But, who was it that screamed a minute ago? I almost had a heart attack."

Casey smirks, and Seth looks away. "Yeah, that was me," she says, turning toward Seth. "He thought he'd have a little fun. He snuck up on me and shot me in the face with his stupid gun. What a jerk!"

"Yeah, real nice, Seth." I try my best to sound like I mean it, but I give Seth a flick of a thumbs-up. "I was trying to come to your rescue when my cape got caught. Grace here saved the day!"

I smile at the tiny woman at my elbow "Grace, these are my friends Casey and Seth. Friends, this is Grace, Lakefront caretaker and superhero rescuer."

"Sounds like Grace should be sporting the cape, man," Seth says as he shakes her hand.

"Dude, capes are for suckers. I'm done with capes," I say.

Grace steps toward Seth. "Blaze says you were doing some rubbings. How'd that go?" As my friends look from one to the other deciding who should answer first, Josie approaches.

"Hi, everyone." Josie smiles warmly at Grace, stretching out a hand and introducing herself. "Are we in trouble for being on the property tonight?" she asks.

"No, just the opposite. I was telling Blaze it's nice to have people visit for the right reasons. Besides troublemakers, no one comes around on Halloween. I was putting apple cider on the stove when I heard a ruckus out the window." Grace looks down at the ground. "Would you folks like to come inside the cottage and get warm?"

Looking from one to the other, we nod silently.

Josie scans the four of us. "What ruckus? What'd I miss?"

"Nothing," Seth answers.

We walk to the cottage and a fuzzy cat bursts out from behind Josie's legs. Josie smiles. "Oh, yeah, by the way, it seems I'm the proud owner of a stray."

The cat lifts his chin high and strides toward the cottage. We follow him to Grace's house in a line like some wacky, impromptu Halloween parade.

Josie Learns the Secret Ingredient

GRACE HAS THE GREEN DOOR to the cottage unlocked before we've managed to climb the porch steps. She clips the key ring onto her belt and works the copper knob. Mounting the porch, Seth eyes the line of shoes by the door and kicks off his dirt-caked Doc Martens. Wordlessly, the rest of us add our shoes to the queue.

Grace props open the door with her body. "That's awfully thoughtful. Thanks."

The scent of cinnamon and warm apples rushes out to greet us. I soak it in and feel something close to calm, a settling of sorts somewhere deep inside. The cat pushes past me into the house.

"Can the cat come in?" I ask.

"Josie, I think he already is." A smile lights up her face and she transforms from plain into beautiful. "He wants to be right by your side, girl." She bends down and scratches the cat between his soft batty ears and he skitters out of reach. Grace mutters, "I haven't seen him around here before. I wonder which stray had kittens?"

Gathering inside the doorjamb, we find ourselves standing in an airy blue kitchen. Small by today's standards, the kitchen feels cozy and inviting. The golden maple wood floor warms my damp stocking feet and I realize for the first time how cold I really am.

"It smells great in here!" Casey remarks.

Grace says, "That's mostly why I put the cider on. Makes the whole place smell like autumn. Now, who wants a cupful?"

We all raise our hands, as if we're in school.

"Well, then," says Grace. "Grab a seat in the front room. It's cozier there. I'll just be a minute behind."

Grace shoos the bunch of us toward an adjacent hallway lined with sepia-toned photographs in tarnished silver frames.

"Do you need any help?" Blaze asks.

"If you wouldn't mind, could you fetch that tray for me, Blaze?" Grace points to a high shelf above the stovetop.

I wander down the hallway and stare into the old pictures looking for what? Familiar faces? Then I watch Blaze and Grace work in the kitchen as if they've known each other for a long time.

Blaze fetches the oversized wooden tea tray and hands it to the woman.

"Thanks," says Grace. Setting down the tray, she opens a drawer and rifles through it until she finds a large soup ladle.

As she spoons cider into mismatched china teacups, Grace calls over her shoulder to us. "Oh, and please eat some of that Halloween candy! My waistline will thank you for it."

I follow a blue flowered runner into a buttery yellow living room. An inviting fire crackles inside a sooty hearth. Two overstuffed gingham print sofas rest face to face in front of a stone fireplace. The coffee table between them is a faded, stocky wooden piece, adorned with a blue and white porcelain vase overstuffed with fragrant pink roses. I think of the rotten flowers on my mother's grave and cringe.

A crooked tower of books on one corner of the table is the only thing remotely messy about the comfortable room. Fuzzy yellow chenille blankets hang across the arms of both sofas. My mom would've loved this place.

Still feeling the chill of the night in my bones, I choose a seat closest to the fire, on the end of the sofa. The cat jumps to my lap, and then vaults onto the arm of the sofa. Kneading the soft blanket with his white tipped mitts, the cat settles down onto the perch for a nap. Seth and Blaze find seats across from me. Blaze looks awkward as he squeezes his tall frame onto the petite, flowery sofa.

Casey ducks into the adjoining entryway. On a tall table by the front door stands a crystal punch bowl filled to the brim with miniature candy bars. As she reaches for a handful, Grace steps into the front room.

Grace nods at the candy bowl. "It's the dumbest thing. I am a sucker for Halloween candy. I buy bags of it every year knowing full well no one's going to knock on a door in a cemetery, so I eat it myself. Sorry, I'm rambling. It's been awhile since I've had visitors."

She sets the loaded tray onto the coffee table. I meet her gaze and smile. She passes cups of cider to each of us and then cuts into a crumbly, golden cake.

Grace hands us each a plated piece and a white linen napkin. "This is an old family recipe: honeycake. Reminds me of visiting with my grandma when I was a girl." After everyone is served, she fetches a wooden rocking chair from a dark corner and drags it to the end of the coffee table. Sitting, she rocks back and forth and scans us with a contented expression.

Seth is the first to dive into the cake. "This is delicious! I didn't realize how cold I'd gotten out there until just now, hungry too!" He doesn't notice the crumbs tumbling off his chin onto the front of his shirt as he wolfs down the food.

I taste the cake. It really is delicious. "I hope it's not a secret recipe, Grace. I do all the cooking at home. Dad and Owen would love this. Is it hard to make?" I ask.

Grace grins at the compliments. "The funny thing is my grandma gave me the recipe. But it wasn't quite right 'til I turned eighteen. That's when she told me the secret ingredient, a tablespoon of stale coffee. Once I knew that, mine tasted perfect. Why she waited 'til I was eighteen to tell me the secret, I'll never know."

The room turns silent as we all dive into the snack. The only noise comes from scraping forks and slurped sips.

"I know Blaze met Father Kujala tonight. His grave is in my front yard." Grace points out the large picture window to her right. "But, who'd everyone else meet?"

I take a drink to gather my thoughts. Before I can say anything, Seth interrupts. "Finding my grave was almost too easy. After we split up, I went toward the middle of the grounds, not far from the entry gates where all the flags are. I figured that'd be where the military cemetery was. It's separated from the rest of Lakefront by a low white picket fence." Then, pausing his own account, he asks, "Grace, is that area part of your responsibility? Or does the government keep up those graves?"

"I take care of them, raise the flags, garden and whatnot. The military folk attend the funerals. Don't do much else."

Seth carries on, "I hadn't walked far when I saw one grave that was covered with wet leaves, like a tree dumped everything it had onto the poor guy. There were so many leaves that I couldn't even see a grave marker at first. I got down and brushed the whole thing clean. It felt like the right thing to do. And that's when it hit me. I'd found my grave. The marker was still a little wet from the leaves, so my rubbing came out a bit blurry. But, here it is."

He unrolls the paper and holds it up for us to see. The rubbing takes up less than a third of the paper. A tiny American flag is etched in the center of the marker.

Grace nods. "I didn't bury him that long ago, maybe the first week of August? He had a military service. A horn played *Taps* for him. Lord, that song makes me bawl. All it takes is the first three notes and I'm done for. Anyway, back to the sergeant's funeral–the soldiers draped a flag over his coffin, did this thing with the rifles. Because there wasn't any family in attendance, they folded up the flag and brought it to me for safekeeping. I've got it in storage."

"That's so sad," Casey says, staring into her teacup. She sets her empty plate onto the coffee table and fusses with her hands. "I went to the children's cemetery; at least, I assume that's what it was. The place with the apple tree, Grace?"

Grace sets her cup onto the table and nods. She stares at Casey as she unrolls the rubbing, reading the words.

"I don't really know how to pronounce his name. Here, just look," she holds up the rubbing and yellow blotches of color shine through the ripped paper. Casey does not get an A-plus on the assignment.

"The name is Ettore Versino, it sounds Italian to me. Anyways, he had these..." her voice shakes and she takes a quick swallow of cider, then continues. "There were all these sweet little toys and cards in the area, but Ettore had a Halloween costume lying across his grave." Casey rolls up the holey rubbing and tucks it behind her on the couch.

I lean in and squeeze her hand. "You seem really shaken up. Are you doing alright?" I ask.

"Of course. It's just hard to think about kids and death, that's all. Thanks, Josie."

Next to me the cat wakes, stretches and dives onto the coffee table, knocking over my empty cup. I set it upright and wipe the drops of spilled cider with a sleeve. "This little guy showed me my tombstone. I was almost ready to rub my mom's grave when he pounced on me. He landed right on my chest. Then he led me to a different grave."

I pause and stare at the faces around me. I shake off the feeling I left something important behind at my mom's grave, but the satchel is tucked beside me on the couch.

"No way!" Blaze holds out his hand to Seth, "Dude, pay up. You totally bet that Josie would rub her mother's grave. Five bucks, now." Seth hands him a wad of bills.

"Yeah, well," I say, "I felt like the cat was a sign. He led me to this place I never knew about before. It was an older part of the cemetery on the lakeshore, and it was creepy. Grace, do you know about that place? It has its own gate, but the thorns and brambles are so thick that you can't get in without a little effort." I think back to the way the wood groaned and cracked as I pushed past. I cross my fingers and hope that I didn't break any boards.

"Those damn brambles! Are they back already? I hacked those to the ground less than a month ago," Grace says distractedly, as if mentally adding the task to tomorrow's To Do list.

She stops rocking in her chair and turns her attention to me. "The place past the brambles is called the Ghost Forest," she says. "My uncle, who looked after this place before me, warned me not to spend too much time there. He said there were a 'bunch of witches buried in that cursed ground.' He also said that the place would make you feel 'funny.' And he always claimed that land wasn't part of Lakefront Cemetery, so it wasn't his responsibility to tend. Said he wouldn't do her bidding; he said that most often. 'I won't do a witch's bidding.'

I nearly fall out of my seat and Casey asks the question on the tip of my tongue. "Witches! From where?"

Grace shakes her head. "Well, I don't know it for a fact, because there's no paper trail for that property, but from what I gather, they put some women to death for being witches and buried 'em there. Must have been over a century and a half ago, because Lakefront was established in 1859, and it happened before that.

"Lots of rumors swirl around about the Ghost Forest. I'm always finding strange stuff back there: melted candles, burned paper scraps, Tarot cards, beer bottles, one time an Ouija board… lots of weird stuff. Kids think the place holds magical powers, so they sneak in the Ghost Forest to try out their own little preschool spells, I suppose."

Casey asks, "Did they really bury witches back there? Are you telling us it's haunted, Grace?"

Grace shakes her head. "I never saw an actual ghost myself. No, the only thing I ever saw back there…" She stops, then starts again with a sigh. "The truth is, silly rumors or not, that place affects me. I'm not a drinker, but I do keep one bottle of the stiff stuff around. After I tend to that place, I leave feeling heavy, low. I don't know what you'd call it, but I'm not quite myself. Afterward, I come straight home and drink down a shot of rum. It helps it all fade away again.

"I guess the best I can tell you is that the people buried back there are sad, forgotten, and abandoned in some way. And the place holds that awful feeling in a physical way, as real as that moss hanging from the trees. Are those the ghosts talking or just powerful memories that linger? I can't quite say." Grace takes a sip of cider and gazes at us.

"The dead don't like to be forgotten," she whispers, and her eyes drift away from us as though we have lost her attention to a memory. Smiling, she stacks the empty cups together and exits to the kitchen.

We collect the last of our detritus and head toward the kitchen. Grace beats us inside and reaches into a low cabinet and extracts a handful of plastic bags.

"Please, take that candy. Each of you, fill up a bag with your favorites!"

We do as we are commanded, and then we return to the back porch to claim our shoes. "Thanks for coming this evening. It was awfully nice to meet all of you," Grace looks down at her feet, suddenly shy. I move to the side of the slight woman and give her a hug.

"Thanks for everything, Grace. It was awfully nice of you to invite us in. If I want to find out more about my grave or anything, may I come back and snoop around?"

"You bet, Josie. You're all welcome here any time. And I'll pick my brains to see if I can remember more about the graves in the Ghost Forest. I'll poke through the old records again, and see if I can find some new scrap of information."

The others gather around Grace and wrap her up in a group hug. Uttering our thanks, we start down the porch steps.

Grace stops us mid-step. "Hey! Keep your eyes out for the ghost dog on your way out. He likes to show up on nights like this," she says mysteriously.

"Ghost dog?" Blaze asks.

"He's a white German Shepherd. Lays on the grave of a child over there," Grace says, pointing to a white obelisk in the distance. "Most folks think he's real and don't pay him any mind. They probably assume he's my pet. But, try and get close to him and he disappears like a puff of smoke. He never stops watching over the child buried there. The poor dear drowned in the lake and that dog was the one who dragged him onto shore. It's the saddest story because the boy was already dead, and the dog joined him soon after. That dog's a real hero." She wipes under her eyes and smiles. "Well then, I'd say that's enough ghost stories for one night. Happy Halloween."

Half-terrified and half-thrilled at the prospect of seeing a ghost on our walk back to the entry gates, we head into the darkness slow and easy. Grace waves goodbye from her porch.

As she turns toward her door I hear her mutter, "Damn, girl! You forgot the front gates again." But she goes inside anyway. The door shuts and the deadbolt snaps into place.

"I guess Grace decided to roll the dice tonight. She's not locking the gates," I mumble.

I shiver to think of the ghost dog that might be watching us as we cut across the cemetery. Not that I would recognize a real ghost even if he ran up screamed, 'Boo!' in my face. I crane my neck and take a final peek at my mom's grave and see vacant shadows under the cedar tree.

What did I leave behind? What am I missing? I clutch my satchel and try to push away the nagging thought.

As we near the entrance gates, I hear a low growl and freeze.

Somewhere up ahead a bark erupts. Casey looks at me and mouths, "What was that?" She grabs my hand and we sprint toward the cemetery gates. The boys jump out from behind an oak trunk in our path and laugh.

"We got you!" they sputter between hoots and howls.

I laugh, but it is a fake, empty laugh. I don't like being the butt of a joke. I know it was just one of their pranks, but I feel suddenly tired, ready to be alone with my rubbing. A knot forms at the base of my neck, the signal a headache is coming on. Casey squeezes my hand.

"Come on, Josie! Can't you take a little joke?" Blaze asks. Seth cuts a finger across his throat to shut Blaze up, his gaze on me. "I mean ghost dog, really?"

My head starts to throb and pushes out all my happy. I release Casey's hand and stomp through the cemetery gates alone.

Josie Bids the Others Farewell

I KNOW WITHOUT TURNING that three jaws drop as I wave a curt goodbye over my shoulder and stomp solo through the cemetery gates. I feel their eyes burn into the back of my head and my ears itch from the chatter I can't quite make out, the wild speculation my exit is sure to have touched off. *What's wrong with her? Is Josie sick? Do you think this is about her mother?*

It doesn't matter. I can't do another second of fake happy. What did I expect tonight? That my mom would come sauntering out from behind her tombstone and read me a bedtime story? I'm a fool. I didn't rub my mother's grave, so what? But, it matters after all. That's why I can't stand company right now.

Ms. Reliable has left the building. No down time at the coffee shop; no sleepover with Casey. Figure it out yourselves. I pass a jack-o'-lantern with seeds and pumpkin guts hanging from its gaping mouth. "That's right. One more fake smile and I'm gonna throw up, just like you."

My freedom comes with a price. As much as I wish it away, guilt and fatigue settle across my shoulders like a wet woolen blanket. My legs feel heavy, like the marrow inside has turned to concrete. I loll my head from side to side to ward off a pending migraine. My mood flits from tired to tense to happy to crushed, in time with my heavy footfalls.

I run a hand along the iron fence that borders Lakefront Cemetery as I walk until I run out of fence at the end of the block. I search for dead leaves to crunch; smashing things will keep me moving forward. The load of hope and desperation in my satchel, the one I forgot to leave at my mom's grave, feels like a bag of stones. I switch the thick strap to the other shoulder and thank God Owen's backpack is so light. I pat my side to double-check that the plush loaner is still in place, but hit my hip instead. "Oh no! I forgot Baby Sacagawea!"

For a blink, I consider backtracking to fetch it from the grave, but dismiss the idea in the same instant. By the time I get home, Owen will be asleep. He'll never know if I pick it up tomorrow instead.

As I mentally rearrange tomorrow's schedule to make time for a quick visit to Lakefront after school, the little cat from the cemetery darts out from the shadows and pounces a fat leaf, shredding it to bits. He shoots between my feet and I nearly trip and fall. "Little menace," I mumble.

As we pass the corner coffeehouse, rowdy customers push through wide wooden doors with steaming hot paper cups in hand. Wisps of live blues escape the closing doors. The cloud of music and smoky aroma drifts to the street and I breathe in the musky scent of espresso. My gaze stops at an empty table, the one by the rugged outdoor pit surrounded by five empty chairs. That's the table where we were supposed to cap off the night.

I hang my head in shame. I pride myself on being the reliable one, but tonight I am not myself. That's what I try to convince myself of, because I can't consider the alternative, that the real Josie Jameson is an emotional wreck.

A muffled ding comes from deep inside my satchel and I stop to check the text. I've missed not one, but three, texts from Casey and one from my father. I read his first.

"J. Need more candy. Went thru ALL. Hope treaters don't get violent! D."

Dad sent the message over an hour ago. A wave of guilt washes over me as I realize I let him down, too. If I come home to a yard wrapped in toilet paper thanks to empty-handed trick-or-treaters, I deserve it.

I finger through Casey's texts sent seconds ago and wince when I blow up the photo she's sent under the words, "Just in case I die." A sketchy man stares into the phone with drug-fuzzy eyes. His dirty hands clutch a piece of shiny silver metal. Is that a knife? Taken from the back of a bus, I feel a pang of guilt. She was supposed to walk home with me tonight, but instead had to ride a bus alone because her house is miles from Lakefront.

Her last text reads, "Think my parents would notice?"

I mutter, "Dang it! How many times have I told that girl not to ride in the back row?"

My fingers shake as I type a response. "Move! Sit by the driver!" I hit 'send' and hope she gets the message before Mr. Scary sticks that knife into her.

I type one more message–"Put on your helmet!" and press send. I realize just in time that I'm about to knock headfirst into a metal signpost, and cut right. Casey's texts send a shot of adrenaline into my veins and I pick up the pace. I just want to get home. The cat runs to catch up, and then sprints into the distance.

We enter the mouth of my neighborhood, and I take more care with my path so I don't collide with the clumps of giddy children that still roam the street. The intensity of their quest boggles my mind. Tomorrow all that candy will be half-price at the grocery store.

When did Halloween stop being fun? Back when my mother was alive, the Baby Group went out together. But then she died. Somehow, my father didn't notice holidays after her death. In fact, if it wasn't for the Baby Group, I might have given up trick-or-treating entirely. As it was, I made costumes for Owen and me out of what I found around the house. We were matching bed sheet ghosts that first year. We went out with the others, but it was me that carried Owen when he got tired of walking. It was me who made sure he had a glow stick or flashlight. It was me who coaxed him home before bedtime. It was me who sifted through his goodies for razor blades and poisoned apples before he ate anything. It was me who made sure he only ate two pieces of candy before bed. Me.

The sky opens up and rain pours down. I shiver. I imagine the cozy bed that waits for me only blocks away and I run. The cat rests in the pool of light under a streetlamp and shakes the rain off his curly coat. A bank of mailboxes serves as his umbrella. Even at this distance, more than five feet away, I gag from the rotten stench. As I close in, I see bits of shell and raw egg dripping from yawning metal boxes. I hold my nose and hustle past, the cat at my side.

Home at last, I reach to unlatch the front gate and trip over something low and solid; a black cauldron props open the wooden gate. I reach a hand inside, but I find only a single full-sized candy

bar at the bottom. My father raided our earthq
kit, I guess.

A note in his familiar tidy script says, "Take
Halloween!"

I lift the cauldron and follow the cat up the walk.

Our Craftsman bungalow looks like something out of a national
park brochure; its leaf-green façade, stained glass, stone fireplace,
and overgrown flower garden make a happy picture, a picture that
warms my heart.

But, tonight I stand beneath the dim porch light and search my
mind for that thing I've left behind at Lakefront. Not Owen's teddy
bear. No. Something bigger and more important.

"God, Josie. Stop it!" I growl. I make a silent vow to stop obsessing
about my decision to rub a different grave. What's done is done.

The cat pushes past me and makes a beeline for the two flickering
jack-o'-lanterns on the top porch step. He pokes a paw deep inside
one of the hollow eyes and bats at the flame. He yanks his paw out
with a hiss, and the smell of burnt fur surrounds us both.

Owen and I carved the pumpkins last night and I am surprised
to see the candles inside have any life left in them. Mine looks primitive
and crude next to Owen's elaborate work. It took him nearly an hour
to sketch the cat face and full moon onto the side of his lumpy
Cinderella pumpkin, and even longer to whittle the design into the
flesh with a dull two-inch blade, the whole time blocking out my
chorus of, "Hurry up, Owen. Aren't you done yet?"

Me? I scratched a crude triangle-eyed face and toothy grin onto
my pumpkin, making quick work of the holiday activity, all the
while texting or talking on my cell. I am a bad sister.

As I turn my key in the deadbolt, I try not to wake the house.
But chances are Owen is still squirming and wiggling in his bed, unable
to zonk after eating too much candy. Dad the early bird, will be out,
dozing off to some an old Alfred Hitchcock on his favorite television
channel not long after eight.

I slip inside the door, but the cat stalls at the threshold. I scoop
him up. "It's all right, little guy. You're welcome here."

Padding down the hall to my bedroom on quiet feet, I wrap the
cat in a thick blanket and plunk him in the middle of my bed. Then I

leave the room, close the door, and tiptoe to Owen's room. In the dim glow of his rocket nightlight, I see his blankets in a heap on the floor. The air inside his room smells like sweaty kid and melted chocolate. I slink over and kiss Owen's sticky cheek and he grumbles, flipping onto his stomach. I scoop the blankets off the floor and straighten and tuck them around his long thin body. When did he get so big?

"I love you, Owen. Sorry I was such a grump about the pumpkins. I'll do better," I whisper.

I rub a hand over the back of his curly red hair and give him one last kiss, which he rubs off in his sleep. I flick off his nightlight and close his door behind me, and then move to the kitchen.

Feeling my way in the dark, I dig through the kitchen cabinets for cat supplies. Finally, I locate an ancient can of tuna and a small plastic bowl from Owen's baby days. Back inside my room I set up a temporary feeding station in the bathroom. I sit on the toilet lid and watch the kitty inhale his makeshift dinner.

Somewhere in the back of my mind I remember something about why you should never feed cats tuna. Seth would know. But since we've never owned a cat, the details escape me and I let him eat. Actually, he eats so fast I don't think I could stop him if I wanted. When he licks the last oily bit from the side of the bowl, I turn on the fan to get rid of the fishy odor that now permeates the tiny room. I pull myself to my feet and wander toward my bedroom. I'll wait until tomorrow to ask my father about the cat.

"Who could resist you, right?" I whisper. "We'll buy you proper supplies after he says yes." I stroke the length of his silky back and feel my body relax in kind. "Are you purring?" He vibrates against my hand. "I hope you like it here."

I examine the room through the eyes of a cat. Soft blankets. Big window. Everything a cat needs to feel at home except...

"Oh no! I don't have a litter box." I crack open the window above my bed and tell him, "In case of an emergency, go out there."

He jumps onto the sill and stares into the black yard. The soft sound of rain beating against the glass makes me feel sleepy.

It takes the last of my energy to unpack my satchel. I start with the roll of paper that pokes out of the bag. Using four silver pushpins, I hang the rubbing on the corkboard above my desk. I stow the extra art supplies inside my desk and set my cell phone in the charger.

A new text from Casey pops across the screen: "Alive. Home again. No sign of parents."

I hope they remembered to keep a light on for poor Casey, but then again, the Starbaugh family usually forgets they have a Casey.

After docking my phone again, I take a step back and study the strange rubbing. Its stark black and white form stands in contrast to my garden-themed bedroom, awash in shades of pastel. As I squint into the mysterious symbols on the rubbing, I can't help but wonder about the person buried beneath the odd tombstone. What do these symbols mean? I graze a finger along the coin-shaped arch at the top of the paper. Was the person buried here really a witch? And what did Grace mean when she said, "I won't do her bidding?" The last question sends a chill through my body. Maybe it's best to leave any deeper analysis alone tonight.

I roll my fatigued shoulders in tight circles, but the stress has settled too deep to release. I wanted an adventure, didn't I? Looks like I got one. Witch or not, she died and her name isn't even carved on her tombstone. And why doesn't Grace mow the grass on her plot, anyway? Is she scared? Should I be scared?

I shake my head. "Crazy thoughts. What I need right now is a bed. Sleep makes everything better."

The cat vaults onto my desk and shoves his head under my hand. As I stroke the length of his soft lean body, the knots in my shoulders loosen. He purrs under my hand, but a tightness forms under my ribcage. I massage the ache with a fist, and hot tears prick at my eyes. I confirm that my door is closed, and then give in to the sadness. As a tear rolls down my face, the cat stands on his back paws and pushes his head against my face. His whiskered cheek tickles my forehead. He smells like tuna. A fat tear drops onto his silky fur, but he doesn't seem to notice.

"Tonight was supposed to be magical. I thought I would feel my mom's spirit with me. Halloween's when the dead speak, just not to me, I guess."

Swallowing down salty tears, I keep talking to the cat. "I'm stuck with a bunch of foggy memories of her. I don't even know which ones are real anymore and which ones I made up. I'm no better off than Owen," I sob.

My shoulders shake as I silently weep. A steady stream of tears rains down on his blue coat. "I didn't sense anything supernatural, just the same old, same old. Then you took me on a wild goose chase to the Ghost Forest. What if that was my last chance to really connect with her and I missed it?"

I press my fingers against my eyes, willing the tears to stop. I want to feel happy again. Chocolate. Must have chocolate. And then I remember the gift from Grace and reach inside my satchel to find a miniature candy bar. The buttery caramel and chocolate square melts across my tongue and the sadness recedes, not away, but into a dark corner. I draw in a deep breath and will myself to stay calm.

"Time for bed."

I grab a fleece blanket from the chair in the corner and spread it across the bottom half of the bed. The cat jumps up immediately and begins to knead himself a cozy spot, working the blanket like a mama cat. "I knew you'd fall for my cat trap."

He curls his body into a tight ball and slips into a dream. I give him a kiss on the top of his sleepy head and smile. "Maybe tonight wasn't a complete failure. I found you, didn't I?"

A flit of movement at the window catches my eye. A black crow perches on the windowsill outside and scans my room with a keen, glossy eye. Then, with a rustle, his feathers ruffle across his body. With another rustle, they lie flat again. Closing his eyes, he seems to settle in. I consider shutting the window but then think about how the cat is supposed to use the bathroom, and the potential mess and stench if I close it. I leave the window open a crack.

Ready to settle down too, I shed my costume. I reach inside the top drawer of my chestnut dresser and pull out a thin white t-shirt, a bold cheeseburger grinning across the front, and ancient plaid pajama pants. I slip them on, pull my hair back in a low ponytail, and collapse onto the bed. I imagine my beautiful, copper-haired mother, the sweet scent of baby powder, and the caress of golden sunshine on our faces, and I fall fast asleep.

In my sleep, I hear a voice crying, "Josie! Wake up. I've locked myself out. Josie! Let me in, please! The door's locked."

My mother's voice oozes through the cracked window. I try to wake up; she wants me to let her in, but I'm so tired. I finally awaken to a chill running down my spine like a cold finger. I check my window and see the smoky black outline of my mom, Sarah Jameson. She looks at me with dark, smoky eyes. "Josie, let me in, honey," she pleads. Curls of smoke shaped like black fingers probe inside the open window then disappear. "The front door's locked, baby."

I stare into her face, made up of the same smoky substance as the fingers; it shifts and pulses before me. Her eyes are soft and pleading. I recognize her and stare into their depths. I lean toward the window and rest my hand on the glass to push it open and she whispers, "Thank you." Her voice is just as I remember and I stare again at this strange, yet familiar form of my mother. Then I catch movement, behind her. Like looking through a thin veil, I see the trees of the yard through her form. As horrifying as it is, I cannot avert my stare.

As I gawk, her eyes shift into greasy black pools, like the crow's eyes. I shiver and back away from the window. At the same time, the cat jumps up, pressing his face into the crack. My mother slams her hand to the glass, and her image explodes into a puff of black ash.

I scurry back to bed and huddle under the covers. The cat jumps off the windowsill and curls against my legs, luring me back to sleep. I pray that the next dream will be made up of normal things.

Josie, Pancakes, and Moving Snakes

I SLAM THE 'OFF' BUTTON on the alarm clock harder than necessary and rub the last gritty traces of sleep from the corners of my eyes. It is a school day, which stinks. I stretch my legs beneath the cozy quilt and spy an empty divot where the cat should be, but instead I see only wisps of gray fur.

Footsteps thunder down the hall to my room and I jolt upright as my door swings open with a hard thud. Owen's freckled face peeks inside.

"Hey, Josie! Get up, lazybones. I found a kitty! A kitty! A kitty!" he sings, and pink splotches erupt across his cheeks.

My brother bounces up and down on tippy toes in fleecy blue space alien pajamas. His green eyes sparkle with mischief as he yanks on my comforter. If only he had enough muscles to pull me out of bed. Soon enough.

"Hey, Owen! You're supposed to knock before you come in!" I point to the sign I made months ago, skull and crossbones under the words, "Keep out!" He pays the sign about as much attention now as the day I taped it up, which is none.

"Sorry. Come see the kitty, Sis. Please, please, please!" Owen says. Without waiting for me, he turns and sprints down the hall and the "Keep out!" sign tears loose and flutters to the ground.

Every morning since way back when, I wake to find my pillow wet with tears from a dream I can never quite remember, and a knot of sadness in my chest. Today, I reach to flip the pillow over, but I stop. It is dry. Not exactly the proud feeling I had when I first mastered my ten-speed bike, but it's something. The feeling in my chest has changed from sadness to something uneasy and complicated. Something about my mom and a dream flits through my mind. I try to gather bits of the dream I had last night and find it is no more productive than sweeping the floor with my hands. She visited me and then she vanished.

Owen hollers down the hall, "Come on, Josie!" I promise to revisit the dream later.

I reach the family room and find the cemetery cat face down in a can of tuna. His full belly grazes the wood floor as he tries to lick the last morsels from the can.

"Isn't he the best, Josie?" Owen crows like a proud papa. The cat glances up at us briefly, a chunk of white tuna smashed across the bridge of his nose. "He's purring! Can you hear him?"

I nod. "Yeah. You sure that's not the noise he makes before he barfs?" As if to prove my point, the cat hiccups and then lops onto the sofa cushions, leaving behind a cloud of fishy gas.

"I found him, Josie. Me!" Owen bursts. "I was getting the newspaper for Dad, and the cat was curled up on the rocking chair. Dad said I get to keep him. He said we have to put up lost and found posters. But if nobody calls, I get to keep him. Forever!" Owen holds his hands behind his back and smiles.

I shake my head. "Sorry to burst your bubble, but this little guy followed me home from the cemetery last night. I was holding him prisoner in my room until I could talk to Dad. I guess he jumped out the window." Owen's smile vanishes, so I add quickly, "You did good, pal! He's in a strange place, so he might've gotten lost or even hit by a car if you hadn't brought him inside. Good job."

I gather him up in a bear hug and lift him off the floor until his feet dangle in the air. As I set Owen back on solid ground, the front door swings open and our dad enters the house, two grocery bags tucked under his arms. "Well, now we have the essentials. Thought I'd pick up some things for our new addition. You've met, I take it?"

A tall, lanky man in his mid-forties, my father's cheeks are tinged with color to match his windblown auburn hair. He puts down one bag and runs a hand through his wild curls. "It's pretty wicked out there. You'll need rain gear today."

As he hands me the bag, filled with a purple plastic box, liners, and litter, he asks, "Who'd like blueberry pancakes for breakfast?"

"I do! I do!" screams Owen. "How come you're making birthday food, Dad?"

"Well, maybe it's *his* birthday," he says, nodding his head toward the cat, who is busy grooming his face and ears. The cat stretches out across the sofa and purrs; his chubby tummy gives a gurgle. "This little guy needs a name. You two work on that, and I'll get cracking on breakfast."

Whistling, Dad strides into the kitchen. He hums a familiar cat food ditty as he pulls ingredients down from the cabinets. Dumbstruck, my feet stay cemented to the wooden floor and my mind spins. When's the last time Dad was this happy? And blueberry pancakes? You gotta be kidding me. Owen always begs him, and Dad always says no. Weird.

I head into the laundry room, slap the litter box together and give it a generous spray down with the catnip-in-a-can, and then check the time on the oversized clock that hangs above the dryer.

"Hey, Dad! You remember it's Monday, right?" I shout down the hall. "Will pancakes make us late for school?"

I walk back to the kitchen and recycle the empty bag of litter. I can't help but screw up my nose at my father, who's flipping pancakes like a veteran fry cook. He looks up from the griddle and winks at me so quickly that I wonder if I imagined it.

"Don't take the shuttle today. I'll drive you guys. That'll shave off twenty minutes. Besides, Jameson's Pancake House is open and ready for hungry customers!" He hands me a stack of steaming pancakes and then turns back to the grill, pouring circles of thick batter on the stainless griddle.

I cut the pancakes into pieces and head into the family room. Owen sits on the couch, stroking the sleepy cat stretched out across his lap. "Owen, hurry up and eat. We need to go soon," I tell my brother as I slip his plate of pancakes onto the arm of the sofa.

He points at the cat in his lap, "Look, Josie. I got him to sleep," he whispers. He strokes the cat and kisses the top of his head. For a second I think to warn him about worms, but I choke the impulse down and make a mental note to call a vet after school to get the cat in for shots.

Passing the kitchen, my father hands me a plate. "Dad, what's this? Mickey Mouse?" I pick up a pancake with ears and shake it in the air. He glances up and winks again. "Am I six?"

Still laughing, I pour a lake of maple syrup onto the pancakes. With a handful of quick bites, I devour the stack. As I place my plate in the kitchen sink, I say, "That was a great way to start the week, Dad. Thanks. I better get ready for school, though. We need to leave in about fifteen minutes."

I pass by Owen and warn him, "Eat fast, buddy! It's not pajama day at school. And I need time to do something with this mess before we go!" I pat the top of his springy red curls and he smirks at me as I race down the hall.

Usually, I'm meticulous about getting ready for school. It's not that I'm vain. Honestly, I'd be more comfortable in jeans and a ponytail. But, I learned the hard way after my mom died that how I look affects how people act around me. I have to laugh when kids at school call me a natural beauty. What an oxymoron. Choosing the right clothes and accessories, applying makeup that looks fresh and natural, and straight-ironing wild auburn locks into submission is a full-time job. There's nothing natural about it.

After my mom died, I missed a week of second grade for the whole funeral and mourning thing. When I came back to school, the class gave me a huge card and a pile of flowers. I know, really nice. But my classmates didn't talk to me anymore. I'd look up from my workbook and catch someone staring, or I'd spot clusters of kids whispering about me on the playground. I think they were waiting to see me have a big sloppy meltdown. It was awful.

Over the course of the week, I felt more and more left out by everyone except the Baby Group. The stares and whispers from the other kids left me feeling like an outcast. That is when I made it my goal to be perfect in every way so they would forget I was motherless. I knew if I tried hard enough, I could make them forget.

I had to dress and act perfectly. The dressing part was easy thanks to my Aunt Karen. She owns a children's clothing boutique. That's right, a boutique, not a shop. She jumped at the chance to fill my closet with the latest fashions. It was an excuse to spend time with me that didn't involve death, I suppose.

The acting part would be a longer journey. For months, I studied my stone-faced father and mimicked his ambivalence, his measured even tone of voice, always calm, nothing bubbling to the surface no matter what. All those years ago, I learned how to keep my true feelings trapped behind a fake smile and lying eyes.

By the end of second grade, I knew my masquerade had worked. After spring break, a new kid joined the class. At recess she found me and whispered, "Who is the girl with the dead mother?" Ah, sweet victory was mine. I pointed to a group of tetherball players on the far end of the playground to throw her off the scent.

Today however, I'm pressed for time, so I do the bare minimum. I dress in the first thing I grab from my walk-in closet: a faded pair of boot-cut jeans and a purple polo shirt. I wrap a multi-colored knitted scarf around my neck and slip into silver ballet flats. A quick check in the full-length mirror, and I call it good.

As I pull my hair back in a high and tidy ponytail, I idly study the rubbing that hangs above my desk. Doting my eyes with purple shadow, I wonder anew about the odd symbols. What do they mean?

I touch a finger to one of the dark quarter-sized circles that grace the top of the art. These look like holes where something ought to be. Is something missing from this headstone? I stare at the giant cloverleaf in the middle of the rubbing as my phone buzzes in its charger.

The screen lights up with a text from Seth. "Jeez, J. You OK?"

I text back, "?" and hit send.

My phone buzzes, and I read, "Your text last night. It said, 'Help me.'"

The hairs on my arms stand up and I grab a cardigan from the closet, suddenly chilled. As I turn to leave, something black flickers to life in my periphery. Did that clover move? Either I am tired or stark raving mad, but looking straight on at the rubbing, I don't see anything special. I focus on Seth's text and have to admit that I might be a touch crazy.

I text back, "It wasn't me. Ask C." I press 'send' with attitude and turn back to the rubbing.

Staring straight on, I see what looks like the head of a snake in one of the clover leafs. Its gaping mouth appears ready to snap off and consume its own spiky tail, creating a strange carnivorous circle. Feeling another chill, I slip on the cashmere sweater.

"Dude, it was from you!" Seth texts.

Owen yells at me from down the hall. "Josie! Brush my hair!"

I huff out my nose and scroll down through the text thread. There it is: a text from me to Seth at 3:15 a.m. that says, "Help me."

I pull my finger away from the screen and stare at the dark powder smeared on my fingertip. Eye shadow? I rub it on my jeans and suddenly remember the details of the spooky dream I had last night; my mom begged to come inside. She was made of ash.

"Josie! Come on!" Owen yells.

I creep closer to the rubbing and count four snakes, not leaves, on the clover. Four self-consuming snakes emblazon the center of this strange rubbing. Goosebumps erupt down my arms and panic bubbles up my throat, taking the form of maple syrup and orange juice. The room feels like it is collapsing in on me, crushing my ribs, and I sling the backpack over my shoulders and sprint down the hall.

By the time I hit the living room, I try to write it off to a lack of sleep. But it doesn't stick. My after school to-do list is getting longer: fetch Baby Sacagawea, make vet appointment, toss rubbing in the garbage? I tug a brush through Owen's hair, and he squirms under me because my mind forgets to tell my hand to be gentle. My mind is too busy trying to make sense of Seth's text and the rubbing. What the heck is happening to me?

JOSIE'S SCHOOL DAY

"DID ANYONE ELSE have bad dreams last night?" I group text to Casey and Blaze.

Blaze answers, "Slept like a baby."

"As in wearing diapers?" Casey returns.

I usually know better than to text on the car ride to school, because texting on this twisty road makes me feel sick. But today I am anxious to find out if anyone else had weird dreams after our field trip to Lakefront Cemetery. I crack my window and wait for the nausea to fade, as Dad threads his silver Euro-sedan to the school Owen and I have attended since preschool: Heritage Preparatory School.

Taking us to school is one big ego stroke for my father, which makes me wonder why he doesn't do it more often. When Mom got sick, Dad signed me up to ride the shuttle to school. It was fun back then because Seth rode the bus, too. It felt like a grown-up thing to do at the time. We always sat together and talked about big things like history and weather and death, things we imagined adults had conversations about on their commutes to work. I found out more about the history of the Beaux Arts Village, the neighborhood that hosts our fair school, than is natural to know at the age of eight. But the village is ripe with historical trivia which Seth adores.

Established in 1908 by a group of architects and artisans, the Beaux Arts society purchased fifty acres of wooded forest to create an idyllic Arts and Crafts community. People were invited to join the new community, as long as they built their homes in strict adherence to the aesthetics laid out in the founding documents. With a goal to be an independent entity, no roads were paved to reach the village.

A ferry system was built to shuttle people across Lake Washington to jobs in downtown Seattle. Nearly perfectly preserved more than a century later, visitors still come to explore this living history book, take in the Arts and Crafts houses and wander the last remnants of the ferry pier.

Midway through fourth grade, my ride to school got very lonely. It was the year of Seth's great rebellion. His perfect world crashed, his parents divorced, and Seth deemed his father to be the worst person in the world. The best way Seth could figure to get revenge was to fail school. But, all he really got was an angry parent and a desk in the public school down the street. And I got to ride the bus alone. No more big conversations. No more history lessons. It was sad, but I adjusted.

When I was in fifth grade, Owen started preschool and Dad drove us to school. Not to have quality time with us, he drove us to Heritage for the opportunity to watch as his drawings became reality each morning. He was the principle architect in charge of our school's major renovation. The project was his first in the historic neighborhood and would bring him a slew of awards and accolades. I knew he was driving us for him, but I did not care. Having a parent at school again felt good and I accepted it under any terms.

I check the screen on my phone for a text as we pull up to the curb at school. I open Owen's car door and grab his lunch sack from the seat. I stroke the wrinkles from the back of his khaki pants and he wiggles past, racing up the front steps to the entrance of our three-story private school.

"I win!" Owen yells and his breath comes out in a puff of white steam. He throws his hands in the air and does a victory dance.

"You always win!" I tousle his hair, undoing all my earlier hard work.

Before pushing inside the heavy front door, Owen and I turn toward the street below and send off our dad with a wave. As his car turns onto the arterial, I open the door and shepherd my brother inside.

As I walk Owen to the elementary school corridor, I take a look out the common area window wall to see if there are ducks on the lake outside, or even blue herons or eagles. Except for a runner with a dog, the park is empty.

My brother lets go of my hand before I can kiss him goodbye and runs down the hall toward a blonde girl with braids hanging down the front of her pink dress. She smiles and waves frantically at Owen.

"Have a good day, buddy. I love you. Think about cat names, all right?" I suggest.

Feeling uncharacteristically late, I make my way down the packed corridor of the high school wing at running speed. The hall is thick with the teens of Seattle's most famous residents, all busy sending one last text, offloading tonnage from their backpacks, flirting, primping, and generally loitering. My padlock is barely open when Blaze and Casey approach.

As I say a quick hello then unzip my backpack and unearth a notebook, pencil pouch, and a slim laptop, stopping briefly to inspect my friends.

Blaze looks at me like he's gauging my mood. "You doing okay? You left in a hurry last night," he asks.

"Yep! I was just really tired," I say.

Casey shuts her locker and comes at me. "I'm going back to the cemetery today. Do you want to go?" Her hair, tied with a thin silver ribbon, swings over her shoulders.

"Yeah. I have to find Baby Sacagawea. Why are you going back?" I ask.

"I want to see if Ettore's parents have been back since last night," Casey answers. "I've got to know if they've changed all that Halloween stuff over to Thanksgiving décor. It's sick, I know." She wraps a rainbow scarf around her neck and adjusts her jean mini-skirt; her calculator slips out from the pile in her arms, dropping to the floor with a clack.

I pick up the calculator and hand it back to her, "You're obsessed, Casey! But, whatever. Has anyone texted Seth to see if he wants to go?"

"No. I'll do that now," says Blaze. "I'd follow along, but I've got Aikido at four." He taps in a message and hits 'send.'

"Has the first bell rung?" I notice the necklace with my mother's ring has slipped free of its hiding place beneath my sweater. It must have slipped free when I went for the calculator. I tuck the ring safely away again.

"Not yet. You have a couple minutes. Relax, little one," Blaze says patting the top of my head. He loves to remind me how short I am. He turns his attention back to his phone.

"Hey! Did you get to keep the cat, Josie?" Casey asks.

"Yeah," I say. My mind returns to the freaky dream and my mystery text. "Hey, did any of you have bad dreams last night?"

"Don't you read your texts?" Blaze answers. "I told you; I slept like a baby."

"Oh, yeah. Does that mean you sucked your thumb?" Casey jabs, again.

She sticks her thumb in her mouth and smashes up her face. Blaze yanks her hand from her mouth, laughing. The two start to scrap and wrestle. Casey's scarf falls to the floor and they grab it at the same time, tugging it until the fabric rips. The bell rings for class and pink-faced and disheveled, Casey and Blaze break it up and turn to their lockers.

"Seriously. No one had a bad dream besides me? We spent Halloween in a cemetery rubbing graves. It's normal, right?" I ask. My friends stare at me like I've grown a third head.

Blaze squints into my face. "Josie, you always have bad dreams. Was something about last night's worse than all the others?"

"Yeah. It's no big thing, though," I say, my face aimed to the ground. "It was about my mom."

"Dude, that's not exactly a bad dream," says Casey.

"Well, she wasn't really herself. She came to me as a ghost, and she wanted me to let her in the house. But, I didn't do it."

My cheeks flush and I duck my head into my locker, pretending to dock my phone, praying they haven't noticed.

"That's creepy," Casey mutters. "But you didn't rub her grave, so…"

Blaze's phone dings and he checks the screen. "Seth can't go tonight. He's got a dad thing lined up. We're gonna be late, folks. Let's roll."

Like the kids around us, we scramble for our things and then race to our classes with a quick goodbye. I'm glad to get away from them before they see any more cracks in me that I forgot to cover up with makeup. Being me can be very exhausting.

JOSIE COLLECTS THE FORGOTTEN THING

GRACE PUSHES a rusty red wheelbarrow across the lumpy grass. "Josie, you are all frowns today. Too many tricks and not enough treats, honey?" she says, studying me with a sideways glance.

I stick on a smile. "Mondays leave me feeling blah, that's all. And I've got a bunch of homework," I lie.

My eyes flicker to the mammoth cedar up the hill that stands watch over my mother's grave, and I cross two fingers inside the sleeve of my raincoat and make a wish that Grace won't see through my dishonesty. I am a mixed bag of emotions and it has nothing to do with homework. I feel sad that I didn't end up rubbing my mom's grave and a little scared to unearth facts about the tombstone I did rub.

"Sometimes when I'm bothered about something, thinking about other people's problems puts mine in perspective. Take the story I read in the paper, for example." Grace says. "It was about a car fire in Fremont. A fellow stumbled upon it by accident and pulled over himself to help the folks trapped inside."

We travel over uneven ground and a hand trowel bounces out of the wheelbarrow. Casey scoops it up and plunks it back inside. "Thanks, Casey." Grace tucks the trowel away and continues her story.

"With the car threatening to explode at any moment, the stranger tugged a door open and pulled a little girl to safety!" Grace says in a rush. "In spite of all that danger, he went back into the car a second time to fetch the driver! Can you believe that?" She takes a deep breath. "Kind of makes worrying about homework seem a little silly, doesn't it?"

Grace gazes at the sky above and a sparkle flickers across her amber eyes as she glances up the hill toward my mother's grave.

Casey says, "Oh my gosh. What happened to the driver? Please tell me he survived, too."

I slip my heavy backpack to the ground next to Casey's feet. We stand next to a glossy black tombstone, not fifty feet from the entrance gates to Lakefront Cemetery, with the name "Marlene Smith" carved across its surface. It's four o'clock in the afternoon and the morning fog has finally evaporated and I squint into the sun, unaccustomed to its brightness. The grounds glow gold, my favorite light for sketching. Though I am in no mood to do art, Grace's story has begun to pull me out of my own complicated, guilt-laced thoughts.

Stuffing a curl under her knitted cap, Grace rubs her hands together and continues. "I wish I could tell you the driver survived. Unfortunately, he didn't. When the stranger got to him, the driver was still alive. He was trapped inside by a seatbelt that wouldn't budge. Instead of leaving the driver alone to wait for help, the stranger crawled inside next to him, held his hand and waited next to him in the passenger seat until the paramedics arrived. Finally, the ambulance made it to the scene. They cut the driver free and soon after pronounced the driver dead," she says. "It's so damn sad." She shakes her head and wipes fat tears from her eyes.

"Anyway, here's the crazy part. A couple days later the man that rescued the little girl was startled awake by the driver of the car. His ghost stood at the foot of the man's bed, probably giving him quite a shock. The ghost asked the rescuer to do one last kind deed for his family; for his surviving daughter and wife. He asked the man to deliver a final message to his family. Strange as it all seemed, the rescuer delivered the message. And that was that," Grace finishes.

"Wow! That's some story. Kind of creepy, though," says Casey, and Grace and I nod in agreement.

I ask, "What was the message he was supposed to deliver?"

"He wouldn't tell the reporter," Grace says. "Said it was for the family's ears alone. But he could see it brought them a great deal of comfort, not just the message, but the fact that we go on after we die." She dusts her work gloves off on her muddy overalls and tosses them on the pile of dead plants in the wheelbarrow.

"That story got me thinking about you kids." She scans the graves that surround us. "How many of the folks buried at Lakefront had one more thing to do before they died? How many have some piece of business that still needs doing? Maybe they need someone to wrap things up for them, neat and pretty. Until then, they stay unsettled.

"It got me thinking, what if that's why you kids were drawn to the graves you chose? Someone underneath may need a hand. After all these years, maybe you'll get to help someone rest in peace. Did you ever think of that?"

Grace looks at me and I think about the grave I was supposed to rub. I glance once more at the hill that holds my mom and feel an urgent need to get moving, collect Baby Sacagawea, and slink home. I say in a quiet whisper, "Maybe. I thought we might be called to a particular grave, but I don't know. Now, it sounds so romantic and unrealistic."

Casey fidgets with her bangs and knots her black hair into an awkward bun at the back of her head. "Well, I'm not sure I even rubbed the right one," Casey mumbles. "Seems like the one I rubbed has plenty of visitors already. He doesn't need me to do anything." She purses up her lips so tightly they lose their color, and I watch Grace back up a step.

"Why do you care about his visitors?" she asks.

Casey scowls at Grace. "I don't care about his visitors. I just doubt a kid has any unfinished business, that's all. Seems like his family members are the ones that have unfinished business. Wouldn't they get over his death after all these years?" She looks past us to something in the distance, and I follow her stare to the far corner of the children's cemetery.

I grab her sleeve and rub her arm. "Does a parent ever get over losing a child? Isn't that a parent's worst nightmare?" I say.

Casey pushes my hand away and wraps her arms around herself. "I'm not sure my family would even notice," she says, without a trace of bitterness.

"That's crazy talk, Casey! A family by definition cares," Grace yanks a weed free from the grass and tosses it in the wheelbarrow. "Come on, now. What's this?"

I look at Casey to see if she is going to tell our new friend about her cold, distant family. She is staring at the ground, so I assume not. How much can I say? We've grown up together, but I still cannot wrap my head around the way her parents ignore her. It's no wonder why Casey spends more time at my house than hers.

"Well, Casey doesn't have what you would call a typical family life. She lives in the shadows of an older brother that is the best ever at everything. Casey hasn't brought home any awards yet, so she is invisible to them." I explain.

Casey laughs without humor. "She's making it sound better than it is Grace. My mom was born in China. As a little girl, her family sent her off to boarding school. She had to earn her scholarship with good marks. If she failed, she would have had to come home and work in a factory. The way she sees it, I'm nothing to her until I prove I am the best at something too." She pauses. "I'll bet that boy, Ettore, was the cutest kid that ever lived. I *know* he was. He doesn't need me for anything."

She yanks a weed free from the grass and with it comes a giant clump of moss. She tosses it into the wheelbarrow.

"Girl, what do you know about him? His name? The day he died? You don't know what he may need now, do you?" Grace says, a smile breaking over her face. She pulls off her knitted cap and shakes her braid loose, curly brown hair flows past her thin shoulders. I feel like I am watching a butterfly emerge as the shell of the tough cemetery lady falls off and a noble, beauty emerges from the layers.

I laugh thinking of the odd grave in the Ghost Forest, the one that scares me a bit. Grace and Casey turn to me. "Well, I rubbed some long-forgotten witch. Don't know exactly what she might need, except for an eye of newt and toe of frog…." Putting it out there, it feels silly to be scared of a rubbing. I was tired this morning. Nothing moved. There are no witches. I relax.

The sun dips behind a thick cloud and I grope for my backpack. "We better get a move on, Casey. I need to find Baby Sacagawea before it gets pitch dark."

I think about heading off on my own, but Casey seems shaky, so I accept that we will stay together. We give Grace a quick hug and walk toward the children's cemetery.

As we approach Ettore's grave, Casey slows. She runs her hand across the snowy white sculpture of the boy. Touching the deeply carved curls on his head with a gentle finger, her brow furrowed, she clears her throat.

"It's beautiful. I can see why you were drawn to it," I offer.

Crisp, bright sunflowers and sprigs of fragrant rosemary are tucked artfully inside a stone urn at the base of the petrified tree. Any hints of Halloween are noticeably absent; the costume, the orange and black floral bouquet, all that Casey described last night, are gone. I glance at Casey, and her face is twisted into a sour expression.

"Casey! Are you feeling okay? You look like you're about to explode."

"Jeez, Josie, cut the Oprah, would you?" Her knot of hair falls apart and spreads out over her face. "All right, that's all I came to do. I can see that his parents came again and switched out the Halloween stuff. Goody. We can go now."

She turns and leaves.

"That's it? That's all you came for?" I ask the back of her head.

"I told you. I wanted to see if his parents came today to change things around. And they did. Let's go." Not waiting for me, she stomps toward the entrance gates, and I hurry to catch up. Grace glances up as we pass and I shrug my shoulders at her.

"Hey, Casey! We can't leave, I've got to…"

But she is already outside the entrance gates and beyond earshot. I walk to my mother's grave alone.

SETH LEARNS SOMETHING IMPORTANT

I'D NEVER ADMIT TO MY FATHER how much I love this desk, the only thing of any value in this hovel of a bedroom. I run a hand over the smooth, glossy finish of the burled walnut. Given to me in second grade after receiving another report card of straight A's, the desk is a miniature replica of my father's desk. The original sits against a floor-to-ceiling window in Seattle's most powerful law firm. Not long ago, my father was my hero and I wanted to be just like him. But, that was a lifetime ago.

Before my lawyer phase, I wanted to be a construction foreman; Foreman Seth. While my older sister toiled at school, Mom and I spent hours at construction sites. She'd pack lunch, then drive us to some hole in the ground, the bigger the better. I knew the equipment by sight; earthmovers, backhoes, cement mixers, dump trucks, and all the rest. I wore a yellow construction helmet everywhere, which drew all sorts of funny looks.

I'd still be dreaming of that career as a construction foreman if it weren't for the bathrooms. During one of our construction site lunches, I had to go. And when you gotta go, you gotta go!

Out of desperation, Mom brought me into a portable toilet on-site. I changed career paths in the span of two stinky minutes. I hung up the old hardhat, put all my die-cast construction vehicles into my memory box, and took a fresh look at my vocational options.

As chance would have it, "Bring Your Kid to Work" day followed soon after. My father had brought me to his downtown law firm to experience a day in the life of a prosecutor. His morning was spent locked inside his corner office with a small group of people prepping for an upcoming trial.

I spent that time in the care of his legal secretary. That pretty blonde lady who looked like a younger version of my mom, taught me the ins and outs of the copy machine, tricks for filing fast, and how to get a lunch catered with barely an hour's notice.

When the heavy wooden door to my father's office opened at last and his glass conference table was cleared of occupants and lunch remnants, I was ushered inside. The panoramic view of the city was incredible, even on that drizzly day.

As I watched the mist collect into fat drops and slide down the windows, I felt the urge to go. That's when my dad ushered me into the executive bathroom. Not only was it the cleanest restroom I'd ever visited, but it was snazzy. Like, straight out of a magazine awesome. When I came out still drying my hands, I announced I wanted to be a lawyer like him. And for the next couple of years, I wore my miniature three-piece suit purchased for a family wedding to school. I carried my lunch in an attaché. I tried to look, act and speak like my father.

The desk I sit at now is polished to a high shine; its burgundy wood shimmers under a green desk lamp. The elaborate Birdseye maple veneer, golden brass hardware, and clawed lion feet are not worthy of the pigsty that surrounds them in my room. Though I no longer wish to be anything like my father, I can't make myself hate the desk. Random rave posters hang crooked above an unmade bed. Dirty clothes lie in piles on the white carpet at my feet. And the garbage can overflows with wads of paper and old food wrappings. I keep my room at Mom's house tidy. This mess I create solely to irritate my father. Why do anything halfway?

There. I complete my algebra homework and print "Seth Anthony" neatly in the corner. Reaching into my top desk drawer, I pull out a pair of scissors from a green felt tray. Carefully, I trim off the last three problems and stow them into a file folder in the locking drawer marked in block print, "Algebra." Like the effort it takes to make my room look slovenly, it takes equal amounts of work to earn mediocre grades. I complete all of my assignments, but take care to turn in only eighty-percent of my work. Pulling at the brass handle one last time to make sure the drawer is locked, I startle as my father ducks his head inside my room.

"Hey, son. We need to get cracking on dinner. I'm starving," he says. "Are you done with your homework?" His perpetual stack of legal files is missing from his arms and I worry suddenly that this won't be a working dinner as per usual. Are we going to attempt to have quality time? I think about grabbing my algebra book off the floor and starting from scratch, but decide to see where this leads.

"Yeah. Just finished."

I follow him to the kitchen where water boils on the stovetop. Nervous about spending time with him without him having a stack of work between us, I grab a potato off the counter and start to peel it. The best word to describe my method is "frenzied" as the brown peels fly across the counter and fall to the floor.

"Why aren't we getting take-out? Isn't that the bachelor way? We haven't had Chinese in a while."

"I thought it'd be fun to start cooking together when you stay with me," he answers, as he removes a saucepan from a drawer. "Maybe it'll be good for us. Besides, take-out food gets pretty old when you eat it every single day."

I think about my mom's great cooking and how I miss it on my odd week at my father's place. The side effects of divorce are never-ending. "I guess you should have thought of that while you were diddling the paralegal, huh? That you might miss Mom's cooking?"

My ears burn red, and my heart pounds in my chest. I grind my teeth to keep from saying more, and chop the raw potato with a little too much testosterone. I sneer at my father as I work.

"I'm not going there tonight, son. I can only apologize so many times for what a jerk I was. All I can do is move forward. You should, too. It's been four years," he says, whisking a gravy packet into boiling water. The brown gravy bubbles and sends a delicious smell across the postage-stamp kitchen. My stomach growls.

After I've finished chopping the potatoes, I drop them into the boiling water and the pan threatens to boil over. As I turn down the heat, the oven timer beeps.

"Can you get that, Seth? If I stop stirring, we'll have lumps in the gravy."

I grab black and silver oven mitts off the counter and open the oven door. A plume of savory steam hits my face. Carefully, I remove a casserole dish filled with bubbling stuffed pork chops. A savory aroma follows the hot pan onto the countertop.

My father says, "Grab some dinner plates, would you? We're waiting on the potatoes. They'll be done soon, seeing that you diced them!"

"I was worried you were going to give us food poisoning. But, this actually smells good. So, when'd you learn to cook?"

"Do you want the real answer or the fake one?" he asks, turning the heat on the gravy down to simmer. He sets the whisk into the sink and turns to face me. His eyes look intense.

"The real answer, I guess."

"Your mother told me this summer that she forgives all my mistakes; the affair being the biggest of them. We got together a few times. Not formal dates, just a lunch here and a walk there. We had some great talks. I wish we'd had more of those when we were married. We even did a handful of counseling sessions together. She told me that she forgives me."

He stops and wipes under his eyes with the cuff of his sleeve. "It's more than I deserve. Anyway, she tried to take some responsibility for my mistakes, which I wouldn't allow. I was the idiot, not her. In the end, we agreed that we still love each other. But, she doesn't want me back. Who can blame her, right?"

I rub my hands together and pace in the tight space. "Thanks a lot for keeping me in the loop. Therapy? Walks in the park? Awesome!" He ignores me and keeps talking.

"So, I signed up for a cooking class... partly because I was depressed and needed something to do. Mostly, I knew it was time for a dose of reality. Looks like I'll be alone for the long haul. Your mother was the one for me, and I screwed it up." He serves us pork chops and stuffing, careful to avoid my angry stare.

"I couldn't risk getting your hopes up, or worse, making you hate me more than you already do. I've done enough damage to this family. And after all this, I realize more than ever that you and your sister are the best thing I've ever been a part of. You're all I have left. Especially you now that Sadie's off to college. It's just you and me."

I stab a fork into the boiling water and one of the bits of potato breaks apart.

"I think the potatoes are done." I can see why he didn't say anything to me before this, but Mom? I thought we were close.

"What do I do now?" I ask.

"Use the lid to drain the water from the pan. Then toss in a couple tablespoons of butter and mash them with this."

He hands me a silver-handled tool with wide holes across the flat end. "I'll pour in a little milk as you work."

Five minutes later we sit down to a hot, home-cooked meal.

"Cheers!" he says, raising a glass of apple cider.

"Yeah, cheers." My mind is still busy processing all that my father has said. I want to jump up from the table and call Mom. The food smells too good and my stomach growls. I decide to eat first.

"So, how'd it go last night? A visit to the cemetery on Halloween with the gang? Did I hear your mother right?"

"Mm, yeah."

I swallow, and then take a long hard look at the man across the table. He leans forward like he really wants to hear something about it. Maybe I'll throw him a bone. "Josie had this tombstone rubbing kit from her aunt. It was pretty cool. I rubbed the grave of a sergeant who was in World War II. We even met the cemetery caretaker, and she told us some cool ghost stories."

Digging into my plate, I take a forkful of meat and stuffing. It melts in my mouth. I can't believe my father made this meal. It's actually good. Still chewing, I say, "I had a dream about the sergeant last night, Sergeant Isaac Paxton."

My father pauses eating and wipes his face with a paper towel. "What was it?"

"Nothing scary. We were sitting across a booth from one another at this fifties diner. We sipped coffee and ate pie."

"Whoa! Since when do you sip coffee?"

"It was just a dream! Anyway, the point is that we were comfortable with each other, like we had been friends for a long time. He told me that life had been good to him. He was able to come back from the war with all his limbs. He was even recognized as a hero, but he didn't dwell on that part. He got a taste of true love. He said life doesn't owe him anything. He told me I have permission to let it go."

"Let what go, son?"

"That's what I'd like to know. The thing is, I can't stop thinking about how his eyes and his story didn't match. His story sounded resolved, complete, but his eyes looked haunted and sad somehow. Does that sound strange?"

"Sounds like you have a mystery on your hands." My father pours applesauce onto his plate from the jar, a great big puddle right next to his potatoes and they ooze into one another, yellow and white mush.

I tear my eyes away from the mess and use my fork to separate my meat from the pile of potatoes left on my plate. "Do you believe in ghosts?" I ask.

He scrapes the last of the mixed mush onto his fork and swallows. Then he says, "Yeah, I do. I even saw a ghost one time."

He gathers up our empty dishes and moves to the kitchen sink, turning on the water. I rise, grab what is left on the table, and put it all in the sink. Elbow to elbow, he rinses off dishes and I place them in the dishwasher.

"When did you see a ghost?" I make an effort to sound calm, like I'm only pretending to be interested. I've spent too long keeping him at a safe distance to go all authentic on him now. I'm sure my red neck is giving me away though. It's my tell, the bane of a fair-skinned guy. The plate rattles as I slip it into the dishwasher with my shaky hands.

"Do you remember that old house your grandparents owned in Spokane? The mansion on Fifth Street?"

"Yeah, the one by the park with all the ducks?"

"Exactly. Well, when I was about nine, we moved there. The house was ancient, even back then. With three kids and one more on the way, your grandparents needed a bigger house. And that house was huge, but it needed a ton of work. It had sat vacant for a decade so it was in disrepair. That meant every Anthony weekend included a meaty do-it-yourself project.

"The day we moved in, I was helping your grandma move boxes into the basement. While we were unpacking, an old, heavily-whiskered man appeared. He was dressed in this old-fashioned suit with a black bolo tie, and he looked to be about eighty or so. He stood next to my mom and said, 'You get out of this house.' He didn't yell or anything, but I just about peed my britches." He laughs at the memory. Six o'clock shadow colors his strong jawline with black flecks. He wipes his thumb under his green eyes and I see the wrinkles around his face that weren't there the last time I really looked. He runs a hand through his hair.

"Oh my gosh! What did Grandma do? Did she freak out?" I want to hear more about his side of the family, people I didn't know well because all our visits were with my mom's family who lived an hour outside of Seattle.

"No. She stood her ground. I don't know how she stayed so calm, but I will never forget how she looked at him and said, 'It's my house now, not yours. It's time for you to get going, mister.' And, by God, that's just what he did. He vanished in front of us like a puff of smoke.

"The next day, your grandma and I took a trip to City Hall. She had them pull the file on our house. Buried inside and yellowed from being a hundred years old was a photograph of our ghost. The paperwork said he'd built that house for his wife. But tragically, she died before the place was finished. They never had a family. He roamed around that huge place alone all those years."

I take a seat at the table and fidget with the plastic salt and pepper shakers, the kind people buy for picnics and other temporary occasions. "Wow! Did you ever see him again?"

"Nope, he never came around. I guess after Grandma told him it was her house, he moved on." My father pours himself a glass of red wine and sits across from me at the table.

"Are you going into work this weekend?" I ask.

My father leans back on two legs of his chair, the glass of wine balanced in one hand. "I wasn't planning on it since you're here. Why?"

"I wanted to do some research on Sergeant Paxton. I bet I could find out more with your network."

"Well, I've always got plenty of work to do in the office. We're about to go to trial on that fraud case. How about we go in Saturday morning, and then cut out early for meatloaf sandwiches at McSorley's?" He leans his chair onto four legs again and takes a sip of wine.

"That'll work." Wiping down the table, I look up at my father. "Thanks for dinner. And the story. Thanks for sharing that with me." "Any time. I can't wait to see what you find out about the sergeant." "Yeah, that makes two of us."

BLAZE AND THE DO OVER

AFTER SCHOOL, I come home to an empty house and a blank wall where my rubbing was posted only hours ago. On the wall above my bed, I'm shocked to find bits of white paper trapped under the red pushpins I used last night to hang up Father Kujala's rubbing, nothing but bits of paper where a full-sized rubbing should be. In the center of my desk sits a yellow sticky note stating in crisp black letters: "Blaze, we <u>will</u> talk about this when I get home. M."

"What did you do with it, Mother?" I say to the air.

I kick over the garbage can under my desk, but nothing spills out except crumpled half-done algebra problems. I race to the kitchen and Miso, my Shiba Inu, shoots through the doggy door from the backyard. He charges at my legs for a biscuit and a thorough petting. But like good dogs do, he senses my wrath before I can rein it in, and he runs away from me.

The recycle can sits empty. I follow the smoky scent into the family room. Miso lies flat on the ground by the fireplace hearth, his face resting on his tan paws. If you didn't know better, you would think he was a rug he is so flat. He stares at me with guilty brown eyes.

"Miso! What did you do?" Where I expect to see a yellow puddle, I find a wisp of singed paper and bits of ash scattered across the brick hearth. "No way."

I ball up my fist, ready to hit something and fume. My bossy, overbearing mother went into my room, tore down my rubbing and burned it. I stomp at the ground and Miso zips away. "You couldn't just throw it away? You had to destroy it? What are you afraid of, Mother? That I brought God into your home? If you don't believe in Him, how can one piece of paper threaten you? Or be powerful enough to influence me? It makes absolutely no sense! It's my room and my life! You had no right!"

I have to get it all out now while the house is empty, because around here real feelings aren't acceptable. Miso has left a trail of yellow from the living room to his doggy door. "Great! Now I have to clean up after you, too!" I bark.

Returning to my room, I toss my backpack on my bed and grab a windbreaker from the closet. I grab a wad of tissue from the bathroom and wipe up Miso's pee with my shoe. I think about leaving the wad of yellow tissues on the floor, but toss them into the garbage can instead. As I stomp out the front door, I text Josie: "PU ruined rubbing. Need stuff to make a new one. U home?"

I don't text my mother. Let her sweat it and wonder where I am. Then I realize she won't be sweating at all because I'm supposed to have Aikido tonight. My phone beeps with Josie's text: "Just got back from there. LOL. Grabbing stuff, could be back at cemetery in 20?"

"Yes."

It would've made more sense to jump on the Metro, but the cold wet air feels good, cleansing somehow, and it washes the last of the smoke from my nostrils. I picture myself as a dragon that's blown fire through his mouth and now paces back and forth in a prison, a thick chain tied around his neck. I walk fast, fuming about the rubbing. It will take me under ten minutes at this breakneck pace to get to Lakefront.

I wait for the light to change green and stare across the street at the small, brown church on the corner; its stained glass windows glow from the inside. Organ music leaks from the stone and wood walls of the church. Surrounded on all sides by two-story houses, the brown cabin-sized church looks like a time capsule, something you would expect in a fairy tale forest, not on the streets of a Seattle suburb.

Before my mind has caught up with my feet, I cross the street. Standing before the tiny church, I listen to the music from the sidewalk. A bell rings from a tower that stands watch over the structure. Its mellow chime resonates in the thick, humid air. A high voice sings along with the organ and a churchy song rings out of the walls to me in sweet, pure tone. The singing cuts off abruptly and the thick wooden doors swing open. A tiny blonde girl runs out toward me.

"Mom wants me to practice, but I'm tired of that song! I'm not going back." The girl looks up at me with giant blue eyes and waits for my answer. I look behind me, expecting someone else to be standing there, but all I see is a trim boxwood and patch of grass.

"Are you talking to me?"

"Yeah, I need help. I thought you might be an angel, you know, here to help me get out of practice today." She smiles up at me and her eyes twinkle. Golden wisps of hair flutter around her sweet round face. And suddenly I feel like the sun is shining on my face, warm and happy.

"No one sent me. Coincidence. That was you singing in there?"

"Yeah."

"You're pretty good for someone so pint-sized," I joke.

She smirks with half of her cute face and continues to stare up at me. Her eyes are so blue.

I try my best to help. "Well, you might not want to practice, but you'll worry them sick if you run off. Go back in and tell them your throat's tired."

"Is that a lie? Won't God be mad?"

"I have no idea. You're tired of singing today though, right?"

"Yeah." She rubs her neck and frowns. "Can you go in there and sing for me?" she asks, grabbing my hand with her tiny white fingers and tugging me toward the concrete steps that lead to the church entrance. I can't help but laugh.

"I'm not much of a singer. Besides, I probably don't know these songs. My heart wouldn't be in it."

"My heart isn't in it today, either. But I guess I better go back. Bye."

And with that, the little blonde whirlwind tugs the iron handles open, parts the heavy doors, and slips inside. Before she disappears entirely, she waves at me and I see her run up the long aisle toward the pipe organ through the closing doors.

I wave and check the time on my phone. Late, I race the rest of the way to the cemetery. Josie must be waiting for me by now, alone. Out of breath, I see her standing inside the gates with an oversized sketchbook under her arm. She waves at me.

"Hi. Sorry I kept you waiting, Josie. Have you been here very long?" I pant.

"No. I just got here. So, your rubbing got ruined?"

"Yeah, my mother ripped it down and burned it in the fireplace actually. Nice, huh?"

"That's pretty harsh, even for the Drama Queen. Here." She hands me paper, tape and graphite. "Do you mind if I tag along," Josie asks.

"Not at all. Sorry you had to come back to Lakefront again. I forgot what you guys were doing after school."

"No problem. If we have time, I'd like to take a look at the grave I rubbed. I think I must have done something wrong; parts of my rubbing look strange." She shrugs a shoulder.

"Strange? As in you didn't get all the details?" I ask.

She bites her lower lip, "Sort of, parts of the rubbing look like snakes and this other thing looks like an octopus. I just want to see the tombstone in person to know for sure." She adds, "Let's get a move on before it gets much darker."

We walk in silence to Father Kujala's grave. A man is stooped over the plot, too busy trimming back strands of dead plants to notice us. The whole area smells like a perfume counter at the mall. When he finally sees us, he stands and we introduce ourselves.

Now that he's standing, I see that he's a good six inches taller than me. He dusts off his hands on a khaki pant leg and holds one out to Josie and me.

I shake it, introduce myself and say, "I'm sorry to disturb you. I only met Father Kujala last night. Well, more like I rubbed his gravestone."

"Hi there," Josie says, shaking the man's mocha hand.

"Nice to meet you. My name is James."

He grabs a navy windbreaker off the ground and puts it on. Beside him sits a white canister filled to the brim with yard waste. He continues, "So, a grave rubbing. What brought you back again? The conversation?" He laughs as he trims another clump of brown with his rusty scissors and tosses it into the container at his feet.

"Something happened to my first rubbing, so I wanted to do it again. Honestly, I didn't even realize this was a grave at first with all herbs and flowers growing over it. The caretaker told us that's part of the Russian Orthodox tradition. Is that right?"

"Sort of. As a boy he attended the Russian Orthodox Church, but his family was from Alaska." He points to a stone figure nestled deep inside the foliage. "That's why this little guy was placed here."

Cobbled out of rectangular rocks in varied shades of gray, the figure stands nearly eighteen-inches high. Out of the greenery pokes a stone man, made up of two stocky granite legs, a brick-sized granite torso, a thin rectangular stone for arms and a round river rock balanced on top for a head.

"Wow! I didn't see that last night. It must've been covered over by the plants. What is it?"

"It's an Inuksuk," Josie answers before James can speak. "They're stone figures left by native tribes to mark something important. My mom told me about these a long time ago. She was from Alaska, also." Her eyes cloud over and she touches the stone man's head.

"Nice! I'm officially impressed," James says, smiling.

"What were they used for, Josie?"

"The figures sometimes helped tribes find their way to a good hunting ground. Sometimes they marked a food cache. Others helped direct people to nearby villages. Some were thought to hold magical powers, so people would leave trinkets, hoping their wishes would be granted. That's about all I remember."

"We built this one to point Father Kujula toward heaven. It was to honor his Alaskan heritage," James says.

"So, were you a member of his church?" I ask.

"Yes. I studied under him as a young man. Then after seminary school, I worked with him at Holy Episcopal Church. Now, I'm blessed to lead the flock there."

"You're a priest? You don't look like a priest."

I realize too late that I should have kept my mouth shut.

The man laughs. "I'll take that as a compliment. What's a priest supposed to look like then?"

"Well, all the priests I've seen in movies are old and white." I hold my hand next to his, both dark brown in the waning sunshine.

"First of all, Blaze, God doesn't just speak to people with light skin. He's here for everyone to enjoy. And secondly, I'll look old and crotchety soon enough. So, savor this while you can!" He grins widely and holds his arms out.

Josie smacks my belly with the back of her hand, "Ha! That was such a Blaze thing to say." She and I crack up.

"And funny. I didn't think priests were supposed to be funny," I add.

"Now, now. I think God does his best work with humor. Well, Josie and Blaze. I should clear this junk out of here so you can get your rubbing done. We're about to lose our light."

He reaches inside a pocket of his windbreaker and pulls out a business card. "Here Blaze. Take this in case you have any questions about Father Kujula. Come by and visit me any time, both of you. I'm right down the street." He hands me the small white card.

I read the card. "Are you kidding? You have a cell phone?"

"Yeah, this is the twenty-first century, Blaze. Some of my parishioners are more comfortable texting than talking to me in person. I write my sermons on an iPad, too. Shocking stuff, isn't it?"

He smiles and grabs his can of yard waste by the handle. "Have a good night. God bless you both." He heads toward the entry gates.

We are both quiet as I finish my rubbing.

"Hey, Josie. Look at this! What language is this?" I point to an odd phrase that decorates the bottom of the Father's stone.

"I don't know. I suppose you can look it up when you get home. Didn't you see that last night?" Josie asks.

"Nope. It didn't make it onto my rubbing either. I must not have done as good a job as I thought. Good thing we came back tonight."

"Yep," Josie says distractedly. "Blaze, would you mind coming with me to my grave? I won't take too long." She stares at something off in the distance, must be where the Ghost Forest is.

"No prob. Let's hurry. I don't want to be caught in the Ghost Forest when the sun goes down! Mwaaah haa haa!"

JOSIE SCRATCHES
HER HEAD

"WHAT THE HECK IS THAT?" I return from the cemetery to find a carpeted barrier blocking the path to the living room. I shuffle sideways and wiggle into the room. "The world's biggest scratching post?" The three-foot high tower is covered in shaggy brown carpet, tunnels, hammocks, ramps, scratch mats, and dangly toys. The new cat lies tummy up in a third story hammock and purrs.

Dad reaches over and snaps off a price tag from the square base. He stuffs the tag deep in a pocket and adjusts the string on a felted mouse so it dangles free. "Actually Josie, you are looking at a deluxe kitty condo. I had to move the sofa to fit this beauty in front of the window. I thought he'd enjoy the view."

My mouth hangs wide open with shock so I snap it shut. "I never thought I'd see something like this in our living room. Does this mean you like the cat?" I giggle at my own understatement.

"I've always loved cats. I've even owned a cat before."

"You're kidding right? When? We've never had a pet."

"Your mom and I adopted a cat named T.R. about a year before we married." Dad peeks at me as he moves around the kitty condo, checking hammock ties and whatnot. "T.R. stood for trial run. Get it? He was our trial run at parenthood, this funny dumpy orange-striped tabby. He had a stump where his tail was supposed to be. It sort of trembled when he was excited or happy. Half his left ear had been ripped off in a catfight long before we owned him. He was a real tough customer."

"Two things. First of all, I didn't know you and Mom lived together before you got married. Scandalous! And second, I don't recall seeing any baby pictures of me posing with an orange cat."

"Yeah, he ran off during our honeymoon. He didn't approve of the cat sitter we left him with. So you never got to meet your furry big brother."

"Wow, that's the capper right there! Others would have shied away from parenthood after that, but not you guys. Nice." I punch Dad's arm, and we both laugh.

"Yeah, maybe not a good omen. But, look how well you both turned out in spite of us!" Happy tears rim his eyes and he chuckles.

Owen runs into the room and laughs without knowing the joke. He turns to Dad and says, "Hey! You look just like in the pictures, Dad!"

"What do you mean? Am I turning back time?" Dad scratches his head and a tuft of auburn hair stands up straight.

"No, I mean around your eyes, the crinkles. You're smiling like in all those old pictures with Mom." Owen runs out of the room, the cat trailing behind him.

Dad laughs again. "Your mother was convinced that at one time T.R. had a gloriously fluffy tail. Ha! I'd forgotten about this. She'd make up these tales of tragedy to explain how T.R. lost his tail. He rescued babies from burning buildings and his tail burned to the nubbins, nabbed bank robbers and lost his tail to a stray bullet, saved runaway trains and lost his tail to the tracks! You name it, your mother thought it up! Ha! Good times." He hugs me, rubbing the top of my head.

I close my eyes to commit the story to memory; another thing I can file away about my mom. As I reopen my eyes, I see my dad's wide grin and notice how good the memory makes him feel. I haven't seen this side of him in a long, long time. "You're not turning into a weird cat lady, are you?"

"I think I have to own at least five more cats before I can be classified as a cat lady."

My stomach growls. "Did you guys eat dinner?" I ask.

"Oh, sorry, Josie," Dad says. "We ate after Owen's soccer game. Your sandwich is in the fridge."

"Hey, Owen!" he shouts down the hallway. "Bathtime!"

"That boy has some serious layers of dirt and grass to scrub off. The soccer field was really bad tonight. I don't think his uniform will ever be clean again."

Ugh. I knew there was somewhere else I needed to be after school. "Sorry I missed the game, Dad. I was helping Blaze with something at the last minute. Did Owen's team win?"

Dad brushes off a puff of fur from the uppermost hammock before looking my way. "They won. We missed you, so try to come next week, all right? It would mean a lot to Owen. How's the homework situation?"

"Not bad. But I better get to it. I forgot my charger at school, Dad. Can I use yours?"

"Yep. It's in my office. I'll read to Owen. You get to work on your studies so you're not up too late."

Grabbing Dad's charger from his office and my sandwich from the fridge on the way, I head to my room. Some quick mental math and I realize I can get my assignments done in study hall first period tomorrow. I boot up the computer and study the rubbing pinned above my desk as I bite into my turkey club.

Unzipping my backpack, I slip out my journal from the inside pocket. I scan the thumbnail sketches I did of the symbols on the witch's gravestone today. I didn't want to keep Blaze waiting, so the drawings are rather crude, but they show details my rubbing doesn't.

What looks like a black circle on the copy I made last night is actually a primitive three-legged creature, its legs swirling around the perimeter of a fat circle. It looks like an octopus. I also confirm what I guessed this morning: the clover in the center of the rubbing is made up of four self-consuming snakes.

I click on Google and struggle with what search words to use, when my phone rings. After I answer, Casey says, "Josie, I'm an awful person." She sighs into the phone.

"Nothing's further from the truth. What's going on? Does it have something to do with your grave? You seemed pretty miffed earlier."

"It has everything to do with my grave. I'm obsessed with little Ettore Versino. You know how all the Halloween stuff was gone? Well, I knew that's what I'd find, but it still felt like a knife in my stomach."

The line goes silent and I assume we've lost the connection, but then her voice comes back. "Josie, here's the deal. That child died almost ten years ago, and he has parents that miss him even now. I'm jealous of him for it. God, it sounds so bad when I say it out loud. I'll just go."

"Casey, stay with me, here. The last thing you need is to hang up and feel awful on your own."

She huffs into the phone. "You're probably right. Then again, maybe awful people like me don't deserve company when they're miserable."

"You are not a bad person. And the way your family treats you isn't your fault."

She must have put a hand over the phone because her sobs become muffled. "I'm jealous of a dead boy. I'm completely insane."

"Here's a thought. What if you were supposed to rub that grave so you could come face to face with your own family drama? What if Ettore's trying to help you, Casey?"

She takes a deep breath into the phone and her voice steadies. "I hadn't thought about it like that. All I've been able to think about is how weird I must be to hate a little boy that doesn't deserve anything but sympathy."

A pang of guilt grips me because I brought all this down on her with my idea for Halloween. I have to make this better. "I think the most important thing is to move forward. If you have to make a daily inventory of his grave decorations, do it. If you need to talk to Grace, do that. And if you need to get some things off your chest with your family, well, by all means do it," I insist.

Casey sniffles, "You're right. It's just that I've spent most of my life making excuses for my family and how they treat me. I'm invisible to them, and it sucks."

My throat closes up with sadness. I swallow and whisper, "You aren't invisible to me, or to Seth or Blaze."

I want to erase the hurt her family caused. I want her to look in the mirror and see what we see. "Casey, you are the funniest, kindest, most perceptive person I know. You see us your friends, warts and everything, and you love us in spite of them. You make us laugh at our own quirks without making us feel bad. You keep us real, and we love you for that too.

"As soon as your brother steps away from football, your family's going to snap out of this fog. And they're going to feel terrible, because they made the choice to miss out on your life. Just wait! When you become a best-selling writer, a comedian, or whatever, your family will come crawling back begging for forgiveness. And guess what? You'll get to decide whether or not to grant it."

Casey gives a weak laugh on the line. I continue, "If it'd help, I'm willing to decorate your locker seasonally. And with teddy bears. I can leave teddy bears for you." I am determined to make her feel better. "You don't need to be jealous of Ettore, because you're cherished, too. We love you, Casey."

"Thank you. And I know that. But thanks for reminding me. Thanks for making me feel better," Casey says quietly. She seems sincere.

"No worries. As strange as it may sound, in one way I think I have it a little easier than you. My mom's gone. So, I'm left with a handful of glorified memories to play and replay, which means Sarah Jameson can do no wrong. You on the other hand, have to deal with living, breathing people, with all their ugly shortcomings... and that is a much tougher thing to do."

"I'm not sure about that. I do know that hoping for my family to change has gotten pretty old. I am sick of waiting for them to care about me."

"Focus on your friends. We care."

She sniffs again, "Yeah, please don't get all lovey again, Josie."

"Fine but when we get off the phone, I want you to think about something that makes you laugh. How about when Seth clobbered me with his Fisher-Price radio when we were two? Remember that?" Casey giggles on the other end of the line. "Then get some sleep."

"You're an old soul, Josie. Thanks for talking me off the cliff. I gotta say, Mylar balloons were probably the wrong reason to pick a grave. Bad move. See you tomorrow?"

"Bye, Casey. See you at school."

As I hang up, I cannot help but wonder what I unleashed when I set up the Lakefront Cemetery field trip. Poor Casey was driven to tears. Blaze and his mother are fighting. At least Seth seems to be fine. Maybe I can make some headway on my grave.

I turn my attention to the Google home screen. I type in "Octopus images" and get ten million hits. Across my screen dance webpages that feature octopuses, crocheted octopuses, glass octopuses, and some that remind me of the art work in *Journey to the Center of the Earth*. None resemble the three-legged creature on the tombstone. I pause that search and turn to the other prominent symbol.

I do a quick search of snake circle images and find a mere three million pictures. Some reference Wiccans, and others date back thousands of years and reference a Chinese proverb that says once you are bitten by a snake, you will fear a rope. I don't think the person buried here feared ropes. My head throbs with the beginning of a migraine. I look through images for close to an hour but find nothing that resembles the snakes on the tombstone. The closest thing I find are the ouroboros from ancient Egypt. They are crude, long, skinny versions of what is carved into the tombstone and stand for eternal life. Frustrated, I shower and fall into bed.

*   *   *

In my dream, I cannot see the women's faces. I hide behind a gigantic cedar and grip its feathery bark. The roots of the tree have pulled free of the earth and tangle around my bare feet and ankles, tethering me to the spot. The two women are only flashes of copper and black hair and blurs of motion. And hands, mercurially quick hands: one pair is ghostly white and the other a shiny bronze. The women attack each other at such speed that I only catch glimpses.

Their screams are not human. Between high-pitched screeches and throaty rumblings, they battle with each other under the low drooping boughs of an ancient tree. The witch with the bronzed hand clutches a rusty trowel. Its silver and red-flecked metal flashes in the full moon that shines above. Held high, the trowel is sharply pointed at the end, not blunt like the one I use to dig in perennials. I struggle to find my voice, trying to scream out for them to stop. I can't muster a warning as the trowel rams into the chest of the black-haired woman.

*   *   *

I startle and wake. It takes a few seconds to clear my mind of the vivid dream.

The unearthly sounds of their struggle echo in my brain. "Am I still asleep?" Then I realize the noise comes from outside my window.

Squatting on my knees, I look out the window above my bed to the front yard, dim in the approaching dawn. The clock on my nightstand says it is nearly five in the morning. Two animals are tumbling in the grass. A dark bird stands on something furry, and attacks the creature over and over with its beak. It's too big to be a squirrel, but it is gray.

I finally get a decent view. "Oh no! It's our cat!" The shock of seeing our foundling trapped in the black talons of the crow jolts the last of the sleep out of me.

I race to my dad's room, screaming down the hall.

"Dad! Dad, wake up! Our cat! Help, Dad! Our cat's being attacked outside."

Dad wakes and jumps out of bed, not bothering with slippers. He's at the front door in seconds, flinging it open and stumbling down the porch steps. The cold humid air rushes inside and envelops me.

I watch him from the open door, holding my arms around myself to stop the trembling. Dad turns on the spigot by the porch and aims the hose at the cat and crow. They remain locked in a desperate struggle until the water hits them. The crow makes one last ear-piercing noise, and then flutters into the night. The cat remains motionless on the ground. The water that pools underneath his thin body is red. Or is it? I squint into the dim light.

"Is he dead? Dad! Is that blood? Oh, God. Did the crow kill him?"

"Josie. Inside. Now! You don't need to see this."

My father turns to me, and his eyes stream with tears that shine in the light of the moon. His image blurs as my eyes flood.

"Can you get him to an emergency vet clinic, Dad?"

"Josie, go inside and get me some towels. I'll do everything I can for him. But you need to get me some towels and then go back to your room. Promise?"

"I guess."

I run to the laundry room and grab a huge pile of old beach towels from the linen closet. Crying, I bring them to Dad, wiping my face with my arm.

As I turn to go inside, I hear my dad sob into his chest. I return to my room and look out the window at the scene beyond. Dad crouches above the cat, tenderly wrapping his limp body with fluffy towels. I'm struck with how sick and wrong it seems that neon beach towels, referencing bygone tropical vacations, are draped around our dying friend.

I lie down in bed and cover my head with my comforter so no one can hear me sob.

Josie and the Cat Miracle

A GENTLE TAP on my bedroom door jolts me from a bad dream. I remember only bits and pieces of it: the cat fighting with a crow, a puddle of blood, a lifeless gray body.

Dad cracks open the door, "Josie, I've got some news."

His voice comes out soft and gentle. Is he getting ready to break really bad news? It wasn't just a bad dream. The fight between the cat and the crow really happened.

I sit up, shoving the comforter off my head. Dad opens the door wider and steps inside tentatively. His expression is happy, but after last night how could it be?

"I can't even believe I fell asleep again after what happened last night," I say. "I woke up and thought it was just a bad dream."

Looking again at Dad, his bright eyes and wide grin, I'm suddenly confused.

"Why do you look so happy? What did you do with the cat?" I rub my eyes and stretch.

"So, it wasn't a dream? You remember the fight too, right?" he asks, scratching his head and grinning.

A quick gray blur runs past his legs and tumbles onto my bed. The curly furred cat purrs and rubs his body against my outstretched hand. Then he circles in my lap, folding himself into a warm, fuzzy heap. I hold my breath; I want to hold onto the cat forever.

"How? I don't understand. He's perfect."

I stroke the cat's body, trying to find any physical trace of the fight.

"Dad, he was ripped apart and bleeding all over last night."

I start to cry and the moisture disappears inside his coat. He's a magnet for my tears. Before I can ask Dad if this is real, Owen rushes into my room bouncing next to the cat and me.

"Josie, you're always hogging him!" Owen grabs the cat under his ribs, sits and plops him onto his criss-cross pajama legs. I lock eyes with Dad, unable to speak. He lays a finger over his pink lips, winks, and then points at Owen. Without a word, I understand that whatever wild theories we've got will stay under wraps until Owen's tiny ears aren't around. I wink back so he knows I understand.

Owen strokes the cat's silky back. "I know his name, guys. It's Shadow. After you tucked me in last night Josie, I had a dream about him. I was with you on Halloween and we found him together. And then we lost him, 'cause he ran into the shadows. Then we found him again. So, that's his name. Shadow."

"I love it. What do you think, Dad?"

"Shadow is the perfect name! Now, time to get ready for school. Shall we hit the pancake house before I drop you off? I'm starving and we've got time."

In answer, Owen and I race to ready ourselves. Smiling, I close my eyes, and feel the weight of the world slip off my shoulders.

"Shadow! You're something else."

He looks up from taking a drink out of my toilet and scurries down the hall.

JOSIE ENJOYS
MOVIE NIGHT

"HEY, THIS WAS A GOOD IDEA, Casey," I say, grabbing a bottle of water from the basement mini-fridge. It has been six long days since Halloween and Casey had the great idea to invite Seth, Blaze, and me over for movie night. I am grateful someone else stepped up to plan an activity and am excited to see Seth in particular, since we don't see him at school anymore. If he made any headway on his research about the sergeant, I am sure to hear about it tonight.

I pick a seat on the lumpy, beige, pull-out sofa that doesn't manage to do any job very well; it's a terrible bed and bad seat too. I stuff a blanket under my rump to keep the metal spring from poking through my jeans. The Starbaugh's media room has walls cluttered with a collection of Drew's football jerseys, and framed articles from local and national newspapers and magazines. They transformed their old play room into a media and games room the summer before Drew's senior year of high school, so all of his friends and adoring fans would be comfortable as they sat around worshipping him. The sofa might have been comfortable four years ago, but not now. Still, we're Casey's friends, not Drew's, so it is the best we are ever going to get.

Casey checks her phone and hands a napkin to me. "Movie night, my favorite! Oh, Blaze just sent a text. Seth's dad just crossed the bridge; they'll be here in a few minutes. We need to hurry up and choose the top five. Otherwise, we'll be stuck watching a *Star Wars* marathon!"

She shoves half a slice of pizza into her mouth, wipes her hands, and then slides open the giant oak drawers that store the Starbaugh's expansive DVD collection... if old high school football games count, that is.

"I'm thinking nothing animated right?" she says before taking a gulp of soda.

"Actually, I wouldn't mind a trip down memory lane. Do you remember Seth's crazy obsession with *Treasure Planet*? I think we're the only kids on Earth that watched that sucker more than once."

"Sorry to disappoint you, Josie. We don't have it." Casey slams the drawer shut and rifles through another. "How about *The Goonies*?"

"No, thanks. Those boys are obnoxious. I'm not in the mood. What about *The Day the Earth Stood Still*? That's a great movie."

Casey nods. "Sounds like a top five to me."

I nod too as I reach for a slice of pizza. She pulls a drawer open extracting the black and white DVD case. "Do you remember the words to say to the robot in case of an emergency?"

Seth and Blaze storm down the steps as she asks this. Seth throws chips and dip onto the long snack table on the sidewall. He looks down at his phone and says, "You're such a nerd, Casey."

He scrolls down his phone screen with his thumb, no doubt finding the answer to the trivia question. "Klaatu barada nikto! Doesn't everyone know that?"

Blaze adds a baking dish covered in foil and a bag of tortilla chips to the offerings. He turns around to Seth, eyebrows raised.

"Klaatoo, what? How does anyone remember that? Only people from the 1950s should remember that, Seth!"

"I didn't remember. It's too obscure even for me. Was the magic of the phone." Seth twirls his black phone in the air, blows on the end, and stuffs it into a front pocket like a gun-slinging cowboy.

Blaze makes a quick bow. "You are now, and always will be, the god of research, Seth. But what I can't believe is that a classic sci-fi makes it to the top five, and it's not even my birthday!" A giant grin breaks out across his face. "Oh yeah, it's good to know my love of science fiction has influenced your lives for the better. Speaking of lives, I might not have one tomorrow if my mom finds out I'm going to church! Say your farewells tonight folks." He removes the foil from the top of a yellow ceramic baking dish with a flourish, and a spicy aroma fills the media room.

I say, "Church? Since when?" My stomach growls from the smells coming from the food table. "Holy crap! What amazing thing did you make for us tonight, Blaze? Smells great!" I bite into my cold piece of pepperoni with no enthusiasm and wonder how rude it would be to abandon it on the coffee table.

"Well, it's my very own seven-layer dip: black beans, tomatillo, cheddar cheese, green onions, salsa, guacamole, and sour cream. Casey, do you have a bowl for these?" Blaze opens the top of the chip bag.

"What! You didn't handcraft the tortilla chips, Blaze? I'm shocked! I'll go grab a bowl." Casey heads upstairs to the kitchen.

"And a spoon! I forgot to bring a serving spoon!" Blaze yells.

Seth loads up a paper plate with snacks. "So, church tomorrow? Boy, you sure take the death penalty lightly Blaze." He laughs at his joke.

"Yeah. I texted James about something this morning and he invited me. I guess I'm curious to see what I've been missing out on. Besides, I've got some questions."

Casey returns and Blaze takes the bowl from her arms, pulling the spoon out of her fingers.

"Blaze, have you really asked yourself what your mother would do if she found out you went to church?" I say as I slip the DVD into the machine.

"What's the worst she could do? Ground me? For going to church? Naw, I'm pretty sure she won't find out and if she does she'll just roll out the old, 'Why organized religion is so awful,' lecture. Big deal."

Casey pauses her eating. "Well, I am proud of you, Blaze. This is the most rebellious thing you've ever planned, Mr. Goody-goody. And I agree with your worst case scenario. You're an only child, so we know she won't kill you."

"Did you tell your dad what you plan to do tomorrow?" Seth asks.

Blaze swallows a chip and wipes his mouth with the back of his hand. "Yup. He's cool with it and I know he won't say anything to Mother because he doesn't like trouble."

"Yeah, well my father has a nose for trouble. He's jumped right into my little project, Sergeant Paxton research," Seth jokes. "I went to his law office today and we dug up some background info."

He plops down on a fuzzy gray beanbag in the center of the room. A black and white cat leaps into the air from behind him and races away with a noisy burst. "Oops, I didn't know Boots was here. Sorry." He pauses. "At this point, the more I find out about the sergeant, the more questions get raised. Does that make any sense?"

"What have you got so far?" I ask.

"I guess he died back in August and has no relatives, and didn't leave a will of any kind. He owns a house down in south Seattle, but since there seems to be no one to inherit it, the state's making legal moves to claim his property. They put a legal notice in the paper three months ago and so far no one has stepped forward. If no legitimate heir steps forward, the state will officially own all his property. Dad said the state will sell the lot and put the dollars into the general fund. He's going to have a paralegal do some digging, but according to our search, the sergeant was never married and never had kids. It's not promising."

"What'd you find out about the house?" Blaze asks.

"He owns a house by the Green River. I printed off a satellite image. It is a little yellow rambler boxed in on three sides by concrete warehouses. It's the only house on the block. Everything around it is gray and industrial. I know it's not much to look at, but if he has a relative, they deserve to inherit that money."

Seth runs his hands over his scalp, making his blonde hair stand up in fluffy clumps. "What about you, Josie? Have you unlocked any secrets to the Ghost Forest?"

"No. But I need to tell you guys something." I scan their faces and wonder if I'll be able to speak the words. The way my father is suddenly sticking his nose in my life makes me mad.

"Dad went all mental on me last night. I mentioned I was going back to the cemetery this weekend to do some research and he freaked. He didn't outright forbid me to go, but he said I've become obsessed with the place. He said to forget about my tombstone and spend more time at home with him and Owen."

Blaze says, "Wow! I can't picture your dad telling you what to do. You sort of wear the pants in your family, Josie. You've held that family together since forever. Why'd the tables turn all of a sudden?" His question cuts through to what confuses me the most.

"I don't know. He's changed over the last week. It's going to sound crazy, but it all started after Shadow came to live with us. That first morning, my dad bought supplies for the scrawny cat. He made us breakfast. And he's driving us to school again. That hasn't happened regularly for a long time. He grocery shops on his own without me writing down a shopping list. He's back, after six years in La La Land. Maybe this is all the cat's fault."

"Do you think he's figured out that he's missed out on almost a decade of bossing you around? Isn't that what parents live for? And he's trying to make up for lost time. That's gotta be it!" Seth sinks deeper into his beanbag.

Casey throws him the end of her blanket like a lifeline. "It looks like you're being eaten by that thing, Seth!" We all give a collective chuckle. She turns to me. "Maybe he's realizing how much time he wasted, how much time he lost getting over your mom, and he doesn't want you to do the same thing. Now that he's found a little joy in life, he wants everything to be hearts and flowers. He doesn't want you wasting time dwelling on a dead person."

I'm caught off-guard by the anger that surges up my torso. I begin to shake, and I tuck my hands under my jeans. Why are they defending my dad? He lost his right to meddle in my life a long time ago. "I don't care. Considering how little I've found out about my tombstone, I'm going to ignore him for now. Do you realize I don't even know her name? So, I'm sorry if it worries him or makes him mad. Frankly, it's too late for him to weigh in on my life."

No one meets my gaze. No one says a thing. Don't they realize they are the only people that have a right to an opinion?

Seth finally speaks from the depths of the beanbag. "He's your parent. He's always going to have a say about your life, especially now that he's back in the world of the living. But that doesn't mean you have to listen to him. Do what you need to, Josie." Though his words are wise, I can't help but laugh as he loses most of his torso to the fluffy, white plush sack.

"I second that," says Blaze. Casey nods.

Boots leaps down the stairs two at a time and onto my lap. He circles, then settles.

"You smell like a litter box," I tell him.

Casey, always the one with perfect timing, presses play on the DVD player. As *The Day the Earth Stood Still* begins, I take a deep breath. Maybe they've known more of the real me than I thought all of these years, this dear, crazy, hodgepodge of friends.

SETH PATCHES
TOGETHER A LIFE

WHEN I DO RESEARCH, I like to peel back the layers of a project like an onion. Most times, I get so deep inside the onion that I can't remember what I was searching for in the first place.

Tonight's research goes no differently. After discovering an article about the drowning of Sergeant Paxton's hometown, I can't help but find out how this fifty-year-old piece of history was saved. And that's how I found Jessie Case, my new hero.

The article about the watery ghost town of Hover would've been lost forever if it weren't for a group of communications students at Columbia Basin College, led by Jessie Case. A child of the Tri-Cities, Seattle's sagebrush sister to the east, Jessie knew urban media outlets like *Seattle Times* archived everything. But the history of dusty farming communities was never considered worth saving by big city folks until she made it her personal mission.

Looking for a valid senior project, Jessie Case found her subject from a blurb in the local paper: the *Tri-City Herald.* In an attempt to cut costs in the bad economy, the paper planned to empty a century of old newspapers and photos from a costly storage warehouse. Jessie got the blessing of her professor, secured funding and organized volunteers to document, scan and archive every old article. She created a website and posted the old newspaper articles online. Slowly, the website became a rich, well-organized virtual library. And three years after earning her bachelor's degree with honors, Jessie Case still leads the foundation, traveling to other parts of the country to raise money by organizing similar programs for all the overlooked rural nooks and crannies of the United States. And that is why Jessie Case is my new hero.

A quick glance out of my window at the star-filled sky tells me that it is nearly time for some shut-eye. I switch on my desk lamp and hunch over a copy of the newspaper article that explains the fate of Sergeant Paxton's hometown. Once a humble farming community on the banks of the mighty Columbia River in eastern Washington, Hover boasted a lively main street that attracted shoppers with tidy brick stores that included, among others, Paxton Hardware.

After returning from World War II, Isaac Paxton had no interest, however, in running the family business. He sold the last of his inventory to nearby Prudhomme Hardware and moved to Seattle to recruit young soldiers for the U.S. Army, an easy post-war job that would bring a paycheck and benefits.

Mr. Paxton is quoted in the article: "I've got no living relatives left. I guess it's time for me to try someplace new. And I certainly don't want to be here when they open the dam and flood this place." The black and white image accompanying the article shows a fit young man, with strong shoulders and arms. But even this grainy image can't hide the pain in his eyes and the dark circles beneath.

When the McNary Dam was opened in 1957, Hover and four other towns down the Columbia flooded. Residents stood on the hill above gawking, picnicking, cheering, crying, and reminiscing as the mighty river claimed Hover one painful inch at a time. Today, the town sits preserved under the wind-chopped river. The streets are empty except for the occasional prehistoric white sturgeon that slithers through the crumpled brick rubble.

My cell phone vibrates, bringing me back to the present.

"Hi, Josie. What's up?"

"I need to talk with a friend." Her voice sounds strained and I eye the clock on my nightstand.

It's eleven minutes after eleven. I make a wish on the lucky digits. "What's going on?" I ask, typing search words into the computer.

"I had one of those weird dreams again," she pauses. "Hey, Seth. Are you in the middle of something?"

I stop typing. "I was looking a little deeper into my guy, the sergeant."

"Have you found any of his relatives yet?"

"No luck. Do you really want to talk about this? You called for a reason."

She pauses, then says, "I'll get to that soon enough. Tell me what you found. You sound focused."

"Yeah, I am, and a little frustrated. The last article I found confirms that he had no family when he moved to Seattle. And public records show that he never married. I guess the state's going to get that house. I don't have a next step yet, Josie. But what's up with you?"

She sighs. "I am freaking myself out with all the weird dreams. The one I had last night was the worst yet and I don't know if I even want to repeat it."

"Come on, Josie. 'Better out than in.' That's what my mom always says. Though she was referencing other things. Really though, I can handle it." I shut down the computer.

"Fine, but it's a doozy." She huffs into the phone. "I was flying above the trees in the Ghost Forest and my jeans got caught on a branch. I started to fall in slow motion. As I fell, I saw a person hanging by a noose from one of the limbs, and as I passed it on the way to the ground, I saw it was *my* body hanging there. A crow was picking at the rope wrapped around my neck. It was trying to untie the knot. I felt myself fall free and then I woke up.

"If I close my eyes, I can still hear the creak of the rope rubbing across the fat oak limb. And I swear, I had a mark across my throat this morning. Why would I have that dream, Seth?"

"Creepy, no doubt. But, aren't you being a little dramatic?"

When she grumbles into the phone, I get serious. "For real, Josie. Are you afraid you're having suicidal thoughts?"

"Seth! I'm not saying that. It just got me worried. Why do I have so many awful dreams and what kind of weirdo dreams about her own death?"

"It's not all that uncommon. Think of death in a more figurative way." My hands itch to boot up the computer and do a quick web search, but I resist. "Do you realize that most cultures view a dream about death as a harbinger of change? Maybe you are seeing the future, but it isn't you hanging on that tree; it's a part of you. Maybe your dream marks the end of something in you that needs to die so you can move forward with your life. It's not death; it's change. Think change."

Josie says, "Change? What exactly do I need to change?" She sounds mildly irritated.

"Well, you were complaining about how your dad is all the sudden meddling in your life. Maybe the change you need is letting him step in and be a parent to you." I pause because I am overwhelmed by my awesome analysis.

"Well, I guess that would make sense. I am not a big fan of change," she mumbles.

"Embrace it. Or distract yourself with other things, like finding out more about that grave you rubbed. Did you learn anything about the octopus symbol? You didn't give us an update tonight at Casey's."

"There's nothing to report. I haven't moved forward, Seth. Not one inch."

I can almost see her cute pouty face over the phone. A laugh slips out.

"Seth! That's not nice. Everyone else is uncovering all this great stuff. Casey's checking Ettore's grave daily, you are just being you and finding answers in cyberspace, and Blaze is diving into the priest's life. I'm nowhere, and you laugh!"

"I wasn't laughing at you. Okay, I was laughing at you, just not for what you think. I was picturing your pouty face. You look like Owen when you're all mad."

"Seth Anthony, you apologize right now or I am hanging up!"

"I'm sorry. Really, like ninety percent sorry."

She grumbles. "Well, then I forgive you ninety percent." She laughs and I relax, because she sounds normal again.

I think about sharing my father's disclosure. Maybe now is a good time. "I want to talk to you about something too. But, I was kind of hoping it'd be in person, not over the phone."

"Whoa, Seth being serious? Should I worry?"

"No, nothing like that. It's just, well, my father dropped a bit of a bombshell over dinner this week. Unbeknownst to me, he and my mom have been going to therapy together."

"That's a bit of a shock." Her side of the conversation grows quiet. I picture the little wrinkle between her eyebrows she gets when she is thinking hard about something.

"They've been spending other time together, you know besides the therapy sessions, taking walks, eating lunch, stuff like that."

"That's big, Seth. Does this mean that they're rekindling things?"

It isn't the first time I've thought about the question, but it irritates me to contemplate the possibility of my mom taking him back. "Not at this point. Dad told me that mom forgives him; that's it." He seems like he is trying to change. I don't want to say the words out loud, because if he doesn't change I will be pissed all over again.

"You know, for the first time I really believe he realizes how much he hurt Mom. Maybe he even sees how he blew it with Sadie and me. He is getting into my sergeant project in a big way," I say.

"It might be his way to connect with you again, Seth. You both love research. You both love a good mystery. Are you going to let him in?"

I feel tired suddenly, thinking of all the energy I expend to keep hating my dad. It takes masses of energy. "I don't know, Jos. I've spent a lot of hours wishing that man was dead. But, while I was reading through articles about the sergeant, I realized it takes a lot of effort to actively hate him, to keep feeling as angry and hurt as I was the day she kicked him out of the house. I'm tired of being a hater, Josie. Maybe I should get over it." I rummage through my desk drawer and find the file marked, 'Algebra' and the two problems I cut off the end of my homework. I debate whether or not to staple them to the back of my homework.

"It isn't going to happen instantly, Seth. Do this in baby steps. Start by being mindful of all the times you try to dredge up the past with him. Take note of it, and then stop. Stop spending your time hating. I'm just winging it here. I've never had to forgive something so big."

I laugh. Letting go of the hate makes me feel lighter. "Our timing is hilarious," I say.

"Clarify?" she clips.

"Well, just now, when we were talking about me and forgiving my dad, it got me thinking. What if you need to forgive yourself before you move forward in your mystery?"

She doesn't say anything back, so I go on. "Forgive yourself, Josie. Forgive yourself for being human, not some superhero that does everything perfectly!"

"I don't think I'm some superhero. Where'd that come from?" she huffs.

"You think we don't know how you try to be all perfect all the time. You never wanted other people to see you as the sad kid you had every right to be!"

She rustles the phone and I check the screen to make sure she hasn't hung up. "You knew about that? But, I don't do all that Ms. Perfect act anymore."

"Ha! Who are you kidding? You keep berating yourself for not figuring out your tombstone yet. Big deal! Did you know you happened to pick the oldest grave in Lakefront Cemetery? I did a little research on those symbols, and…" I pause while I fumble in my hanging files for the manila envelope with the words, "Josie's Tombstone" written in the tab.

She sniffs into the phone. "Are you kidding me? You did research for me?"

"That's what I do," I say, and she laughs. "Anyway, I looked up that snake circle and the octopus image. Josie, those symbols date back more than a thousand years. Though the snakes go back even further to Ancient Egypt. But the ones on your grave have both Celtic elements and, I don't know how else to say this, but they are pretty scary."

"Out with it! No, wait. I think I'm going to move into the living room. I feel like the rubbing is watching me from the wall. Wait a minute." I hear her make her way through the house and her father shout something about a hairball.

"All right, I'm back. Shoot."

"I searched the octopus image first and think I found a connection to an old Celtic symbol called the triskelion. The triskelion is a design with three strands or trunks that remind me of waves. It is a very old symbol that by itself means movement, change, or growth. This website called What'sYourSign.com stated that the symbol means three things: personal growth, human development, and spiritual expansion."

Josie comments, "So far, what you've told me isn't ominous. Personal growth isn't bad. Weren't you telling me a minute ago to embrace change?"

"Because I haven't applied the triskelion to *your* symbol... the octopus. Think of it as, Triskelion + Octopus = evil. The octopus changes everything!"

I run a hand through my hair and flip to the printout of Celtic animals. "Imagine how terrifying an octopus might seem to people hundreds of years ago. To them, an octopus wasn't a smart little jar opener. No, it was a mysterious man-eating monster from the depths of the ocean. Not a good thing.

"Do you see? When the carver of that tombstone morphed the triskelion into an octopus, I think he was saying that this symbol stood for the opposite of growth, development, and spiritual expansion."

"That gave me chills. What about you?" Josie asks in a hushed voice.

"No. I've known about this a couple of days now. The shock value's gone for me. But I understand your reaction, that was me when I puzzled it out. Now, about the snakes."

"Oh, great! Do I even want to know?"

"Ha! I can tell from your voice you're dying to know the rest," I say, shuffling through papers in the file folder. I thumb through the pages until I find the print out titled, "Snake-Witch Symbol."

I say, "As far as the snakes go, I couldn't find anything that matched exactly. I pulled a dragnet through websites working under the assumption that the snakes are Celtic because the way they rope around each other on your rubbing is like a Celtic knot. Though interestingly, your snakes circle in the opposite direction of the normal snake symbol. I did manage to find a stone that was discovered in a cemetery in Gotland, Sweden that is called the "Snake-Witch Stone." The red carving on the stone has some striking similarities to your grave. They found the stone in a cemetery a while back and dated it to 500 A.D.

"I also found out that some cultures, including the Celts, regarded snakes as a symbol of immortality because they lose and regrow their skin. But, again Josie, I think your snakes mean something different. Because those snakes appear to be eating themselves and circle in the opposite direction, I think they mean the opposite of immortality... maybe mortality. Not like a statement of truth, more like a curse." I pause so she can take it all in.

She taps the phone with her fingernail, so I know she's thinking. I can imagine her biting her lip as she digests the information. She finally speaks. "It's like the people who designed her tombstone didn't want her to come back."

"Come back from where?"

"From the dead. They left curses carved on that stone to keep her from coming back from the dead. Those people were mental. What could she possibly have done to make people hate and fear her that much? The whole thing is so mysterious."

I wonder about the person buried below the curse-ridden tombstone. "How bad of a person would you have to be to warrant a tombstone like that? Did you ever consider that the person buried there might be bad after all?" I ask.

"Oh my God!" Josie barks. "Are you buying into all the witch rumors now? Really?"

"I'm just saying, if the person buried there tended to the sick, fed the hungry and all that jazz, they wouldn't have put such strange symbols on her grave. They would've carved her name, written something nice, and etched flowers. Normal stuff. It is just something to consider."

"Well, what do I do now?" she asks. My ear hurts from being on the phone this long, but I know better than to put her on speakerphone. Josie hates that.

"I have no idea. Maybe just sit with all this for a while, and then see where it takes you."

"Gee, could you be more vague?" She laughs into the phone, hard enough that I have to pull it away from my ear.

Her voice grows serious. "This morning I was thinking about how we started that wave we do to say goodbye, the frozen hand in the air. Do you remember how that started, Seth?"

"Sort of. When our play dates were over we'd get stuffed into our respective cars, crying, fussing, you name it. I remember slapping my hand on the car window as we left. I remember the greasy print I'd leave on the glass every week. I think it had something to do with that."

"Yeah, mostly. We'd wave goodbye, but then we'd hold our hands against the glass waiting for someone to touch their hand against the other side of the window. A frozen wave. When we do that now, I think about our outstretched fingers, the pieces of a hand. We're better together than we could ever be apart. That's what all of you mean to me. I couldn't have survived this long without any of you."

She sniffles into the phone. "Are you crying, Josie?"

"A little. I'm sorry."

"You mean my little superhero has feelings? And she's showing them? Hmm." She lost her mom six years ago and stopped letting herself act like a kid about the same time. I am relieved to see her real feelings leaking out.

I hang up the phone and revisit the article about the sergeant. I stare into the print out until his features blur. What do I do next? I think about the little house surrounded by warehouses that will be forfeited to the state and feel an urgent need to find someone the sergeant left behind. I wish I had an address book or list of phone numbers, something that would point me to a relative, even a friend. I think about his abandoned house, waiting to be claimed by the state and then it comes to me in a wild rush. The house. I need to search the sergeant's house for an address book.

JOSIE VISITS THE FORBIDDEN PLACE

I WALK TO LAKEFRONT CEMETERY on this mild Sunday morning under a blue sky, but my mood is anything but sunny and bright. I long for the typical gray Seattle skies to return, because they make a better backdrop than sunshine when one wants to ruminate on their difficult parent and complicated life. Where are my gray skies when I need them?

Seattle wears its gray skies like New Yorkers sport black clothing, daily, but with subtle variety. Some days our Northwest sky is a canvas of primer gray, sprayed on with a celestial air gun and flat, drab paint that is easy to overlook. I call those the blah days.

On more drama-filled days, foreboding charcoal clouds sag above the skyline, barely keeping their fat, rain-gorged bellies from scraping the tops of buildings. I call those the green days, because our palette of trees and moss-carpeted terra firma never appears more vibrant than under those ominous formations.

Then, there is the winter sky, where earth and atmosphere meld together into a single milky entity. The fog lifting off the ground blends into the muslin-draped atmosphere. You spend the day with your mind and body entombed in clouds, as if watching the world through a shroud. Those are the times when locals long for a sunny island or a quick jump off a high bridge.

My favorite sky, the one I call the birthday cake sky, is filled with gravity-defying pillows of white and pink like a Rousseau landscape set in motion. This is the sky that accompanies me to Lakefront on this Sunday morning, a week after Halloween. A blue sky usually brightens my spirits and inspires me to unearth a sketchpad and pencils from the dusty bottom of my bag. But as I near the thorn-encrusted wall that marks the Ghost Forest, my father's voice rings in my head.

"You're going to the cemetery again? It's the fifth time this week, Josie. Your preoccupation has to stop. You are absolutely forbidden to go to Lakefront!"

I grind my teeth as I think back to our one-sided conversation. I tried to tell him two of those visits were for other people, but he wouldn't listen.

Casey's been here every day since Halloween. She's practically on Grace's payroll. I haven't been here nearly enough. While I stand by and watch the Baby Group unlock mysteries, I've made no progress. Seth's made more progress on my search than me! But, let's cut to the chase, Dad. This isn't some new preoccupation-with-death phase. News flash, it's a lifestyle. I've been preoccupied with dead people since I lost Mom six years ago. You just never cared to see that until now. Why didn't I think to say that earlier? That would have shut him up.

As I step onto the soft mossy earth of the Ghost Forest, I spot a tiny figure toiling under the rose trellis in the distance, the lake shimmering through the archway. "Is that you back there, Grace?" I yell.

"Yep! That you, Josie? I knew I'd see you today." She snaps at a thick cord of woody thorns with long pruning shears. Her pinstripe overalls hang off her small frame and her hair frizzes out wildly around her face. "Hey, can you give me a hand? I'm up to my elbows in roses." She wipes the back of a gloved hand across her forehead, leaving a streak of dirt behind.

I reach the arched trellis in quick strides. Rays of rare autumn sunshine sparkle and dance across the choppy waters, past the pile of dead roses, gardening tools, and Grace. I glance up at the oak limbs that weave a spider web above our heads and a chill ripples down my back as I think back to the freaky dream I had of me hanging from a limb.

Grace shakes her head. "My hands won't cooperate today. I thought the sunshine would drive off the bad of this place, but it's getting the better of me. You might be my saving grace, girl." She reaches into a front pocket of her overalls and unearths a pair of pruning shears. She hands them to me, and then stuffs a coil of hair into a fuzzy red cap, frowning.

She tugs at a knot of thorny dead stalks and grumbles something I don't hear under her breath. I ask, "What's got you all worked up today? Don't tell me you spotted a ghost!"

My feeble joke fails to make her smile. I decide my best plan of action is to pitch in and help. I gather an armload of plant detritus and add it to the heap of yard waste.

"I feel them, the spirits. They're as real to me as the moss hanging off those branches." Grace points to the tufts of silvery lichen that hang off the naked limbs with a gloved finger. "Josie, ghosts are real. Just trying to tell their story, most ghosts whisper, but the one back here screams, maybe because it was me that found him dead back here, right in this tree." She scans the limbs above our head and hugs herself. "I didn't want to talk about it Halloween night because your visit was so nice. Didn't want to clutter the evening with dark memories."

She pauses from her work and scratches her forehead. "That night you asked if I was afraid of this place and I told a half-truth; I'm sorry about that. The plain truth is that I'm scared of the Ghost Forest. It wasn't always that way, but five, maybe six years ago I came through that gate and found a boy's body hanging from the oaks."

My heart pounds and I take deep, calming breaths like I learned in yoga class. It was just a stupid dream. Seth told me death means change. Change, I chant in my mind.

"He hung himself from those oak branches above us. When I found him, I screamed until my voice sputtered out. The police swarmed over the cemetery for a couple days like ants on an abandoned picnic. Turned everything upside down. Seemed like a cut-and-dried thing to me; he'd killed himself. But they had some questions about his death. Couldn't figure out how he'd gotten up so high in the tree without a ladder. Of course, he climbed; that's what boys do, they climb trees."

I use my sleeve to wipe the layer of icy sweat off my face, hoping Grace hasn't noticed my mini-meltdown. I try not to pass out. Forcing my voice to steady, I ask, "Did they eventually rule it a suicide?"

"Yeah. He wasn't much older than you, but decided he'd had enough living. He was an outcast at the local high school, a target for bullies. But his teachers said it was nothing serious. You ask me, I'd tell you all bullying is serious. You change a kid forever when you bully him. Anyway, they figure he climbed up there, tied the rope, and then jumped."

"Help me understand something. If he chose to die in the Ghost Forest, why does he haunt you? Because you found him?" I rub my neck where I felt rope burns after my dream. I peek into the treetops expecting to see a shadowy image of a boy. Stop. Thinking. About. It.

"First off, it upsets me that the family buried him somewhere else when he handpicked this spot. They tossed his ashes in the Pacific. But mostly, he tears me up because a life as new as his shouldn't end that way. His heart, limbs, mind, and body didn't fail him. But his soul did. Can't explain it any better than that Josie. Just to say that in my darkest hour, it never crossed my mind to stop living. Somewhere inside, I must've had a grain of hope. So, I guess his worst day was more than I ever faced."

"When you say 'haunt' then, you mean his memory sticks with you, right? Or have you actually seen him back here?" I ask. Wind blows over the lake, sending a chilly gust through the Ghost Forest.

Grace's gloved hands hang at her sides and her pruning shears slip to the ground with a heavy thud. "Both. He stays on my heart, don't think I'll ever erase that image of him in the tree. As far as an actual ghost, I haven't seen anything, more like feelings. I've thought about that boy many times." She wipes a curl off her forehead and continues. "Maybe at the heart of it all, I wish he'd thought to knock at my door. Maybe if he'd been shown a simple kindness, it would've changed his mind." She uses the bottom of her sleeve to wipe away the traces of a tear on her cheek. The tear leaves a shiny trail, washing the dust off her cheek as it falls. She darts her eyes to the pruned bush, avoiding my gaze, and then grabs up the rusty shears.

I wrap her in a hug before she can stop me. Her hair smells like coconuts and baby powder. For the first time since meeting Grace, I realize she's my height.

I tell her, "For the record, if he'd knocked on your door that day, he'd still be with us. You're one of the good guys. I have no doubt that you would've helped him find a grain of hope, not just for a day, but forever. I know it."

She busies herself snipping through dead roses. "That's awful nice to hear, but maybe we should get back to these roses. You know what I was thinking before you came by?"

"About roses?"

"Ha! You sounded like Casey just then. No, I was thinking how the iron gates of Lakefront are like the cover on a good book. They hold stories inside, Josie–strange, sweet, spine-tingling stories." Grace digs into the last of the rose bush.

I can't help but think of my dream as I look up at the heavy limbs overhead. I wonder if Lakefront has a special hold on me, too. I'm tempted to tell Grace about my dream, but doubt and worry trap my words deep inside. Crouching to gather bits of roses from the spongy ground, my feet slip and I tumble onto my bum. Grace offers me a hand up.

"You feeling all right? Maybe we should quit for the day."

I brush off the back of my jeans. "I'm fine. I lost my balance. Let's finish. Then I need to visit my tombstone." It's high time I gave the grave I rubbed some attention.

In no time, we've tamed the ragged roses into submission. We make our way over the gravel path; our fat wheelbarrow bounces and plant debris tumbles to the ground. I stop at my tombstone and sit, taking care to avoid any cast off chunks of gravestone that surround it. Grace abandons the wheelbarrow and sits beside me.

"This is the one, huh?"

"Yep. I don't even know her name, Grace. The others are busy unraveling these awesome mysteries and I'm stuck on square one."

"Well, I can't say I've looked too close at this particular stone. Sad as it sounds, I tend to ignore the put together ones. I spend more time trying to fix the ones that fell and broke to pieces. It's old, though. And the shape is unusual."

Grace squats and runs her hands over the face of the stone. She pokes a finger into one of the quarter-sized circles that dot the top. "Now, this here. It's like something used to be set inside here, like a jewel or small coin. Maybe got picked out and pocketed long ago."

She rubs her hands along the backside of the stone and quickly twists out a clump of dandelions at the base. A handful of silky moss comes out with it. Grace tosses the clump of weeds onto the pile in the wheelbarrow. It tumbles off, landing dirt-side up on the ground. A fat pink worm crawls out of the clump and starts to dig itself back into the living earth below.

The lowest part of the tombstone is now exposed to the light of day. I rub my hand over its cool, sandy surface.

"Look how the stone's lighter down here!" My fingers trace a deeply etched line and catch on sharp bumps. "Grace, what is this?"

She crouches down to get a better view and scowls. After removing her gloves and stuffing them into a back pocket, Grace runs a hand over the dark peaty line and pokes a fingernail inside the cavity. "This might open. Quick, honey! Hand me that trowel."

I dig through the cast-off roses in search of the red-handled trowel that rests in the belly of the wheelbarrow, cutting my hand on thorns as I go. Grace grabs the trowel from me and turns back to her work.

As Grace digs and scrapes, a nervous tingle crawls up my belly. Crows flutter above the treetops, making a noisy ruckus. I watch them circle, and one breaks off from the group, diving down and landing on the rusted edge of the wheelbarrow. He stares at me with an inky black eye, puffing his feathers.

Oblivious to our visitor, Grace diligently scrapes away dirt from the hole like a wizened archeologist exposing fresh bones. "Think I've got something here." We hunch over at the same time to get a better look and conk heads. "What's that a picture of? It looks like a fancy heart," she guesses.

Smooth loopy swirls surround the carved heart, like the sweet doodles of a love-struck teen. Grace digs deeper, adding scoops of the moist, sandy soil to the growing pile at her feet. She uses the sharp tip of the hand trowel to poke and prod the stone.

"See these grooves, Josie?" I nod. "I think they go all the way into the tombstone." She picks and scrapes away dirt, then rests on her heels.

Carved into the brick-sized surface below the heart are twin dragons. They coil together around a blackened silver knob; fire juts out of their sinister-looking mouths.

"You see that knob?" Grace asks, her voice high-pitched and excited. "I'll bet you a nickel this is a secret compartment. My uncle used to carve wooden puzzle boxes and he always had a secret drawer built into them."

I caress the cold stone with my hand and run a finger over the detailed carving. "They're dragons, Grace. And that's not a heart! Those are tongues and fire all curled around each other. Creepy." Grace clears another few inches of dirt without answering. The hole is a foot wide and roughly six inches deep.

"I've got the dirt cleared away." Grace pulls off her gloves and touches the knob with her fingertip. "It feels like meddling, Josie. I know it is exciting, but if there's anything inside this drawer, maybe it's none of our business."

I wrap my fingers around the knob. The metal is cold to the touch and goose bumps erupt up my arms. "The person buried here needs us to open this drawer. She has no name, no history, nothing. What if we find something that helps us give her back her name?"

Grace stares into my eyes and nods. "Yeah, everyone should be remembered. Go ahead and open it."

I grab onto the slippery knob and pull. The drawer slides free with a gritty gasp. Grace and I knock our heads together for a second time as we try to look inside the dark cavity.

"Should I just reach inside?" I'm gripped with fear, and silently pray Grace will do the retrieving. "We are respecting the dead, right?"

"Of course we are. You were right, I don't know any more about this grave than my uncle did, or the person who came before him. I think this person here deserves to be remembered, like all the rest." Her eyes never stray from the knob. "Now, do you want to do this or what? It's your adventure that led us to this place. You should be the first one to see what's inside."

My hand trembles as I reach into the hole. My heart pounds. "I'm afraid something is going to bite me like a monster spider. It's dark in there."

"Nothing could survive being shut away for a hundred years."

My wild imagination almost gets the better of me. I pull my hand away from the hole and rub it against my jeans. All the parts are still there. I remind myself why I came to Lakefront today, to find out something new about this grave. I can't walk away from this. I push my hand inside the hole again. "Then, here goes nothing."

I expect to feel giant spider fangs sink into my fingers, but I only find a stiff roll of parchment tied with a thin ribbon. Feeling emboldened, I hand the paper to Grace and probe inside the drawer again to make sure I didn't miss something. The crow shrieks at me from his perch on the wheelbarrow. I hiss at the sky, "Get away pesky crow! Get!"

I contort my wrist to squeeze my hand into the back of the drawer and poke a finger into the corner. My fingertip grazes a cold, smooth lump, and I coax it out into the light of day. Tied with a piece of twine, the gray lump I extract fits easily into the palm of my hand.

Before I fully register the warmth that emanates from the lump cupped in my hand, a rush of feathers and caws descend on me. I feel a hard whack on the side of my face, and fall to the ground.

JOSIE READS
THE PARCHMENT

I WAKE TO A FIERCE PULSE of pain across my jaw. *Where am I?* Yellow walls, soft couch, blue blanket, the crackle of a fire and whispers.

I squint and see Grace and my father on the couch opposite me, heads down, talking in quiet tones over a crinkled piece of paper as if they have known each other for years. Imaginary question marks hang above my aching head. The fire in the hearth pops and spits.

The twosome turns toward me and notices I am awake. Grace rolls up the paper, ties a tidy red bow across the middle, and sets it on the coffee table.

"Hey, honey. How're you feeling?" Dad brushes a hand across my forehead.

Pain pulses across my face as I answer. "All right, I guess. My head hurts a little. Why are you here? How did I get to Grace's?"

"She called from your cell phone and said a crow attacked you. At first I thought it was a joke, but then she started hollering. Grace said you were knocked out and there was blood. So, I raced over."

His hair is a mess of wild curls. He has no doubt been running his hand through it over and over out of worry. "Josie, I told you I didn't want you coming here today. Maybe next time you'll listen."

Grace enters the room and sets two glasses of lemonade onto the coffee table.

"Drink up! Grant, you too. This'll help."

Grace lifts the ice pack from my jaw and replaces it with a fresh one. She tucks the blanket around my feet and studies my face.

Worry crackles her forehead. She bends over me, looking tired and worn, not like the spunky forty-something woman I've come to know. Her eyes dart to the roll of paper on the coffee table.

It is out of my reach. "What did it say? You read it, didn't you?"

I sit up too fast and white stars shoot behind my eyes. As soon as my sight clears, I reach for the lemonade, and the stone heart that was tucked inside my hand falls to the floor and bounces out of sight.

"What's this?" My dad grabs the strange object from under the couch and holds the heart, turning it over in his hand.

"It was stuffed behind the papers in the secret compartment. I don't know what it is," I answer.

"It's a heart carved out of stone. Maybe basalt? Or blue stone? I'm not sure." Dad gives it back to me and I hand it to Grace, whose eyes are bright with curiosity.

"Is this what you pulled out when the crow smacked your face?" Grace scowls down at the object. "Why's it warm?"

"I had it in my hand the whole time, I guess. It's weird, isn't it? What'd the paper say?" I ask again.

My dad sets his empty glass on the coffee table. He sits up so his elbows rest on his knees, looking like a granite sculpture in the park. "There were two documents in there, Josie. Strange things, really. And this heart makes it seem all the more mysterious. Read them. One says that the woman buried at that site was found guilty of witchcraft and put to death in 1851.

"The other is a letter from the mayor of New Market, Washington from a long time ago. In it he asks that the woman be reinterred somewhere far away, as she was, 'even in death,' bringing bad luck to his town. Very melodramatic."

Dad hands the roll of parchment to me. I slide off the red ribbon, uncurl the document, and a small yellow letter flutters to the ground:

29th of October, 1851

Dear Sirs,

Herein lay the remains of Mrs. Bain McLaren. As Mayor of New Market Township, I presided over the trial that led to the sentencing of Mrs. McLaren. Tried by a jury of her peers, she was found guilty of practicing witchcraft against citizens of our Godly town. She was sentenced to death by way of public stoning one month's time after the trial's completion.

It is imperative to note that, before her sentence was carried out, the High Council attempted to cleanse Mrs. McLaren by way of sage and cedar, the means proven to be most effective during the historic witch trials of the 1600s, to no avail. Mrs. McLaren swiftly and ruthlessly employed her dark magic to poison two council members and coax a third to take his life. I myself suffered physical manifestations of her magic as well.

With the death of Mrs. McLaren, may all her sorcery go to the grave as well, ashes to ashes, dust to dust. At the direction of the Council elders, her home and surrounding acreage was burned to the ground and the McLaren homestead covered in rosemary and cedar boughs.

Within her headstone rests her last vestige, a crudely carved stone fetish she was never without. All attempts to destroy the fetish were met with failure, thereby leading the Council to bury it with the witch. It should be made known that the strange fetish was among the stones that were used to press Mrs. McLaren to death.

Your humble servant,
Mayor Smythe

"Are you kidding? They stoned her to death? I thought witch hunting went out of vogue 200 years before that?" I rub my aching jaw and look to Grace and then to my frowning dad, who says, "That's what I don't understand. But there's more. Read this." Dad hands me a sheet of yellow parchment written with sepia ink in a slanted script. I read the document and my head starts to pound again.

On the twentieth of December, in the year one thousand, eight hundred ninety nine of our Lord, we implored the assistance of northbound travelers to reinter the last vestiges of witch Bain McLaren to the northern city of Seattle, Washington, which would be their final destination.

Since executing Bain McLaren, New Market has been plagued with illness, famine, and failing commerce. Our young children and our eldest citizens struggle with ill health. It is our most solemn prayer that with the removal of witch Bain McLaren from our lands, we will no longer suffer her curse. It is our deepest hope that with the removal of her remains this cloud of evil will lift from New Market and that our town may once again know peace and prosperity.

God bless those willing to exorcise this cursed Bain far from New Market. God bless the husband and daughter of the witch who had both wisdom and forethought to return to their homeland, Ireland, thereby severing all earthly ties to the witch and allow their family an unencumbered future. If only we had acted sooner.

God bless New Market, Washington, which will be rechristened under the name Tumwater upon the removal of this Bain from our soil.

My hands shake; I grip the paper with such force. "Wow! Makes you feel sorry for all the people of New Market. Maybe they should've blamed themselves for their bad fortune. It's karma, if you ask me. Putting a woman to death? Rejoicing when her family deserts her? I don't believe for a minute that she was a witch. But, I know the things they did to her were unforgiveable. You put all that human wreckage into the universe and it comes back to bite you in the rump! I mean, 'pressing her to death' with stones? God." The ice pack slides off my face and I set it on the table with the paper.

Grace fumbles with the paper after refilling my glass. She squints into the page as if concentrating will help her make sense of the words. There is a rap on the door and Grace abandons the paper to answer it.

"Well, hey there, Casey! Come on in, will you?" Grace gives Casey a hug as she passes.

"Hello, everyone," Casey says. "I didn't realize I'd be joining a party." She gives me a sideways glance and looks to my dad, her brows crumpled into a question mark. "Do you still need my help putting in the winter cabbage?" she asks.

Grace answers. "It's been a busy morning around here. How about you visit for a while, and then we'll see if we feel like digging in plants. Does that work?"

Casey nods and grabs the heart fetish off the table. She tosses it casually from hand to hand. "Sounds great. So, what's up?"

I say, "Grace and I were checking out my mystery grave and we found a secret compartment." I point to the curls of parchment on the coffee table. "The lady buried there is named Bain McLaren and they stoned her to death for being a witch. They used that fetish in your hands during the death sentence."

Casey drops the object like a hot coal, and it bounces to the rug with a soft thud. "Christ! That's awful." She looks at her hands as if they are tainted with blood and wipes her palms across her jeans.

"The mayor was convinced she was bringing the town bad luck, even in death, so they had her body moved to Seattle."

"Whoa. What's that saying? 'The truth is stranger than fiction.'" She shoves her hands into her hoodie pocket. "I guess that means the rumors about the Ghost Forest were partly true. Right, Grace? At least the part about witches back there." Casey picks up the stone heart and places it by the rolls of parchment. She touches a finger along the thin string of beads that run across the fetish. "What is this thing?"

Grace stares at the object uncomfortably. "Most cultures have charms, amulets, talismans, what have you, that they carry with them for good luck. Maybe this was Bain's. But the folks of New Market with all their crazy talk about black magic must've assumed it held evil powers. Makes me feel squeamish, and that's the plain truth. But, it probably has more to do with those villagers using it to kill a woman than anything else." Her eyes never leave the strange object. "I'm just, um. I just thought of something. I'll be back in a minute," Grace says and then leaves the room.

Dad takes the object off the table, and turns it over in his hands. "This must be a Celtic talisman. Didn't the letter say her husband and daughter returned to Ireland before they tried Bain for sorcery?" He fingers the beads strung across the stone heart. "What are the beads for? See this? They're glass beads tied around the heart with a braid of metal. Gold? It's beautiful. It must've taken someone quite a while to craft this. It's art, really."

Grace treads with purpose into the room carrying a large wooden box. "Josie, I wanted to share this with you. Remember I told you how my uncle used to make puzzle boxes? Well, this one reminds me of the drawer we found in Mrs. McLaren's grave. Maybe you girls can get this thing open." She hands it to me and I stroke the smooth golden wood. "See if you can find its secrets. I'll be back."

Grace disappears out the front door as Casey inspects the wooden puzzle box. It resembles a piece of doll furniture, fit for an infant princess. Smooth on the top, the front of the box has two tall doors with notches where the handles would be on a full-sized armoire. I dig a nail into one of the divots and try to pry a door open.

Casey scoots close to me on the couch. "Let me have a try. I love puzzle boxes!" She smiles. "I think this is Douglas fir, but the veneer is cherry."

"Spoken like a cabinetmaker's daughter, Casey," my dad says. Grace reenters the room with more lemonade and a bowl of microwave popcorn.

As she sets the refreshments down on the table, she pushes the strange fetish out of reach all the while watching as Casey probes the box. Something clicks.

"I got the door open!" Casey bursts.

Grace laughs, "Think you made quick work of it, huh? There's about nine more steps young lady." She glances at my dad who smiles and they end up laughing together about nothing.

I want to grab the fetish, tuck it under my legs because that odd piece of Bain feels too far away. Why did Grace have to push it way over there? I reach for the heart and my dad plunks down on the other side of me on the couch.

He says, "I'm sorry you got hurt out there. I guess it was for a good reason though. You uncovered some interesting things today. Still friends?"

"Friends," I whisper and kiss his rough, unshaven cheek.

SETH BREAKS INTO THE SERGEANT'S HOUSE

SOUTH SEATTLE is the gritty underbelly of the Emerald City. Dowdy industrial streets lined with concrete warehouses, gas stations, and asphalt parking lots give off as much color as a dead beta fish. Truck exhaust hangs in the air and trails from the port to the freeways like an aerial troll net. The antithesis of a dream catcher, the net scoops up angst and holds it fast to the dour geography. The only evidence of humanity in south Seattle is the occasional slumped wretch limping his way inside a windowless tavern, searching for a brief diversion from his pathetic life.

For local historians, south Seattle remains the purest example of the city's lumber origins. The epicenter of Northwest commerce in the 1850s, its sawdust-filled air was testimony to the city's bustling lumber industry; ponds burgeoned with logs waiting to be transformed into lumber. Cut down, stripped naked, sawed, and shipped south, the boards hewn here built a young San Francisco.

Sometime during the last century, the buzz of sawmills and the whistle of cargo trains gave way to the squeak of exhaust brakes and the incessant drone of airplane traffic. If south Seattle had a grain of charm left, local historians would rally for its preservation. But it has no charm. So no one rallies. In fact, most people go out of their way to avoid this part of town.

Snaking through the heart of south Seattle is the Green River, famous not for its sluggish waters, but for the bodies dredged from its depths and the serial killer that sunk them. Sandwiched between the warehouses and gas stations are a handful of homes, former brothels and taverns from days of old. Built a century ago, they wear thick coats of peeling taupe and ash gray latex and sit largely forgotten.

I step off the Metro bus and scan the map on my phone, hoping my GPS won't fail me. I check the schedule nailed to a weathered bus stop sign and assure myself I have a ride back to the land of the living.

A walkway of cracked concrete cuts a path to the front door of a tan, single-story rambler. Surrounded on all sides by overgrown brown grass and a slumping wooden fence, the house sits midway down Green River Road. An oversized white sign is hammered into the front yard and states that 413 E. Green River Road will be claimed as property of the state of Washington six months after this posting if no living claimant is revealed to the courts.

Weekly circulars in varied states of decay are strewn about the yard and porch. I gather them up and toss the stack into the bowels of a blue recycle bin tucked at the end of the lumpy brick and concrete driveway. I climb the front steps, noting the peeling white paint, and open a wobbly screen door.

Out of habit, I knock. With the sergeant dead three months, I don't really expect an answer and shift to the right to get a look inside the giant picture window: orange shag carpet, brown furnishings, and brass light fixtures. I'm looking at a time capsule from the 1970s.

Thinking back to the family trip we took to the Smithsonian's American History Museum last summer, I expect to see Archie Bunker's favorite easy chair tucked into a corner. Instead, I find a wood and pleather davenport facing a two-tiered coffee table; its top littered with magazines and coasters. Next to the smoke-stained fireplace hearth sits a brown plaid easy chair. A brass floor lamp stands beside the chair.

I return to the front door and debate for a millisecond whether or not to jimmy the simple knob lock. I jiggle the knob and the door swings open. "Didn't expect that," I mutter as I walk inside slowly, wiping my shoes on the felt mat that lies over a yellow patch of linoleum.

A tattered flag hangs to the right of the door. Old and beautiful, it is no doubt filled with stories from a battlefield half a world away. My eyes film over. I've got to find some answers. I touch a finger to the soft fabric and a moth flies free toward my face.

Other than relics from the 70s, the front room is outfitted trim and neat for visitors, without any sign of personal items. I have a hunch he didn't do much living in this space.

I open a coat closet off the front door. A milk crate rests on a particleboard shelf above the coats and empty hangers. A quick glance through its plastic skeleton reveals nothing more than a mix of gloves and scarves ready for the two days of the year that dip below freezing around here.

On the floor rest a pair of rain boots, snow boots, and a long black umbrella. The umbrella confirms what I already know: Sergeant Paxton wasn't born here. No one born in Seattle uses an umbrella. Hoods, yes; umbrellas, no. I close the closet door and move toward the sunny kitchen at the back of the house.

In my bones I know that this is where the sergeant spent most of his time. The room holds the faint scent of coffee and long since eaten slow-cooker meals, but the aroma comes from my imagination. In real life, I stifle a dust-induced sneeze from two months of stagnant air.

The butter yellow walls and white scalloped curtains make the space light in spite of the vacancy. A window above the kitchen sink looks out onto a tiny yard. A bird feeder sits empty. Two Adirondack chairs grace a flagstone porch beyond the kitchen window. A hodgepodge of planters are scattered across the backyard: ceramic vessels small, fat, and tall in various shades of blue. Fist-sized rotting tomatoes lie on the ground unpicked, along with a handful of weeds, within a hooped wire cage.

Along the back fence, painted a clean white, is a dried out garden. Pole beans and corn stalks hover over rows of carrots and lettuce gone to seed. A few bees zip from plant to plant looking for some pocket of forgotten pollen.

I scan the perimeter of the fence and see another flank of fence, bare of fresh paint, on the right side. A gallon of paint, sun dried, is tipped on its side in the dry grass. A paintbrush with stiff white bristles pokes out of the grass next to it. Is this where you died? I try to recall the slim death notice that ran in the paper; was a heart attack listed as the cause of death? I take a moment and say something like a prayer, and then I turn my attention back to the search. The moment ends with a loud blast from a car horn from the alley behind the yard. I cringe as a car crawls down the narrow road. The fence is six-feet high, but what if they saw me? I slink back inside the house to finish my search, but worry the car will circle to the front of the house. Then what? Would they call the police?

Adrenaline pumps through my veins and I eye the kitchen with a sharper focus. The room is small and well-ordered. Underneath a white curtained window is a chrome and vinyl dinette; its sleek top shines in the natural light. As if plucked from a fifties diner, two pristine chrome and vinyl chairs face each other across the shiny table. Under the curtained window, above where I'd expect to find a tabletop jukebox, rests a blue ceramic pot filled with folded white linen napkins, slips of paper, and pens.

I rifle through the papers and find a grocery and To Do list. Water tomatoes, check. Empty garbage, check. Finish painting back fence, no check. Goose bumps rise across my arms. Tucked behind the napkins I find a water bill and garbage bill, both due August 30, only weeks after he died.

I return everything inside the blue pot and turn my attention to the white cabinets that frame the room. Most of them are filled with dishware and glasses, but a slim door above the black rotary telephone holds promise. Phone books, blank envelopes, a roll of stamps, and an address book– now, that could be helpful! Still worried the car will return, I keep an ear tuned to the street noise. But the house is quiet.

I flip through the pages of the tiny book and open the P section, finding Colin Paige its lone entrant; no Paxtons are listed. The size of a thick business card, the small book tucks easily into my jeans pocket. My heart pounds.

Determined to comb the house before the eleven o'clock Metro pulls up out front, I return to the front room and begin to make my way down a long hall, but slow as I pass the large picture window. A car crawls past on the street. I squat down and hug my knees, trying to remember if the reflection of light on the glass kept me from seeing into the house. I had to press my nose to the window to see inside. It's been what, maybe fifteen minutes, but my memory is fuzzy. I slowly rise and peek out the window. The car is gone. It was probably just normal traffic.

I hustle down the hall and duck inside the first doorjamb. Inside, I find an efficient but comfortable guest room. A twin bed rests underneath an equally diminutive window. There are no cars on the street out front and I breathe a sigh of relief. The only other furniture in the space is a cherry rocking chair. I do a cursory check of the closet, bare except for a couple of wire hangers on a thick cedar rod and a retired kitty condo like the one in Josie's living room window. Otherwise, nothing.

The largest room is at the end of the hall – the sergeant's bedroom. A dark ebony sleigh bed with white bedding is centered along the back wall. I'm tempted to pull a coin out of my pocket and confirm that it would bounce on the tightly bound bed, but I resist. Two ebony nightstands with stained-glass lamps flank the stately bed.

The furnishings stand out for their beauty, but mostly because they don't quite fit with everything else, like a shirt in your closet bought by an aunt that lives a thousand miles away. Did you inherit this from your parents?

The master closet holds no cardboard boxes filled with memories and photographs. In the darkest reach though, covered in the thin plastic film of a dry cleaner bag, is an Army uniform. My heart thumps in my chest. What had blurred into a voyeuristic exercise instantly sharpens to an exercise with a purpose. The sergeant deserves better than to have his property claimed by the state, and this is my best chance to find a living relative. I check the pockets of the uniform, but they are empty.

The last unexplored room is an office. A retro tan metal desk and chair fill up the undersized room. I sit in the chair and spin, rolling the casters across a hard plastic carpet protector beneath. Above the desk hangs a corkboard stuffed with a jumble of postcards, photos, and clippings held on with black pushpins. It's the only thing I've found in the house that lacks precision.

I pull at the top drawer and expect to find it locked. But, like the front door, it slides open without resistance. A tidy assortment of office supplies lines the bottom of the metal tray: a few sticky notes, pencils, paper clips, pens, notepads, and a thin calculator. I tug at one of two heavy drawers. Metal hanging files swing and clatter as I slide the drawer open. Each has a tab neatly printed in capital letters: 2009 IRS, 2010 SSA, and so on. Nothing pops out at me. I pull open the last drawer and find a similar array of hanging files. Surprisingly, these tabs are labeled with dates that have yet to occur. And I thought I was organized!

A noise from outside the house stops me. I hold my breath and listen. There is the steady rumble of a car idling out front. Or maybe the car is across the street? But why would it sound so loud? I don't want to stand up and look out the tiny window. I decide I'd better leave, slow and quiet like. I can slip out the back door and walk through the alley, catch the bus a couple blocks down from here. I'll just set this room to rights.

As I shut the drawer, all the empty files slide forward with a metallic clatter, and I see a black leather-bound book lying underneath. My whole hand tingles as I reach inside the drawer. It looks like a journal. I raise my hands with the book in a victory pose and then freeze. I hear thuds from the front of the house – footsteps? I clutch the palm-sized book to my chest and spin out of the chair. When the chair finally stops spinning, I face the corkboard. My dizzy eyes focus on the photos and postcards and land on a yellowed newspaper clipping from a long time ago.

The black-and-white image is familiar to me, because I printed off its digital cousin last week. Sergeant Paxton stares out with vacant black eyes. He wears army pants with a clean white button down shirt. He looks young and fit, but his eyes look haunted. Before I can talk myself out of it, I rip the photo from the corkboard and stow the fifty-year-old article inside the journal. A rustle from the front room makes me freeze.

"Seattle Police. We know you're in there. Come on out!"

I slip the journal inside my jacket pocket. I steel myself and dash to the back door, blood rushes through my ears. I brace myself. Whatever happens next, it was worth the risk.

JOSIE UNEARTHS
A QUEST

A RUSTLE AND TUG on my shoulder jar me from a cozy dream. The bleary outline of Owen stands at my bed. "Josie, wake up. I had a bad dream. Josie," he whimpers.

"Do you want to crawl in?" I ask and he sniffles and nods. I raise the comforter and all the yummy warmness vanishes, replaced by my brother's cool, thin form. Thank goodness he has on flannel pajamas.

"Want to tell me your dream?" I ask. I stroke his wild curls, and brush away the hair from his forehead. He doesn't answer. I stroke a gentle hand over his face that is turned away from me. His eyes are closed. He is back to sleep already.

Glowing numbers on the alarm clock read 4:26 a.m. No wonder the sun isn't up yet. I lie in bed trying to sink back into my sweet dream once again. Seth was in it. He was telling me a story about when we were kids. We were laughing. Try as I might, I can't get back to sleep. I stare into the window above my bed, but all I see is the dark outline of tree branches.

"Caw! Caw!" I jolt at the loud noise outside. It sounds like many crows all at once cry and shout. I crouch on my knees to peer outside, but see nothing. Sleepy Owen sleeps through the noise. I wiggle out of bed and wrap him in blankets. I root slippers out from beneath my bed and follow the noise to the back of the house.

From the kitchen window I see black movement. Flits and flutters. I unbolt the back door and debate going outside. Something rubs my leg and I jump. "Oh, it's just you, Shadow."

The cat growls deep in his throat. He rises on back paws and scratches the door with the front two. *Scritch, scritch, scritch.* His paws fly up and down and carve vertical trails into the wood door. I clap at him. "Stop it! Shadow, quit that!" I can't blame him for hating the crows. One beat the heck out of him only days ago.

The cat hisses and caterwauls. I fear he will wake up Owen or worse, so I crack open the door. Shadow slips into the darkness and the crows lift from the yard and scatter into the sky. I step onto the back porch. A harvest moon hovers above the unkempt garden, washing the furthest reaches in amber light. The copper roof of a tiny building flashes in the moonlight, catching my eye.

A crow swoops in front of the path and lurches for Shadow with a piercing "Scree!" I step onto the pea gravel and wave my hands.

"Leave him alone, you! Get!" The crow glides past my face. I raise a hand to block him in case we collide and he soars to the top of my mother's art shack, a small wooden building in the furthest reaches of our yard. He perches on the roof and stretches out his neck.

"Caw, caw, caw." He pecks at the copper shakes that line the small roof and waits for me to catch up. I follow the path to the shack and overgrown rosebushes grab at my pajamas.

The shack is roughly fifteen-feet wide and twenty-feet long. The small building is held together with rusty nails and a web of wisteria and ivy. I reach for the copper knob and let the door swing open to reveal the dusty space. It is a time capsule of my mom's life. This is where she brainstormed, sketched and carved. It's no wonder I couldn't feel her near me Halloween night. My mom lives here, not in that hole at Lakefront Cemetery. It has been some months since I last visited her shack. I got too busy, somehow. I make a mental note to spend more time here in the days to come.

I step inside and my slippered foot lands on fur. "Rrroww," Shadow howls. I lift my foot and he turns, scratches my leg and hisses. I clutch my leg where he swiped and pull my hand away to find drops of blood.

He hides under a chair in the corner and growls. His eyes flash green, then red in the dim light. He looks scary, and I shiver.

Maybe he is just scared. "I didn't see you there. I'm sorry," I say. Shadow shoots out from behind the chair, between my legs into the garden. I swing the door shut behind the cat and rub my sore leg.

Tired, I settle into a wicker rocker. I cast my eyes around the space and take in the dusty nooks and crannies, struck by how what always felt so large as a little girl now seems tiny.

My eyes rest on a chestnut brown shadowbox hanging above my mom's worktable. Miniature objects dot the twelve openings: soapstone masks no bigger than a quarter, a doll-scaled porcelain pitcher, an old coin. My favorite, a thumb-sized painting of palm trees, sits dead center. I spent the months following her death staring at this odd collection of treasures, feeling that if I could unlock this visual riddle I would come to understand a part of her that no one else did. I gently stroke the objects and my fingers tingle to hold her hand again.

At eight years old, I wasn't quite mature enough to grasp the concept of forever. When my mom passed away at the hospital, my young mind concocted a story to explain her absence, one that didn't include death. I told myself she'd gone on a trip, maybe traveled to a place where they had a cure waiting for her. When my mom decided to come home, I knew her art shack would be the first place she would visit. I slept here secretly, waiting for her return. I'd slip the blankets off my bed and tiptoe across the yard. I worried I'd get in trouble if Dad found out. But, looking back, I could've fallen off the face of the earth and he wouldn't have noticed. His mind was far away from us. Maybe he was making up his own stories to get through those cruel days.

After a few weeks, it sunk in that she wasn't coming back. I think it was the dust that convinced me, or rather the lack of it. Carving stone for a living, Mom created a steady stream of productive dust. Carving, sanding, sanding again, polishing, sanding another time; dust covered every surface like a gossamer drop cloth. Productive dust like that looks so white it almost glows. The dust that clung to the surfaces after her death was different. It was tan in color and lighter than bits of stone. It made my nose tickle.

Years ago, my mom appointed me the official duster of her art shack. Looking back, I think she made up the job so I'd feel important. I wore my title proudly though, and had the dirty feather duster to prove it! After the funeral, I came here to dust, maintaining the old routine brought me some small comfort. Cleaning the soft layer of debris from her space made the muffled voices from the house bearable:

'She was taken too soon;' 'How are the children taking it?" 'I am sorry for your loss.' Owen slept in the rocker while I puttered.

After the story about how my mom was on a long trip wore thin, I pretended she was like the elves that cobbled shoes at night. I convinced myself that she hid away in the day and toiled through the night on her craft. I imagined that the pieces she created were so beautiful that God brought them straight up to heaven to delight the angels. But my fiction had holes. The truth was, I spent most nights sleeping in the rocker but was never startled awake by her work. She left no white carving dust behind. She was gone.

I hug myself and try to comfort the little girl that figured out in slow motion that her mother was dead. Her death settled over me like that dust. It settles over me still, one small particle at a time. Dust that weighs down my thoughts, dust that forms layers over me and her memory until I can't see through one to the other. "I miss you, Mom. I wish you were here now." I wrap myself with the old knitted blanket from the back of the chair and let the tears come.

Above my head, there is a scraping noise. I cover my mouth and listen. It is a scratching, tapping noise, beak on metal. It's the crow. For some reason it makes me angry, his noise, his apparent destruction of this sacred space. I rise and lift a low, wooden stool, turn it upside down and bang it on the ceiling of the small building. "Stop that! Go away!" I shout.

I slam the stool hard, and a painting on the wall falls off of its nail and thuds to the floor. The canvas smacks against the wall and a slip of yellow paper flies out from underneath its wooden frame.

I return the painting to the empty nail and reach for the yellow paper on the ground. The yellow sheet is folded in careful quarters, having come from one of countless legal pads Mom used to jot down notes and sketches. Expecting a thumbnail sketch of the fallen painting, I open the paper to find a letter addressed to me. My hands tremble as I sit on the rocker and read.

Dear Josie,
My first-born, my wish-come-true girl. I miss you so much, my darling. When the doctors told me my fate, I knew what I would miss most in this life was you and dear baby Owen. We were supposed to grow old together,

remember? You were going to be my bridge partner at the old folks' home. We were cheated. Well, I will save you a seat at the table up here after you've had a long, fruitful life on earth. I pray you'll still want to be my partner at the card table after you know everything there is to know about me.

I've looked into your eyes and I can tell you exactly who you are, Josie. You're a masterpiece. You are smart, giving, capable, loving, and artistic. I hope you haven't lost yourself as you've tried to make life complete for Owen, and make life right again for your father. Those were never your jobs, but I'm sure you took them on, didn't you? Promise me you will find yourself again if that has happened, my girl.

Your father will have been devastated by my death, but not for the reasons you might guess. I was never what he thought I was, and if he found that out it is because he ignored my final wishes, which were to die at home and keep my body untouched, unexamined. When my throat cancer went to stage four, I asked the doctors to stop the chemo. I wanted my final weeks to be at home, unaltered by drugs. I asked that they not touch my body when I died. I didn't want them poking and probing me after death. But, I fear they did. And if your father won't speak of me, then I know they did.

If there was an autopsy, they will have found what I spent my entire life hiding. But, I need you to know the truth, so you can finish my journey and let me rest, finally and completely. My throat hurts from the secrets I've had to swallow in this life. I don't want to pass that pain on to you.

It all started in Alaska. You remember my mother was a member of the Unangan tribe of Aleuts? Well, it was when my father came to the Atka region to study her tribe that they fell in love. We settled in Anchorage, where your grandfather taught at a budding new university. My mother moved with him to Anchorage after they married, but stayed close with her family, taking me on many wave-swelled journeys to forge bonds with her kin.

When I was five, I came down with an illness. Though your grandfather was English and had faith in modern doctors, my mother did not. So when I became sick, as my illness took over and the fever rose higher, against his wishes my mother took me to her village for treatment.

Six weeks later, I returned to Anchorage completely healed. I don't remember anything about that time, but I was left with a four-inch scar under my left breast as a reminder. My mother and father never spoke to me of that time.

When I turned sixteen, my mother took me aside and handed me a dusty, wooden box. Carved out of Sitka Spruce, Golden Cedar, and Douglas fir, it had to be opened in a specific sequence to reveal the contents within. I thought it was the most amazing present I had ever been given. But Mother did not act like she was giving me a present. She never smiled. And she repeated the instructions on how to open it to me over and over until I had committed them to memory. But, even odder, she demanded that I never perform the last step of the instructions. I was never to reveal the contents hidden inside.

You know me too well to be fooled, Josie. Of course, not that day, or the day after, but soon I did complete the instructions, and within rested something withered, red, looking like a burgundy knot from a giant tree. My mother, shocked at what I had done, explained to me that it was my human heart that rested inside that puzzle box. She begged me to close the lid and protect it, because as long as it was never joined again with my human body, my magic would persist. Magic? I touched the scar below my breast and wondered what could possibly beat beneath my ribs. Was the magic my mother referred to, the thing they put inside me that kept me alive when I was a sick child, kept me alive now? I was scared, horrified, and excited all at once.

I ran away, or rather, I ran to find the answers on the island of my mother's kin, Atka. Elders filled my head with stories, remarkable, unbelievable stories. They told me my life was foreseen by elders generations before my father would ever visit the island and take away my mother. They told me of a jade stone that was found and carved into something the size of a fist. It was hollowed out and filled with herbs, then thrown into a communal fire to burn through the night. The village sang and celebrated as the stone heart burned they cheered as it was removed from the ashes. The elders kept the stone safe until it was needed, when I was returned to the Atka region for healing. They explained the power the stone gave me. They told me it was my destiny to become the tribe shaman.

You can guess the rest can't you, Josie? That stone rests beneath my ribs and beats as I write this letter. I am a stone shaman. Things grow for me that shouldn't. Luck is always in my favor. I heal people and animals that are hurt or sick. But, I have swallowed this secret too long, and my throat has rotted from the effort. You need to complete my journey for me. In order to rest completely, and end my residual earthly magic, you need to find my puzzle box and bury it next to my human remains. Only then can I move on to the next life and meet you at that bridge table. I would like to rest now.

You are the best thing I ever did, you and Owen. You are my greatest stroke of good luck. I miss holding your hand in mine. Please finish this for me.
I love you,
Mom

Seth Plays Dodgeball
and Hears a Confession

"**ALL RIGHT, SPILL EVERYTHING, MAN!**" Blaze paces a five-foot stretch of sidewalk. He wears shiny athletic pants and a Heritage sweatshirt, doing the whole sports look for our field trip to Skyjump Sports Center to play trampoline dodgeball with the girls. "Seth, I need details." A broad smile transforms his eyes into crescent moons.

"I can't believe you're here!" He smacks my arm. "Tell me how your dad worked the system."

"Yeah. I'll tell you, but not in front of the girls. They don't know about the police part, and I want to keep it that way. Gotta protect the old reputation, right?" I think about the non-sibling feelings I have been having about Josie lately and how my criminal dabblings would put her off. That is, if she has any feelings for me. Which I hope she does. I check my phone to see if I've ignored a text, but the screen is blank. "What time are they due?"

Blaze stops pacing long enough to check the time on his phone and then resumes. "They'll be here soon, so talk fast." His slick black athletic pants *swish, swish* with each excited step.

I begin. "It was terrifying. You know I've done a thing or two in the past to piss off Dad, but nothing big enough to keep me from getting into college." I tell him about the visit to the sergeant's house and when I reach the part where the men in blue stormed the house I slow up.

"So, the police dragged me out of the sergeant's house and stuffed me into a cruiser. They took my cell phone and wallet and gave them a good look over while I sweated it out. They asked if I was Seth Anthony, which they read off my student ID. Then, the guy in the front seat asks if my dad's a county prosecutor, if I'm *that* Anthony. Says my dad was on his softball team a couple years back. I didn't recognize him. But, just spitballing, I asked him if he played catcher. And wouldn't you know it, he lights up. Yes, he's still the catcher, but their pitchers were lousy last year. He asks me if there's any way I could get my dad to play next season."

"At some point, the other police officer must have called ahead, because by the time we got to the Justice Center, Dad was there to meet us. Immediately, the police officer pulls my dad aside and whispers something. He nods my way. Everyone shakes hands and that's it."

Blaze strokes a hand across his face. "You are one lucky dude."

"Yeah, lucky and connected. Anyways, the whole ride, I was bracing myself for the tirade but he was cool."

Blaze's phone dings, and he reads the screen. "They're almost here." I blink, still not believing how badly it could have gone and yet didn't.

Stowing his phone away, Blaze shakes his head. "No yelling? No life sentence? No, 'You are such a disappointment, Seth!' Nothing?"

"Nothing. I was bracing myself for the lecture. Instead, he asked if I'd found anything in the sergeant's house. And in all the excitement, I had almost forgotten about the journal. I handed it to him and he just laughed, grabbed it from me and thumbed through a couple pages, trying to drive at the same time. He's even more excited about this than me." I search the parking lot to make sure the girls aren't here.

"Anyway, Dad said he worked out some informal probation with the police. I have to do some legal research, do some volunteer hours, write a paper about how sorry I am, and that'll be the end of it. Oh, and Dad agreed to pitch on the softball team this coming season. I guess when you work for a living to put bad guys behind bars, the police cut you a break sometimes."

Blaze asks, "Have you read the journal yet?"

"Nah, man. Just a couple entries. The sergeant wrote like a doctor; it's all chicken scratch. Dad's better at deciphering his handwriting, so he's typing it up for me to read. I'll keep you posted as we go. But, the biggest development is that Sergeant Paxton visited Hawaii after World War II. I'm trying to talk the family into chasing down any possible island leads over Thanksgiving."

"Man, that little nugget in the journal isn't much of an excuse to visit Hawaii. Or was there more than that in the journal?"

"Well, he goes on for a lot of pages about this Hawaiian woman he met. She showed him the island. I don't know. He says in the journal he loved her, but I don't see anyplace that she followed him back to Seattle and had babies with him. Probably nothing." I check for the girls. They are a little late.

"I don't know. Might lead to something, Seth. Maybe there's a lovechild somewhere," Blaze laughs.

"Probably a long shot, but so far it's my only shot." My mind races to find a search term, some new direction for my mystery, but finds nothing. I notice Blaze watching for the girls.

"Hey, I meant to ask you about church. How was it?"

Blaze messes with the drawstrings on his hoodie. "It was very interesting. Dad drove me, but didn't come in, not like I expected him to or anything. The sermon was really good, though I have no means of comparison, but still, it moved me. Then, all hell broke loose."

"What happened?"

"My mother made a surprise appearance at the end of church. She must've followed us as we drove there or spotted Dad's car in the lot. Anyways, as I was leaving the church, saying my goodbyes to Father James, she pounced. You know her temper; she didn't just tap my shoulder and pull me away. No. She had to make a scene. The entire congregation got a free show. No doubt Father James has already added her to the Concern List so the congregation can pray for her salvation."

"Man, I'm sorry." I say.

"That's just how she is, Seth. Bossy. Loud. I got over that a long time ago." Blaze laughs and glances at the silver sedan that pulls to the curb. We wave as the girls empty onto the sidewalk.

"Who's ready for some dodgeball?" Casey shouts and grabs us up in a sloppy bear hug.

An hour later we sit down, sticky and sweaty, to dinner at the pizza place across the street. Casey nurses her jaw with an ice pack, our solo casualty. I'm starving, so even though I should be following the conversation, I track our waitress obsessively as she delivers pizzas to other tables.

As Blaze recounts the church incident, our waitress sets down an extra-large combo pizza and plastic plates. Without a word, Josie serves up slices and dishes them around. I'm waiting for her to squirt hand sanitizer in our palms, but she doesn't.

"So, during Mother's rant in the courtyard, Father James walked up real slow. He had this calm face, this determined look, and he stared down my mother. Not in an aggressive way. He just gave her all his attention.

"When she was done with her lecture about sneaking off to church and the horrors of organized religion, blah, blah, blah, Father James asked something like, 'Don't you think we should let Blaze explore this side of himself? I've seen kids banned from things and those things always end up meaning too much to them.' And my mother was silent. She didn't say anything at first. My mother, the one who always has something to say.

"Finally, she asks him if it might be natural curiosity, nothing more. And he says, 'Probably.' He tells us this story about the Bing children. They grew up on the same block and weren't allowed to eat sugar. No trick-or-treats. No sugar cereal. No movie candy. Nothing. So, they went off to college the same year he started seminary. When they all came home for summer, guess who had gained fifty pounds? Yup! The Bing children.

"He told my mother that it's better to let kids explore things in small doses and find their own limits. His story worked like magic. On the car ride home, Mother said church should be officially out of my system. And that was it." Blaze adds red pepper flakes and Parmesan to his slice and takes a huge bite.

Casey looks at him. "So, is it out of your system?" She accidentally sloshes root beer out of the pitcher onto the table as she talks. Josie flings napkins on the puddle.

Blaze smiles. "I don't think so. You know how a roller coaster ride makes you feel? Heart-pounding? Thrilled beyond belief? That's what church does for me. I suppose it's possible that what Father James said to Mother is true; I care too much because I've never been allowed to do the religion thing.

"But, in my gut, I know it's more. I feel at home. The people are really nice. That little girl who ran out of the front doors and started talking to me that day? She saw me walk into church alone. God, I was nervous. She marched down the aisle, grabbed my hand, and sat with me in a back pew. The sermon made sense. It made me want to do better. I don't know how, but I'm going back."

"Good for you," I say. "I'm just glad we have connections at a local cemetery. You might need a plot soon!"

Blaze nods his head and laughs. "No doubt."

Josie eats in slow motion, her eyes focused on something in the distance. I turn behind me to see a red brick wall. Nothing more. "You all right, Josie? Did we kick your butt on the trampolines?"

"No, nothing like that. Just a little out of it." Her focus is so far away from us.

She bites into her slice and doesn't notice the pepperoni that falls off. I reach across the table and stuff it into my mouth, then duck down low. Josie would normally smack me for that, but she doesn't seem to notice.

I wave a hand in front of her face and she blinks. "Hey, Josie. What's up? Where'd you go?"

"Sorry, I'm just a little tired. I was up early." She rubs her eyes to prove the point, but I don't buy it. She is thinking about something, something she doesn't want to share with us.

I try to catch her eye; I suspect she had another nightmare. I'm not sure I should mention it in front of the others. I decide to ask her about the grave she rubbed instead. "Have you found out anything more about the witch?"

She stares at me and then glances around the table like my question has broken her trance. "The witch? What do you mean?"

"You know, those documents from the secret compartment. Did you find out anything about the husband and daughter?"

She plays with the pizza crust on her plate, pushing it around with a finger. "Oh, yeah. That. No. I don't know anything more about them. But, did I tell you the town she came from, New Market, was renamed Tumwater after they disinterred her body?"

"You mean the Tumwater south of us? The one outside the capital?" I ask.

"Yep. So, I'm hoping Dad will take me there for a visit. Maybe they have a pioneer museum. If I go, maybe I can find more information about their homestead, although by now it's probably buried ten feet under a strip mall," Josie says.

I stuff the last of my crust into my mouth and take a quick swig of soda.

"You know, Ireland has a good network of genealogical societies. You could send copies of the documents you found. Maybe they could track down the McLaren family or locate a living descendant."

"Great idea, Seth! I'll check it out online. Thanks." Josie pastes a smile on her face and bites into her pizza.

She thinks we buy her act, but I'm not one of the groupies at school. I know her. And she's not in a good place right now. Something's eating her up. But before I can ask, Casey shoves a picture in my face.

"Check out what I dug up last night?" Casey pulls out a color snapshot of four toddlers flopped face-down across a gray plush rug. "Do you remember this?"

I laugh. "We're laid out like we need a coroner and body bags!" I pass the picture across the table to Josie.

"Hey! This is at my house. That awful burgundy leather couch will be etched in my brain forever. Look at our matching Baby Gap outfits! We were so cute. And our little bubble butts!"

Josie shows the picture to Blaze, who says, "Our diapers were full. How'd the moms get us to nap at the same time? Did someone slip Benadryl in the milk?"

Casey squints into the picture. "How old are we? Two? That's so sweet. We're all spread out across the floor, but we're still holding hands." She leans on Blaze's arm.

"Maybe that's how we invented our goodbye thing," Blaze says.

"No. We got that from our car tantrums. We were just talking about that the other day." Josie smiles and holds her hand into the middle of the table. We all clump a hand in the pile and laugh.

"Where would I be without you guys?" Josie asks. "We're better together than we are apart. We're consistent. We're face-value. Genuine. I wish everyone was like that." Josie's eyes get fuzzy and she stares off into the distance as she rubs a hand over her front pocket.

Casey leans in, nose to nose with Josie. "Wow! Where's this coming from?"

Josie pulls away. She frees her hand from the pile and rummages through a pocket, "I found a letter from my mom. She wrote it to me before she died."

Blaze asks, "How does a letter stay hidden for six years?"

"It was in her art shack stuck behind an old painting. I accidentally knocked the painting off the wall and found this."

"So, what'd it say?" I ask, reaching for the yellow paper. Josie pulls it away.

Josie unfolds the paper and skims the letter. "She said she loved me and would miss watching me grow up. She knew, even then, that I would do everything I could to help Owen and Dad. She said that if Dad didn't get over her death, it was because he found out who she really was."

Blaze asks, "What's that supposed to mean?"

Our waitress moves slowly past our table and eyes our unpaid check. She taps her foot and stomps away.

Josie tells us about the strange letter, the even stranger visit to the Aleutian Islands, details of a jade heart and the nature of her mother's last wish. Her voice drops to a whisper. "She told me I have to find some puzzle box and bury it with her remains. Then she can rest."

Blaze asks, "Puzzle box? Did she leave a treasure map to find it?" Josie hands the letter around the table.

"Man, Blaze."

"I'm only saying. You knock a painting off a wall to find an old letter, the letter exposes a side of your mom no one knew, one with a stone buried under her ribs, and she tasks you to find an old puzzle box and bury it with her body," Blaze says. "It's pretty wild."

"Does the letter give you any clues to help find the box?" Casey asks. Blaze hands her the letter. "That's the next step. You have to find the box before you can bury it. Your mom must've wanted it to be some type of adventure, otherwise she would've told you outright where she hid it. End of story." She hands the letter to me.

The waitress comes to the table again and sneers at the bill. Everyone pretends we don't see her. I can't help thinking that if this was a table full of thirty-somethings, our waitress wouldn't be pressuring us to pay and go. It irritates me and my voice comes out tight and gritty as I ask her for a few more minutes.

"So you think there really is a puzzle box? Or am I going on a wild goose chase?" Josie slides the last piece of pizza onto her empty plate and takes a bite. The crease across her forehead disappears.

Blaze answers. "I think there is a box, Josie. Maybe it's been right under your nose all this time waiting to be found. And it wasn't supposed to happen until now. Our visit to the cemetery, that cat. I mean, you were going to rub your mom's grave and didn't. But even so, you are getting a mom-based adventure. Cool." He pulls out two twenties and puts them down before the waitress can skulk past again.

Josie nods. "It's true. I was banking on something happening that night. I can't believe I'm admitting this. I had myself convinced that Mom's ghost would appear because it was Halloween. I know. I'm an idiot!" She studies the Formica tabletop and stacks our plates in a tidy pile. The waitress spies the money and scoops up the plastic tray.

Casey takes the plates from Josie and sets them on the neighboring table. She grabs Josie's hands. "It all worked out, didn't it? You got a two-fer."

Josie smiles, holds onto Casey and laughs. "I guess I did."

"Need any change?" Our waitress snaps her gum and shoves the bills deep inside her apron pocket.

"No. Keep the change," Blaze says.

"Thanks, guys. Come back again soon!"

JOSIE SEARCHES FOR THE BOX

I KNOW IT IS SETH before I answer the door because of his corny knock. Sometimes door-to-door sales people knock that way so you'll mistake them for an acquaintance and rush to answer the door. What they don't realize is that their little scheme multiplies the customer's disappointment tenfold. That's no way to ask someone for business. Not that I'm buying.

I open the door and take in Seth's natural dirty blonde hair. It is cut shorter than normal. He still looks like himself, just calmer somehow. "Wow, Seth! I like the hair. You look better. Does this mean you're done rebelling?"

He steps inside. "It's not a personal statement, Josie. I was just sick of tending roots. So, no luck finding an Irish genealogy website?"

I touch a finger to my lips. "Wait! We'll talk in my room."

Owen thumps down the hall in heavy black soccer cleats and rushes at Seth's legs.

"Hey there, little man! You got a game today?" Seth scoops Owen up in a hug.

"Yeah! Last one of the season. Can you come?" Owen squirms in Seth's arms and slips back down to the ground. He dusts crumbs off his shiny red Little Kickers jersey, then fiddles with his laces.

"It depends on how fast I can help your sister get done with this thing. What time's the game?"

"Warm-ups are in an hour." He grunts as he double-knots the long laces and then stands up again. "It's right across the street. Please come! Please!" Owen pleads with Seth and ignores me. He assumes I'll be there, I suppose.

"What d'ya say, Josie?" Seth puts a hand across his face, but he's too late. I see traces of a smile beneath his fingers.

"I say yes, as long as we can get cracking on my project now! To my room!"

Owen grabs my sleeve and pulls me back. "Hey, Josie. You know the rule. No boys allowed in your room, remember?"

"Owen, Seth's not a boy. He's family, so it doesn't count. Do you want us to make your game or not?" I walk down the hall and drag Seth behind me.

We shut the door. Seth sits at my desk and wakes up the computer. His face is red. Did I insult him when I called him family? It was supposed to be a compliment.

"Josie, this is the perfect website. You found it!" He taps the keys and scrolls to the bottom of the website.

"Yeah, about that! I found a great contact and mailed copies of the documents to her. It'll take a while because I'm relying on snail mail. I don't have a scanner and the digital picture was too fuzzy."

"That's perfect. So then, why am I here?" Seth shuts the computer down and spins around in the chair. When he finally stops spinning, he faces me.

"I couldn't say over the phone because Owen was around. I was wondering if you could help me search for the puzzle box; that is, if there is one."

He sits upright and smiles, "Little Miss Independence needs help?"

"I'm too close to it to think straight." I sit on the floor and stretch my legs like in yoga class. Stretching helps me think. "I feel like it's a test and I'm failing miserably, Seth. I don't know my mom. I thought I did, but this letter makes me realize how little I really knew. And my memories of her are getting fuzzy. Maybe you can use logic to get us to the puzzle box."

"I don't think it's a logic thing, Josie. I think it's deeper than that. It's a gut thing. But I'm glad to help. So, where do we look first?" He taps the computer keyboard though the screen is blank.

"I already tore apart her art shack. And I tried going through my parents' room, but my dad kept popping in. He moved her stuff out some time after her death, so there's not much there anyway." I bend and do a yoga pose and Seth spins around again in the chair. His ears, very prominent now that his hair is so short, are red at the top.

He stops spinning and faces me, but his eyes linger on my backside. Is he checking out my butt? He clears his voice. "Did he give all her stuff away? Or is it stored somewhere?"

I rise from the yoga pose and reach into my closet for a baggy sweatshirt, one that will cover my booty in these tight leggings. He was checking me out. Is that a bad thing?

"Josie, her stuff. Did he give it away?" Seth asks.

"Sorry, I was trying to remember. I think he gave away her clothes. But the rest is in boxes in the garage."

"Did you go through those already?" he asks.

"Not yet. Should we start there?" I take him by the shoulders and spin him in the chair.

"Seems like as good a place as any."

As his chair slows, he stares at me. "Nice sweatshirt. Sexy."

"God, Seth. Don't let Owen hear you. His teacher had to send a letter home because someone said that word during circle time." I laugh.

"He's in second grade and they still have circle time?" he asks.

"No, that was in first grade. But, it made a big impression." I think about how he called my baggy sweatshirt sexy and how I caught him checking me out. I should be offended or something, but instead I feel a quiet thrill as we walk to the garage.

Five cardboard boxes are all that's left of my mother. And her art shack. That was more a part of her than anything, except Owen and me. We find the boxes in the garage and Seth removes the lid off the first one. He says, "Dad's office is filled with these boxes. They're a lawyer staple. He hangs files inside and writes the case number on the outside. I didn't know other people used them."

Rifling through the contents, he pulls out a stained glass box decorated with dried flower petals. He piles stacks of photos onto the concrete floor and hits bottom. "That's it for this one. Come take a look."

I lift the lid off the small square glass box. Inside is a tangle of necklaces, bracelets, and dried flower petals. The brown petals crumble as I dig out the jewelry.

"It's a mess! All the chains are knotted together. Look! There's a locket." I pull out a silver locket and half the jewelry follows. I slip the silver chain out from the knots and unclasp the locket with a fingernail. Inside rest two pictures. Inset into the left side is a portrait of a much younger Mom and Dad. Their smiles are wrinkle-free. Their cheeks are flushed with new love. "This was taken before I was born. Maybe it's their engagement portrait."

The other side has a picture of me as a baby. I was maybe six months old, toothless and mostly bald. I'm gnawing on a teething toy, and a stream of drool has drenched my bib. I'm seated in front of a brick fireplace on shaggy brown carpet.

"She couldn't have put a better picture of me in here?"

"Let me see it!" Seth grabs the locket and grins. "You were so chubby! Look at those cheeks."

"Okay, give it back!" I snatch it out of his hands and pull the chain over my head. The locket sits against my heart. Seth works through the next box marked "Sarah" with a bold black marker. "These are all letters, cards, notes, stuff like that. Do you think she would've left a written record of where to find the puzzle box?"

"No. If she wanted to write it down, it would've been in my letter. I don't think she would risk writing it in two places."

I grab a letter at random and unfold it. The yellow-lined notebook paper has my mother's familiar block print. I read through the contents and quickly refold it, tossing it back inside the box. I grab another and another and find the same thing.

"These are love notes my parents wrote to each other in school."

"Gross!" Seth says. "I don't want to think about *my* parents writing love notes during class. That's what we do, not them!" His face turns red, and he digs into the third box without looking up.

"You've written love notes? To who?" I ask.

"I've never written a love note. But, I'm just saying…." Seth cuts his sentence short, and pulls out a black chain with a small rusted black key hanging from it. "What's this?"

"It looks like a piece of Goth jewelry. I can't remember my mom ever wearing it. Let me see." I grab the chain and examine the key. "There's a word etched on here. It looks sort of familiar. Can you read this?" I hand the key back to Seth.

He squints with effort. "It's not English, but I can't make it out. It's too dark in here to read."

I take back the key and slip the chain around my neck where it *clinks* against the locket.

"We can examine this closer inside the house." I lift the lid on the fourth box and find stacks of sketchbooks. I take them out and flip through pages and pages of drawings. Seth thumbs through another box.

"It's obvious where you get your art talent, Josie."

I gaze into the sketch, all fluid strokes and strong composition. The drawings look effortless and remarkable at the same time. "Thanks, but I could never do this. And I couldn't sculpt anything to save my life."

"That makes two of us." Seth puts the sketchbook back and takes the lid off our fifth box. "As much as I'd love to be wrong, I don't think we're going to find her puzzle box in here."

"Yeah, I agree. But maybe it'll give us some clue." I tuck the lid back on my box and slide it back onto its shelf. "Why would my dad leave those love notes in the garage? If I lost my wife, I would keep them close to me. And the pictures? Why'd he put these in here? I would put them in albums so my children could enjoy them. It's weird. He's hidden away every trace of her."

"Kind of goes with what she said in her letter, doesn't it? He found out her secrets and maybe mourning her became complicated. All this box has are receipts and photos of sculptures she sold. I don't think we'll find anything here."

A scarf covered in bright sunflowers slips out of the box. I snatch it up before it hits the ground and wrap it around my head.

Seth gives me a thumbs up. "Nice."

"I remember when my mom lost her hair. It didn't come out gracefully over a period of days, small clumps in a brush, like they show in movies." I wrap and rewrap the scarf around my head. "She lost her hair overnight in giant wads across her pillow. I ran into her room to see her one morning and she was mostly bald. I had to bite the inside of my cheek so I wouldn't cry."

Seth stops rummaging through the box in front of him and listens. "She looked in the mirror and started to laugh, a big belly laugh. Maybe she faked all that to keep me from crying, I don't know. It didn't seem fake. Then she pulled a wire basket out of her closet stuffed with all kinds of scarves. This was one of them." I touch the scarf on my head. Seth tucks one of the dangly ends of my scarf into my head wrap. It is such a tender gesture. I feel the little wall I built those years ago begin to crumble.

"We tried the whole basket on in a spontaneous fashion show. I wrapped this one around my mom's head. The colors made her eyes sparkle green and gold. She looked like an angel.

"Dad came in to see what all the laughter was about. He stood in the doorway, maybe soaking up the moment. Then again, he probably knew what the kerchief covered and that's why he clung to the doorjamb. Mom was one step further from him." I pull the scarf off my head and tuck it back inside the box.

"At the time, Dad was a good sport; he laughed with us. He even let me tie a scarf on his head. Owen must have been asleep in his crib, or else he'd have pulled Mom's scarf off with his sticky, chubby fingers. He would've exposed her bald head in a moment, a blink, just to stick something new in his mouth."

Seth reaches out and touches my cheek. "You've had to be strong for so long, Jos. I marvel at your awesomeness." I put my hand on his and we stay like that for what seems like forever, but probably amounted to seconds. Weird and wonderful at the same time. Something trills, his phone or mine, and it breaks the spell.

The screen on my phone says we have ten minutes until it is time to leave for Owen's game. "We have to hustle." Seth rummages through the remains of the last box.

"Hey! I didn't know your mom did this sculpture!" He holds a photo of a statue of a mother and little girl. "I walk by this every day on the way to school."

Sculpted out of green stone, the two figures sit together on a park bench, the girl curled up asleep in her mother's arms. Even though the photo has yellowed with age, it captures the loving face of the mother beautifully. She stares at her sleeping daughter in adoration.

"I'd forgotten about this statue. I remember going to the dedication right after Owen was born. I had a tantrum. It was hot and I didn't want to be dressed up. God, I was such a brat."

"Take it easy. You were too little to know what you were doing."

"I was six, Seth. I knew how to behave. It's just that after Owen was born, I had to share my mom all the time. I didn't deal with it very well."

"Look at her purse!" Seth points at the green stone purse that hangs off the sculpted mother's shoulder. "Is that a keyhole?"

"It's hard to tell from this. But it might be..." I touch the black key that dangles around my neck. A warm tingle runs up my fingers. "We need to go see it in person!"

I take the picture from Seth and stuff it into my pocket. We replace the lids on the boxes and slip them back onto the shelves as Owen stomps into the garage, his clunky cleats thumping and clacking across the concrete.

"Are you guys done? Can you go to my game now?" Owen looks at the boxes that have "Sarah" written on them and cocks his head to me.

"Yes! We finished our work. Time for a little soccer, right Josie?" Seth grabs my hand and pulls me out of the garage.

I suppress an urge to kiss his cheek as we follow Owen out the door.

BLAZE'S RIDE TO CHURCH

"THANKS FOR STICKING YOUR NECK OUT like this, Dad. But, if Mother finds out you're taking me to church, not Aikido, she'll kill us both!" I laugh a little and then turn to my silent dad.

He grips the steering wheel, his knuckles stark white skin against black leather. He takes a deep breath and sets his eyes on the distant road ahead. I wonder if he's heard me at all. He casts a sideways glance at me as he pulls into the church parking lot and turns off the engine. The man is seriously tense. "Blaze, taking you to church may be the right thing to do, but it doesn't make this easy."

"I appreciate the ride, Dad. She won't find out, I promise." The man will do anything to avoid conflict. I hadn't thought about what a risk he was taking to drive me to church.

"I'm not afraid of her finding out. I've made my decision. I am your father and I deserve a voice in your upbringing. And I say you should be allowed to attend church." He uncurls his fingers from around the steering wheel and rolls down the window. A mixture of cold air and rain drops blow inside the car. "Your mother's always had her opinions. Observers of our marriage would say she wears the pants. But I've got opinions about things also, Blaze. I just don't shout to have them heard. It's the biggest difference in our upbringing, I suppose."

"What do you mean, Dad?"

He wipes the raindrops away from the car door with a sleeve. "Growing up in Japan, my parents taught me to follow rules and avoid making waves. Your mother's upbringing was very different. She grew up in the deep South, with a politically vocal family standing up to inequality. She left for the Northwest in hopes of finding a place where her skin color was as irrelevant to her trajectory as her eye color. She had to be strong to endure the prejudices she faced as a child.

"And I fell in love with that strength and married her for it too, Blaze. And I still love her. But, I wonder what the toll has been on you, watching your mother decide everything, lay down all the rules. In the meantime, I keep my head down and stay silent. Maybe you don't even see me as a man anymore. I don't know." My dad's face flushes with color. He looks down at his hands.

I think about his words. What he said is true, but I can't come out and say it. The truth is, I avoid upsetting my mother, too. I'm no more a man than him. "Mother basically runs over the top of both of us. She always has. I roll down my window and breathe in the cold air. "So, why now, Dad? What's different this time to make you stand up to her?"

His face is smooth, calm like he was carved out of white marble. He gazes out the windshield as he answers. "When my family moved here from Japan, I was a little boy. I was struck by how big this country was. We were on a train for many days to get from New York to Seattle. As I grew up, I watched my parents with great admiration. They left our country with very little and created a business, a successful business, in America.

"And that's when I realized how great a gift being an American is. In this country, we have freedom. We can carve our own path. We can become anything we dare to dream." Color washes over his pale face and neck. He grips the steering wheel and continues his story.

"Your upbringing has been anything but free, Blaze. Our house is not a democracy. But at fourteen, you're a young man. You need to follow your curiosity and decide what kind of man you want to be in life. As long as you live in our house, you won't be able to choose your path, unless I help. You could be trying to experiment with things far worse than religion, but you haven't. I'm determined to do everything I can to let you check this out, to find your own path. And if your mother finds out about our deception, I will handle it."

"Well, thanks for the offer. But I can defend myself," I say defensively. My first attempt at being manly comes across a bit overdone.

My dad turns his gaze to me. He takes me in. "That's true. But I am here for you regardless. You have your mother's strength and conviction, so I know you can do anything." His words hang in the air between us. I want to believe them. I hope he sees something in me I have yet to discover. I want to hug him, but wonder if hugs are manly.

My father decides for me. He reaches an arm across the seat and gives me a sideways squeeze. "You better head on in. It's ten o'clock."

I swing the car door open as one of my little friends from Sunday school passes by. She grabs my hand and leads me into church. I turn back and wave at Dad. And he waves back.

CASEY EXTENDS
AN INVITATION

"WHAT ARE YOU DOING back so soon, Casey? You show up this often, I'll have to put you on the payroll." Grace stops digging and rises to her feed, she puts her gloved hands on her hips for emphasis. She laughs and her denim overall straps slip off her thin shoulders. Suddenly, I wish I'd brought a belt with me.

"You like my help, right?" I ask.

"Oh, darling. Of course I do. In fact, lately I find myself looking for you automatically around four. You're my unofficial apprentice," she squints. "You're comin' this often to learn about gardening, right? Or is there something else that brings you by so much?"

Yikes. I cringe at her question and search the grounds until my stare lands on the gnarled apple tree by Ettore's grave. "I kind of like to check back with the grave I rubbed on Halloween. Someone leaves him new stuff all the time," I mumble, keeping my eyes on the ground. I don't want her to see my face.

"How's this your concern? You're supposed to be off doing teen stuff. Hanging out with your friends. Picking out nail polish. Calling boys. You're too young to spend this much time with dead people. Not that I'm eager to lose my apprentice." She smiles and tugs at my sweatshirt. "C'mon. Walk with me."

I'd no more refuse her than a dead leaf could refuse the wind. As we walk past a row of graves, Grace hands me a red-handled trowel and a purple winter pansy. I have to stop to itch my calf, which suddenly erupts in a red swollen welt.

"I think something just bit me." I scratch at my leg and drop the pansy.

"Nah, keep moving. It'll go away," says Grace. "Hurry, now!"

I grab the pansy and move. After a few steps, the burning irritation disappears. I stare at Grace in amazement. "How'd you know it'd go away?"

"It happens to everyone. I've seen perfectly content people come past this one grave and start to bicker. I've seen kids scratch at their heads like they have bugs. The person buried here seems determined to cause a general irritation to anyone that comes close. Don't go all the way back there, but if you can, read that name," Grace directs.

I strain my eyes to make out the name etched into the stone. "It's familiar. Is she the writer?"

"Yep. A famous mystery writer."

"Are there lots of celebrities buried in Lakefront Cemetery?" I ask.

Grace laughs. " Yep, we've got our fair share. Now, looky here." She points up the hill to where a few cars are parked. "See all those cars?" I nod. "That's where the rock star who killed himself is buried. Over there is the poet who died of drugs." She points in front of us. "Over yonder is the Hollywood star who dropped dead during a stunt. He's the reason I felt it necessary to install all the wood signs." Grace pulls a clump of weeds from the base of a wooden arrow at our feet with names scrolled across it and arrows pointing in various directions. Sure enough, I recognize all the names and fight the urge to follow the tourists to see the famous graves.

Grace dusts off the top of the grave we stand near, the one that makes me itchy. "This lady gets her fair share of visitors, too. She made a lot of money writing over fifty books, and a TV series. They even turned some of her books into movies. Before she died, she bought a small island in the middle of the Pacific. I don't think she meant to live there, though. The writer wanted to be buried in the middle of nowhere. It was all recorded in her last will and testament, according to the newspaper.

"One thing I've learned from doing this job is it's best to follow someone's last wishes. It always goes bad when you don't. After she died, her relations ignored her last request and buried her at Lakefront instead. And I'm just speculating, but based on how folks react to her grave, itchy welts and all, guess how the writer feels?" Without waiting for me to respond, Grace moves quickly toward the entrance gate.

We make an abrupt stop at the enormous planter bed that greets visitors as they enter the cemetery. Grace parks her rusty wheelbarrow at the edge of the concrete curb that circles the mulch mound. "All right, now. We're going to plant in an arc. The first rows will be the winter pansies. Try to alternate the colors: dark purple, light purple, white, and yellow. It looks better that way.

"Then, if you're not too worn out, we'll move on to the cabbage. Those go behind the pansies so they can spread out some. Finally, if you aren't near death, we'll cut back these damn grasses." Grace shakes her head as she surveys the fluffy mounds of grass at the back of the planter bed.

"My uncle loved grasses and planted over a hundred on the property. I used to tease him, asking him if we were looking to raise cows at the cemetery. You have to cut them to the quick every year just so they look decent. A hundred infernal clumps of grass. Every year." She shakes her head, as if finishing an internal argument with the long dead uncle.

As I set to work, Grace eyes me. "What's your family think about you spending all this time at a cemetery?"

"Are you joking? They don't even notice I'm gone. It's football season."

"Oh, big sports fans, huh? And I take it you don't like sports much?"

"Actually, I always did like sports. I just wasn't a natural at anything like my brother."

"A natural? Let me tell you a secret; no one's a natural at anything. There are people led to believe they're naturals by overzealous parents and under-experienced coaches. But, it's the magic of being believed in that makes a talent." Grace stares into my face to check if I'm following and continues.

"It feels good to be singled out, so they spend all their time practicing to make it happen again. And more practice means better skills. And better skills lead to recognition. And recognition leads to more practice. You see? It's like a success machine. Built because someone had beginner's luck. That's all."

Grace digs in another pansy. "I take it your brother plays football?"

"Yeah. He's really good, a permanent fixture on the SportsCenter highlight reels." It feels good to bring some of my family drama out in the open. "Drew's the star quarterback of his university team. My parents spend every weekend in the fall traveling to watch his games. When winter comes, the hype for the bowl game starts. It pretty much consumes the whole family."

Grace asks, "What about you? Do you go on those trips?"

She hands me a pansy and I slip off the thin plastic container to reveal a knot of white roots bulging from a sprinkle of dirt. It gets me thinking about my relationship with my family, which makes Drew the roots and me the dirt.

I say, "I don't need to go on a trip that's all about Drew. I'm invisible enough without doing something like that. I stay home."

She stops digging and shakes her head. Her lips are pinched together and then she huffs. "Nah! That's not right. You stay home alone? How old are you?"

"Next week I'll be fourteen, on Thanksgiving."

"You don't belong at home by yourself. Why not stay at one of your friends' houses?" Grace asks.

"Most times, I stay with Josie. That usually works out," I say. Grace looks concerned about me. It is sweet. In the last couple weeks, she has become a dear friend.

"You'd be welcome here, too. I have a guest room that only gets slept in when my nieces visit."

It strikes me how much more of a friend she's been to me than my own mother. Something appeals to me about the invitation, but she lives in the middle of a cemetery. "I don't know if I'd be able to sleep here. I'd get the creeps. I'd probably have to pee in the middle of the night; and then I'd imagine some ghost waiting for me with a bloody axe in his hands and wake up in a puddle. Maybe I could hang out with you during the weekend days and stay with Josie at night."

Grace laughs. "I don't want to cause any accidents, Casey," she laughs again. "But, yeah, I see your point. You'd be more than welcome to spend your days here. I'm sure I'd be able to find plenty for us to do when you're not doing school work." She hands me a yellow pansy as if to make her point.

"Okay, since you've been all nosy and bossy about me, I have a question for you. What are you doing for Thanksgiving?" I ask, digging another hole into the soil.

"Nothing. More of this, I figure." Grace gestures to the planter bed in front of them.

"I'm having Thanksgiving with Josie's family. Why don't you come, too? I go over first thing in the morning before the Macy's parade. I help cook, watch football, all that stuff."

"Don't want to be a tag-along or anything," she says.

"You wouldn't be. I swear. I've already asked, and Josie said she'd be really excited to have you over. What do you think? Do you want to spend Thanksgiving with me at the Jameson's house?" Grace always makes me feel better. I would love do this little thing for her, surround her with family to celebrate a holiday, double holiday actually, if I count my birthday.

Grace smiles. "It's been years since I had a proper Thanksgiving. Always seemed silly to cook an elaborate meal just for me. I usually eat a frozen dinner." She tucks a hand in her pocket and chews her lower lip thinking. "Yep, I'll come along. But, I'll only go if you let me cook something for the meal."

"That's an easy yes. I'd bet whatever you bring will be appreciated. Josie normally does all the cooking, so you'd be helping her out."

Grace rests from our planting and takes a seat on the curb that circles the planter. "That girl does carry a heavy load. Misses her mother, I bet."

Josie does such a convincing job of being perfect, I sometimes forget how hard it must be for her to take care of Owen and watch after her father. "Yeah, her life is complicated. She spends all her effort trying to make life normal for her dad and brother," I say.

I sit next to Grace on the curb and set down the shovel. Grace says in a hushed voice, "I recognized who she was on Halloween night. She and her family had brought sunflowers for her mother a few weeks prior. I even remember seeing her at her mother's funeral, too, way back when. The rest of her's grown up, except her eyes. They're exactly the same as when she was a little girl, sad but trying to appear happy."

Automatically I defend Josie, perfect, put-together Josie. "Really? I've never seen her in a bad mood. And I've never seen her feel sorry for herself either. She's incredible." My mind drifts back to Halloween and how Josie just left us standing there. It hurt that she forgot about our sleepover. Maybe I am more familiar with the side of Josie Grace described than I thought.

"Trust me. I know what I'm talking about." I nod my head because I already get it. "That girl hasn't had a chance to grieve properly. When she lost her mother, she decided to step into those huge shoes and keep that family going. One day she's apt to crack, and Casey, you'll need to be ready to catch the pieces." Grace dusts off her hands and stands. "Grief can be poisonous you know. Did I tell you about the grass?"

"This grass? Under our feet?"

"No dear, the grass on Sarah Jameson's grave. It was my uncle who told me that tears from grief are poisonous. If they fall on bare dirt, grass will never grow. As God is my witness, that's what happened to her grave. After her funeral, I was determined to get the grass to grow again over her plot, so I bought rolls of sod, watered them every day, but they turned yellow. I tried seeds next, but they never sprouted. Finally, I thought to shovel off the spoiled dirt and replace it with compost and that did the trick. The grass came back. But I knew for a fact after all that effort that someone had cried poison tears on top of that grave."

GRACE SPENDS THANKSGIVING WITH THE LIVING

THANKSGIVING COULDN'T COME soon enough!

After being invited to spend Thanksgiving with the Jameson family, I sit down with a cup of coffee and a notebook to plan out the pies I will bake. Pecan is my best recipe; everyone loves that thing. I will bake a pumpkin pie; wouldn't be a holiday without one on the table. Then there's my recipe for Pioneer Cranberry Cream Pie. It's more like a cheesecake. And, of course, I'll do a tray of cupcakes to celebrate Casey's birthday.

I spend the next week combing markets to gather fresh ingredients. And the night before Thanksgiving, I keep the kitchen TV tuned to satellite radio for background noise as I mix, roll, pat, pour, and bake. By one in the morning, the pies and cupcakes are cooled and packaged for the trip down the street.

After that I try to sleep, but don't. I am so damned restless. I toss and turn until five and decide it is best to dive head first into the day. After sipping two cups of coffee, I check the pies on the counter, grab the paper off the porch, and tuck myself into a rocking chair.

I rock back and forth as I skim through the paper, making myself a little sick with the motion. I get up to pace, rub my hands together, and think about how nice it'll be to celebrate a holiday with a family again. It's been too long, over ten years.

Hands down, Thanksgiving is my favorite holiday. As a child, I spent the day inside these cottage walls with my aunt and uncle. I don't recall my parents being here, but then again, I've scrubbed them out of most memories.

My aunt was usually getting started on the stuffing as we rushed through the door. We'd watch the big parade on the black and white TV and chop celery and sweet onion. My uncle was the official stuffing-seasoner and I was the official taster. He'd add salt, pepper, poultry seasoning, and Lawry's. Of course, I'd try the stuffing two or three times to make sure it was just right, wink, wink. Then my aunt would stuff the bird, tie the legs down, and set it in the oven to roast.

When the bird was in the oven, all the attention turned to pie making: pumpkin, apple, pecan, and sometimes a strawberry-rhubarb if my uncle asked nice enough. The steady procession of crusts and fillings stopped only for the singing of the Star-Spangled Banner, which marked the beginning of the day's football marathon. Everyone in the house paused what they were doing and stood hand over heart to sing the National Anthem.

I shake my head at the memory. We weren't a perfect family, we had our problems big and small, but it was enough to keep me from feeling bitter about the ugly stuff. Today, I hope to make happy memories with new people. Maybe they will be enough to push away all the lost years, the number of holidays I spent in isolation to punish myself for what I did a decade ago.

The grandfather clock on the hearth reads five after eight in the morning. I have nearly two hours before the Thanksgiving gathering begins. Itching for the time to pass, I decide to check my clothes. Being in a dirt-under-the-nails occupation, I don't have much occasion to doll up. In fact, until now, I only owned two dresses. One was for funerals and the other was for making my closet look less empty. But I didn't want to embarrass Josie for inviting a gravedigger to dinner, so I went to the mall and tried on a handful of new dresses and after some debate with myself, I picked a pretty floral number with short sleeves and a fitted bodice.

My new dress hangs on the closet door; the skirt ripples as I push past into the bedroom. A purple cashmere button-down sweater sits neatly folded at the bottom of the bed, next to matching purple heels. It's like something I'd wear to church if I wanted to find a date. Oh, golly. Just thinking about the word date gets my heart pounding.

This isn't a date, just an innocent holiday gathering. I know all the people that are coming except Aunt Karen. New people don't bother me a bit, so what's with the nerves? It might have to do with Grant Jameson. The day he came to the cottage for Josie, we had time to visit while she recovered. He is funny and handsome. My heart flutters and I step away to eat a nibble of crumb cake to settle my nerves before cleaning myself up. I want to look pretty in the hopes Grant will notice me. Been a lot of years since I cared what a man thought of my appearance.

I don't usually wear makeup, so it takes me forever to copy what the department store lady did yesterday. I apply it with a heavy hand and have to wipe a little pink off each cheek. I blot my lips twice. The effect is a tad overdone, but not terrible when I squint into the mirror.

I touch a hand to my bare neck and wonder again what I was thinking when I let the stylist hack off my long hair. It looks so different and makes me feel naked. All these tiny curls took a pea-sized drop of shampoo to wash. But, maybe it works now that my makeup's done. I take one last peek in the mirror before heading out.

"Not bad, Grace. I've seen worse. Lord, I've been worse!" I say to my reflection. It's as close as I come to a pep talk.

I make an effort to breathe as I mount the steps to the Jameson home. Every window's lit in the sweet Craftsman house. I smell the wood smoke when I am getting out of the truck, and I know I'll find a cozy fire crackling inside.

Thanksgiving spent with a family? The last time was ten years ago. We met my aunt and uncle at a big hotel to eat buffet food. My uncle had been hospitalized, and no one was up to hosting, so we made a reservation for six at a Thanksgiving buffet. My little brother was in town. He wanted to cook supper and sneak it into the hospital, but our aunt said, "There's no sneaking a turkey!"

The hotel served a full Thanksgiving meal. The sign boasted, "All the fixin's!" That musty, dusty indoor atrium was as depressing a place as I'd ever seen. And this coming from a lady who is used to spending the holiday in the middle of a cemetery says something! The atrium was dripping with fake, sun-bleached plants and harsh fluorescent lights. The glass panels in the roof let in a smattering of filtered light through a decade's worth of dirt. I was worried dust bunnies were going to break free and fall into my food.

Our table was too long and too empty. A phony Christmas tree sat in the center of the room, probably plunked down by some ambitious hotel employee trying to get a head start on the next holiday. Of course, the food like the décor had no taste. I remember thinking the hospital cafeteria would've been an improvement.

Shortly after, but not because of, my uncle suffered a massive heart attack and died. Without any drama, my aunt joined him a month later. I moved into Lakefront Cemetery after to take over the family business, tending the dead. And in less than a year, the last of the local family would join my aunt and uncle in the grave. That's when all my holiday celebrations ended. Hard to celebrate alone.

I lean in close to the picture window that stretches the length of the Jamesons' front porch. My breath steams up the glass. A giant cat condo blocks most of the view inside. I straighten the front of my sweater and ring the doorbell while admiring the planters at my feet overflowing with rosemary, winter pansies, and dusty miller. My foot taps with nervous energy. The door swings open, and Josie gives me a broad smile and scoops the pies out of my arm.

"Hi, Josie."

"Hey, Grace. Don't you look beautiful."

I touch my bare neck and giggle. "Honey, I've got one more load. I'll be back in a minute." I return to the truck for the cupcakes and third pie. Beads of sweat collect at the back of my neck. I sweat when I'm anxious. The cool air calms me. I take my sweet time gathering up the orphaned pie and Casey's birthday cupcakes before I head back to the house.

As I wipe my shoes on the mat, Josie returns, propping open the door with her foot. Her pretty hair spreads out over an emerald green sweater dress. "Come on in. Casey's already here, but Aunt Karen's going to be late." Josie's cheeks are flushed. "Man! I love your hair! It really sets off your face."

I step inside the house and Shadow shoots past to the garden.

"I'm just getting used to it. Thanks again for having me over." I glance past the entryway in search of Grant.

Josie commands, "Owen! Help Grace with that!"

A cute, redheaded boy runs toward me, his bare feet slapping down the sidewalk. He wears a brown suit with a crisp white shirt.

"Thank you very much. Can you carry this?" I point to the pie that threatens to slip off the top of the plastic cupcake carrier. As he grabs the pie off the top of the stack, I stare down at his sweet little toes. "Are your feet cold, Owen?"

"Wow! You know my name and I know yours. It's Grace! You don't look like a cemetery lady. My sister says you're funny and nice and tell spooky stories. Can you tell me one today?" The boy doesn't stop to breathe. I smile and feel all the nervousness fall away.

He fumbles with the pie and finally settles it into his thin hands. Emotion wells up in my chest and I'm overcome with an urge to take this sweet boy in my arms, but no doubt that'd spin off a case of stranger danger in him.

I say, "Maybe I'll share a story today. Somehow though, they sound better when you're at the cemetery. It might not fit at a Thanksgiving gathering." I give him a genuine smile and climb into the front room feeling welcome and happy.

The house smells heavenly and I know who's behind it. I duck a head into the kitchen. Casey stands at the counter with Josie, mashing potatoes. "Hey, Grace. Oh, don't you look nice. I feel underdressed now." Casey looks down at herself, but she looks positively darling in a short, flippy skirt and denim jacket.

"Nonsense," I tell her. "You are pretty as always." Holding up the cupcakes, I ask Josie, "Do you want these in the kitchen or the dining room?"

Casey stops mashing and wraps me in a hug.

She whispers in my ear, "I love the hair. You look absolutely gorgeous." Casey knows I'm nervous about seeing Grant again and meeting Aunt Karen. I search again for any sign of Grant, break out of her hug reluctantly, and wait for orders from Josie.

"Put them in here." Josie points to an ebony buffet that runs along the dining room wall. I set the cupcakes down and step inside the kitchen and see Grant. He smiles and says hello as he puts on oven mitts.

"Casey! Can you pull the stuffing out of the bottom oven for me?" Josie wears a bright green apron with a felt turkey across the front. Her auburn hair sprays around her flushed face, shiny with a layer of sweat. Behind her, Grant wrestles an oversized roasting pan out of the oven. The pan begins to tilt, and I dive in and grab an end. He's able to regain control and sets the pan onto the countertop.

"Thank you! I almost lost it there for a minute. It is nice to see you again, Grace." He holds out a hand and I shake it. "Did the pan burn you?"

He keeps my hand in his, pries my fingers open, and inspects my palm. A little shiver runs up my spine. "Looks fine to me."

I move to Casey's side and help her hold a red bowl while she spoons in hot stuffing.

"Nice to see you too Grant." I say, mostly to the countertop because I feel suddenly shy. "You've got quite a chef there. And it smells like she cooks a heck of a feast."

Grant removes the crisp-skinned turkey from the roasting pan and sets it on the black stone countertop. "Thank heavens for her, or Owen and I would've starved years ago." He sets the roasting pan on the stovetop and retrieves an electric carving knife out of a drawer. The knife buzzes to life as he carves the bird in tidy motions. I move to his side and arrange pieces of tender meat across a white porcelain-serving tray. Oh, girl. You are being bold now.

Josie ties back her hair from her face and smiles at me across the kitchen. "Baking's not my forte though. So thanks again for bringing dessert Grace."

She spoons flour into the roasting pan and whisks. Steam puffs from the pan and the air fills with the smell of gravy. My stomach rumbles. I empty a can of black olives into a bowl and shuttle it to the dining room table. I find a blank spot for the bowl and stand back to admire the glorious display.

"Who set this table? It's gorgeous!" I yell into the kitchen.

A garland of red, yellow, and orange leaves threads through the middle of a sleek walnut table. Three bouquets of sunflowers and purple asters nest inside the colorful garland. Tiny pumpkins with delicate white place cards sit in the center of elegant white china plates. Thin white taper candles flicker from little glass jars filled with dried beans. *Beans?*

Owen runs to my side, hands on his hips, and assesses the table. "The good stuff was all my idea! Like the candles in the beans; I thought of that. We got to do art with dried beans at school. It was a substitute lady. I made a tree with black ants in it. My friend Becky put a dried pea up her nose. She had to go to the hospital to have it removed."

I pat the top of his head and try not to picture the bean that was removed from the girl's nostril. "Well, the table looks very professional, like the cover of a magazine. And I like the beans best!" Owen wrinkles his nose at me and runs off to answer a knock at the door.

"It's Aunt Karen!" Owen screams to the household as he slams the door shut.

"Happy Thanksgiving!" A woman blows in the front door behind Owen. "Sorry I'm late. We had a pipe break at the store, so I've been up to my elbows in blowers. Josie, should I put the cranberries on the table?" Aunt Karen's colorful silk wrap flutters around her as she sets a bowl on the table and takes a bottle of chardonnay from her bag. "Grant, can you open this?"

Her eyes are like Josie's and are framed by ash blonde and gray hair that swings above her shoulders. Grant swoops in and whisks the wine away giving Aunt Karen a quick kiss on the cheek.

He shouts over his shoulder, "Grace, I'd like you to meet Aunt Karen. Karen, this is our friend Grace." He emerges from the kitchen with an uncorked bottle. "Grace, may I pour you a glass?"

"Just a sip. I'm not much of a drinker."

"Join the crowd. Any more than a glass and I'm out for the night," he says.

Grant pours the wine and offers a glass to me. He clinks my glass with his and the crystal goblets ring crisp and clear across the room. "Cheers! To new friends and new traditions!"

With everyone gathered around the table, we join hands in prayer. I close my eyes and enjoy the fellowship, sending my own prayer up to God. It's the second one this season! Owen stands up abruptly and races to the front door. "Shadow! Shadow, come, boy!"

The little blue cat shoots through the door and ducks underneath the dining room table to be close to the turkey. I break off a tiny piece of meat and toss it down to him, and he scratches at my fingers. I drop the meat and pull my hand away from the aggressive cat. I check my hand for blood and glance around at the others to make sure they didn't catch me. Beneath the table, the cat wolfs down the meat and rubs against a leg for more. I toss down another chunk, but don't give him the chance to bite my hand. He chomps it down and bolts out from under the table, skittering down the hallway, out of sight.

"He's a jumpy little thing." I say, mostly to myself. Grant's eyes crinkle at the edges as he grins sideways at me.

"Maybe he knew you were done sneaking him turkey." He smiles again and refills my wine glass with sparkling cider.

"Ha! Looks like one very pampered pet," says Karen. She must be talking about the massive kitty condo I've yet to see the cat touch. "So Grant, your yard hasn't looked this good for years. Sarah always said you were allergic to yard work."

I hold my breath, waiting to see if the mention of his dead wife cracks all the good feeling at the table.

"Ouch! Grace, can you take the knife out of my back?" Grant takes a swallow of wine and laughs. "It was about time I pitched in around here. I was just going to trim back the roses. But once I started in, I couldn't stop. It feels like there is room to breathe again."

"It's nice," Karen says. I bite my tongue, because this may be an improvement, but I can spot at least fifty things I could do to that yard to make it shine even brighter.

Conversation takes a back seat as folks dive into the meal. For a good twenty minutes, the only noise in the dining room comes from the scraping of utensils across plates and passing of platters.

After finishing my second helping of everything, I settle back in my chair, hand over my full belly. "So, I know Seth's in Hawaii trying to track down some mystery lady, but where's Blaze spending Thanksgiving?" I ask, feeling a furry head nudge me under the table. I raise the tablecloth and whisper, "Shoo!" to the cat. I don't want to get scratched again.

Josie stacks dirty dishes and answers. "He always volunteers at the Salvation Army. He serves meals. I don't know what they do after. They might just eat at the shelter. I guess I should ask." She stands with her pile of dishes and makes a move toward the kitchen.

"Josie, sit! I'm taking care of clean up tonight." I spring up from my seat and grab dishes off the table. Karen and Grant trail me into the kitchen.

"You're a guest here, Grace! You're not doing dishes." Grant takes the plates from me and puts them in the sink. He opens the dishwasher and gets to work.

I know when I'm defeated, so I busy myself with the teakettle, putting water on the stove to boil. "Well, I wish I could Grant! In my family, cleanup was the best part of the meal. I remember standing in the kitchen elbow to elbow with my aunt and brother. We'd speed gossip our way through dishes. My aunt would sip a glass of wine and we'd laugh. I don't remember working. I only remember the small talk."

I turn on the coffee maker and rummage through the fir cabinets for cups, saucers, and dessert plates.

The two girls have their heads together whispering as we return with dessert. They startle apart and Owen races to my side. "Grace, can I have a little bit of everything?" I notice the finger-sized wipe of whipped cream missing off the pumpkin pie and smile.

"I think I can manage that. Couldn't choose, huh?"

I slice into the pies, thinking how much I miss the stark honesty of children. He couldn't pick a pie, so he wants a bit of them all. It's the ultimate compliment. I hand Owen his overstuffed plate and then make my way around the table.

I finally sit and Grant sets a cup of peppermint tea in front of me. He must have remembered from the cottage. I take my first bite when Owen says, "Now can you tell a story, Grace?" I wipe the crumbs off my lips and laugh. This is everything I'd prayed it'd be.

After cleaning up a second time, we all settle down in the family room. I'm not sure if it's time for me to gracefully exit, or if I should take a seat. The fire blazes and crackles in the hearth and as I stare at the flames, Owen takes my hand in his.

"Grace, can you tell us a story now? Will you sit next to me?" He leads me to a worn burgundy leather couch and pats the cushion beside him. I sit.

"Josie said you know bunches of spooky stories and see ghosts and everything. When she goes to the cemetery you always tell her one of your stories." Does that boy ever stop to breathe? Owen looks up at me like a dog that heard the word "walk."

"I don't tell the stories to hear the sound of my voice, Owen. It's like if you run into a school friend while you're out with your dad. You stop and introduce one to the other. That's all I'm doing. If we happen to pass a grave on our way somewhere, it'd be rude not to introduce you to them, right?

"To me, the people we pass are more than a name carved in a stone. They lived, made their mark on the world, and sometimes after they die, they keep on speaking. It's my job to tell their stories so no one forgets the folks buried in Lakefront."

"Like my mom? Do you tell her story too?" Owen kicks his feet against the couch with a *thump, thump, thump.*

I rest a hand on his busy legs and offer up an answer. "Ah, Owen. She doesn't need me to tell her story. You do it just fine, you and Josie. You carry her story inside you. Who do you think gave you that sparkle in your green eyes? Sarah Jameson." I stop talking and look down at my hands. Owen grabs one up and gives it a squeeze. And with that, I begin to tell an old story, one born over a century ago.

"I think I've got a story you might like. One of the city's founding fathers, the fellow buildings, streets, parks, and freeways are named after, had a colorful past. Coming from Virginia and determined to be a big fish in a new pond at last, Mr. Hank Yessir homesteaded here 150 years ago. He brought enough people with him to clear land and begin building a city. Had so many folks working for him they soon nicknamed him "Yes-sir," because wherever he walked there was a chorus of "yes, sir" right behind.

"The backbone of his new city would be a lumber company, general store, and a fish cannery. Not long after they were built, people flocked to the newest and most prosperous city on the West Coast of the United States. Not his wife though. Mrs. Yessir wouldn't follow him out west 'til she was assured acres of that infernal forest were replaced with civilization. Her husband grew lonely from the waiting and took an Indian bride to tide him over. This was far more common than our history books care to reveal, by the way. She was the beautiful, young daughter of Chief Seattle. The two fell deeply in love." I take a quick glance at Grant and regret my boldness immediately.

"Maybe it was the newly completed theater, maybe it was the whispers about a copper-skinned lover, but the wife finally headed west. In her honor, Mr. Yessir built the city's first mansion. For his comfort, both body and soul, he built a second house behind the first, equally modern, for the Indian princess that ruled his heart. Both homes stand today in an older part of Seattle, though the latter has been partially rebuilt after a mysterious fire broke out soon after the wife's arrival from Virginia.

"Mr. Yessir died two decades later after he amassed a fortune selling wood. He left his riches to his wife with two exceptions. The General Store income and the house on the back lot would always belong to his Indian bride. Can you imagine how his wife and adult children felt about this? But even though the family hated the idea, they made little effort to fight his wishes. You see, the Indian princess was beloved by the city of Seattle. Known and cherished throughout the city for her patient ministrations, she was known as Mother Medicine for the lives she saved and the suffering she put to rest.

"In fact, her medicinal herb garden thrives to this day! In a serene, rarely traveled part of a bustling university, sits a tranquil secret garden where her seeds continue to grow. Young lovers have been known to stumble unknowingly into the garden, and as if a spell has been cast upon them, fall madly in love and stay that way for life.

"Anyhow, Mr. Yessir was buried with all the pomp you'd expect of a man of his stature. He would rest for eternity under a mammoth gravestone at the peak of Lakefront hill. His final request was to have his Indian bride buried by his side when she passed on. This request was recognized and upheld when the princess died a few years later, mostly because of the pressures the Yessir family felt from her adoring public. After a little time had passed and the family felt the princess was sufficiently forgotten, they had her body exhumed and moved down the hill a ways.

"Thinking all was right in the world, the Yessir descendants gave no more thought to the tryst. But, the princess would have the final say. Within a month of the princess's reburial, the entire Yessir family would die out. Old Mrs. Yessir died at a crowded dinner party, face down in a plate only seconds after eating a wild mushroom. The eldest son died of respiratory arrest after collecting wildflowers to adorn his mother's grave. And the last Yessir, left with a remarkable fortune at her disposal, died of a simple bee sting. The Indian princess got her way. Revenge was exacted on the Yessir family."

Owen, who by now has nuzzled himself into my ribs, pipes up. "But, she's still buried at the bottom of the hill Grace! She didn't get her way?"

"You wanted a ghost story didn't you? Believe me, she still gets her way. Every evening the Indian princess journeys to the top of Lakefront hill and sits on top of her lover's grave. I've seen her too many times to count. She's as regular a fixture around there as the entrance gate. She always has on a fur coat that hovers above the ground as she winds her way to his grave, her silky black hair glistens across her back when the moon shines just right. Nothing can keep her from her lover, Owen, not even Death himself."

"That was an awesome story, Grace. Thanks!" Owen jumps up and races down the hall.

My face warms, not knowing what the others think of the long-winded tale. Before I can give it too much thought, Owen rushes back into the room his hands hidden behind his back. "I want you to have this." He opens his hands and inside a piece of rock glistens. "We went to the Gingko Petrified Forest last year and I found this. It has a fossil in it too. Isn't it neat?"

I take it from his hand and give the boy a squeeze, blinking back the tears that fight to leak out. "This is very special. I'll take good care of it." I hold the rock in my palm and give thanks for this day, this moment.

Josie stands, slipping inside the kitchen with her father. After a minute, they emerge with the tray of cupcakes all lit up with fourteen candles. Owen scoots behind them with a small stack of presents. We join in and sing "Happy Birthday" to a blushing Casey as she mumbles a couple *you shouldn't haves* as we finish up the song. There is so much to be thankful for these days.

SETH HUNTS FOR THE SECRET POND

IT IS THE DAY BEFORE Thanksgiving, our first full day in Hawaii and my mother is being militant about the sunscreen. "Mom! What am I – five again? I can get my own."

My mom grimaces as she squirts a pool of SPF 50 into the palm of my hand, which I slap on my legs and arms, then rub in to erase the slick white streaks. She says, "Stay still!" through clenched teeth as she wipes down my forehead and I stop rubbing at the white blobs.

"Seth honey. The Hawaiian sun is very intense." A knock at the hotel room door startles both of us. I jolt and Mom jabs a pinkie into my eye. "Sorry! Flush that with water and I'll answer the door."

She wrestles the thick wooden door open as I splash cold water into my flaming eyeball. My dad strides inside the hotel room. Fresh off the plane from Seattle, he looks crumpled. I'm glad we flew in last night. My parents hug, which still manages to surprise me. "You made it," she says.

"Hi, Dad," I say from the sink. He pulls a plastic container from behind his back. Mom stares down at the string of white flowers inside and smiles. It is a Hawaiian tradition to offer those you love flowers and the thought of Mom and Dad and flowers leaves me feeling a bit mixed up.

I swab my weeping eye with a white washcloth and say, "Don't give that woman flowers! She just wounded your only son." They are too engrossed in each other to notice me and I shrug. Wasn't this part of my motivation for the trip to Hawaii? Of course, I wanted to research the sergeant, but I also wanted to bring all four of us together again for a holiday. Then why is this cozy scene making me feel so uncomfortable?

My mom giggles as my dad snaps the container open and slips the flowers around her neck. "Oh, Dave. Thank you." The pungent white flowers tangle around her long hair. Dad bends down and kisses her cheek, then slips away to find the next recipient.

"And my flowers are..." I say, knowing full well there are no flowers for me. That would be just plain awkward.

Dad strides past with a smile through the open sliding glass doors where my sister Sadie lies across a chaise lounge, hard at work on her tan this morning. She lies on the lanai with a philosophy book stretched across her lap, trying to cram for a post-Thanksgiving exam. She crinkles her nose and giggles, clearly irritated and delighted all at once at the lei Dad places on her. Finished dishing out flowers, my father finally turns his attention to me.

"Seth, I made an executive decision. In lieu of flowers, I got you chocolate mac nuts."

"Nice. Thanks, Dad." I stow the gold box in the mini fridge for later.

"You ready to head out?" he asks.

My stomach rumbles, so I dip back inside the mini fridge and take out two chocolates and stuff them in my mouth. Between chews, I answer, "I have to grab my stuff."

I rummage through my unpacked suitcase and grab the pouch that holds the sergeant's journal and my trusty camera. I duck through the sliding door to the lanai and throw the wet washcloth at my sister.

"Bye, Sadie." My sister shrieks and tries to throw the washcloth back. Her Kierkegaard book slips off her lap and falls beneath her chaise lounge. "Thanks a lot! I'm trying to study here!" Sadie gives the book an overly dramatic dust-off.

I laugh at her. "Sadie, did you know Kierkegaard gave the world the concept of 'a leap of faith'?" She rolls her eyes at me. "I think you should skim the rest of your reading, and then take your own leap of faith. You've probably done enough studying at this point, right? Go swim with turtles. You'll do fine on the test."

I turn to leave and Sadie says, "It's not natural for one person to know so much about so many things. It's freaky."

My parents stand elbow to elbow in the entry. I might have interrupted something, but the room is only so big. Mom has a dreamy look on her face and holds the flowers to her nose, breathing in their scent. Whose idea was it to bring the two of them to a tropical island? Oh, yeah. It was my idea. I slink past them to the door. I want to melt into the sisal rug under my Keens.

"So, we'll see you at five for dinner?" My mom says. Her voice is coated in sugar.

My dad babbles something that sounds like yes, and I shove him out the door. A gecko scurries away from the door and leaps onto the trunk of a palm tree. He must be allergic to awkward moments, too.

On our way to the parking lot, we pass an acre of fishponds alive with spotted orange koi and darting yellow tangs. We pause at a pool of baby turtles and watch them scrape and clamor on top of one another to get a look at us, splashing water onto the shiny blue floor tiles.

"What's the plan for today, Seth?" he says as we navigate across the massive parking lot to his rental car.

Relieved he's pulled out Cupid's arrow, I share, "Well, you remember how the sergeant mentioned the secret pond in his journal?" If it wasn't for my dad's ability to decipher difficult handwriting, I would never know what was written in the old journal. But he translated the beast a page at a time and typed up the entries for me to read. Thus far, half of the journal has been translated.

My dad nods. "Yeah, he spent time at some secret pond with his Hawaiian sweetheart. He said the water was so clear, you could see three feet down without any distortion. Is that where we're headed, then?"

I say, "It's a bit more complicated than that. According to my web search, there are two ponds the locals call 'secret ponds' on the Big Island. One of them is here on the resort property, less than a mile from the breakfast buffet. The other one's in a national park, Kekaha-Kai Park, about a half hour south of here. It's referred to as a secret fish pond, but I figure that's close enough to warrant a visit."

My dad scratches the five o'clock shadow on his jaw. "I am all for walking in the sergeant's footsteps. But realistically, what can we possibly find after fifty-plus years?"

I adjust my pouch across my back. "I'm not sure we will find anything. My hope is that by visiting the two ponds we can narrow it down to one, the one with the crystal clear water, and then we will be closer to finding out about the mystery woman Leilani. Didn't he mention in the journal that she worked at a hotel near the pond?"

"That sounds familiar, yes. But it seems like a vague quest."

"No doubt," I agree. "Well, what say we hit the secret pond at Kekaha-Kai State Park today, and check the second one tomorrow after breakfast? That way I'll have an excuse to eat an extra coconut waffle."

Dad pats his stomach. "Sounds like a plan."

We approach a shiny blue boat of an SUV. It honks obnoxiously when Dad hits the unlock button on the key. I have to laugh. Mr. Prius in a riptide blue Escalade? I take a picture on my phone and text it to Sadie as I climb into the shotgun seat. My feet dangle off the end of the hot gray leather because the seat is so massive. I feel like a dinky menehune, one of the mythical little Hawaiians that gets credit for all the cool buildings on the islands.

Dad drives at a crawl past a flock of geese that loiter in the middle of the street. After a series of honks and engine revs we scare them off, managing at last to reach the Queen's Highway without killing anything. The road is mostly empty this holiday morning, except for the occasional cargo truck that zips the opposite way en route to Kawaihae Harbor.

"Hey Dad, do you think the park will be open today? I hadn't thought that part through." Dad cracks his window and whistles. I whip out my phone and type in 'Kekaha Kai State Park hours.'

He slips on his sunglasses, "What's the phone say?"

As I wait for the website to load, I try to remember what I read about the park and stare out the window. The landscape through the glass looks like another planet altogether. Stark lava rock rolls in black waves to the foot of lush green mountains. The ocean stretches to the horizon and sparkles under the bright sun. I snap a few pictures out the windshield, but the result is flat and distorted. I wish Josie were here. She'd find a way to capture this on paper with her magic watercolor pencils. I crack my window and flower-scented air blows inside the rental.

I read the screen. "Okay, the park is open until noon." I check the digital clock on the dash. "We've got almost five hours, plenty of time." Back home it would be ten in the morning.

Dad takes a hand off the wheel and reaches into the suitcase-sized glove box between us. He plops a stack of papers onto my lap. "I finished translating the journal." I flip through the typed pages. "My secretary says my handwriting is beginning to look like the sergeant's. Must be all the hours I've spent squinting into his journal that did it."

I'm skimming the print-out as fast as I can for some new clue, when my dad tosses a folded piece of newspaper onto my lap. "Did you know about this? It fell out of the back cover of the journal."

"Bonus!" I say. "I didn't know there was a back pocket. Thanks." The paper feels old and fragile. Carefully, I unfold it to reveal an ad from the *Honolulu Advertiser* newspaper.

I skim the paper and my heart pounds. "The sergeant took out an ad to find Leilani? When was this?" The page is dated December 25, 1958. The sergeant visited the Big Island after his service in the army during World War II. He said in the journal it was his attempt to ease back into civilian life. "Why would he try to find her ten years after he left the Big Island? What a waste."

My dad stares at the road ahead. "It's never too late. Maybe he regretted his choice to live alone. What did he say in that journal entry? He didn't think he had it in him to make a 'forever vow?' What if he was lonely for her and decided to take one last chance instead of choking down regret the rest of his life?" Dad sounds like he is talking about something close to home.

We pass a sign that says, "Donkey X-ing Next Mile," which he reads out loud. "We might see a Kona donkey…"

"… also known as the Kona Nightingale," we spout at the same time. I laugh.

"Keep your camera handy." Dad stares out the windshield toward a clump of low trees and the car slows. "Is that a donkey?"

"Where?" I set aside the journal printout and search the side of the road for movement. "Oh, that's a goat. There are three of them! It's hard to see them because their fur is the same color as the scrub brush." Standing under a clump of shade trees, a mother and two baby goats graze on grass sprouting from the black rocks.

"This is so great! We've seen goats today! Goats!" Dad tries to take a picture with his phone and the car veers toward the shoulder of the road. "Did you know I spent most of my childhood wishing for a goat?"

"Really? You grew up in the middle of a city. How could you raise a goat?" I scratch my head and tuck the camera away.

"That's the thing right? How do you raise a goat in the big city?" Dad scratches his chin. He hums to himself and snaps on the radio. Sweet music pours out of the Escalade's mega sound system. "We just saw goats!" he announces out the window.

With Hawaiian slack music strumming in the background, we zip past black lava decorated with white coral. We buzz past declarations of love, smiley faces, and hearts on the black lava. "Is this the coolest graffiti ever?" I ask. Remembering what I read in the guidebook on the six-hour plane ride last night I add, "It's white coral. People collect the coral then use it to form messages on the lava. It's supposed to be good luck. I guess if you paint rocks white, Pele, their fire goddess, gets mad."

I pop the scan button on the radio and slow, sweet bits of music pour out at every stop on the dial. "What's with all the sappy music?" We pass the Kona International Airport and I check the rental map to confirm how close we are to the park.

"I don't know, Seth. It's seems like the perfect music for a place like this. The air smells like flowers, and the ocean is crystal clear. Hard rock doesn't belong in Hawaii." Dad hits the scan button and the dial rests on the slack key music for good. "I have always loved this island!"

Our car approaches a stack of lava rock supporting a sign that says, "Kekaha-Kai State Park."

"This is it, Dad." A winding road leads us to an empty parking lot and a small visitor's center. Surrounded by black lava and scrub brush, I'm not getting a warm and fuzzy feeling as we park. "Man. Did I drag us all to Hawaii for nothing? What if we don't find anything?" Suddenly I feel like an idiot for talking Dad into this trip. The sergeant wrote about Leilani in his journal. He mentioned that she worked near a secret pond. But he also made it clear they parted ways after he returned to the mainland.

"First, you didn't drag anyone to Hawaii. We had many a pleasant family vacation here before the divorce. I for one, am glad we returned together. Second, both of us have done the research. The sergeant has no other living relatives. The most we can hope for is to find some love child and finding Leilani is our only chance of that. It's a long shot, but we've got nothing else. And third, two history fiends are at a national park, a place we've never been. I'm not leaving without having a good look." Dad turns the engine off and the air in the car heats up in an instant. "It's the journey, not the destination right? We're here. Let's see where your puzzle takes us next." He pats my arm and opens his car door. A gush of fresh air blows inside the car.

"I just hope this wasn't all for nothing." I grab my fanny pack off the car floor and stuff the camera and newspaper ad inside, slipping the thin black strap over my shoulder.

After a quick walk through the small but informative visitor's center, we follow the park signs to the trail that leads to the secret pond. It's a mile-long trek on easy terrain through lava fields, wooded forest, and sand dunes.

"All right, Seth. Keep your eye out for the planters that hold ancient crops. If you want to earn that Junior Ranger's badge, and I know you do because you pulled the flyer on it back at the visitor's center, you'll have to identify taro."

I punch him, but not too hard. He's the man with the water bottles and candy bars, and I'm already melting on the black asphalt path under the eighty-five degree sun. I guess we Northwesterners are not as rugged as I thought.

Dad stops walking. We're surrounded on all sides by sharp craggy lava rocks and the ocean is nowhere to be seen. Except for the occasional fern spear this land is devoid of life. It gives me the creeps, even in broad daylight.

My dad uncaps a water bottle and hands it to me. "The secret pond is about another quarter mile from here. This must be the burial site the map indicates." He points a finger to a red area on the park brochure and eyes the landscape. "Hey, Seth! That must be a burial mound. And there's another one!"

"How do you know?" I see the outline of mounds, but nothing indicates a burial to me. Then again, maybe that's why I have this uneasy feeling creeping up my neck.

"While you were scanning history books in the gift shop, I was reading the park brochure. This island's history is amazing. After we go through the forest, we'll see petroglyphs. Ancient Hawaiians raised fish on these grounds! They practiced their religion and buried their dead, including kings, on this land."

Dad sticks his nose back in the brochure and nearly runs into a sign at the side of our path. "And checkers! Hawaiians invented their own game of checkers. We'll see that too."

To my father's delight, we reach the carvings Hawaiians used for a game of strategy similar to our own checkers and he tries to talk me into the game, but I spot the sign that points to the secret pond fifty feet ahead on the trail. Now that we are only steps away, I'm anxious to get there. "Sorry, Dad. I've got to see the pond," I say.

At the end of the boardwalk, I find 180 degrees of ocean, but not the secret pond I expect. Salty sea mist, nature's air conditioning, sprays our faces as we climb a high sand dune. We drink water and take in the view, and I can't help but feel disappointed.

A man in a ranger uniform approaches and introduces himself as Sam. "Howdy! Do you folks have any questions?"

Dad jumps in with loads of questions and I ditch them to climb the sand dunes down to the water. Past the lava rocks that line the ocean shore, boats bob on the waves   My dad and the ranger reach me. "This is a secret pond?" I ask, thinking that Hawaiians have a penchant for understatement.

"No, it's a fishpond, a bay in the ocean that Hawaiians utilized to raise fish," explains Ranger Sam. Damn. I knew we were wasting time. Secret fishpond does not equal secret pond.

As we walk back to the car, the ranger mentions a secret pond, kept out of guidebooks by the locals, like a secret pond to the nth power. Typical of the Hawaiians to hide the real historic places from tourists, I recall a bumpy ride over rocky red dirt years ago. We heard a rumor from locals about the birthplace of King Kamehameha I and ignored 'Private Property' signs and dodged potholes to reach the windy spot. Tourists were definitely not welcome to the historic place. We snapped a few pictures and left as quickly as we could.

Sam describes a place called Kaloko that is a quick mile drive from here. Rumored to be the final resting place of King Kamehameha I, it is the confirmed burial place of the king of Maui and other legendary Hawaiian leaders. When Sam mentions there is a restaurant and bar at the harbor, my hunch is confirmed that this might be the right secret pond. Maybe our visit to Kehaha-Kai wasn't a total wash.

Sam points to a leafy green plant on the walk back. It looks like a regular bush except for the odd half-flower that blooms in its center. The ranger tells us the legend about this strange half-flower. A similar plant thrives in the misty Hawaiian mountains. Legend has it that a jealous and enraged Pele turned two lovers into these plants and forbade them to be together. One was banished to the ocean shore and the other was trapped in the mountain peaks.

My skin erupts in goose bumps. I rub my arms and make a silent vow not to make Pele mad during our short holiday. I ask the ranger, "She likes rum and cigarettes, right?"

When he nods, I make a mental note to offer Pele something before heading back to Seattle; maybe she'll smile on me and help to unlock the sergeant's mystery.

I am excited to explore Kaloko before park hours end. We say our goodbyes and drive to Kaloko. Next to a busy modern harbor and nearly invisible from the road, it can be identified only by a small earth-colored sign on top of a thin aluminum pipe. I think about how the sergeant said Leilani worked near the secret pond and know a harbor provides many jobs. This could be the place.

My phone vibrates in my pocket and I pull it free. The screen shows my contact photo of Josie; she scowls at me over the top of a sketchpad.

"Hey, Josie, or should I say, aloha?"

Her voice comes out in a rush of words I can barely make out over the sound of the ocean pounding the surf a few feet away. "You have to speak up. I can't understand you," I nearly shout.

I push the phone against my head and hit the volume button repeatedly and finally make out her voice, but the words don't make sense. "I found the puzzle box, but I can't get it open. I need help, Seth. Can you help me?"

Something isn't right about her voice; it sounds far away. It makes my hands shake and I clutch the phone to my ear. Dad walks to the black asphalt path and looks back at me to follow. I hold a finger up to indicate I will be a minute and return to the car.

"Hey, where'd you find it?" I ask. But part of me is hurt she went searching for it without me. I check my watch and do the time zone math. It is almost noon in Seattle. "Was it in the sculpture like we thought?" She talks right through me.

"The top! I got the top off and, oh man, it smells bad." She coughs over the line. "It stinks like rotten meat. Hold on! There's something else to this. I can hear like a marble when I shake it. What do I do next? Help me."

"Oh, there's probably an internal maze. You have to tilt the box different ways to get the marble through the maze. It's impossible unless you have instructions, Josie. Why don't you wait until I'm back? We can do it together," I plead.

Her voice continues quietly over mine, and I check to see that I didn't hit the mute button on the phone. I didn't, so I don't understand why she is ignoring me.

"I got the first piece open. The marble was in a maze. I got the drawer open. Oh my gosh. I'm going to need something to pry this piece off. Wait a minute," she says.

I hear a thud of her setting down the phone and the clatter of something else. "Do you think a nail file will work? Dang. This is really stuck." She grunts.

"I did it! There's not enough light." She coughs. "I can't see what it is, but it smells so bad. It feels like feathers…" And then she is silent.

"Josie, are you okay? Are you still there?" I check the phone screen to make sure I didn't lose the call. "What's happening? What is in the box?"

"This is so gross. It looks like part of a bird, a black bird. Oh, God! It's a head; it's the head of a bird!" She screams.

"Josie put it down! Go get your father. Don't look at it!" I command. The line goes dead.

My dad runs across the lot. "Seth, what the hell is happening?"

"I don't know. It's Josie. She…" I try to call back her cell, but it rings through to her voicemail. "I've got to call her house."

I try to remember the house number, but I haven't needed it since forever. A familiar series of digits comes to mind and I punch in the numbers with shaky hands.

On the third ring, Mr. Jameson answers the phone. "Hello."

"Hi, Mr. Jameson, this is Seth, Seth Anthony. I'm calling from Hawaii."

"Oh, hey. How's the vacation?"

"Mr. Jameson, I'm trying to get ahold of Josie. I lost her call, and she was freaking out about something. Can you go check on her?"

"Do you know how mad teenage daughters get when you wake them up on a vacation day? No way."

"You don't understand. She called and sounded weird. She said she was...." I stop, because I don't know whether or not to mention the puzzle box. "Just please go check on her."

"All right, already. I'm going. Hold on!" The minute it takes him to get to her room is so tense I want to throw up. He comes back on the line. "I'm outside her door and there is not one squeak of noise. She's asleep, I promise."

"Mr. Jameson, please check on her. Please. If she gets mad at you, blame it on me." I hear him breathing into the phone and imagine him cracking open her door, peeking in, and finding what?

He comes back and whispers, "She's asleep. Are you happy now? The cat's on the bed, right next to her. She is sound asleep, Seth. Just like I said."

"She is? Does she have her phone with her? I swear, I was just on the phone with her."

"Yeah, well maybe she dialed you accidentally. It's beside her."

I feel like a heel. "Well, I guess she called me in her sleep. I'm sorry to have bugged you, Mr. J." Part of me wants to stay on the phone and have him wake up Josie, see if she remembers the dream.

"No problem. Now, if I'd woken her up that would be another story! Hey, tell your folks hello for me."

"Yeah, I will. Bye." He clicks off the line.

I wipe sweat off my forehead and sit on the curb next to the car. Dad sits next to me. "What was that all about?" he asks in tandem with my own thought.

She's had awful dreams before, but this was the worst one yet. Maybe it just felt that way because I was on the line with her while it happened. I've never gotten a first-person account of her nightmares until now. "I don't know. Josie was having a bad dream and must've called me in her sleep."

"Gotta love teens. Half human, half zombie as far as I can tell." He laughs. "Shall we?"

Photos next to the short footpath to the pond illustrate the recent reconstruction of the fishpond. Masons worked stone by stone to rebuild this traditional fishpond for over a dozen years. They described the painstaking process as "listening to where the stone wants to go."

I find it hard to believe that the sturdy rock wall we stand on was laid by hand. It is solid under my sandals and I feel certain this is the place because the water the stones hold in is crystal clear just as the journal described. I watch tiny fish dart between the black rocks. Leilani showed this historic place to the sergeant. My worry about Josie flicks away as we reach the restored fishpond.

The Hawaiians packed the wall tight enough to walk across, but loose enough to allow baby fish to slip inside the underwater structure. After a few days of eating, the fish were too big to slip back out to the ocean, and were trapped forever like aquatic Hansels and Gretels. The fish would live and thrive in the fishpond until a hungry Hawaiian harvested them.

The pond is not a little puddle, but a small man-made lake. I realize I'd need a small boat to explore the pond fully. I can see the recesses in the walls that Ranger Sam told us hold the bones of ancient Hawaiians. This place holds something special, not only remains, but a unique energy.

Dad grabs my camera and snaps shots. "We should try printing these shots in black and white. The textures are fantastic!"

On the drive back to the resort, my mind drifts to the story about the half-flowers banished to the mountains and ocean. I am certain it is the story of Leilani and the sergeant. I feel sure she would have taken him to see this significant spot during his months on the island.

I flip through the sergeant's journal and stop at a sepia-toned sketch of a flower, or rather a half-flower.

"Dad, is this the same plant we just saw? The one that inspired the Pele legend?"

Dad furrows his brow and the huge SUV careens to the road's edge.

"Yep! That's the same one."

He was here. I'm on the right path to finding Leilani. I need to find out her last name and then question her about her time with the sergeant.

"Do you think Leilani worked at the harbor?" I ask.

He switches off the radio and turns onto the highway. "It's possible, but I thought she was a dancer or something. I can't remember why I think that, but I pictured her working at a restaurant or hotel. Was there a restaurant at the harbor?"

I stare into the map on my phone screen. "There's a small deli and store, and it looks like there used to be a big restaurant. But, it's closed now. Shoot. I had a good feeling about that place."

I text Josie, "U OK?"

We return to the resort and take a swim before getting dressed for dinner. We meet Dad in the lobby. Mom looks beautiful in a new dress. Sadie is gorgeous as always, but as her sibling, it's my job to keep her feet planted firmly on the ground, so I point out a flaw or two. Dad wears a new butter yellow Tommy Bahama shirt. He seems happy and relaxed.

With time to spare before dinner, we sit in the open-air lobby and listen to live music. We were lucky to find an empty loveseat that fits three people. Dad tucks a chair on the end next to Mom. Slack-key music pours forth from the coffee-colored instrument strummed by a pale Hawaiian.

A young hula dancer interprets the sweet lazy song with her body, and I'm hypnotized as I watch her brown feet glide across the shiny blue tiles. An elderly singer accompanies the duo. Her smooth voice sings a song in an ancient language I do not know, but that I understand somehow. It tells the story of two lovers banished to the mountains and sea, but eternally united in love. The elderly singer's shiny gray hair falls in waves across a red and white muumuu. She wears a string of white flowers and her husky full voice resonates in the open airy space.

A breeze blows through the lobby and sets the palm trees in motion. They sway with the beautiful dancer, their gentle leaves adding soft percussion to the Hawaiian performers. It's all so perfect and I long for my friends, especially Josie, to see this place. It would be nice to share this place with Josie. I take a picture of the dancer and musician and text it to her.

The night is filled with a magic the photo cannot capture, but I promise to remember the feeling forever. My mom reaches out a hand for my dad. And I pretend not to notice.

Josie Watches as Grace Reclaims a Garden

"I SPEND MORE TIME with the living than the dead now, Josie," Grace reveals as she prunes back a row of hedges clipped flat enough to set a plate onto. "On Thanksgiving, I couldn't stop looking out the windows and wishing I could put on some gloves and cut back this mess. Sure Grant said he did some work on the yard, but it wasn't near enough. It was like some cottage garden gone wild. Now, look at it!" She appraises a newly transformed Jameson garden. Over the last three weeks, she has come over with her garden implements and dug into our overgrown yard one planter bed at a time.

She smiles as she does a visual assessment of the yard. Everything is trimmed back and tidy. In fact, I am hard-pressed to find one thing she could possibly do to make it better. I scrunch my face at her to ask, and then the truth hits me. She has come over every Sunday to see us. Her visits aren't about gardening. She spends more time with the living now... Duh.

"I have to hand it to you. Our yard hasn't looked this good for a long time," I say, and I mean it. "My mother did all the gardening. After she died, the rest of us never stopped to think about it much, well, at all," I expect the words to make me sad, but sharing this feels good, like pulling out a splinter.

"Well, I'm happy to get it back ship-shape." She tosses her hand trowel into her wheelbarrow and extracts a pair of hedge trimmers. I laugh. At this point, what she needs is a pair of those itsy bitsy scissors they use to trim miniature bonsai trees. We are down to the fine details; busywork is what my mother called it.

"What are you giggling about? Seriously, just wait until spring, Josie! These roses and rhodies are going to wake up to a layer of fresh mulch. I bet you will get twice the normal blooms. Wait and see!" She holds her hands on her hips and smiles. I'm glad we could provide such a satisfying project for her. She glances past me to my approaching father.

He is all smiles. "Hi, ladies. How's it going? Is anyone ready for burgers and milkshakes yet?" He takes a finger and gently wipes away dirt from Grace's cheek, and she puts a hand over his.

Owen stands in the picture window making smooch faces. I frown at him and signal for him to stop before either Grace or Dad spot him. He is being a goofy spectacle and I turn my back, deciding distraction might be the best course.

I touch Grace's sleeve. "I'm starving. What about you?" I ask, standing close to keep her from seeing my idiotic brother.

"I need ten minutes." She hands me a heavy blue container. "Would you mind tossing a capful of this under each of the rose bushes? It won't do any harm to add a little slow-feeding fertilizer before winter." I scatter the pellets of plant food and hum a cat food commercial.

Dad straightens the collar of his blue and white striped polo shirt. "So, Grace. Did you find someone to help you out around Lakefront Cemetery?"

"Mmhm. I found a guy. He's an eager beaver. Likes to do the digging and has experience in construction in case anything breaks around the property. Pretty soon he'll be doing more around there than me." She rakes under the bushes and collects a handful of yellow leaves.

Dad tosses the leaves into the yard waste can and smiles at her. "Lakefront's a big place. It's about time you got some extra help. I still think you could use a full-time gardener so you can concentrate on the things you like to do best, like keeping the records straight, putting in the flowers, things like that. You mentioned building a website for Lakefront, remember? Maybe now you'll have enough time to do that."

She shrugs, stowing the last of her tools in the wheelbarrow. My dad steers the wheelbarrow to the street, and lifts it into the truck bed with a grunt.

"Okay, I'm ready anytime." she says. I set the plant feeder into the truck and dust off my hands on my jeans.

Owen sees us load up and rushes down the front steps, "Lunchtime! I'm getting a banana milkshake today!" He grabs Grace's hand and pulls her toward the car.

"Do you want to pile in with us, Grace?" asks my father and she nods.

"I'll sit in the back with you, little bro. Grace should sit in the front." I wink at Owen and he giggles.

As we drive to Tasty Burgers, I think about how Grace ignored my father's question about the website. With a college degree in library science, she could land a good job anywhere. What holds her to Lakefront? It's not only childhood memories; there is something more to it. I wonder if she will ever trust us enough to tell *that* story.

Owen jabs me with one of his sharp, little elbows. "Ow, Owen! Why'd you do that?" I grab my ribs.

He stares, a finger to his lips to hush me up, and I follow his eyes to the front seat. Grace and my dad are holding hands. Owen and I thunk our heads together and giggle as we drive to lunch.

JOSIE DISCOVERS WHAT THE STATUE HIDES

"**SO, WHAT MOVIE** are we supposed to be at?" Blaze asks as we step off the bus onto a bustling corner in downtown Kirkland. The air is cold and crisp and smells like snow and wood smoke. Usually, the chance for some of the white stuff would make me excited, but not tonight.

It's the first day of Christmas break and the Baby Group has ventured to Park Lane, a lively pedestrian-only street sprinkled with galleries and coffee shops, to examine my mother's statue. I thought it best to stage this little field trip after nightfall, since we might have to tamper with a piece of public art in order to find the mystery puzzle box.

Seth is convinced we will find a puzzle box, and I worry he might be right. It's the thought of finding her box and revealing an actual heart inside that has kept me postponing this trip the last three weeks. I am stuck between wanting to find something, and scared to see if my mother's letter is true. Emotions churn inside my gut with the spaghetti and meatballs I ate for dinner. Anxiety and dinner bubble up my throat.

Blaze asks again. "Movie? Anyone? So we have our stories straight."

I stare at the twenty-five-foot Douglas fir we're standing under until the white lights blur into stars.

Seth answers Blaze before I can collect my thoughts. "Dude, I panicked. My parents asked me where we were off to and I forgot about the Christmas shopping cover we'd agreed on. I don't know why I said we were going to *The Sound of Music*, sing-along version. I just got a tweet about it and it was stuck in my brain."

"Dang," Blaze shakes his head.

"Yeah, I know." Seth laughs. "Although if my Dad buys that, he'll A) Wonder what blackmail the girls have on us and B) Take a step back to admire my newly sprouted moobs. Heck, he may even take me shopping for a training bra tomorrow." Seth's laughter turns the heads of the sedate gallery walkers wandering the lane. They cast stern looks our way.

Casey says, "Whatever. That's our story and we're sticking to it." She pulls a furry hood over her black hair, resembling a sweet Eskimo girl.

I wrap my scarf around my neck a second time and blow out a puff of fog. I feel a gentle wetness on my cheek and look up. Snowflakes fall down around us. Giant, puffy flakes drift to the sidewalk. We're in a life-sized snow globe.

"Next time, let's pretend to play paintball!" Seth ruffles my hair as if I'm Owen and fake ice skates the half block to my mom's sculpture on the thin slippery snow. I tuck my head into the hood of my holey UCLA sweatshirt and zip up the front of my down vest to protect against the cold.

When Seth was in Hawaii, he says I called him in my sleep. I didn't want to believe what he said was true, but my phone held the proof, a four-minute, thirty second call with Seth at 11:56 a.m. Usually I remember my nightmares, but this one was different. I only know what Seth told me, that I said I'd found the mystery box and there was a crow's head inside. Disgusting. I may not remember the dream, but the sick, sinking feeling in my gut that day is with me now.

Seth shouts from the distance, "Hey, Josie! Toss me the key. I want to see if it fits."

I race down the sidewalk. Blaze scrapes at the ground and tosses a walnut-sized snowball at my head as I pass.

"Keep it down," I hiss. "We've got to fly under the radar." Excitement makes my voice rise and crack. Finally at the statue, I gawk at the dark sculpture of a mother and daughter. The snow collects in the folds and recesses of the stone art. I brush away a layer of white from the mother's face.

I extract the black chain and rusty key from a warm spot near my heart and fumble to undo the clasp. "Can someone help me? I'm having a hard time with this thing." I can't get my fingers to work as a team.

Casey takes hold of the chain and does her magic. The key slips free. She tucks the chain into the pocket of my vest.

"Thanks." I hand the key to Seth, and his eyes dart around for unwanted witnesses before he squats down to examine the stone purse. He studies the keyhole decoration in the sculpture and fiddles with the key. He uses a finger to scrape bits of ice out of the keyhole.

"I don't think there's any mechanism in here." Seth hands back the key. When he sees my expression, he says, "Josie, don't look so bummed. Maybe it was just meant to be a hint. The key and keyhole were metaphors to get us to this point, to this sculpture, right?"

Blaze rubs my back. "So, what now?"

Casey takes a seat on the stone bench next to the mother and child. "I didn't know this statue was one of your mother's. It's amazing. Look at the book in her lap. Her daughter fell asleep in her arms while she was reading something. What book is that?"

Blaze rubs the powdery snow off the cover of the book.

"I can't make it out," he says. "It's too dark. Does someone have a flashlight?"

Seth draws a tiny Maglite out from his pocket and hands it to him. Blaze switches on the light and flashes it across the soapstone cover. The green stone shimmers in the beam's light and the metal around it looks flat and boring in comparison.

"*The Runaway Bunny*," Blaze reads.

My legs wobble, just for a second, and then calm washes over me, as if some invisible force has steadied me with strong hands. My voice comes out louder than I mean it to. "It's here. If she carved that book, I know she hid the puzzle box inside. That was our special book. She read it to me every night."

I run my hand over the face of the sculpted mother. I run it down the back of the slumping toddler asleep across her mother's chest. I pull my hand away from the icy cold stone. A strap of the little girl's overalls slips off her tiny shoulder, and I want to lift it back into place with a fingertip. It's hard to imagine how someone could carve stone to look so lifelike. I expect them to stand, stretch, and walk away.

"Josie, she dedicated this to you!" Casey squats and shines the light she wrestled away from Blaze onto a brass plate at the base of the statue. "Listen. 'Dedicated to my daughter, Josie.' Casey drapes an arm across my shoulder. "She must've known she was dying when she carved this."

Blaze clears his throat, "No, man. If what Mrs. Jameson says in the letter is true, she had to keep the box safe until she died. After that, she would need someone to find out about it and bury the box with her body to end her magic. Everyone dies. She just didn't know she'd die so soon."

I look into the sky and watch the fat white snowflakes fall out of the black night. "Why'd she pick me to do this?"

Casey drapes the chain with the key around my neck. "Who else would do it? Your aunt?"

I shake my head. "No, Karen is the older sister. It had to be someone young, someone she thought would outlive her." I pull my hood up to hide. The thought of my mother planning for her death, even if it was supposed to happen at a ripe old age makes me sad. "And she dedicated it to me." I touch my name on the plaque, then retrieve my phone from a pocket and snap a picture.

Seth circles the sculpture, dusting off the snowflakes that collect on the cold stone. He chews his lip, thinking. "This is the clue. The key was supposed to lead us here. She knew someday you would find the key and think of that lock." He pokes a finger into the keyhole, and then rubs his hands. "She didn't think you would be looking for any puzzle box until you were much older. So, what did she think you would do next?"

She thought I would be able to find the box. I feel like I'm standing within reach but can't grab hold. "It's so frustrating!" I bark.

Blaze taps the brass dedication plate with the flashlight and the metal shifts ever so slightly. "Isn't this a little crooked?"

"Good going, Mr. Maki!" Casey says. "You broke it."

I swivel the plate so it is straight again and leave fingerprints across the metal. I use the sleeve of my sweatshirt to wipe it clean and the plate slips to the right. I push it hard to the right and the plate slips off, falling to the ground with a *clink*. I notice the end of a dark object and Blaze directs the flashlight beam into the cavity. I pry a box free with my fingernails. It's smaller than I imagined, and heavier.

Wordlessly, my friends arc around the sculpture and shield me from curious onlookers, though the street is mostly silent as the snow begins to stick to the pavement. Seth reaches for the brass plate and replaces it in front of the empty cavity.

"We should probably move along, Josie. Tuck that someplace and let's get going." Seth's voice sounds tight and edgy, and I feel a surge of paranoia. I look behind me and the street is empty. But, now I'm worried.

I don't want anyone to take this box from me. They can't have it. I tuck the box into the kangaroo pocket at the front of my sweatshirt and move. Seth points to a dark coffeehouse, holds the door open, and we slip inside, taking over a booth on the far wall. Casey orders hot chocolates from the barista, pays, and squishes into the booth next to Blaze. "So, can we see it?"

"No!" I want to hide it, protect it, and probe it in private. I want to keep it away from everyone, even the Baby Group. Shame burns my ears. I wouldn't have found it without them. Why am I being so greedy? I grip the box inside the pocket. Am I afraid to find out what my mother said was true? What would they think of me then? All this chasing clues, and what if it ends with me finding out that my mom really was a stone shaman. It's all so unbelievable.

Blaze laughs, because he must think I am joking. "Josie, come on. Hand it over." He holds a hand out for the box.

I draw in a deep breath. They are my closest friends. They've stood by me through all the hard times. And if what Seth said is true, they've never fallen for my Ms. Perfect act. I trust them. After fighting a second wave of greed, I slip the box out of my pocket and place it on top of the table. I mumble, "Alright, fine. But, be careful."

Casey is the first to reach for it. She turns the box over in her hands and inspects the intricate wood. "It's absolutely beautiful. They used lots of different woods to create this. Solid woods, not veneer. Did your mother give you the instructions to open it, Josie?" She pushes at the top and feels around with a fingernail for seams in the wood.

"Your dad's taught you a thing or two about wood, Casey," Seth says.

I rub my hands together and grip the cup of hot chocolate before me. "The letter I found says that my grandma gave my mother instructions, but she told her never to open it. Mom didn't leave any instructions for me, not that I've found at least." I take a long sip of the cocoa.

Seth slides the box out of Casey's hands. Watching the box pass from person to person makes me feel nervous for some reason. I don't want them to drop it. What if someone accidentally opens it? Seth holds the box next to his ear and turns it over and over. *Klunk! Klunk!* His eyes lock on mine and I know he's thinking about the dream I had.

"Something's rolling around inside." He studies the box. "It's a metal ball. There's probably a maze that you have to solve."

Blaze takes it from Seth and gives it a gentle shake. *Rattle, rattle.*

"This doesn't sound like a metal marble. This sounds like something lumpy. Metal would make a different sound because it's smooth and symmetrical. Whatever this is seems small...."

Casey takes a sip, sets the cup down, and stares across the table at me. Her voice comes out in a near whisper and we all lean in close to hear her. "Josie, what if you aren't meant to open the box? Maybe that's why your mom didn't give you instructions. All she said was for you to bury it with her remains, right? She didn't say open the box, gawk at the contents with a bunch of friends, and *then* bury it with my remains. Maybe I'm spending too much time with Grace, but I think it's always best to follow a person's last wish to the letter." She pulls out her ponytail and combs her hair with her fingers.

What she says speaks to a part of me buried deep, under layers of ugly thinking, where the do-the-right-thing-Josie lives. But I ignore that part of myself. "I think she wanted me to open it. I just haven't found..."

Casey interrupts. "No, Josie! Lakefront is full of stories about people who ignore last wishes. That mystery writer, for one, who makes everyone itchy when they walk by! Your mom didn't say to open the box. If she wanted you to do that, she would've put it in the letter with the instructions. You need to follow the directions she gave you, or I'm here to tell you it won't end well!" Blaze places the box in the middle of the table.

"Maybe you have a point." I slide the box across the tabletop until it rests in front of me. A cloud of sadness starts to gather around my head, and then Casey's voice bursts through.

"Did I tell you about that one grave of the married couple that hated each other? They bought their plots and headstone before dying.

Grace's uncle remembered selling it to them because they fought the whole time. The missus wanted to be buried by the shore, and the mister wanted to be buried the cheapest way possible. So, they got a double-wide plot halfway up the hill.

"Anyway, they ordered this double headstone, probably to save money. The idea was that when the first person died, their information would be etched onto one side of the stone. Then when the other person passed away, their name would be etched on the blank side."

Without thinking about it, I hold the puzzle box under the table and slide it around in my hands, twisting it every which way while Casey tells the rest of her story. I turn, fumble, and listen.

"I guess, soon after, the husband died. He was buried in their plot. His name and dates were etched on the left side of the stone. But, the wife lived another twenty years! And in those years, she'd changed her mind about that double-wide plot.

"She bought herself a lakefront grave and revised her will accordingly. But when she died, her kids ignored her final wishes and buried her next to their father. And do you know what happened? That tombstone cracked right down the middle! Honest to goodness, the stone split in two! Dead people want their final wishes to be carried out, Josie. That's what I think." Casey takes the lid off her drink and spoons whipped cream into her mouth.

Blaze scratches his head and gathers up our empty cups. "Man! Are you sure you're not spending too much time with Grace? You even tell a story like her now."

Click!

I jump as I realize all my toying with the box under the table has unlocked something. I set the box on the table and glance at the others. They must know by the look on my face that something just happened. I struggle to find my voice. "I think it's open. I was messing with it and something clicked. I wasn't trying."

Blaze says, "You know, I'm sure I can figure out a way to close it again. You don't have to look." He reaches for the box.

I tug the box away from Blaze and lift off the lid before anyone can argue the point. Inside sits a gnarled, walnut-sized lump. In the dim light of the coffeehouse, the surface gives off a flat burgundy hue. A cinnamon odor lifts from the box.

"It looks like those things the Hawaiians suck on, those salty prune pits," Seth whispers as he gawks into the box.

Casey recoils from the box and huddles into the corner of the booth. "Wouldn't that be about the size of a heart? You know, after it's dried out?"

I feel a black curtain fall over me and my head hits the table.

I wake to Casey wiping a wet towel across my forehead. The barista stands next to our table, phone in her hand.

"What just happened?" I ask.

Concern lines Blaze's face. "You were out for a minute. I had the barista call for a cab. We'll go to your house Josie, since it's the closest. There's no way you should ride a bus after that." He bends down and whispers, "Seth has the box. Don't worry."

I am worried. I want it back. I plan to keep the box close from now on.

The barista asks us if she should call someone, but Casey assures her I'm in good hands. She says something about me being hypoglycemic and the barista backs away from our table. She must think it's a contagious disease.

We wait outside for the taxi to arrive. A green cab with chains on the tires pulls to the curb. Seth wraps an arm around me and helps me inside. Casey slides in next to me, and Blaze begins a conversation with the driver about the weather from the front seat. Before we pull away from the curb, I take the box from Seth and stow it away.

The snow comes down fast and piles up thick as we ride home. A winter advisory on the radio says the storm will extend through the night, so we decide it's best if the Baby Group stays over at my house tonight.

Dad pulls out old sleeping bags and blankets, and we make a huge padded nest across the living room floor. Owen joins us, wrapping himself in a comforter on the couch near Seth and Blaze. He lasts about fifteen minutes before his snoring rumbles over the room. I'm not far behind. I stash the puzzle box deep inside my pillowcase and fall into a fitful sleep.

Grace Shadows the
Christmas Visits

IT IS EARLY CHRISTMAS EVE as the four teens enter the front gates dressed in their Sunday best, long coats and shiny shoes. Each of them carries a package or bag wrapped in pretty paper and fancy bows. They might as well be part of a Christmas production. They thread into the cemetery, the girls in high heels walking a little slower than the boys through the last remnants of the big snowstorm. What were once pretty white drifts of snow have melted into ugly mounds of dirty ice.

I navigate a wheelbarrow filled to bursting with fir wreaths and red bows toward the kids and raise an arm. The kids turn my way and give me a quick wave, then it's back to business. Me, putting holiday embellishments on the graves that haven't had any kin visit, and the kids, I suspect, off to visit their Halloween folks. I follow them with my eyes until Blaze and Josie get too far away on the property to track. Hope they have nice visits.

Seth makes it to the sergeant's grave, not fifty feet from the entrance gates. As luck would have it, I've got wreaths to place in that direction. As I wrap a large red ribbon around a tombstone, I watch Seth through the white picket fence that borders the military graveyard. Talking to himself, he unwraps a funny assortment of things from a blue and white bag. He sets a swimsuit-clad Santa on the sergeant's grave, and then opens a plastic container to remove three flower leis. Some of the flowers are purple, some white, and one yellow. He takes care to arrange them across the sergeant's grave. He steps back from the grave, hands on his hips, I imagine to take in the full effect. He sees me and smiles.

"Looks nice, Seth."

The boy smiles again and gathers up his debris. "Yeah, but I didn't think to bring an American flag, you know, since he served our country."

I hand him a red bow from the wheelbarrow. "What you did was perfect. If you want a little color though, you can have this." He takes the bow and says thanks.

"Those flowers sure smell nice," I say. Seth sets the bow next to the sergeant's marker. He kneels on the frozen ground, and I know he's having a private talk with the sergeant, so I scoot along.

I push the barrow in the direction of my cottage where Blaze is wrapping things up. He nods as he sees me approach. He's placed white candles, maybe twenty of them, across the Father Kujala's plot. They're all shapes and sizes, but all of them are white, snowy white. He's talking to the father as he lights the wicks, one by one. He's filled a blue vase with white flowers. The silver accents twinkle in the flickering candlelight. I'll have to make sure that my little house doesn't burn down tonight, but I sure can appreciate the aesthetic of the thing.

"Well done, Blaze," I whisper, because he's deep in thought, maybe talking to Father Kujala in his head. He smiles and I lumber away.

The Jameson family came yesterday to honor Sarah. I added a grave blanket made of cedar boughs and wrapped a red ribbon around her headstone. So, I figure Josie came today to visit her witch, but I can't bear to enter the Ghost Forest today. I have to assume Josie's done something lovely and perfect for her witch, for Bain McLaren. Lord, I'm happy she has a name again. That's Christmas gift enough, if you ask me.

I lay wreaths and ribbon bows on the blank graves between the cottage and the children's cemetery, which is where I find Casey. I notice she doesn't have anything with her, no bag of holiday cheer to sprinkle around the grave she rubbed, little Ettore. I wonder what she's planning to do to her grave. As I come closer, I see that her face is puckered up in a scowl. What's gotten into that girl? With a face like that, I know she's not singing a Christmas carol for the boy.

As I live and breathe, less than five feet away, I watch Casey take the Christmas stocking off Ettore's grave. My whole body shakes with the injustice. I stomp at her until she finally looks up at me. Her eyes get all big and she freezes with the stocking in her hand.

"Casey Starbaugh, you put that back this minute!" I must look crazy, because Casey loses what little color she has, falls backward and drops the stocking. Little presents that had been tucked neatly inside scatter across the ground, like Santa's come to visit but got sloppy. I fall to my knees and gather them up, then tuck them back inside the stocking. I try to wipe the smears of mud off with my jacket sleeve, but it just spreads the dirt.

Casey gets up and dusts the snow off her jeans. She pastes on a fake smile. "What the heck, Grace! I thought you were a ghost. What are you doing here?" If she were a cat, I'd expect a yellow feather to poke out from behind her bright teeth.

"You're going to wish I was a ghost after I get through with you! What'd you do to that boy's stocking?!" I set the red sock at the base of his tombstone. My hands shake with anger. I'm so mad I don't dare reach out to her for fear my touch will be a might too firm. I grit my teeth instead. Casey backs away a couple steps, smart girl, and hits her head on an apple tree branch. Good.

"He's someone's baby. The boy that lies under that dirt is someone's dear and precious child." I jam a finger over and over toward the grave and the dirty stocking. "Someone laid those things across his grave so he'd know he's loved! And you were going to take them? What the hell's wrong with you?"

As Casey cobbles together some feeble excuse, I thunder away. I am not in control of my anger, not about this. Sometimes it's best to get going and stay gone.

The next morning I wake to the sound of church bells. It must be nine, time for morning Christmas services. I haven't slept past seven in a decade, so my brain feels a little foggy. I think about what Casey did to Ettore's things and thanks to the Christmas spirit, forgiveness takes the place of the anger. I remember my mean words, and guilt cozies up to my worn and weary heart. I throw some clothes on and walk to the far corner of Lakefront to sit a while and think.

I hear it before I see it, the clank and chug of tinny metal. A shiny toy train chugs across Ettore's grave on a roundabout track. It slogs along at a snail's pace after running through the night. The batteries must be low. Painted in glossy red and green, doll-sized Christmas lights stretch from car to car and blink as the train travels.

I cry into my hands at Casey's kind gesture. She must have come back last night. Right then and there, I make a promise to show that girl some kindness the first chance I get.

That girl hasn't been shown much kindness. Yeah, she's got a great group of friends. I'm thinking about family kindness, more like family ignorance. Maybe it's my job to help her look into the mirror and see she is worth her weight in gold. Maybe it isn't always our parents that teach us what love is.

I whisper, "Merry Christmas, Ettore," and sit until the train batteries run dry.

Josie and New Year's Eve at the Maki House

"CAN YOU BELIEVE IT? In six hours, we get a whole new year, Josie! I can't wait to make my midnight wish," Casey says as she crams into the back of my dad's car.

I stuff my backpack under my feet, hoping she doesn't notice it, because then she may ask what's inside. God, that'd be awful. Casey adjusts a large flat container across her lap. The smells that leak out from the foil-wrapped container are full of garlicky, buttery goodness. The smell makes my stomach rumble.

Did I eat today? Somehow, since I discovered the puzzle box, I forget to do things like eat. I have become obsessed with the box, and the strange object inside. I've read my mother's letter maybe forty times and know what I am supposed to do, bury it. But, the box was my mom's, might contain a piece of her, and I don't want to be away from it. That's why I snuck it into the backpack and brought it with me tonight.

I click Casey's seatbelt for her since her hands are full and she eyes the backpack. "Why do you need to take your backpack to a party? You planning on studying as the ball drops?"

Owen chirps, "That's not school stuff." I kick my brother's leg. "Ow! Josie, that hurt!" he whines.

He saw me putting the puzzle box into the pack and teased me about it. I made the mistake of telling him to keep it secret and of course the first chance he gets he starts to blab. I say, "God, Owen. You're such a brat sometimes."

"Ouch, a little harsh, aren't we?" Casey cocks her head sideways, but I ignore her.

I wish I could reach inside the bag and touch the box, just a quick poke, but everyone's paying too much attention to get away with it. I crack my window instead to take my mind off my compulsive thoughts. Icy raindrops splatter inside the glass.

"Close your window! I'm freezing," Owen says.

I shoot him a death stare and he shuts up. When did he get to be such a pain? I flick his hand away from Casey's container of food as he tries to steal one of the appetizers tucked inside. He has to wait like the rest of us!

Casey bobs up and down on the seat, little movements that Owen's tracking eyes mimic. "I'm so excited. Maybe this year my wish will come true," she says.

"Hold on a sec! We get a wish at midnight? I didn't know that!" Owen glares at me. "Thanks a lot, sis." He frowns and crosses his arms.

"I told you about the wish! Last year, and the year before that! The problem is that you've never been able to stay awake until midnight. That's why you don't have a clue about it." I reach across Casey to squeeze Owen's knee and he slaps my hand away.

"Dad! Owen just hit me."

My dad casts a dirty look in the rearview mirror. "How old are you, Josie? Four or fourteen? Sort it out yourself." He grabs Grace's hand off the armrest and squeezes it. The two bend their heads together and continue their secret conversation amidst the domestic storm brewing in the backseat.

"Two hands on the wheel," I say, half-kidding and half not. It's been a week since Grace and my dad officially started dating. I love Grace and I really love having Dad happy again. This is about him insulting me and me giving it back; that's all.

Owen won't let this dead horse of a topic alone. "I have too stayed up 'til midnight! Last year, remember?" He shoves a finger for emphasis, and Casey lurches away to avoid a poke in the eye. "We watched the fireworks and a big apple fell off the Space Needle."

He is thinking of the Times Square celebration we watch on television while we play games. Yup. There's the proof he only made it to nine. Casey giggles.

"Hey! Don't laugh at me. That's mean," he barks. He rams an elbow into Casey, which causes her to push into me.

"I'm not laughing," she says, but I can feel her body shaking from the giggles she tries to hold in. "Owen, you fell asleep after dinner at the Maki's, like every other year." Owen moves his hand to the container of food again, and she snaps it away, mumbling, "Brothers," under her breath.

"What are you going to wish for, Casey?" I ask, even though I'm pretty sure I already know. She'll wish for things to be better with her family this year.

My mind travels back to the puzzle box at my feet; and for the first time I understand how much it must hurt Casey to watch her fragile, hopeful little wish die before it ever gets the chance to become real. Like the wish I vow to never say aloud, I worry mine will be crushed by my mother, like Casey's mom will crush hers.

Casey looks out the front windshield where the tall pines that line the road sway in the wind. "I'm going to wish the same thing as last year." The windshield wipers swish back and forth fast and furious, barely keeping up with the downpour. She changes the subject. "Mr. J., are we in for a storm?"

"Yep. They're saying we could have a power outage," he says, smiling at Grace. "Power outages can be cozy? Right?"

Casey has her eyes closed. I wonder if she's making her wish and my heart breaks. She keeps her eyes shut so long I think she's fallen asleep. "Hey, Casey, don't zonk on me."

"I'm trying not to." She yawns. "Grace and I had to get up in the wee hours to cook the food for the party. We made stuffed mushrooms, crab sandwiches, and bruschetta. It was five hours of washing, chopping, mixing, and broiling."

"You left out the sautéing and simmering, honey," Grace adds. "Oh, and wrapping; we did a fair amount of wrapping," she adds. "Those secret Santa presents didn't wrap themselves."

Casey is wearing a sweet holiday dress and has made up her hair and makeup for the party. I say, "Hey, Casey, you look really nice tonight."

"Thanks! Grace dolled me up. Do you like my curls and makeup?" She puckers her pretty pink lips.

"You're gorgeous," I say.

Casey grins.

Out the car windows, a wild winter storm is getting cranked up. The wind blows hard enough to rock the car and I worry my dad is too distracted by Grace to watch the road. I'm sure if Seth were here, he'd spout some statistic about car fatalities and windstorms. Maybe then Dad would focus on his driving.

Casey reads my thoughts. "You know, Josie, if we get taken out by a tree branch, at least we'll have food to eat white we wait for the tow truck."

"Do you think they'd have to use the Jaws of Life to free us?" Owen asks.

Casey raises her eyebrows. "What does a seven-year-old know about the Jaws of Life?"

"Ah, you know. I get around," he smirks. Casey laughs. "So, can I please have just one piece of bread?"

She digs under the foil and hands over a garlic crouton dotted with chopped tomatoes. "Shh, don't tell," she whispers.

He stuffs the offering into his mouth. Between chews he says, "Don't worry. I am good at keeping secrets." He looks like a little leprechaun with that green sweater and wild auburn hair. He sure has the impish attitude down pat. My ears burn because he may technically have kept my secret for now, but he sure is having fun hinting around at it.

Owen blows on the window and etches a smiley face onto the fogged glass. "Ah, man. Well, this year I am definitely staying up 'til midnight," he says, more to himself than us. "Do you want me to show you how to make ghost baby footsteps?" He smashes the side of his hand into the steam, and then dots five times across the top of the print with his pinkie finger. It really does look like a baby footprint. Creepy!

"That's weird, Owen." Casey wipes the window clean.

The car rolls to a stop. "Hey, we're here!" Owen opens his door and sprints up the front walk, then abruptly turns and runs back to us. "Do you need help?" he asks as Grace unloads.

"Honey, if you can switch your speed to turtle, I'll let you carry this." Grace hands over a canvas tote bag filled with crackers, sliced bread, and games. She pats his head as he tiptoes away. Grace wears a slip of a silver dress that shimmers under the streetlights. She pulls a black knitted shawl around her tiny form and ducks back in the car for her handbag.

My dad and I pull Secret Santa gifts from the trunk of the car, the lone vestige of Christmas allowed inside the Maki home. My emerald chiffon dress swish-swishes as I follow the stone pavers that lead the way to the front door. I like the thud of the backpack because I can hear the puzzle box clatter inside as I walk.

The Maki home is not draped in Christmas decorations; there are no nativity scenes or blow-up Santas here. But it is beautiful, nonetheless. Simple white rice lights skim the fence line of their single-story home and hug the bare trunks of three Japanese maples.

We toddle over the pea gravel path that meanders to the front door through their lovely garden. Like an image on a postcard, a tiny concrete bridge crosses the dry creek beneath the Maki's towering oaks. Stone lanterns hug the ground and line the path that wanders between dwarf conifers and Japanese maples to the front steps. As I wait for someone to answer the doorbell, I think about all the playdates we spent in this garden, building forts and staging plays.

Blaze opens the front door and greets us with a broad smile. The warm air that surrounds him smells spicy and savory. My stomach grumbles. He wrestles the food tray away from Casey and whispers, "You look gorgeous," to her and I am left to scratch my head. Does he like her?

We all hang coats and take off shoes and Blaze's dog Miso pushes past to get to Owen. He barks and yips until Owen pets him.

The dog stands on his back legs and licks Owen's face. "Miso, off!" Blaze pulls his Shiba Inu off Owen and pats the dog's side. "Sorry, pal. Miso's a little excited to see you again!"

As we move toward the kitchen, Blaze and Grace walk ahead, talking about tonight's fare. Red beans and rice, gumbo, and sushi. I am suddenly starving. We follow Blaze down the hall as Owen scoops a rubber ball from the stone floor and runs out the front door, Miso at his heels.

Blaze and Grace lay out the appetizers as the rest of us settle into the front room to nibble and visit.

Casey grabs my hand, "This is the best night of the year!" I love her optimism.

Seth slips off the sleek black leather couch to say hello. Our parents exchange pleasantries then tuck into the chairs by the fireplace to talk about the economy, upcoming elections, blah, blah, blah.

Casey plants herself next to the food and wolfs down a handful of salt-crusted edamame and we surround her on the sofa.

Seth leans over Casey and grabs a napkin off the table. "You two look great, by the way!" I glance down at Casey's salty hands and salt-dotted leggings. I brush what I can off of her legs and straighten out a stray curl.

"Do you want me to turn on the game, Casey?" Seth teases. I pinch his ear lobe and leer, but he ignores me. Casey's face blanches like someone kicked her in the stomach. She drops the last of her soybeans back into the bowl.

"Not. Nice," I say.

"It's for the National Championship and it's at the Rose Bowl, no less. Come on, at least let me check out the score," he says.

Casey studies the rug.

Seth loads a napkin with fresh edamame and sets them in front of Casey. "I didn't mean to make you mad. It's just that the whole country is talking about this matchup." Casey stares at him and her features soften.

She picks up the napkin and smirks. "The game is tomorrow, Seth. And if I cared about the outcome, I would've traveled there with my family."

"Got it. Again, I'm sorry," he sputters.

I try to change the subject. "It was nice of Grace to let you stay at the cottage. How's that going?"

"It's terrific," she answers. "Actually, it's weird having someone look after me. Nice weird, I mean. I've never been this well fed. Last night, we stayed up late watching old movies. It was super fun. By the time we got to bed, I was too tired to think about being in the middle of a cemetery. I fell asleep before my head hit the pillow." She blinks as if she's suddenly remembered something. "Hey, did you know that Grace has a brother?"

I shake my head. "Nope. The only family I've heard her talk about is her aunt and uncle, the ones that used to run Lakefront Cemetery."

"Yep. He's like ten months younger than her. He and his family live in New York City. I guess he writes children's books. Grace was telling me about them last night. She has two nieces who might visit in February. Did I tell you they are twins?"

Seth glances across the room. His mom and dad sit next to one another and nod in unison at a comment from my dad. Seth's eyes crinkle and he gives me a quick wink. "Who are twins? Grace and her brother? Or the nieces?" he asks.

"Her nieces are twins, eleven-year-old twins. I hope we get to meet them."

The front door slams open and Owen thunders inside with Miso. The dog shakes and water splashes onto the walls and floor. "It's pouring out there! Josie, I need my rain jacket. Where'd you put it?"

Grrr. How many times did I tell him to bring a coat? Brothers! "Hey! Shut the door, Owen." I command. He's old enough to remember his own stupid coat and know how to shut a dang door. I get so sick of being the parent. And then I feel guilty for being so short with him.

If my mom were still alive, she would have patiently reminded him to shut the door. She would have tucked a raincoat for Owen into the car, knowing he would want it sooner or later. Thinking of my mom reminds me of the puzzle box, the last traces of her life so close to me. I itch to open the box again and smell the cinnamon scent. Owen caught me talking to the box today. He made a cuckoo gesture and told me I was crazy. What's strange about that? Besides, he's not supposed to come in my room without knocking. I shove the backpack further under the coffee table with my foot and pout.

Miso collapses at Seth's feet. He nudges my bag with his nose. Seth notices and says, "Hey, why'd you bring homework?"

He reaches for the bag and I smack his hand away. "What's your problem? Can't a person bring something without people being nosy?" Ugh. I should've just told him I had art supplies in there and he would have left the pack alone.

"What the…" Casey asks, from me to Seth to me again.

In the nick of time, Blaze comes around the corner from the adjoining dining room, a "Kiss the Cook" apron tied around his middle.

"Hey, dinner's on!" he announces.

The others rise and march to the dining room and Seth yanks Casey aside. I know they're going to talk about me. I perk up my ears as I wander to the entryway and tuck the backpack into a cubby. I hear Seth whisper, "How much do you want to bet the puzzle box is in her backpack? She takes it everywhere now. She's obsessed."

"And she is so moody these days," Casey comments. I linger in the entryway and listen.

"Yeah, I never know when she's going to snap at me. I don't know, Casey. What if she decides to keep the box? What will happen if she doesn't bury it?"

I come around the corner and they stop talking, mouths wide open. I spin on my heels and stomp away, but then change my mind and turn back. I tug the two of them back into the front room so the others won't hear.

"You guys have no idea what I'm going through. This box is all I have left of my mom and if I bury it, she's gone for good. But, if I don't, then I am an absolutely terrible, selfish person. It tears me up, guys. I want to do the right thing, I just can't yet." I feel their arms reach around me. I bite the inside of my cheek to keep from crying.

"God, Josie. We are here for you," Seth says. He leans his head into me and so does Casey. I feel like we are in a football huddle, but I know better than to mention it. One of them rubs a hand on my head.

"I'm not saying I understand, but I do get it. You want to hang onto the box for awhile," Casey says. "Why not? If you promise to bury it eventually, what difference does a few weeks make?" Seth voices his agreement and I relax. Yes, I will keep it to myself for a little while. I feel peaceful.

We join the others seated around the table. Everyone sends compliments to Mr. Maki for the feast spread across the long table and he's quick to mention his wife, who is stuck at their restaurant until later tonight. A steaming platter of gyoza sits directly in front of me; there's also sushi, a heaping bowl of jasmine rice, a fragrant crock of shrimp gumbo, a bowl of Satsuma mandarins, and red beans and rice. Who knew two cultures could come together so well?

I don't know where to start. Grace bows her head to say a prayer and Mr. Jameson elbows her. They share a quiet laugh over the near faux pas.

"My mother is still stuck at work. She'll have to catch up on the eating while we play games," Blaze states. "So, thanks for joining us to celebrate New Year's again. Dad, do you want to say something?" Blaze looks across the table to his father. Mr. Maki picks up a champagne glass and raises it in a toast.

"Thanks for coming this evening. Please, raise your glass with me. Here's to friends, both old and new. Here's to daring to live up to our potential. And here's to a happy and healthy year." Mr. Maki takes a quick glance at the front door. "And since my wife isn't home yet, God bless!" He winks and empties his glass in one long sip. Everyone laughs and joins the toast.

As we pass platters filled with amazing food, someone knocks at the front door. Blaze rises to answer it, but his dad motions for him to sit.

Mr. Maki answers the door. "Father James, you made it. Please come in. We were just dishing up."

He invites Father James to join us. Mr. Maki grabs another setting and places Father James between him and Blaze. We all say hello, but I'm sure we're all having the same collective thought. If Mrs. Maki comes home early, it could get interesting around here!

After dinner, in my case two heaping platefuls, we pitch in with cleanup. Owen curls onto a furry beanbag and Miso snuggles next to him. They fall asleep before the dishes are done. I snap a picture with my phone while Grace slips a blanket over them.

We break out Apples to Apples and Father James keeps everyone in stitches with his quick wit. I try to sneak into the entryway to collect my box, but it seems people are all eyes tonight.

About nine o'clock, Father James says his goodbyes. His escape, though, is apparently not quick enough. As soon as he leaves, Mrs. Maki storms into the house. From the couch, I hear shouting, but the walls muffle the actual words.

I want to leave. As if catching the telepathic message, my father rises. He scoops Owen off the beanbag and flings him over his shoulder. Grace quickly gathers trays off the coffee table and exits to the kitchen, away from the fight in the entryway. Taking their lead, I grab all that remains of the food and flee.

In hushed tones, we make a plan to finish out the night. Grace invites us over to the cottage while Casey and I repack the appetizers.

Blaze stands in the middle of the activity, shoulders slumped and biting his lower lip. He looks lost. "Can I come along? I don't want to stay here." He chokes out the words.

"Of course," says Grace.

As we ready to leave, I realize my backpack sits in the center of the maelstrom. There is no easy way to slip between the fighting pair and claim it from the cubby. Should I leave it here overnight? The thought makes me feel sad and empty. No, I have to bring it home with me.

The others exit through back door, but I remain. Imagining I am invisible, I try to slip inside the entryway, hoping they will be too focused on their argument to notice me. Blaze's parents freeze as I give a too-cheery wave, mumble a quick goodnight, gather the pack, and scoot out the backdoor. Not very smooth, but I got the pack.

I tuck it away and we ride in awkward silence to Lakefront Cemetery. No one is eager to talk about the surprising end to the Maki party. At Grace's cottage, we reboot the festivities. It takes only minutes to set out food, unearth a few board games, and commence the evening.

This year, even Owen makes it to midnight. He closes his eyes, and I wonder what he could be wishing for. Possibly, a nicer sister. I was going to wish for something else, but the new wish I think up feels right. I reach for my backpack, and realize I left it in my dad's car. I was going to hold my mom's box while I made the wish. I decide to go on without it. I close my eyes and wish.

This year I wish to honor my mother's last request. I wish to bury her box.

The finality of it all makes me feel shaky. Too late, I realize I didn't mean my wish. I rush to take it back. The thought of burying the box feels so final and tragic. I try to make a new wish, one about keeping the box to myself, forever, but the magic moment, midnight on New Year's, is gone. I am eager to hold the puzzle box and say a rushed goodnight at the door.

Casey hugs me as do the others. She says, "I'm so glad I get to stay one more night at Grace's."

"Enjoy it, and we will talk tomorrow, right?" I say, distracted.

"Yep. Happy New Year."

Once home, I don't bother with pajamas or tooth brushing. Instead, I curl up with the puzzle box, falling asleep with it nestled into my middle like a teddy bear. I think about how Seth and Casey basically gave me permission to keep it to myself for a time and smile.

"Happy New Year, Mom."

GRACE CHANGES THE LINENS

IT IS SUPPERTIME on New Years Day, and as I snap dirty sheets off the guest bed and add them to the pile of towels at my feet, I tell myself sternly to "Get over it, already." I'm having myself a good ole' pity party, wishing Casey's folks had stayed gone one more night.

She hasn't even been gone a day, and I already miss her. Without Casey running around asking questions, rifling through every drawer and cabinet in this house, and eating me out of house and home, time stands still. My little cottage seems too quiet, too big, and too damn empty. I wrestle the flowery sheets into the washer and turn on the TV for a bit of background noise when someone knocks on my door.

"Hold your horses! I'm coming!"

At a loss to guess who might be here, I swing the door open and look into the face of a grown-up Casey. Unless that girl went and invented herself a time machine, I have to assume this is her mother standing on my porch.

"Mrs. Starbaugh? How do you do?" As I stare at her, I realize she doesn't look as much like Casey as I first thought. Her eyes are mean. Creases stretch out from the corners like fractures in a cracked windshield. Those wrinkles weren't made smiling, I'd bet.

"Not well. Where's Casey? I thought you would have brought her back home by now. I don't appreciate having to pick her up after dark in a cemetery!"

She checks behind her for the bogeyman, and then steps inside my home, dirty shoes and all. She clutches a black, faux fur coat to her so tightly her hands turn bone white, and she does a little shivery thing, like she's allergic to death or something.

We are not going to get along, that much is crystal clear. I draw in a deep breath to cap my rising blood pressure and curse myself in silence for making that God-awful resolution to hold my temper. I make an effort to keep my voice light, but it comes out too high, like I've been sucking on a helium balloon.

"I'm confused, Mrs. Starbaugh. I dropped Casey off myself after lunch. She's not home?"

"No. She's not. Obviously. Otherwise, why would I be here?" Her lips are all puckery, like she's spent her life sucking on a lemon wedge. Poor, poor, Casey. She was born to a woman that doesn't own a good mood.

"I dropped her back home at one. I watched her go inside and everything. Maybe she's at one of her friends'? Have you tried calling Casey's cell, or Josie?" I think about how if this woman knew her daughter at all, she'd have checked in with her friends first. Then again, maybe Mrs. Starbaugh doesn't have her friends' phone numbers.

I try to help, to think back on the few hours we spent together before we packed her things into the back of my truck and drove across town. She'd been quiet, damn quiet. I assumed I'd worn her out with all the cooking and gardening around here. Casey had said she had a big project due for history on Monday. I told her it seemed cruel to assign homework over Christmas break, and she agreed. "Hey, remember, she has that big project? Could she be at the library?"

"I don't know. I suppose." Mrs. Starbaugh scans what she can of my cottage from the entry hall. Her black eyebrows arch. Is she surprised to find out I don't live in an oversized coffin?

I catch myself staring at her eyebrows and it hits me that they are fake, fake, fake! She drew them on with a black crayon. Oh, my goodness! I shiver and take a step back. I don't know why that strikes me as funny, but a bitty laugh gurgles out of my lips before I can do a thing about it. I cover my mouth and hope she didn't notice. I straighten up my posture and try to get serious about helping the woman track down Casey.

"I didn't go into her room. We arrived home around three. After we unpacked, I noticed I hadn't seen Casey. I even yelled for her!

Why would I look in her room? When she didn't respond, I assumed she was still at your … house." Mrs. Starbaugh wanders into the living room and she puts her hand over her nose like she caught a quick whiff of something awful.

"Would you like me to call her friends?" I ask, trying to do something to help.

She fusses with her phone, "No, I'll send them a text. God, why does Casey always turn off her phone? If I could just reach her on the phone, all of this would be resolved by now," she huffs.

Mrs. Starbaugh stares into her phone screen, worry lines cracked across her pale forehead. Somewhere between the front door and the kitchen, her irritation has turned into genuine worry. I say, "Maybe we should check your house first. She's probably fast asleep on her bed. I worked her to the bone around here." She looks at me and nods.

Without giving her a chance to think it through, I follow her to the black BMW sedan parked in the driveway, grateful she's caught me in tidy clothes and spiffy shoes. I don't think she'd let me ride with her if I was wearing my work things.

Maybe she'd make me ride in the back seat on an old towel like a dirty dog. I bite back another laugh and remind myself this is no funny matter. Casey needs me. But in the silence, I think about how this icy woman treats her own flesh and blood! She unpacked without tracking that girl down for a hug first? Hmm.

I spend the car ride tamping down angry thoughts in silence. It was my New Year's resolution to hold my temper. I didn't realize how soon I'd be tested. My hot head steams up the passenger window. I try to crack it open with the slick black button, but it seems she's got the passenger controls turned off. I add "control freak" to the list of things I dislike about Mrs. Starbaugh.

Itching to get out of this tin can, I tap my hands on the front of my khakis. I wish I'd thought to call Josie before we left the cottage. We pull into the driveway of Casey's house. Only a few lights are on in the house. "Where's the mister?" I ask.

"He's staying a few more days in California. Drew doesn't go back to school for another few days."

I take my shoes off near the front door, and Mrs. Starbaugh stares down at my stocking feet with a puckered up face. Nope, we are definitely not going to be friends.

She leads me down a long hall to Casey's room. It's the only bedroom on the ground level of the house. The hallway wall space is chock full of framed pictures. Hard as I try, I can't find a single one of Casey. What the hell is wrong with these people?

Mrs. Starbaugh flicks on the lights and we step inside Casey's bedroom. Floor to ceiling, everything is a shade of purple, except for the white furniture. It's a girly girl room. I can't picture a boy wanting to step inside. But, then again, maybe that's the point. Her bed's made and a pile of dirty clothes lies on top. I recognize the outfits because she wore them when she stayed with me. Her mother fingers the clothes and extracts an aqua cashmere sweater.

"Well, she was here. Just like I said," I add.

Mrs. Starbaugh frowns. She fingers the aqua sweater and slings it over a shoulder. "I didn't give her permission to take this. It's mine."

I need distance from this cold, unfeeling woman or I'm gonna blow my resolution, so help me God. My hands itch to slide around her throat, so I take a step backward and bump against Casey's desk.

On top of a flowery desk blotter is a note. I reach for it and Mrs. Starbaugh snatches it away. She reads it to herself and rants under her breath. I can't make out what she's saying. She wads up the letter and tosses it to the floor. I add 'drama queen' to my growing list.

"Well, she'll come crawling back after a few nights out in this weather. Serves her right!" Her voice comes out tight and strained with emotion. She wipes at her eyes and I wonder if the Ice Queen is melting.

And with that, Mrs. Starbaugh, having forgotten me completely, turns and leaves Casey's room, her shaking hand clutched around her silent cell. The aqua sweater flops off her shoulder to the carpet, but she doesn't seem to notice.

I grab the paper wad off the floor, and iron it out with my hand so it lies mostly flat again. I read:

Hello Parental Units,

Yes, I've run away. You might not notice for a week or so, but I'm gone and have been since January 2 at roughly 3:30, in case you need that information for the police report.

My time with Grace was eye opening. She was nice to me and seemed to genuinely enjoy my company. What a difference from my reality under this roof. I'm not the star of anything, so it's like I don't exist. I won't go back to living like a ghost in this house, so I'm going to live in a park somewhere until I can figure out my next step. I'll be deeply touched if you actually look for me. And I'm glad Drew's team lost!

Casey

The letter oozes with immaturity, though I have to laugh at the girl's brash gumption. She could work on the delivery a bit, but she's got spunk. I guess she decided it was time to stir things up a little.

"I suppose I'll show myself out then," I mumble to no one in particular.

Before I leave Casey's room, I check the bulletin board that hangs above her desk. A black pen and ink hand-drawn comic is pinned in the center of the otherwise blank corkboard. A little anime Casey rests inside a pup tent with a giant smile across her face.

"She's been planning this for some time." I touch the wide-eyed drawing of my friend, and then turn and leave.

I stand on the wet sidewalk and look up to the sky, letting fat raindrops hit my face. I reach inside my purse for keys when it strikes me: I didn't drive. Casey's mom brought me here.

I wish I'd paid more attention on the drive in because I'm lost in a maze of development houses. All the houses look the same, especially in the dark. I know I'm not far from a main street. If only I can make my way out of this knot of houses, I can hop a bus. I wish I'd brought my cell phone.

I get about a half block away and a car honks at my back. It's Mrs. S. She pulls to the curb with a sharp jerk and I freak for a split second. *She's gonna run me over!*

But, then a tinted window rolls down and she shouts, "I'm sorry, Grace! Let me drive you home." Her eyes look softer than before, like sadness blurred all the sharp edges. I climb in the car and we drive to Lakefront Cemetery.

"God. You must think I'm a monster," she says clutching the steering wheel, "the way I acted when I first came to your house." She clutches the wheel and talks. "It's just that Casey's little attempts to get attention are nothing new. Ever since Drew was called out for being exceptional at football, she's been complaining about being..." Her words stop and she sobs. I root a tissue out of my purse and hand it to her. "I'm sorry. I was going to say, she complains about getting lost in the shuffle. Oh, God. What if she really is lost?"

She parks in my driveway and I say, "If you don't hear from her friends soon, I'd recommend you call the police. And if I hear anything, I will call you. Thanks for the ride." The woman reaches across the glove box to give me an awkward half hug and I do my best to receive it.

The back door to my cottage hangs open and I slip off my shoes and pour myself a half-glass of Merlot left over from the bottle Grant and I shared over dinner the other night. I sit next to the fireplace and call Josie. It's eight o'clock. Time to find Casey.

I don't remember falling asleep, but when I wake up the phone is clutched in my palm. I read the time and it says 11:30 p.m. No one's sent a text, but I keep the porch light on in case Casey shows up on my doorstep. My brain knows she's fine. She probably scouted out a place to camp weeks ago, but I'm still heartsick. That girl has become some kind of precious to me.

When the phone rings, it is Grant. He tells me they haven't heard anything, but he has his fingers crossed that Casey will show up at school tomorrow, which is today, according to the clock on the mantel that says midnight. Grant says something sweet and tells me to sleep well and I click off the phone.

After we hang up and I get to thinking about what a good man Grant is. He is funny and kind. Last night over dinner, he told me a story about an eccentric client he's working with to design a waterfront mansion. The guy shows up every meeting with a posse of people, one a former Navy Seal who sports a Glock on his hip and another, an overeager videographer who rolls hours of tape every day. His job has its challenges, no doubt.

I opened up and shared with him about the time I fell into an open grave. I managed to climb out with the help of a slightly freaked out visitor who heard the shouts and thought it was his grandmother screaming at him from the grave about the player piano he broke when he was five. We laughed and agreed Grant's job might be a little less dangerous than mine.

By the end of the meal, our conversation turned serious. He shared the story of how he and Sarah first met. They literally ran into each other while walking across campus in college. He knocked all her books to the ground, and as he scrambled to gather them up he knocked his head on a stone bench. He was bleeding, so Sarah took him to the student hospital. The two of them laughed for years about their first date that ended in three stitches and a heavy dose of Ibuprofen.

I don't know why, but I told him about my husband, and how happy our life had started. Soon though, all the love ended up crumbling away like sand from your feet when it dries. I mentioned how my husband drank too much and sometimes it turned him into a monster. He apologized for what my husband had done to me. Grant told me not to apologize for the tears that ran down my face. He said I should be proud of my own determination and strength.

As I clutch the phone to my chest, I start to cry a mix of sad and happy tears. I am like a broken vase. It has taken years to glue myself back together piece by piece. And now, someone has put a flower inside and added a splash of water to keep it alive. It feels good, but the water leaks a little. I fall asleep right there on the couch, phone clutched to my heart, and the fire still crackling in the hearth.

It's the bitter cold that wakes me. My whole body trembles and I can't figure out where I am. It's dark and wet. I reach a hand down and grip damp clumps of grass with my frozen fingers. I have a kink in my neck and my face hurts from being smashed against something hard. I straighten up.

It is Ettore's tombstone. Did I walk here in my sleep? My sweatshirt and leggings are damp through and I have bare feet. "Damn. I'm gonna catch a cold." I stand up feeling like the Tin Man in *The Wizard of Oz*. I have to work to get the rust out of my joints.

Past the iron fence that runs past the children's cemetery, I see the top of an orange tent. It glows from within, but I don't see any movement inside. Casey must be sound asleep.

I slip into the shadows toward the cottage and rehearse what I will say to her mother on the phone when I call to let her know her baby's all right. I plan breakfast in my head for Casey, portable food that I can pack into a basket for the girl: muffins, a breakfast burrito, and a thermos of hot chocolate.

That ought to do. I smile, and the kinks across my body melt away.

CASEY SURVIVES

"YOU GUYS! I can't breathe! Let me go," I say, not really meaning it. It's the first time I've felt warm in 24 hours and I'm the last to break free from the group hug.

"Casey, we're just relieved you're alright," Josie says. She and Blaze let go and I look down at my feet, happy my awkward bangs block my face. We stand by our lockers at Heritage Prep. Grace dropped me off a few minutes ago. She promised she wouldn't tell my mother where I'm hiding for now. But, she's only giving me until four this afternoon to figure out a plan, and then she says she'll call my mother herself.

Blaze unloads his backpack and watches me at the same time. "So, Casey. Have you called home yet? They must be worried."

I kick at the gray wool carpet. "Yeah, right. Worried. I'm sure they're out of their minds. I was counting on them not noticing at all for a few days. Now I'm not sure what to do. Do you ground someone for running away? It's like beating your dog for digging under the fence after he turns up home again. Doesn't seem right."

Josie brushes my hair back with both hands and kisses my forehead like I'm a little kid. And I love it. I smile and try to talk but my voice won't cooperate.

She says, "I went out looking for you last night. Dad and me. He called all the runaway shelters in case you showed up there. But all night, I had my fingers crossed that you were at Grace's."

I'm overcome with love for these people. What's wrong with me that this isn't enough? So what if my own blood doesn't care about me? I'm fine as long as I have the Baby Group and Grace.

Josie glances at her phone and says, "Man, I wish Seth still went to Heritage. He is freaking out with relief that you're safe! Mr. Anthony gave the King County sheriffs an informal heads-up last night. Seth wants to know if you need him to look up Washington state emancipation laws." She tucks her phone into the charger and slams her locker door shut with her hip.

I gather up my notebook and calculator, then shut my locker. "That seems a little drastic for now. I'll go back, eventually. I guess I already got what I was trying for. Now maybe they won't completely ignore me. You know what Grace said to me this morning?" I soften my voice into my best impression of her. "She said, 'I've got trees that hang onto their dead leaves. It takes a good storm to shake those leaves free. Maybe you're like my trees; you needed a good gust to blow off the dead stuff. But, the thing is, you caused the storm, girl.'"

The bell rings and we scatter for class. As I turn into my algebra class, there is an announcement over the intercom. I cringe and silently hope it isn't about me.

"Pardon the interruption. Would Blaze Maki please report to the office? Thank you."

Blaze freezes in the doorway to class and frowns. He shrugs a shoulder at me and spins on his heels, disappearing down the hallway. I watch him jog away and cross my fingers.

This year is off to a very rocky start!

BLAZE AND THE WRATH OF GOD

"YOU CAN'T LEAVE ME. Where would I find the strength to go on without you?" My mother's choked voice sputters into the hallway and stops me in my tracks.

I knew it was bad when the Head of School drove me to the hospital herself, so I ran all the way to the ER. It comes as a blow to see my fiercely strong mother doubled over onto my dad. Noisy medical equipment surrounds his bed. Tubes crawl up both his arms and poke inside his nose. He doesn't look anything like Dad. I clutch the doorjamb to keep from falling inside the sterile white hospital room.

She has her head across my dad's chest and whispers secrets, releasing her pain in raspy bits. I try not to breathe, because I want to hear what she is saying–maybe need to hear it– as much as my dad, who struggles to live. I hover by the doorjamb out of sight to keep her talking.

"I brought this heart attack on you." I can barely hear her voice above the hum of the machines and the noises coming from the busy hallway.

She clutches a handful of tissues in one brown fist and grips my dad's hand with the other. "I should have walked away when I saw you in that church. I should have checked my temper. I wish I had it to do over."

She is talking about their fight last night, the third one since New Year's. She followed Dad and me to church and busted us at the end of the service. The worst part is Dad came into to church with me, said he wanted to give it a try himself. I should have talked him out of it, because that to a mess of trouble. My mother blames herself for his heart attack, but I am beginning to blame me.

Mother wipes her face down and stares at the ceiling. I duck behind the doorjamb and listen to her juicy sobs. She blows her nose and then chokes out, "God! I should have checked my temper the last fifteen years." I promised my dad I would defend him if she found out. I was consumed with Casey's disappearance last night, but still. I should have stepped in to defend Dad.

I jump as a hand touches my shoulder. I stifle a yelp and turn my head. It's Father James. He's about to say something when I press a finger to my lips and point inside the room, my black eyebrows knit together in a furry line. The sight of him in his black shirt and white collar gets my blood boiling. He put us on the prayer list at church, something about God bringing peace to our family. What good did that do? My dad is tethered to machines in the ER barely clinging to life. This isn't peace. Where's God now?

As per usual, Father James does the noble thing. He recedes down the hallway. I hope he's ready to wait a while, because I have things to tell him. Anger rises in my throat. I swallow and turn back to the hospital room. I want to tell him what I think of this God of his, one that would strike down a man who showed courage enough to stand up to his wife and attend church. But, right now, I need to listen to what my mother is saying to Dad.

My mother weeps at my dad's bedside. "Oh, honey. I know you think I'm strong, but I'm not. I'm just loud. It's you who holds this family together. Please don't die." My knees buckle and I clutch the doorjamb to keep from falling into the room.

"Excuse me," a woman in scrubs pushes a man in a wheelchair past and I step aside. Suddenly exhausted, I look for a chair. A woman in a white coat approaches and takes my elbow.

"Are you the son?" she asks. I nod.

She guides me by an elbow to a place across from his room that has seats. I slump into the closest one. "Your mother will be here in a moment. We need your father to ourselves for a little while. He's stable, but I can do my job better if I have more room to work," she says. Her voice is calm and soothing.

I try to choke out a 'thanks,' but can't. She seems to understand, as she wanders past me to where Father James sits, elbows on his knees, hands clasped together deep in prayer. She bends down to his ear and he rises to his feet, following the ER doctor into my father's room.

My mother's voice pierces the air. "No, I need to stay here with him!" And then she quiets. Moments later, Father James exits the room with a hand on her shoulder. As he speaks in soft words I can't make out to her, my mother listens. She nods, wipes her eyes with tissue and they walk over and sit next to me. Father James continues to speak to her, soft and gentle, and I find it hard to be as angry with him as I watch my mother's face grow smooth with peace.

He looks at me and mouths, "Are you okay?" I nod.

Father James puts an arm around my mother. "Oh, God. What if my temper killed him?" she says and fresh tears run down her face. Father slips a handkerchief, clean and white from his pocket, and my mother accepts it.

"Nonsense," he says. "You saved his life." I don't know the story of what happened.

I lean in. "He left the restaurant, didn't he?" Father James asks.

"Yes. He was making the specials list for the day and he said he didn't feel well." My mother wipes her nose. "I sent him home, told him I could do it. He needed to rest."

"Right. And you went back to the house and checked on him?" Father asks.

"Mmhm. I found him in bed. He said his stomach hurt and his back. He's never sick! That man hasn't had a sick day in his life," she explains. "I knew it was bad when he started telling me he felt like he was going to die." Her hands shake and I reach out to her and she clutches one of my hands in hers. "I called the ambulance then."

Father James says, "And as I said, you saved his life." She shakes her head.

"No, I didn't." She peers at me like she is deciding something and then says, "That poor man spent fifteen years trying not to make me mad. Oh, sometimes he'd give his opinion on things, but then I'd steamroller over him and he'd just...decide to agree. That's got to take a toll on a person over time."

I wipe the traces of white tissue from her black cheek. "Father James is right, you saved him," I say. She squeezes my hand.

"Naw. He's paying for my mistakes. He married a woman who sleeps with one eye open, even when she's nestled safe at home. He deserved better than me, better than this. The thing I never told you, Blaze, is that I've been fooled in my life. Fooled into loving a God that never loved me back! That was the worst of it." She looks to Father James and I expect him to jump in to defend his religion, but he stays silent.

Her words hit home and my body trembles with emotion. "But, now looking back, I never deserved His love. I am a bad person. I am too opinionated, too bossy. I hurt the people I love. No wonder God doesn't love me." She stares at Father James, daring him to challenge her. I wait for him to step in with the perfect words to make my mother see how much she is loved by God, by Dad, by me, by everyone but he just sits there quiet. Every second he stays silent, my blood boils.

"Mom, I love you. I know Dad loves you."

She kisses the side of my head. "You're a good boy."

Father James clears his throat, "Mrs. Maki, there is so much ignorance– no, ignorance isn't the right word–misunderstanding in your opinion. God made you the way you are; you are one of His perfect children. He made you strong and bold for a reason. Can't you see that those are the traits that have carried you through this life? And as far as you believing that you are not good enough for God to love, well, none of us deserves His love. We are all flawed, broken in some way. But He loves us anyway. That is how He shows His grace." Father James pauses. His expression is tight and tortured. "You may not want to hear this, Mrs. Maki, but I feel pressed by the Holy Spirit to speak it. God is using this situation to bring you closer to Him. Maybe He tried in more subtle ways to get your attention, get you to look up and acknowledge Him, and those things didn't work. He went big this time. I would suggest you take a step toward Him before this gets any more serious. I will be praying for you and your family." He rises to his feet and walks down the hall.

I send a glare down the hallway to Father James. God did this to get my mother's attention? He is sick. My dad might die because he defied my mother and went to church. My dad took a giant leap toward

God, and where did it get him? Almost dead? Is that how God works? I hate Him and I hate you for making me wish for something I could never have because it isn't real!

I hope Father James feels the hate that burns behind my eyes. I'm filled with steel-colored hate. I can't stand to be here another minute, so I get up and walk to the puny institutional window at the end of the hall instead.

The sky outside is clear and blue. If you didn't know any better, you would think it was a hot summer day in the Pacific Northwest, not January. But, I lay my hand against the glass and the truth sears cold against my palm. It's below freezing and there's not a cloud in the sky. No clouds means no moisture. No moisture means no snow. No snow means worthless cold. Worthless cold. Worthless cold like what nests in my angry, frozen heart.

I glance down to the street where a homeless person pushes a cart that carries everything he owns, strapped down with bungee cords. He searches through a garbage can for what? Dinner? Something to burn to make heat tonight? I clench my jaw and think, *I don't care.* I ignore the tears that sting at the back of my eyes and harden my heart. I don't see anyone helping me survive today, so why should I give a damn about strangers right now? Screw that!

My hands shake. I should have stood in front of my dad when she attacked him yesterday. I said from the beginning I could defend myself. I said I was strong enough to stand up for myself. I am! Or I thought I was.

I wander back to my dad's room where medical people are busy helping. I squat outside the doorjamb and listen to the beeps and gasps of the machines. He's lying on that bed because I wasn't as strong as I thought. I bend my head into my arms and fume. But like the sky outside, my eyes are dry. No tears come. Something's broken inside. I sit on the floor and rest my head on my knees.

My legs are numb. I have no idea how long I've been sitting here. Hours. I know I can't stand to listen to the machines anymore, but I don't have the strength to rise. I manage to get across the hall, where I fold myself into a stiff sofa in the waiting area. I fall asleep and have terrible dreams.

A sharp, keening squeal wakes me. The sound comes from my dad's room. The machines shriek for help. I try getting up and joining the nurses and doctors that rush inside, but my numb, worthless legs refuse to hold me and I fall backward like an idiot to the hard sofa. My cheeks burn with shame as I struggle to stand. And that's when I see them down the hall, the Baby Group. They walk toward me, arms full of flowers, and balloons, and stuffed bears.

Relief washes over me. Maybe now I can gather the strength to stand.

GRACE DREADS
HOSPITALS

MY BUM IS FROZEN to this metal bench I sit on outside the hospital waiting for Grant to arrive with the kids. Mr. Maki had a heart attack this morning. Since his condition has been stabilized, Grant wanted us to bring the kids for a visit after school, not so much to see Mr. Maki, more to comfort Blaze and his mother.

I haven't stepped foot in a hospital in over a decade, ever since my heart was broken forever. The plain truth is, they terrify me now. As I wait, I grow more nervous by the second. Even the smell of the brownies that oozes from the plastic container next to me can't ease the butterflies fluttering in my stomach. Maybe brownies were the wrong thing to bring for people, should've brought antacids.

Try as I might, I can't bring myself to walk through those automatic doors. The thought of stepping inside makes me shudder. You'd think a woman that buries bodies for a living wouldn't be bothered by anything medical. But hospitals bother me. They bother me a lot.

People come here with fingers crossed, hoping to find answers, a solution, or a cure. People come here to be healed, but the reality is that some of those people won't come out alive. I've seen firsthand how all the fancy tools and clever doctors in the world can fail to make a heart beat again. Hospitals aren't a place of hope to me.

At first glance, a cemetery doesn't seem like it should inspire hope. It is an ending. It's a place to visit someone you lost and still miss. But for me personally, it is a place of stories, the stories of lives that were lived that should be remembered. In that way, a cemetery is a hopeful place. It means that your life mattered. You made a difference. Maybe you didn't win a gold medal or write a Pulitzer Prize-winning novel, but someone was touched by your life and made a little something out of theirs as a result. A cemetery doesn't promise anything, only holds the bones of the people we've loved. But, if we take time to linger, those bones may speak. And if we listen, those words might teach.

I am about to pry a brownie out from under the lid out of pure bad habit, not appetite, when the Jameson family thunders toward me from the parking lot. Owen reaches the bench first and wraps his arms around my middle as best he can in that silver marshmallow-shaped coat of his. Josie says hello and Grant takes a seat to my right, never peeling his eyes from my face. I've told him how I feel about hospitals. He gives me a soft kiss on the cheek and rests a hand on top of my fidgety fingers. He bends down to me. "Thank you for meeting us, Grace."

Owen is midway through a song about K-I-S-S-I-N-G when Josie interrupts him. "I don't mean to be rude, but I want to go see Blaze. Who's coming with me?" Owen follows her.

She heads for the hospital door then turns back. "Do you think it's a good idea for Owen to spend time in there?" I ask.

Grant rises to his feet, but before he can respond, I offer in a desperate rush, "I'd be happy to watch after him. We could sit in the truck and get his homework out of the way. What do you think of that, Owen?"

The boy jumps up and down looking like a piston in his round silver coat. "Yeah, Dad! I don't want to go in there. Hospitals smell gross! Can I stay with Grace?"

Grant strokes the stubble on his chin and nods. "Hospitals aren't my favorite place either, but I think we need to support the Maki family."

Josie huffs impatiently and says, "I can't wait. I've got to go be there for Blaze." She turns and storms through the doors, her hair flying out behind her like a bright flame. That girl is all fire and ice, no doubt about it. I wish I had half her strength!

Owen, Grant, and I watch wordlessly as the doors slide closed.

Grant breaks the silence. His voice is gentle, as if he might scare me off if he's too loud.

"Grace, I sat by Sarah's bed watching the life drain out of her. I'd cringe before every shift change because it meant another nurse had to get up to speed on things, even Sarah's name. I'd watch them read the paperwork and do the mental math. We didn't have days; we had *hours* left together."

He absently strokes my hand and looks down at the ground. "When that happened, the Maki family was there for us. They looked after the kids, stocked our fridge with food. They put out the cans on garbage day. I don't know everything they did, but I know I couldn't have made it through without their support. I need to be there for them now. And, I don't think I can do it without you by my side. If I'm asking too much, please tell me."

I rise, grab his hand, pull Owen by a silver puffy sleeve off the bench and walk through the automatic doors.

"We'd better ask at the information desk for his room." I say, trying to be brave.

Grant smiles at me and mouths a silent thank you.

As we exit onto the fifth floor I almost collide with Casey. She looks sideways at me. Her face reads desperate. I see Mrs. Starbaugh, and she catches my eye.

She approaches and says a quiet hello to me. She holds me by the shoulders and whispers, "Thanks for finding her. But, I have to be hard on her. You understand?"

Casey backs away as her mother approaches, holding up a hand, "God, Mother. Wasn't the lecture on the ride to the hospital enough? Back. Off." Mrs. Starbaugh pulls Casey into a nook by the elevators.

"You ungrateful girl! Go ahead and move out of my house. See how that works out for you," she barks.

I'm stuck between a rock and a hard place. I want to run interference between Casey and her mother and feel the need to climb back in the elevator and push the 'down' button.

Casey Gets
the Boot

WE STAND NOSE TO NOSE. Spit flies from her angry mouth into my face as she hisses about what an ungrateful child I am, careful to keep her voice down so the rest of the hospital can't hear her rant. As if enough isn't already happening in the crowded corridor.

Chaos swirls around us as every person with a badge responds to a code red in Mr. Maki's room. They've cleared out the family and friends to the waiting room at the end of the hall. I'd be thankful for the distractions if it weren't for the terrible reality of my life.

I look down the hall where I imagine the Baby Group huddles together in corner chairs, whispering, consoling one another. I long to be with them, but my mother's whispered criticisms cut that wish in half.

"Your life is so easy, Cassandra. Too easy. It's our fault, we spoiled you. You've had life handed to you on a silver platter. You don't work for your school tuition, your food, your phone, any of it." She doesn't even stop to take a breath.

"When I was a little girl in China, my family expected me to work dawn to dusk. And, I had to be the top student or else they would pull me out. I had to get up before the sun to work in the bakery. If I wasn't working there, I was cracking the books. I'd study until my eyes stung. There was no such thing as free time."

My mother sounds like a Pekinese, yipping and snapping. Her face is red and contorted with rage. Strangers call her beautiful, but I think she looks like a rabid lap dog.

"Your problem is you have too much free time to whine about your life. Now, look at your brother, Drew. He's too busy making something of his life to catalog the ways we've short-changed him as our son. Why can't you be more like Drew?

"He was grateful for thirteen years of private school and he shows it by making top marks. He worked hard as an athlete and earned a full scholarship to the university saving us thousands of dollars every year. He brings honor to our family. And what do you bring? Nothing! You bring us nothing but grief," she shakes her head and sighs.

I bite my lip and let her blather until the wave has passed. My glance wanders to the overstuffed backpack at my feet. It is the bag that contains the supplies I need to survive on my own. My mother sneers at the muddy, holey bag and sniffs her nose in disgust. She draws in a deep breath. Instead of running away from her during the pause like I've done in the past, I surprise myself and stand firm. She watches me, waiting maybe for me to say something or flee. I am not apologizing. I didn't do anything wrong.

She draws a deep breath, getting ready for the final kill and I find I am pulsing with white, hot anger. "Mother, how dare you compare me to Drew! You treat him like a little prince. As far back as I can remember, you've gone to his practices, his games, his award ceremonies. When's the last time you came to my school for an award ceremony?" She puckers up her face and stares at the tiled floor. "Yeah, that's what I thought. Well, I'm sick of being nothing to you and Dad. I'm sick of it. I hate you!" I scream the words and clench my hands into fists. I want to smack the wall. I want her to yell back, and show she cares. But, when she speaks, her voice comes out calm and even, which makes me even madder.

"Well, Casey. If you feel that way, you can find somewhere else to live. And if you want to come home, you'll have to apologize first." She glances at me and I scowl. She turns and stomps down the hall to the elevators, not once looking back. She peppers the down button and stands rigid at the elevators, as if willing herself not to turn around.

It's not about me. It's not about me. It's not about me, I think as I choke back tears. I limp on shaky legs to the waiting room where I find Blaze, Josie and Seth. Seth's dad sits next to Mrs. Maki and Mr. Jameson. Josie scoots over a seat so I can be between her and Blaze. Someone touches my back. Josie tucks a piece of hair behind my ear and I cry. I can't hold back anymore.

I sit inside their cocoon and weep, partly for Mr. Maki, but mostly for myself. When I've purged all the self pity, I take a shuddering breath, wipe away the snot and tears with my sleeve, and eat the brownie I'm handed on a tidy napkin.

I think back to my fight with my mother. I remember something about seeing Grace and Owen. "Hey, where did Grace and your brother go?"

Josie says, "When Mr. Maki coded, my dad asked Grace to take Owen home. He doesn't need to see this side of life, not yet at least."

Between bites, I ask after Mr. Maki. The stint they put in earlier in the OR to open up his mostly blocked artery didn't work. He is in surgery now where they will try to find a better fix.

I almost start to cry again but stop myself. Instead, I reach for Blaze's hand. He rests his head on my shoulder and we stay like that for a time. "I'm so sorry, Blaze," I tell him.

"Thank you. Sorry you and your mom got into it," he says. I watch the adults across the room, the men trying to do their best to be there for Mrs. Maki. I'm glad I have my friends with me and I'm glad we're here for Blaze.

I prop my feet on my backpack. "What's better do you think? Going on with life as usual even though things are all wrong? Or taking a chance and stirring things up on the off chance that might make life better?"

"Can I wait to answer that? Say after my Dad comes out of surgery?" asks Blaze.

"Absolutely," I answer.

Seth glances to the clump of adults and says, "Man, I think for me I have to vote for, God, I don't know."

Josie tugs at his sleeve. "Come on, answer! Safe or change?"

"Change, then. Doesn't mean I have to be relaxed about the changes, right? I'm thinking about my parents." Seth brings his voice down to a hush. "Mom is so happy; so is Dad. It's nice to see them together again. But, then there's a part of me that worries about what happens if this doesn't work out."

I smile. "That's called being guardedly optimistic. I guess that's what I am, too. It was awful to listen to my mother. I officially have no place to call home, but even though it scares the heck out of me, I feel like it's better than living in that house like a ghost." Blaze gives me a side hug.

"You can come live at our house," Josie offers.

"Or mine," Seth says.

Blaze shrugs. "Gonna have to delay my offer. We're sort of up to our necks in drama right now."

"Thank you," I say to my friends feeling grateful and sentimental. "You are my favorite people in the world, and it's terrible that I haven't said it more."

As the Baby Group squeezes me in a collective hug, I feel Blaze pull away from us. His mother stands at his shoulder. Her round brown face has deep lines etched across it.

Her eyes are bloodshot and her voice comes out in a quiver as she says, "Honey, you need to come with me." I hope for the best, but his strong mother seems sad and drained.

Blaze hangs onto her shoulder and lets her lead him down the hall to his father's room.

The Baby Group clutches one another and whispers wishes to the sky. Father James joins us in the waiting room and hums, then whispers a religious song:

> *Are we weak and heavy-laden,*
> *Cumbered with a load of care?*
> *Precious Savior, still our refuge—*
> *Take it to the Lord in prayer;*
> *Do thy friends despise, forsake thee?*
> *Take it to the Lord in prayer;*
> *In His arms He'll take and shield thee,*
> *Thou wilt find a solace there.*

The song and companionship settle around me like fairy dust and my bones start to warm. The cold that had burrowed deep inside me since running away yesterday is slowly thawing. My eyelids feel heavy. After spreading a sweater across the next chair, I give in to the weariness and lay down to close my eyes a second.

"Casey, wake up, honey," Grace whispers in my ear. "We need to take you home. It's late."

Someone shakes my shoulder softly, and as I begin to wake, I realize it is Grace. I open my eyes a crack and see her gazing down at me. The round light fixture in the ceiling glows behind her head making Grace look like an angel with a halo. I try to remember where I am. I'm still at the hospital, but it is quiet now.

"Oh my God! How long was I out? What's happening with Mr. Maki? Did he —?" I can't say the word.

"No, no. He's gonna be fine, just fine. The doctors got him stabilized. He's sleeping. We sent Blaze and his mother home to get some rest. Father James is spending the night in the chair next to Mr. Maki's bed. He'll call if there is any change, but things look good, Casey. The doctors expect a slow, but full recovery. They're saying it's a miracle. But, now it's time to get you home. I'll drive you. Do you have a house key or should we call your mother on the way?" Grace asks.

My gut clinches and I wrap my arms around myself. "I don't have anywhere to go. My mother told me not to come home. Ever." I pull the sweater off the chairs and wrap it around myself. I glance toward the dirty backpack that contains my worldly possessions and wish that I'd never woken up. I squint my eyes shut.

"Well, I wouldn't have changed the sheets so soon if I'd known all this was about to transpire. But, you're welcome to come back to the cottage. I'll put you up until your mother comes to her senses." Grace swings my backpack across her shoulders and offers me an arm for support.

JOSIE'S FIELD TRIP TO BAIN'S HOMESTEAD

WITH LOWLAND SNOW in the forecast, Dad, Owen, and I pile into the car for a hurry-scurry trip to Tumwater, Washington, a small city south of the state capital. I hope to find a cold, hard trail of facts that will show that Bain MacLaren wasn't a witch and then restore her good name. I'm in search of documents that might pinpoint the location of the MacLaren homestead and reveal the first names of her husband and daughter.

I want to walk in her footsteps as best I can, and comb for facts about the original homesteaders. I hope to find proof that corroborates the Mayor's letter that stated her husband returned to Ireland with their daughter and left Bain behind to face her execution alone.

In addition to the fact-finding, I actually have a personal goal today. I feel like I've been going through the motions with Bain, thinking of her more as a project and less as a human being. Sure, my anger is genuine when I contemplate the community that fingered her as a witch, and then stoned her to death. But, I don't have any sense of Bain as a mother and a wife. I hope today changes that and I come away understanding Bain the woman, the wife and mother abandoned by her family in her time of need.

Tumwater, or as it was known in the 1800s, New Market, is recognized as Washington state's first community. Nestled at the foot of the spectacular Tumwater Falls along the banks of the Deschutes River, the settlers were drawn to the area's abundant natural resources.

Last night, I printed a list of local historic sites that seemed relevant to the MacLarens. Because of their extensive collection of pioneer records, the Henderson House Museum is our first stop. The two-story house was constructed in the 1860s, and includes modern amenities that New Market's settlers would never have known. Regardless, it is easy to picture life as it was for families nearly two centuries ago as we wander through the house.

As we get our bearings in the museum, a lady in period costume approaches. She introduces herself as Elizabeth, but demands we call her Lizzie; she explains that she is the docent on shift. Her white gingham bonnet bobs on top of her wiry brown hair as she regales us with stories of the pioneer days.

Lizzie sways back and forth in her floor-length yellow dress as she lists the ways pioneers perished on the 2,200-mile trek from Missouri to Oregon. I love the information but watching her makes me a little dizzy, so I read interpretive signs as I listen.

On a roll, our docent throws herself into describing the brutal conditions that the brave pioneers faced at the end of the trail. It wasn't an Eden that waited for them on the West Coast; it was tree-riddled farming acreage, angry natives, harsh weather, and crippling illness.

"How awful do you think life must've been for 'em back home to uproot and come out West?" Lizzie asks.

Owen chirps in, "Man, it must've been awful. Either that or they didn't do their research before they left!"

"Young man, this was long before the internet. Yup. Word of mouth was all these folks had. And maybe a government that made things sound better than they really were, because they needed warm bodies on that land to claim it for the United States." Lizzie looks satisfied with herself. "So, what brings you to Tumwater?" she asks.

I tell her, while Owen's eyes glaze over, about the tombstone I rubbed on Halloween, the Celtic symbols I identified across its face, the speculation that Bain was a witch, my correspondence with genealogists in Ireland, and our discovery of the secret drawer in Bain's tombstone. Lizzie nods her head, and her fair freckled cheeks blanch white. She rubs her hands in a way that makes me feel nervous.

After I wrap up, she scurries to a back office and shouts questions from the deepest recesses of the house. When she reemerges, she hands me paperwork that lists a Mr. and Mrs. McLaren in a roster of New Market's first inhabitants. I still don't have a first name for Bain's husband, but a charge races up my arms anyway.

"The originals are in the care of the Smithsonian. You can keep that. It's a copy," she says, handing me the paper. McLaren, not MacLaren, I read.

For the next hour, until Owen's iTouch battery loses its charge, my dad and I sift through logs of old paperwork, copies bound in leather, looking for the address of their homestead, but come up empty. Lizzie tidies up our stacks and says, "Chances are, it's in the original New Market settlement, which is still called the New Market neighborhood today. It lies in the center of Tumwater. Here, I'll draw you a map." She sketches a rough layout of the roads that will lead us from here to there.

My heart pounds as she hands over the map and suggests we take a side trip to the Pioneer Calvary Cemetery. She adds a small star on her map and hands it back to me. "It was officially established in 1873, but it'd been holding the dead for at least twenty years before that. So, odds are it was the original resting place of …the witch…before they moved her up north." She pauses. "Now, did I hear you mention there was a secret drawer?" I notice she rubs her hands together again and wonder if the subject of Bain makes her feel unsettled.

I shut the leather-bound book and pull out the manila file from my purse to show her. When I look at Lizzie again, I'm worried she might have a heart attack. She's red all over. And for some crazy reason I think of that old joke, "What's black and white and read all over?"

She skims the relics, being careful not to touch anything but the edges of the old parchment. I ask her if she wants to make copies, and she ducks into the back office and returns with my documents. She hands them to me absently as she reads through her copy, mumbling to herself. I tuck the originals away and before I can start toward the exit behind Dad and Owen, Lizzie tugs at me.

She takes a quick glance behind her shoulder, and then puts a finger to her lips in a silent hush. She has to stand on tippy toes to reach my ear. "I know about the witch," she whispers. She watches Owen who is deep in concentration with his favorite app. "Don't want the boy to overhear." My dad is still nose down in a leather-bound volume. He is snapping pictures of documents with his phone. We step into the entry room away from Owen's ears and Dad's eyes.

Her voice comes out in a throaty rasp that sends a chill down my spine. "My mother told me stories, the same stories her mother told her and her mother told her. Bain was a witch, I tell you. She was a stone cold witch!"

For some reason, I think about the puzzle box that sits on my desk back home. I didn't want to take it here, the last piece of my mother. I let the tickle in the back of my mind fade away as Lizzie shares the ancient lore. "She murdered the village wives with her black spells and kept the husbands for herself. Rumor has it that all her black magic ruined their homestead. Her husband–Jacob, I think his name was–couldn't get a darn thing to grow on that land. Anyhow, you can't make a living off moss and weeds! Any idiot knows that. To this day that land sits barren."

"Aha!" I bark. "So, you do know where her homestead is!" I say.

Lizzy reddens. "Maybe it was near the Pioneer cabin, on that bare land in the park. My mama always told me to steer clear from that area. It still holds the evil that woman did in her lifetime. And you don't want to track any of that back to your life."

Her expression reads fear, raw fear, and I wonder what kind of horrible bedtime stories Lizzie heard as a child. "Don't go stirring her up again, Josie. She can reach you from beyond the grave. The folks of New Market learned that the hard way." She clutches the sleeve of my sweatshirt so tightly that it wrings taut across my arm and cuts off the blood flow. As I wrench my arm free, she looks down at her own hands. Without a word, she stumbles back into the recesses of the house. "I'm sorry. I didn't mean anything by it," she sputters.

I flee into the main room and my dad startles from his reading. "Come on, Dad. Let's go. Seems Lizzie has been drinking the same tainted Kool Aid as the rest of the town. She is convinced Bain's a witch," I say. Dad rises and joins my side, pulling Owen behind him like a floppy teddy bear.

"Your town brought bad luck on itself by killing an innocent woman! It's karma, baby. Google it!" *Crazy people*, I think as I storm down the wooden stairs to the street. I try my best to shut Weird Lizzie out of my mind as we drive to the cemetery, but her coarse whisper echoes in my head and sends ripples down my arms as we pull into the dark, wooded parking lot of the Pioneer Calvary Cemetery.

"Not much here, Josie," Dad mutters as he shepherds Owen out of the backseat.

That's an understatement. The cemetery is a small cobble of stones not much bigger than the parking lot next to it.

"Dad, can you take pictures of these interpretive signs?" I ask as I make my way across the bumpy earth. The graves are time worn and most are impossible to read. I do a quick thumbnail sketch of a stone that reminds me of Bain's, then climb back into the car. Dad hands me his old-school Nikon before turning the car toward our last stop of the day. My stomach aches for lunch. I can only hope the next stop goes just as fast.

Man, what is wrong with me? Here I am walking in Bain's footsteps and all I can do is count the minutes until lunch. I dismiss the guilt-laden thought as quickly as it forms. It's natural for me to dismiss this little town after what they did to Bain. No wonder I don't feel anything, I rationalize. My father rolls the car to a stop in a postage-stamp parking lot. We've reached the Pioneer Cabin.

Not the original but historically accurate, the cabin was built in the same way as those of the first settlers to the area. Peeled fir log sidewalls and split cedar shakes on the roof, crude cobbled stone chimney, and, even with the drone of traffic in the background, it is easy to imagine someone, even Bain, bustling inside these four walls cooking, sewing, watching after baby McLaren, and cleaning.

I have to question how a person six generations removed could dare call this brave, hardworking pioneer woman a witch. I feel a rise of emotion for Bain, the first of its kind since Halloween. I knead my jaw muscles and ball my hands into fists.

"Did Lizzie call you a stone cold witch? What's a stone cold witch?" I ask under my breath. Lizzie's whisperings fan the flames of my anger. There is a tickle of familiarity to the term 'stone cold witch,' but I can't find the link. All I can think about is how odd New Market's people must have been to resurrect witch rumors hundreds of years after the Salem Witch trials.

Perpetuating such vile, false rumors is such an ignorant thing to do! I run toward the back of the lot and Dad's Nikon slams against my back. I navigate through rocks and weeds to get to the giant gnarled cedar in the distance. I want nothing more than to sit under its branches and brood. I grit my teeth and sprint over the treacherous land.

As I run my dad yells, "Hey, Josie! We gotta head out. Owen needs a bathroom!"

I turn back to him and swallow down my anger before I holler, "I need to take a couple photos of the cabin. It'll just take a minute, I promise!"

Dad turns hand in hand with Owen and lopes toward the parking lot. I simmer. They can wait. This is more important! A surge of anger and impatience for Owen rises in my chest. I run faster toward the cedar knowing I'm on a short timer thanks to him.

I drop my things on the rocky soil below the cedar and take a series of photos of the cabin from across the field. I pull out my Moleskin journal and pen to make a quick thumbnail sketch when I think about poor Owen, waiting to go potty. I'm hit with a wave of guilt and I scurry to my feet, collect my scattered things, and run back toward the parking lot.

Don't do her bidding. It is such a soft whisper that I fear I'm either going bananas or a ghost is standing behind me. It is just Grace's words I hear repeated in my mind. The ones her uncle said when he talked about the Ghost Forest. Feeling nervous and vulnerable, I pivot and stare across the blank field. There is not a soul in sight besides my two guys in the parking lot.

It strikes me how the gnarled cedar I was standing beneath is a twin of the one that guards my mother's grave. For the second time, I register some tickle of familiarity. I stare over my shoulder at the tree as I run toward the parking lot, and my foot catches in a deep hole. My ankle twists and I fall onto the cold, hard ground. As the pain sears up my leg, my dad's camera falls free of my shoulder and bounces across the ground, giving off a sudden flash.

A flock of birds bursts out from behind the cedar, like a winged black mob. I don't know how I know it, but somewhere at my core I realize they are coming for me. I scoop up the camera by its wide strap and struggle to my feet. I limp as fast as I can manage on my sore ankle, but as the noise grows behind me I speed up.

I take a quick peek behind and see the black birds, crows, careening toward me. There must be a hundred of them. And the noise is so loud. I don't dare cover my ears because then I'm done for. I swallow down spit and tears and run for the car.

As I reach the cabin, I glance back again. Under the ancient cedar tree, stands a smoky black figure. The crows block my view, but as they move and flutter, I see the figure stoop over the cedar roots. She chisels at the hard earth with a rusty hand trowel. Her black hair flutters behind her as she spots me and, even from this distance, stares into me with mercury-colored eyes. She rises off the ground and points the sharp tip of the trowel and the birds caw and shriek, only feet away from me now. I tremble and my legs shake.

The mass of crows circles away from me and blows through her smoky form, breaking it into a million dusty pieces. I rub my eyes and make out nothing beneath the tree. Was I dreaming? Or am I going crazy? I race toward my family, the car, and safety.

The ride home is a quiet affair, because I am stuck in my own thoughts, trying to make sense of what I witnessed. A bathroom visit. The warm meal in our bellies. The hum of the tires on the freeway. Owen falls asleep in the backseat as Dad drives us home, and I drop into a fitful sleep as well. When I wake, it's easy to convince myself it was all in my imagination. There are no witches. There are no such things as ghosts.

Now safe in my room, Shadow purring in my lap, I stare into the computer screen at the images I took during our field trip. One by one, I blow up the photos and send them to the printer down the hall.

The last image is one I didn't take. It was captured when the camera fell to the ground. The image is of the sky and the crows as they rushed at my face. There on the right is a cloud of smoke, or mist, something fuzzy and white. I enlarge the image 200% and the white becomes something with substance. Shadow jumps onto my desk and rubs a cheek against the side of the computer and purrs. I print a copy of the photo and dash down the hall to fetch it off the tray.

It is unmistakable. The words, "Leave me alone!" are etched across the photo as if scratched into the paper with a thin nail. My hands shake with violent tremors and I drop the print. My dad retrieves the photo, giving it a quick scan. He scowls and runs his fingers through his hair.

"This is a little creepy, Josie. Did you use Photoshop to make it? I hope it isn't a new sign for your bedroom door." He laughs and hands it back.

The words seem to glow on the paper. "Leave me alone!" My fingers feel hot. They burn. I drop the image and it flutters to the ground where it starts to curl and writhe, like one of those fortune-telling fish. It turns into strips of gray ash and crumbles across the carpet.

My dad stomps a foot on the smoking paper. "What the hell just happened?"

"I don't know, Dad."

He bends down and touches the smear of gray in the carpet. "Don't use that printer anymore, Josie." He opens up the paper tray and top hatch of the laser printer and gapes inside. Can toner cartridges cause fires?" he asks, removing the cylinders from the printer's belly.

I put my arms around myself and try to get a grip on my emotions. Dad sets down the last toner cartridge and wraps me in his arms. He holds me tight as if I am a small child until the trembling stops.

SETH COMMITS A FEDERAL OFFENSE

IT'S MY WEEKEND WITH DAD. Man, that sounds peculiar now that my parents spend so much time together, but for the time being we stick to the old custody schedule. It is Saturday afternoon, and I am bored, done with my homework and caught up on my reading for Lit.

Dad has a big murder trial starting Monday, so he stayed up all night going over files. It's his ritual. With the cram session behind him, he won't touch the case until court. And he won't take calls about it either, unless there's a change in the calendar. Only then does his office manager have permission to text. He's fired people for screwing with the ritual, so chances are his phone will be silent today.

This morning, he sleeps in until ten and wakes up hungry for Dick's Drive-In. Who can say no to a cheeseburger? Not me, that's for sure. So, against my better judgment, I set my research paper aside and climb into the shotgun seat.

Dad has the radio tuned to the classic rock station, and I immediately regret not wearing headphones as he belts out "Faithfully" by Journey at the top of his lungs. I double-check my seatbelt as he squeals onto the road. Mercifully, the station switches to a grunge song by Pearl Jam. "Are you kidding?" he shouts at the radio. "This isn't classic rock, people! It's too new! I remember this song from law school days. Tell me I'm not that old, Seth! Come on!" His voice is two notches too loud.

Am I going to die in the shotgun seat, for a cheeseburger?!? To distract myself, I think about the origins of the saying, "shotgun seat." The phrase came from stagecoach days. According to Wikipedia, "The person sitting beside the coach driver carried a shotgun to defend the coach and passengers." But today, it's not a masked bandit that scares me. And a shotgun would do me no good. I recall reading something about fresh air making sleep-deprived drivers more alert and crack my window a few inches.

Between the lack of sleep and the buzz he has for Monday's trial, my father is downright giddy. Besides talking and singing too loud, he's cracking lawyer jokes and talking to the drivers around us, making random comments about their bumper stickers. "Club sandwiches, not seals! That's a great one!" he shouts to the car in front of us, pumping a fist in the air.

I see the driver's eyes in the rearview mirror and hope we don't end up the victims of road rage. I slouch down to dodge the bullets I imagine are about to fly, and roll my window all the way down as we zip across the floating bridge to Seattle. I tune the radio to an easy listening station in hopes of taming the beast, and it seems to help. My dad hums along and strums a ditty on the steering wheel.

"So, what's the latest on our sergeant mystery? Where are we at?" he says, sliding his sunglasses over his nose.

"Well, after our trip to Hawaii, I made a list of hotels and resorts on the Big Island. There were fifty different properties. According to the sergeant's journal, Leilani entertained at one of the properties that have a restaurant and bar, seems like they would be the ones to hire musicians and dancers. That cut the list in half." I root my phone out of my pocket and look up the notes I took. "I sent the list to a lady at the Big Island Travel Bureau. She crossed six off the list. Of the remaining nineteen properties, I've heard back from six of the managers, one has record of a Leilani working as a dancer, but she's not the one because this Leilani still works there, and is only thirty years old. I'm hoping to hear better news from the remaining resorts. But, in the meantime, I've got no other leads to follow."

I tap the calendar icon on my phone and say, "We've got less than two months to find a living relative, or the state takes the house." I huff out a breath. "I'm running out of hope, Dad."

"Never run out of hope! In fact, I was thinking after our breakfast burgers, that we could visit his house. I've never seen it and maybe it will inspire a new research direction."

I was told not to go near that place for the rest of my life or the police would make sure my little field trip in early November appeared on my record. "Dad! I can't go back there. We'd both get arrested this time!" My palms coat with sweat and the phone slips to the floor. Dad taps the brakes for traffic, and I bonk my head on the glove compartment. "Ouch!"

"Sorry, Seth, but that guy clearly doesn't understand how to merge. No one lets two cars in. Zipper, buddy; it's a zipper!" Dad mutters at the windshield. He uses both hands to emphasize the point, and I speculate he is steering with his knees.

"Your driving may kill us before we get the chance to visit south Seattle."

"So, you admit we should go to south Seattle, then?" Dad asks.

I rub my head across the growing lump above my eyebrow and use the middle buttons to roll down his window an inch. "God, I don't know."

Somehow we manage to make it to Dick's alive.

With a belly full of food, Dad calms until his affect seems almost normal. As we enter the freeway, his driving is smooth and non-confrontational, a major improvement. I take a long pull of my banana milkshake and settle in for the ride home. "Dad, you have to get left for the bridge exit."

"Nope, Seth. I'm a man on a mission. We can sit around and wait for thirteen busy resort managers to get back to you, or we can take action," he says.

"Technically, both things are taking action."

"Excellent point, but 'wait' is a boring verb. 'Explore?' Now that's a great verb."

Fifteen minutes later, we are idling in front of the familiar brown single-story rambler that's haunted me since November. The house sits dark and lonely. And I see that the front door has been boarded over with a giant plank of particleboard, a "No Trespassing" sign nailed across it.

"Hey, Dad. Where's the big sign? You know, the one with all the legalese?" I ask across the seat.

"Hmm. Must be some mistake," he says. "The state's legally required to keep it posted until the closing date." Dad slaps me on the back. "Son, we may have just bought ourselves a little time. I'll have my assistant look into it after the trial. If they removed the sign prematurely, we should have a few extra months to find a relation."

My eyes rake the empty yard and I count a dozen rotting newspapers scattered across the yellow lawn. I swing open the car door and collect the mushy papers, tossing them into a blue recycle can with satisfaction. Dad has already moved onto the front porch.

Two more circulars dot the peeling porch steps. I stoop to collect them and notice letters and junk mail scattered across the porch. The metal mailbox that hangs from the wall is so full that the rusty lid yawns open. There are flyers for pre- and post-Christmas sales from every retailer west of the Mississippi, offers for credit, all addressed to "Resident" tossed across the welcome mat.

"Dad, do you think it'd be all right if I put these in the recycle bin?"

"Well, the law's a little fuzzy about mail that's fallen out of its intended receptacle. But, if it's generic junk, nothing posted to Sergeant Paxton specifically, I'd say it's probably fine. But, I wouldn't go posting this on your blog…"

"Hey, thanks for the short answer, Pops."

I gather up the flyers and head to the blue bin again. I open the lid and toss the flyers inside one at a time, stepping back in time with every millimeter of dead tree, after-Christmas blowouts, pre-Christmas sale busters, Black Friday price-cutters.

I'm about to toss in the rest of the bundle when I see a crisp white corner of a business-sized envelope poke out the side of the pile. I slip the envelope free and scan the crisp cursive writing:

Sergeant Paxton
413 E. Green River Road
Seattle, WA 98168

There's no return address, but the postmark says Hawaii. Without a thought, I toss the last chunk of ads into the can and race up the porch steps. Dad has his face pressed against the picture window in the living room. His hot breath has fogged up the glass around his face so he looks like he's wearing a fuzzy hood.

"Dad! Check out what I found! It's from Hawaii. This could be the big break we've been waiting for!" I flutter the envelope in front of his face and tap him on the nose with it.

He grabs the envelope from me and reads the postmark. His eyes get as big as saucers, and I watch the excitement flicker across his face and color his cheeks and neck. He turns the envelope over and over, traces the line of the envelope as if he's dying to open it but can't. He knows the rules better than most people.

"Oh, man, Seth. This is different. This is a federal offense!" His voice comes out in a coarse whisper. "We can't open this. We need to put it back! Come on, son. Now! Put it back in the mailbox." He hands the envelope to me.

His eyes flicker to the street and back to the letter in my hands, back and forth, back and forth. He looks like he's watching a tennis match, except his crazy eyes and sweaty face look distinctly paranoid. I can almost hear the bubble burst, our last bubble of hope. Pop! My heart sinks.

I touch the rusty lid of the mailbox, but can't make myself tuck the letter inside. And then the anger takes hold. It burns up my torso.

"No, Dad! Our only hope is right here in my hands. I thought you of all people would get that." I'm so mad that my voice comes out high and tight. I feel twelve all over again, waiting to become a man. "This was *your* field trip, remember?"

"Trust me, Seth. Put the letter back," Dad commands with steely coolness. A minute ago the man was excited and nervous, as if he was on the verge of doing something rash. His abrupt change in demeanor fuels the flames. My hands shake and I grip the envelope with white knuckles. Damn! He always has to do the legal thing.

My dad examines the street and neighboring buildings with careful eyes. "We need to go."

I stuff the letter inside the open box and slam the lid closed, but I don't get any gratification because the volume of mail inside keeps the metal from clanging. Not waiting for Dad, I run to the car and bang the door shut.

I kick the glove compartment with my mud-caked boot and smile when I see the brown scuff I've left on his fancy Italian leather. I stare out my window with dead eyes as my dad climbs into the car. I don't have a damn thing to say to that man.

He revs the engine and guns into the street. The tires squeal on the damp pavement as he zips around the block. I snap my seatbelt on and stare out the window next to me. The glass is fogging up thanks to my hot head. As I squeegee off the mist with my sleeve, something flops onto my lap. It's the letter.

"Now I'm the criminal, not you," Dad says. The greasy food in my stomach does a flip-flop. "I've already opened it, so go ahead and read it. Aloud, if you don't mind."

I read the one-page letter. It's written in tidy print on stationery from the Mauna Lani Resort, the same place we stayed at Thanksgiving. My arms break out in goose bumps and I read out loud:

Dear Mr. Paxton,

I hope this letter finds you well. My mother was an old friend of yours, Leilani Akaka. I send this letter to share the sad news that my mother passed away on New Year's Day.

As I was sorting through her things, I found the picture I've enclosed of my mother and me performing at the Mauna Lani from 1988; a black-and-white photo of you in your army uniform taken after World War II; and a page from the Honolulu Star-Bulletin dating back to 1954. I also found a letter she wrote to you in 1955 but never sent. When I came across it among her belongings, I knew it wasn't meant for me, but I read it anyway. That's how I got your address. I've not included the letter because I would very much like to hand it to you in person.

You see, I'm no detective, but I wonder if you could be my biological father. I have fair skin and blue eyes, which set me apart from my family members. My fair skin was always dismissed as part of being born prematurely. But, my parents could never explain away my blue eyes, the eyes no one else in the family had. At family gatherings they called me, "Polu." It means blue in Hawaiian.

I loved my mother, and still do. I harbor no bad feeling. She did what she felt she must do, is my guess. We were extremely close, as I was with the man who raised me as his own, the man I called Father. I loved them too much to stain their memories with bitter tears.

I wonder if you might be able to fill in the blanks for me now that both of them are gone. I will keep my fingers crossed that this letter finds you well and might be enough to bring us together at last.

Mahalo,
Mel Akaka

I slip a color photo out of the envelope. A striking Hawaiian beauty and a young man stand together on a blue-tiled floor and perform, he with a slack-key guitar, and she singing into a microphone, Leilani and Mel. I know these faces. I've sat within inches of them as they made beautiful music, though their hair was graying by then and their faces filled with lines. This photo must have been taken in the eighties, based on the clothing and hairstyles of the audience. Big hair, fluorescent socks, and Frankie Goes to Hollywood tees scream eighties. Sorry, Dad. It's classic rock, baby.

Dad plucks the picture from my fingertips and stares into it as we wait at a red light.

"Is that—? Are they the musicians we saw performing? From the Mauna Lani?" He hands the photo back to me and rolls forward as the light turns green. "Damn. We can't chalk this up to chance, Seth. It's fate."

"Yeah, I'm at a loss to explain it. We were that close to solving the puzzle at Thanksgiving, and didn't even know it." I try to recall the details of the performers in the Mauna Lani lobby. I remember the shiny blue tile, and the smell of flowers, and my parents being happy. Wait, I think I took a picture of them and texted it to Josie.

"Well, what do we do next?" I ask. My fingers itch to tap a computer keyboard as we turn into the apartment complex. I bet I can find Mel's phone number in less than a minute.

Dad slides into the parking space, and before he can kill the engine I jump out, vaulting the stairs two at a time to his third floor apartment. I strum my fingers on the doorjamb and finally hear my dad hit the landing.

He unlocks the door and swings it open with a heavy thud, hard enough to dislodge a high stack of legal files from the shelf. Manila files with papers flutter to the floor. I kneel down and scrape up the mess of papers into a pile as Dad watches. I read the tabs and see they are files for his trial in two days.

Dad mumbles under his breath, staring at the pile of papers. He slumps onto the leather sofa and runs his hands over his salt and pepper curls, eyes focused on something I can't see out the window. He continues his one-sided conversation, elbows on his knees. He runs his hands over his head, creating a fluffy Mohawk down the center of his scalp.

After taking a deep breath he finally speaks, and I remember to breathe. "Seth, you're not going to like my opinion, but I think we should sit on this for a few days. Ruminate. Maybe we can figure some way to approach Mel without freaking him out. We don't want to set off alarms, right? We don't need him getting any boys in blue involved in this thing. If he did, this could ruin my career."

"Ruminate? Are we goats now? I'm not! I think it'd take me all of ten seconds to track down a working phone number for Mel. I'll call him and explain the whole thing. I think he'd be stunned at first, confused, but that'd give way to understanding and maybe even relief. I don't think it'd cross his mind to call the police on us for opening a letter," I say, my voice dying out during the last of my spiel.

He stands and paces across the flat gray rug, back and forth, back and forth. He stares down at his shoes as he says, "I knew you'd want to dive right in. But, can you please trust me on this? I have a feeling this could go south for everyone in a hurry. God. I can't have my reputation dissolve over this, or this trial. Jesus. It'd be just what the defense would need to make a circus out of the whole court proceedings. Give me time. That's all I'm asking for, two days tops." He stops pacing and sits on the arm of the sofa, still not meeting my eyes.

"Oh yeah! Heaven forbid we do anything to risk your precious reputation, Dad. You are being a selfish bastard. And for your information, I think I'll do whatever I damn well choose."

I stomp down the hall and slam my bedroom door. I want to slam my head against the wall when I realize my phone is on the living room floor with the pile of papers.

Wham! The pictures rattle on my walls as the front door slams shut. I push my ear to the door and listen. Silence. He's gone. It's safe to get my phone and whatever supplies I might need for a two-day siege. I'll stay locked in my room, far away from that S.O.B. until school on Monday.

I grab the phone off the floor and it vibrates. A text pops up on the screen. "When will you trust me? Never, right? Do what you want with the letter. Dad."

I sink into a pile of blankets, phone in hand and try to fall asleep to make the time pass. But, the guilt and anger keep me wide awake.

BLAZE GAINS
PERSPECTIVE

MISO SEES HIM before I do, the furry traitor. He yanks the leash so tight across his throat that he chokes himself just to get to Father James. Frothing and gagging, Miso drags me toward the corner of the cemetery and I slide, unable to get a grip on the mushy grass.

It's been a week since the scene in the hospital, the one where Father James told my mother that Dad's heart attack was meant to bring us closer to God. Thanks to modern medicine, Dad is in stable condition. The second attempt to stint his collapsed artery worked like a charm. We hope to get him back home early in the next day or two, if all goes well.

"You're my dog and I'm not talking to that man, so get a grip!" I command the dog.

At least Miso isn't barking. Father James is too busy praying or doing something equally saintly to notice us make our way toward Kujala's grave. I should turn around and go home. Instead, I grit my teeth and stomp onward.

Why should I back down? Today is Father Kujala's birthday and I came to leave something on his grave to honor him. I can't let Father James stop me! My duffle bag, full of holiday offerings, slams against my back as I walk. A secret and cowardly part of me hopes Father James will turn and leave without noticing me. It's rainy and dark. It'd be easy to slip back into the shadows. But he doesn't budge.

I clench my fists and jaw, steeling myself for a fight. I haven't said one word to the man since the scene at the hospital. And now that Dad's in the clear, Father James probably expects me to sing his praises for all his prayer vigils, but I don't owe him a damn thing.

Answered prayers? I don't think so. It was medicine. Skilled doctors. Caring nurses. That's what fixed my father. Not being on some prayer list.

I reach Kujala's grave and slide my duffle to the ground. I pull up my black hood, hoping it makes me look intimidating. Father James turns to take a step my way, a hand up in greeting. And then he squints into my shaded face, reads my eyes, and his friendly face becomes guarded. He grabs something off the ground by Kujala's gravestone and walks away.

"He's all yours!" Father James says over his shoulder as he jogs into the shadows. He flicks his hand up in a half-wave without so much as a glance backward.

I'm caught off balance. My adrenaline still pumps, but serves no purpose. *He didn't even say hello.*

I barely form the thought when the front door to Grace's cottage slams open. Casey stumbles down the steps and wraps her arms around me, giving me a quick squeeze. She appraises me and frowns. "You look a little scary. Here," she says. She flips my hood off my head. "There! Much better. So, what're you up to?"

"It's Father Kujala's birthday today. I wanted to leave something for him," I answer. I squat down and unzip my duffle. I also brought something to celebrate the Japanese New Year's for her and Grace. I reach in and pass the object I pull out to Casey.

"What's this? It's beautiful." She turns the white porcelain object over in her hands. "Is it a cat?"

"Yep. It's a Japanese lucky cat, a *maneki neko*. It's for you and Grace. I filled him with rice candy in honor of the Japanese New Year. Set him by the front door for good luck." I pull out the cat's twin and tuck him inside Kujala's grave/garden.

. Rosemary bursts around the lucky cat and fills the air with a savory herbal odor that makes me hungry. I reach down and pluck a leaf off the rosemary bush and rub it between my fingers, breathing in the scent. It reminds me of my parents' restaurant and I long for the next time we will be together cooking in the restaurant kitchen.

"All right! Thanks, Blaze." She inspects the shiny gold and white cat in her hands, "I don't want to, but I've gotta go. The lit paper calls! Did you finish yours?"

"Almost."

Casey squeezes me around the middle again, and I can't find my voice, though for a different reason than the squeeze. I am overwhelmed with emotion, sweet feelings for Casey that don't feel very friend-like.

She thanks me again. I want to tell her something, but I'm not sure I know how. "Casey?"

"Yeah."

"Thanks for always taking my side." I want to say more, something about how pretty she is, how good she always makes me feel, how kissable her lips look. I blush.

Casey and Miso have the same look on their faces as they stare up at me. Their heads are both cocked to the side and they gaze at me with bright brown eyes. All Casey needs to complete the transformation are perky golden ears. I smile. I really want to kiss her, but it feels inappropriate on so many levels, not the least of which is that I am standing over a priest's grave.

"Of course. Always!" She runs up the stairs and disappears inside the cottage with a slam.

I kneel down to nestle Father Kujula's lucky cat deeper inside a hidden spot in the rosemary when I spy an origami crane, red and gold wings spread wide, ready to carry him far, far away.

"Did Father James leave this?" Before I can stop myself I crush the crane into a wad. This glittery bird makes me angry on so many levels I can't even put words to it. I stare at the crumpled bird in my palm and feel sick guilt gurgle from the pit of my stomach. I tug at the wad of paper, twist, straighten and smooth, but I can't make it look like a bird again. I killed it. I flatten the paper between the palms of my hands and a slip of white paper falls to the ground. In Father James' blocky script are the words:

From a Letter to His Daughter
RALPH WALDO EMERSON

Finish every day and be done with it.
You have done what you could.
Some blunders and absurdities
no doubt have crept in;
forget them as soon as you can.

Tomorrow is a new day;
begin it well and serenely
and with too high a spirit
to be cumbered with
your old nonsense.
This day is all that is
good and fair.
It is too dear,
with its hopes and invitations,
to waste a moment on yesterdays.

These are the words Father Kujala found for me when the weight of my collar was too much to bear. I hope his words help heal what must be broken in you.
James

I bow my head and blink my eyes as I realize he left this for me. Regret wilts the last of my red-hot anger. When a soft hand lands on my shoulder, I almost scream. But I recognize the muddy brown boots in my peripheral vision. I take in a gulp of air and turn.

"Hi, Grace. I didn't hear you."

Grace fusses with the zipper of her raincoat and then zips it up to her neck. She towers over me and her gold eyes seem to be inspecting me. "Well, I can be sneaky when I want. It's one of the perks of being little."

Her eyes skim the poem in my fingers. She finishes reading, nods and says, "Now, that hits home, doesn't it? I never was much for poetry. I always thought myself too practical minded to bother with it. But these, these are words to live by, aren't they?"

Grace holds out her hand to me. I grab it and manage to rise, even though my legs tingle from kneeling too long. "Thank you."

"Any time," Grace says. She looks at me sideways, her lips pursed together as if she's holding something back.

"What's up? Say it, Grace."

She appraises me and reaches out a gentle hand to my shoulder. "I'm wondering how long you plan to harbor a grudge against Father James? You know, your dad's heart didn't give out because of him. You'd be just as well to blame Miso, or the pizza delivery guy, or that tree. It's a waste of time, is all." Grace shakes her head and strokes a hand across Miso's smooth back. He raises his chin and lets her scratch his favorite spot, and then rolls over to show off his fluffy white tummy, her fake accusation long forgotten.

As angry as I am about Father James' explanation of why the heart attack might have happened, I know it was the fight between my parents that brought on the heart attack. And they wouldn't have fought if it weren't for my silly foray into religion. "It was my fault, Grace. I brought that heart attack on my dad."

"Now you're cranking up the crazy! Really? It was your fault, Blaze?" Grace shakes her head again and then a rumble of laughter splits her face into a grin. She covers her mouth. "I'm sorry." Her face crinkles around her crescent eyes, and I know she is still laughing at me.

"It's fine. Have a laugh. But, I made my dad sick. I prayed for him to be stronger and to actually stand up to my mother, to be a man. And then he did it! He actually stood up to her about me going to church. And look what it got me?" I tuck my shaky hands into my pockets. Miso rubs his muzzle against my leg and whimpers. I pat his head and he settles, smashing down the plants on Kujala's grave.

I take a breath. "I can take responsibility for that part of it. But, the other part is on Father James."

"How's that?"

"After my dad went into cardiac arrest, Father James was trying to comfort my mother. And then he basically told her that God might've brought on the heart attack to get my mother's attention. Said He probably called her in more subtle ways, but then had to go big when she ignored all the other attempts. Grace, I am the furthest thing from an expert on this, but I don't think God causes heart attacks to make us pray. It was a mean and terrible thing to say to my mother. It was awful. I wish I could go back in time. Sure, I could still rub Father Kujala's grave, but then I would stay away from that church, never come to believe in the words Father James said. I wish."

Grace fidgets with the long, plaid scarf around her neck. She mumbles down at the ground so I barely make out the words, "Well, what this comes down to is that you wished for your dad to stand up to your mother. And when he did, we all found out his heart wasn't up to the task. So you think you brought the heart attack on with one little wish?"

I nod. "Something like that." Though from the looks of it, Grace is off in a memory, far away from this place.

She turns to me and says, "Come on. Sit awhile. I need to share something with you."

Grace offers her hand and drags me to the porch steps. She rests on the step below me and unravels her scarf. She reaches inside her coat pocket and pulls out a milky white stone. She rubs her thumb over and over it, gazes across the cemetery, and begins.

"Almost ten years ago I sent up a prayer, a prayer I've regretted ever since because I blamed myself for the consequences. But now I think I might see the silver lining. I'm looking right at it." Grace stares into my eyes and then back out across the grounds. "It became clear on Halloween night when you four stepped through that gate and found your tombstones. That night, I made four new friends."

Her voice sounds quiet and meditative. "I suppose like anybody, I'm a product of my greatest achievements and worst mistakes, Blaze. I grew up in an angry house. That's the first thing you need to know. My parents must've loved each other at some point, but I was only around for the hating. And the drinking. And the fighting.

"My brother and I escaped that house every chance we got, and when we were old enough, we left their angry house for good. My brother went to study art in Chicago, and I hopped a bus to Oregon. I worked my way through college and studied to become a librarian.

"I went to work at a public library in Eugene after graduation, but not for long. One day I was shelving books and found myself staring through the empty shelf into the eyes of my future husband. He was such an exotic creature with olive skin and dark eyes, I thought, compared to my black skin and hazel eyes.

"Within a month, we wed. Pregnant with our first child, we decided to make a life for ourselves in Seattle. Things were so happy back then. Our different skin color made no difference to the folks in our Georgetown neighborhood.

"Renaldo, my husband, opened a coffeehouse, then another, and another. Our son grew and we bought a fancy new house in the Magnolia neighborhood. The folks there didn't pay much attention to us for the longest time. And when they did, they assumed I was the maid because of my dark skin, I suppose. So, things at home got tricky.

"Then the bottom dropped out of the economy. We couldn't make enough money to keep up with our debts. That's when Renaldo started drinking. He'd come home at all hours of the night, drunk and smelling like other women.

"I swallowed it all down and pretended not to see it. But, he was a mean, nasty drunk, and he'd go after me. He'd accuse me of cheating on him. Like I had the time! I was too busy being a mother, a maid, a teacher, and a taxi cab driver. I didn't have time to cheat! But, one night, our fight got really ugly and Renaldo hit me. He pushed me to the ground and raised his foot to kick me in the head. I thought I was going to die."

Grace pauses to rub the milky white stone. Miso slinks across the porch and slumps his head onto her lap. Grace pets his face absently and continues. "That night I crawled into bed next to my son and I prayed. I prayed for Renaldo to die, so help me God." Grace cups her face in her hands and weeps. I feel helpless, but I reach out and place a hand on her shoulder. I can feel her bones through her thin coat.

Grace wipes away the tears. "So, the next evening, when Renaldo took our son to see a baseball game, I stayed back and packed. I packed everything my son and I would need to start over. I called my aunt and uncle and warned them they'd have two new residents at the cottage that night. My marriage was over.

"I waited on the couch until all the light drained out of the sky. I fell asleep at some point and jolted awake when the doorbell buzzed. I was half-asleep, so my first thought was that Renaldo had forgotten his house key. When I swung the door open and saw that state trooper on my porch, I knew."

She rubs the milky white stone and blinks away the moisture in her eyes. I want to reach out, but then she might never finish her story. "They were killed in a car accident on their way back from the stadium. Renaldo died at the scene, but my son held on for a week, only the machines keeping him alive.

She takes a shuddering breath. "I gave him permission to go, Blaze. He was hanging on for me. I promised him I'd be fine if he left. I told him he was a good boy."

Her tears start again. She doesn't even try to keep them inside this time, and I reach for her hands. They tremble in mine, so I hold them tighter until the shaking stops. Grace takes a deep breath, pulls a fresh tissue from her pocket, mops down her face, and clears her throat.

"It was only a little bit ago that I started forgiving myself for that prayer, Blaze." Miso nuzzles his head under Grace's arm and whimpers. She pets him and he shuts his eyes in pleasure.

The prickle that crawls up my spine tells me I might already know the answer. "When?" I ask.

"On Halloween night." She shakes her head. "See? God answered my prayer that night, but not in the way I expected. When I first saw the four of you, I assumed you were vandals. But, then Josie passed around things for the rubbings and I felt terrible for my accusatory thoughts. I said a prayer. I asked God to let you have an adventure that night."

She laughs. "I never imagined I'd play a part in your journey. I didn't mean to pray for myself. But here I am four months later, Blaze, knee-deep in all your lives. Me!" She laughs into her hands and tears fall from her eyes, but she catches them with her fingertips before they have the chance to seem sad.

"At first I enjoyed taking care of Lakefront Cemetery because it was other people's loved ones, then mine joined the strangers buried here, and finally I buried myself. That's the plain truth. I hid myself away from living folks. And somehow I thought I deserved to be alone, isolated from the rest of the world, because of what I prayed that night. But all at once, when you four came to the cottage, included me in your adventure, I realized God listens to all our prayers, but He only answers the ones He wants, the way He wants to. Even the bad prayers.

"The thing is, Blaze, God didn't kill them that night. Renaldo did. I didn't understand that for the longest time. But, I do now. Renaldo drank those beers. He drove that car into a wall, not God. God couldn't save my little son, but he saved me. Oh, Lord help me. He left me behind to make something of my days. I feel sick about all the years I spent being angry with God, but it is what it is. I don't feel that way now, Blaze. I can look back and see the whole picture, the one God saw all along."

Grace takes a deep breath, determination written across her striking features and I wonder if I am witness to an exorcism. "You didn't cause that heart attack, Blaze. Your father chose to stand up like a man, finally. But his heart couldn't handle it. That's all."

Grace pats the top of my hands. "One day you'll see the silver lining in this experience. I promise. Until then, I want you to have this." Grace passes me a milky white stone. "It's a worry stone, a crystal. It comforts me when I'm troubled. Now, it's yours."

I pluck the stone from her palm and give it a rub. The crystal warms to my touch. "Thank you."

"You're welcome, honey. Use it to sort through your misunderstanding with Father James. After all, Father James is just a man. He makes mistakes, just like us. What he said to your mother was harsh, and I believe was absolutely false. But, maybe it came out different than he meant. He's been a friend to you and your family and deserves another chance. Everyone does."

Miso stands up and shakes off. I stand too and give Grace a hug. "I need to think about that for a bit; then I guess there's someone I need to go visit. Thanks, Grace."

"You're welcome. And Blaze?"

"Yeah."

"That story, the one about Ettore and Renaldo, was for your ears only, okay?"

"Okay, Grace. Thanks for sharing it."

"You're welcome. And good luck." Grace smiles at me as I turn to leave.

CASEY DODGES CUPID'S ARROW

AS I STEP ONTO THE PORCH to wait for my ride to school this Valentine's Day, I lurch to a halt mid-step and somehow manage to keep my clumsy feet from knocking over the mass of roses on Grace's doorstep. I attempt to pick them up, but there are at least two-dozen stems stuffed into the thick crystal vase.

My arms aren't strong enough to lift them. I swing my backpack to the ground and use it as a door prop. As I lift the vase, I concentrate to keep my steps smooth so I don't slosh water all over the place. Shiny red stones shimmer at the bottom of the vase. Red glass stones, flat at the bottom, like the ones I've been stealing from Ettore's grave since Halloween.

I almost lose my footing and slam the flowers onto the entry table, then jab a hand inside my pants pocket. My fingers graze a ball of lint, a house key, and finally touch the round glass stones that rest in the creases.

I listen down the hall to make sure Grace is in the shower. The water's running, so the coast must be clear. I unearth the stones from my pocket. Ettore's red stones shimmer across my palm, one, two, three, and give me a secret thrill. These stones show up on the base of Ettore's grave every now and again. When I spot one, it makes my whole day to slip it off his white marble grave and claim it for myself.

I need to add the ones in my palm to the stash of others in the jewelry box that sits on my nightstand back home. But how can I do that now that my mother's kicked me out? I must have at least twenty stones by now, all shiny, round, and red like these. Seems like quite a coincidence that the same stones rest at the bottom of Grace's valentine bouquet. Then again, they're common items, sold by the bagful at most gardening stores.

I perk up my ears and listen as Grace stops whistling and shuts off the shower. I stuff the stones deep inside my pocket and yell, "Bye, Grace! Cupid left something for you!" and rush out the front door.

My ride to school rolls to a stop in front of the cottage. I collect my backpack from the porch and stumble down the steps. I fall into the backseat next to Owen and he says, "Happy Valentine's Day, Casey! Do you want a kiss?" He puckers his lips, leans over the hump in the seat, and chucks an envelope at my face. Taped to my first valentine of the season (and most likely my last) is a bag of foil-covered chocolate candies.

"Ha! Ha! Kiss! I get it, Owen," I say, rolling my eyes at Josie, sitting in the front seat.

"Hey, Mr. J. Were those flowers on the porch from you? Or is someone else vying for Grace's affections?" I only have a two-inch by five-inch peekaboo view of his face in the rearview mirror, but I'm sure his cheeks match the red across his neck.

Mr. Jameson clears his throat. "Ahem! That would be exactly none of your business ma'am." He looks back at me through the rearview mirror and smiles.

Owen croons, "Grace and Daddy, sittin' in a tree, K-I-S-S-I-N-G!"

"That never gets old." Mr. J. laughs and pushes the 'on' button to the radio and smooth jazz pours forth, washing out the last of Owen's juvenile song.

Josie cranes her neck and gives me googly eyes. She says, "I got a mystery valentine today, too."

She wears a powder pink cashmere sweater that makes her hair look like liquid copper. I look down at myself and realize I threw on a dirty gray Heritage Prep sweatshirt. I forgot it was a holiday when I got dressed. I comb my fingers through my ponytail and pinch my cheeks hoping to make myself look perky and fresh.

"Really? Already? Must not be someone from the school crowd. Maybe a neighborhood Romeo? Spill the details, lady!" I say. I pick a pink sprinkle off the front of my sweatshirt, a breakfast stowaway, and realize my only piece of holiday spirit now lies on the rubber mat at my feet, the lone pink sprinkle.

Josie smiles. "It was on my windowsill when I woke up! There was a single rose in a little porcelain vase and a sweet poem. Of course, the poem was a bit damp, thanks to the rain. But, it was sweet anyway."

"Did you recognize the handwriting?" I ask as I give Owen a stern look and the international hush sign. Of course, both Owen and I know who the mystery man is, but we are sworn to secrecy.

"Nope! My Romeo was sneaky. He cut out words from a magazine and pasted them together. It sounds corny, but it was really artsy and cool."

We reach Heritage Prep and pour out of the car. It looks as though Cupid barfed all over the front steps in heart-shaped confetti, pink streamers, shiny Mylar balloons and flowers. I swing open the heavy front door and slink to my locker, clutching my valentine from Owen in my fist. *I got a valentine, too.*

I dump my backpack on the floor and open my locker when someone clears her throat behind me. I spin around to find my mother standing just inches away. My first thought is that I'm trapped. She's blocking the only means of escape. Then I look at her, she doesn't look mad, more like slightly irritated and somewhat impatient to be done with whatever this is about to be. I paste on a smile, tuck my long bangs behind my ears, and say hello.

My mother's eyes flick to the open locker. I realize too late that she's appraising the squalor inside, no doubt adding "messy" to her extensive list of my faults. A double-wrinkle creases her forehead, and I swing the metal door shut with a shoulder.

She is wearing the black blazer and blue blouse she wears for all of her client lunches. The combination is supposed to instill confidence in her services as an accountant. She is all business today, it seems. "I'm here for two reasons. The first is that you received your mid-term report card. You achieved straight A's, so congratulations on that." She hands me a traditional Chinese red envelope filled with crisp new dollar bills and I see her hand shake a little. She tucks them behind her back and straightens her posture. I realize I'm slouching and try to stand up straight like her. The silence is awkward and I bite my tongue so I don't say something stupid, but the effort makes me feel a little woozy. I rock backward and feel a strong hand steady me.

"Hey, Casey! Happy Valentine's Day." Blaze smiles, and then adds, "Oh, hey, Mrs. Starbaugh. Nice to see you."

My mother's expression shifts from icy and indifferent to warm and friendly. "It's nice to see you as well, Blaze. How is your father doing?"

"He's doing really well. Thanks for asking. Oh, and thank you for the fruit basket. We're still making our way through it. My parents loved the Satsumas the most." Blaze's eyes track from me to my mother, back and forth.

"Well, I had to do something. We are so relieved your father is going to be fine. Will you let me know if you need anything else?"

At this point my mother, who might as well have sprouted a second head, reaches for his hand and gives it a squeeze. My mother doesn't do shows of affection! She doesn't do nice! I am completely dumbstruck by the contrast between how she treats Blaze and how cold she acts towards me.

"You've done enough already, but thanks." Blaze is the ultimate gentleman. "I've got to head to the library. Casey, when you have a minute I need to go over that project with you. Sorry if I interrupted. Take care." Blaze raises a hand and spins toward the library, humming under his breath as he walks down the hall.

"He's grown into a nice young man," my mother says in a tone that suggests it is a miracle such a decent person would be friends with me. Her voice is back to the familiar cold timbre I've come to know so well. "Now that we can get back to our conversation, I had a second item to cover. When do you plan to come home?"

I am blown away by her question. I was expecting her to hand over an invoice for the storage fees I've accrued to date for the things I left behind in my room, not this. "Well, I didn't think coming home was an option for me. Is it?" I ask, trying not to sound too... what? Eager? Pitiful? I've been at Grace's for a month, and although I like her, I miss home. Maybe they miss me, too.

"Silly girl. Of course you can come home. I haven't rented out your room."

"That's great, Mom! I've been wanting to move back." I think about how fast I can pack up my handful of belongings at Grace's cottage. It will take me longer to say goodbye than pack.

"Yes, well this silliness needs to end." She purses her lips and her cheeks blush red. Her expression softens, "I'm so…" I think she might apologize, but then she cuts off her own words. She takes her cell from her pocket and reads the screen. Her expression changes back to indifferent. "Let's just call it a silly misunderstanding and get you moved back. Both of us are stubborn, but I think it's time for the bigger person to give a little."

It's not exactly an apology; actually, it's nothing like an apology. In fact, she called herself the 'bigger person' of the two of us. I want to cry with disappointment. She doesn't get why I left in the first place. Things won't be any different if I move back. I blink back tears. I wish Blaze had stayed behind with me. I need him.

"Fine, then. It's decided?" I stand there silent as she continues her one-sided conversation. "What a relief, it was getting a little awkward. My co-workers were at the house for a team-building thing last week and asked about you. And next week is book club. I'm running out of excuses to explain your absence!"

Something inside me that wasn't broken before snaps. I want to cry but would die before I let her see that. I want to run to the library and take refuge in the arms of my friend. As I go over her words again in my head, the self-pity bubbles into anger.

I try to mimic her cold tone as I say, "So, you want me back because it's become inconvenient?" My throat constricts, and I try to swallow but can't.

Her features are frozen into a slight scowl and her penciled-in eyebrows, drawn in high arches make her look perpetually surprised. The combination of her frown and eyebrows strikes me as odd. "Not inconvenient, but it is a bit embarrassing. You are my daughter and belong under my roof. I will pick you up today after school, and then we will go fetch your things from Grace's house."

She turns on her heels to leave, and I grab her black sleeve and give it a healthy tug. Her face registers shock. Just as quickly, she makes her face flat and cold again, unreadable. I realize I might be in for the speech about her being sent to boarding school in another country at the tender age of eleven, but when she opens her tight lips, nothing comes out. She snaps her lips shut again.

"Mother, I'm sorry if I've embarrassed you, but I don't plan on moving back," I say. I'm shaking inside but push forward. "You are barely human. You have the emotions of a rock. A normal mother would cry and say she misses me. She would beg me to come back because she loves me. So no, I'm not moving back."

I grab my backpack from the floor and race to the library, refusing to look back to see if my mother is watching. As I turn the corner, I remember the red stones in my jeans pocket and smile, but not a warm and fuzzy smile. I feel like the Grinch after he's stolen all traces of Christmas from the Whos down in Whoville. *I stole too!* Someone left these behind for precious Ettore to let him know he was loved. And now they're mine. It is my love.

The smile drops and I let the stones fall to the bottom of my pocket. I take my hand off the handle to the library door and let it swing shut. I slouch down the hall to my first class trying to shake the sick feeling in the pit of my belly.

When the first bell rings, I'm surrounded with activity. Kids pour into class, talking and tossing stuff around, and I almost forget Ettore's stones. Almost.

"Hey, Casey. Where'd you go?" Blaze asks, thumping his things on top of his desk. "I was hoping I'd have a minute with you before class." He kicks his backpack under his desk and leans across the aisle.

"My head's spinning, I guess. My mother has that effect on me." I drop my voice to a whisper as the teacher moves to the board.

Blaze opens his algebra book, but he gives me a sideways glance as he tosses me a note. "I have something for you. When?" it reads.

"Lunch, I guess," I scribble onto the paper as I try to shush the questions racing through my head. He's got something on Valentine's Day for me?

Three hours later, as the lunch bell rings, I race to my locker and find Blaze, a red cellophane wrapped plate in his grip. "Hurry, before everyone else is here," he says, glancing down the hallway for unwanted eyes.

"It's Monday. Josie has lab, so she'll be late," I say, staring at the cellophane-wrapped treats. I smell chocolate and notice white powdered sugar where it crumbles out from beneath the wrapping. "If you're afraid there's not enough to share, I think you're wrong. What is it, anyway?"

"They're handmade truffles. Happy Valentine's Day." Blaze stares at his shoes and I take the plate. This was so sweet, but why is he acting all weird?

"Can I eat one now? Or should we wait?" I tuck a finger into the cellophane and a chocolaty ball tumbles free. Powdered sugar explodes across my hand. I giggle and lick a finger.

"It's up to you if you want to share them or not. But, the thing is, I made them for you." He rubs his ear with one hand, and I'm struck with a sudden memory of when I was three years old. We were both three. He was letting me use his shiny new birthday trike. He was so worried I would destroy it during the ride that he fiddled with his ear the entire time. Oh, and he kicked at the ground. I guess maybe we've grown up a little bit.

"Of course you made them for me. Duh. Who else is standing here? Why are you so nervous, Blaze? It's just me here, goofy, clumsy Casey, right?"

"Yeah, well you're a little more than that to me," Blaze says, his voice loses its head of steam and breaks into a shaky whisper at the end.

"Oh! These are for *me*." I finally understand. Blaze made them to thank me for supporting him and his family now that his father is fully recovered. Light happiness wraps around my heart like a ribbon. "You didn't have to do this. I'll always be there for you. Besides, you would be there for me if something like that happened to one of my family members."

Blaze scuffs the floor with his foot; his face drops into a slight frown. "Okay, that's nice. Well…well, I guess we should head to lunch." He reaches out for my hand and I spread my fingers wide, making the Baby Group wave. He holds his hand up to mine, and then peels away all his fingers but one. He gives me a sideways glance, drops his hand, and walks toward the cafeteria. And I'm left wondering exactly what I missed.

At the lunch table, all the talk is about Josie's secret admirer. It is nice to focus on something besides her obsession with that puzzle box. I notice the mini backpack strapped under her hoodie, but I let it go in favor of pretending to guess the identity of Josie's mystery man. Blaze's guesses go from ridiculous to wild and I wonder if Seth left him in the dark on this. All I know is Josie is happy about her holiday surprise.

"So, is everyone excited about the dance tonight?" she asks. "All I can say is thank heavens seventh graders aren't allowed in! Otherwise I'd have zero fun."

Josie takes the lid off a box of chocolates and passes it around the table. "These were a gift from one of the sevies; I think his name is Logan. It rhymed with slogan. That's what he said, anyway, before he ran down the hall and got high-fives from his buddies."

"Dude! Be nice!" Blaze jumps in. "Give him credit for being brave, right? He took a chance, did something bold. Show some respect." He stares down at the last half of his sandwich, and then glances at me; his eyes are all sad-puppy dog.

"Exactly! Be kind." I chime in. "It wasn't so long ago that you were a lowly seventh grader. And you know you were hot!"

Josie asks, "So, does anyone know if Seth's coming tonight?" She reaches for one of the chocolates, bites in, and then gracefully spits it back into her napkin. "Ugh! Cherry!"

"I haven't heard officially, but why not?" Blaze says.

I mop up the last drops of chili with the corner of my maple bar. "Best! Lunch! Ever!" I say, and then realize I will never ace charm school with these manners. I dab at the corners of my mouth and add, "Well, obviously, I forgot about the dance. Look at me! I only have five outfits total at Grace's. And I need to do laundry; this is the second round for these undies."

"Jeez, Casey! T.M.I. I could've lived without knowing that," Josie says, plucking another chocolate out of its paper cup and taking a tentative bite.

"But, you are going to the dance tonight, right?" Blaze asks. His face lights up with enthusiasm.

"No way! I'm spending tonight in the middle of a graveyard, thank you." Blaze frowns and looks past me. "There's an awesome joke in there somewhere, but I am too slow today."

Josie yanks at the sleeve of my sweatshirt. "C'mon, Casey. Come to the dance. Call Grace, and then come to my house after school. I'll help you get ready. You can borrow clothes from me. Please? I don't have a date, so we can be each other's plus one."

She looks me over and her eyes freeze midway down my chest. I peek down and see a blob of chili across the Heritage Prep logo. "Nice! I keep getting more and more attractive today!" I imagine the look on my mother's face if she could see me now and chuckle.

"What's so funny?" Blaze asks.

"Ahhh, where to begin?" I say. "I guess I was thinking about how shocked my mother was when she saw the inside of my locker this morning. 'In China, I would have been beaten if I had made such a mess of my locker.' No wait!" I say in the best mother accent I can muster, "'In China we never got lockers. Our books were strapped to our backs.'" I laugh.

"Seriously, Casey. Why'd she come to school today?" Josie asks.

"So, get this. She wants me to move back home because having me gone has become socially awkward." I take a swig of milk and add, "I'm not moving back home, at least not today."

"Why would you when you've got it good at Grace's? Isn't she like some kind of super mom?" Blaze asks.

"Yeah, she's great, all right." I clear my throat. "The thing is ... when my mother asked me to move back, I thought it was because they missed me. Turns out it was to avoid all those pesky questions her book club will be asking when I'm not around next week. Can we stop talking about this now?"

Josie reaches for my hand. "In a second, but I want to say something. People show love in different ways. Your mother's a first generation Chinese immigrant. Maybe she shows she cares the same way her parents showed her, by being tough on you. I realize cookies go down easier... what's that saying? You catch more flies with honey than vinegar? She's vinegar, but at least she's trying."

"Yup." The lunch bell rings and I jump up from the table with my empty tray. "Thing is, honey goes down a lot easier."

JOSIE DEALS WITH VALENTINE'S CARNAGE

"OH MY GOSH. That phone call was a train wreck, Shadow." It is late, and my feet ache from bouncing too much at the Valentine's dance. I'm becoming the cat lady I used to make fun of as I stroke his sleek back and drone on about my woefully awful phone conversation with Seth that ended just moments ago. Shadow is curled up in my lap purring up a storm, one eye on the television that's tuned to an animal show about predators and prey.

"It was sweet, to be sure, a secret Valentine and that poem. No one's ever done something like that for me. But, I don't want to lose him as a friend. So, we can't even think about becoming anything else, huh? I need a friend more than I need a boyfriend at this point in my life, right, boy?" The argument sounds convincing, but even I don't buy it.

I kiss the top of his furry head and he jabs a paw at me, irritated that I blocked his view of the African lioness, no doubt! I straighten up as the big cat pummels an antelope. Shadow purrs as she breaks the animal's neck with a quick flex of her jaws.

A key twists in the front door and Dad steps inside, whistling. "Well, hello my first-born!"

"Hi, Dad. How was your date?" The broad smile across his face is answer enough.

"Fabulous! We went to that new steakhouse across from the arboretum. We both had surf and turf. Ready for your life tip of the day, Josie? Date a carnivore!"

His eyes flick to the animal channel in time to see the lioness slice open the antelope's belly. Pink guts fall to the ground. Dad groans and holds his stomach.

"So, how was the dance?" Dad slips his jacket off and sits across from me on the easy chair. Shadow vaults from my lap to his.

"Did you just steal the cat?" I say. "How rude."

Dad scratches Shadow under his chin, and then studies me. "Are you avoiding the question? Was tonight, what do you call it, an epic fail?"

I'm not sure I'm a fan of my newly evolved father right about now. In the olden days, he would have been asleep by the time I got home. Good time or bad, he'd be blissfully unaware. I didn't realize how convenient that was until this moment. "It wasn't great."

"Do you want to talk about it?"

"I don't know." I flick off the television and decide gaining some perspective might be a good thing. "I found out at the dance it was Seth who left the mystery valentine."

"And that's bad because…" Dad asks. Shadow jumps off his lap and waddles down the hallway.

"I love him; you know that. We've been friends our whole lives. But I refuse to think about him that way."

My father looks relieved to hear this. "Great news! Because at fourteen, I don't want you thinking about *anyone* that way, otherwise I'd have to invest in a gun." He pauses. "Does this make things different between you now?"

"It was a tad awkward at the dance. But, we just got off the phone and things are fine. It's all cleared up."

Not exactly the truth. I want it to be settled, but I can't help but notice how unsettled I truly feel. Could I want more than a friendship, too? I push the thought away. I smack the remote against my palm and the television flicks on again. The channel flits to a shopping network. "What kind of person buys underwear from a television show?" I ask.

"Mmmhmm." Dad sits with his elbows on his knees and regards me through a tuft of curls. "I know I'm meddling here, but I was a teenage boy once. I feel I need to shine a little light on your situation."

"Go ahead. Meddle, Dad." I turn off the television and sit back into a mass of cushions.

"Well, my advice is to take his gesture as a compliment, plain and simple. He's got to be mortified, so move on without mentioning it again. That's the merciful thing to do."

Dad stands and Shadow skitters back into the room. He rubs against Dad's legs and purrs. Someone's hungry. Must've been the display of guts that got his appetite going.

"Oh! I almost forgot. I've got something for you." Dad rummages through his coat pocket and brings out a black velvet box. "Here! Happy Valentine's Day!" He kisses me on the forehead like the olden days.

I crack the box open, but think about what I found inside my mother's puzzle box and hesitate. "Go ahead," Dad coaxes.

Silly thoughts, I rationalize and I peek inside. A nickel-sized heart sits on a fluffy white pillow of cotton. Its red facets glint and sparkle, and I pull the silver chain free of the box. The heart twirls on the chain and I hold it to my chest. Dad reaches around and fastens it around my throat. "Thank you," I whisper.

"It was sixteen years ago that I gave this to your mother. And now it's yours." He touches a finger to the red heart and smiles. His eyes are wet with tears. "You look so much like her, Josie. It's uncanny, especially your green eyes. She had a twinkle, too. Exactly like yours."

"Thank you. The necklace is beautiful. What's the stone? Garnet?"

"Yep, it was Sarah's birthstone. I had it made for her."

"Wow! That's pretty smooth, Dad. Do you remember what Mom got you?" I touch the garnet and it feels warm and smooth.

As if my question gives him pause, he rubs a hand along his cheek. "She gave me a confession of sorts. But, I didn't bother to listen."

Dad sits down on the couch and puts his head in his hands. He runs his fingers through both sides of his scalp and what curls weren't standing up before are now.

"A confession? What'd she try to tell you?" All of the sudden, the warmth I felt from my necklace evaporates, and I feel weak. I think about the puzzle box that lies on my bed, which I neglected to attend a cheesy Valentine's dance.

"It sounds crazy, but your mother was convinced she was different." He lays his hand across his heart and stares at the wall. He tells me that Mom tried to confess to him what she revealed to me in her letter.

"Dad, it was true, wasn't it?" I need to hear it from him, that her confession was real.

"Man, Josie. You're going to think I've lost my marbles, but I need to get this out. The whole thing was true. I guess, at the time I explained it away as a distorted memory, something brought on by Sarah's childhood illness. What she said scared me, so I wouldn't let her talk about it after that night.

"She almost died as a child, that much I knew to be true. Her father told me as much the first time we met. And later I found out the rest was true, too. But I confirmed it by going against her dying wishes. God, Josie. I've been so afraid to tell you this, not just because it sounds like the rantings of a madman. To tell you the whole thing, I have to confess what a complete jerk I was."

He confesses how he went against my mother's wishes. He checked her into the hospital at the end of her life. And after she passed away, he let them do an autopsy. He weeps into his hands, but no sound comes out. His shoulders shake.

When he raises his head, his face is slick with tears. I untwist the scarf from around my neck and offer it over as a makeshift hankie. He wipes down his face and takes a breath.

"Josie, I hated myself for going against her wishes, until Grace helped me work through the whole awful thing. It was wrong." He pinches his lips together, like he's said all he is willing to say, but I have questions.

Garnet clutched in my palm, I say, "I want to know what they found, Dad. What did the doctors find inside Mom?"

"God, Josie! That is a secret that should never have seen the light of day." He shakes his head.

I tell my father about the letter Mom left for me. He seems relieved to know that I already knew her secret. His eyes soften.

"When they cut her open, they found a heart made out of stone under her ribs, next to her the remains of her human heart. The doctors couldn't believe it. I don't think they even knew what to say. They brought me in to see for myself. And I was the ultimate Doubting Thomas. I touched the stone to see if it was real. God. And the thing is, I knew from a college geology class that the stone inside her ribs was Alaska jadeite. Our hearth is carved out of that stone."

He stares at the heavy spotted stone that sits above our fireplace and holds an assortment of family photos. "The doctors didn't write down anything in their tidy little reports about the jadeite heart. No, that part was conveniently omitted.

"And when I found out the truth, the truth she tried to tell me so many years before, God, I was angry. All these years I thought I was angry with her for deserting us or deceiving me. I don't know. I used every excuse to point a finger at Sarah. It was easier to blame her than look in the mirror. But, when I met Grace I knew it was time to take a good, hard look at myself. What kind of man stomps all over his wife's last request? She deserved better than me."

Something twists under my ribs. A dying wish? A last request? Am I doing the same thing by keeping the puzzle box for myself? Casey was right. I need to bury her box. Why didn't I see it until now?

"Grace helped me forgive myself. She helped me see I'm not that man anymore. She showed me that life is full of things that you can't touch, but they still exist. Like love. And magic." My dad reaches down and holds my cheek in his warm hand. "We knew your mother was special, didn't we?"

"Yeah, she was wonderful."

"She had amazing gifts, beyond human." He smiles at me and the tears start all over again. "She was magic, a living miracle in fact. Everything she touched she made better, just like you, Josie. You have that gift. I hope I can spend the rest of my life appreciating all she did for the world, not the least of which was giving me you and Owen."

Tears stream down his cheeks, and I reach my arms around him and cry. We stay like that for a long time, and when we break apart I know what I need to do next.

I retrieve the puzzle box from my bed. I brace myself with a long breath and silent prayer. I touch the garnet that dangles near my heart clinking against the key and walk back to the living room, ready to share my own story about a clue and a mysterious box, a box that needs to be buried to honor my mother's final request. If I confess this to Dad, maybe he will make me see the burial of the box through; otherwise, I'm afraid I will put it off forever.

He turns the box over in his hands, and asks for me to repeat the details of what we found inside. "We need to bury this for her, Josie."

And I know he's right. We hug each other again and afterward, I take the box with me to my room.

It is well past eleven when I drop into bed. The cat curls behind my knees like an old pro and we sleep.

*   *   *

I've got to bury the box.

I don't bother with shoes or a coat as I rush through the house. She won't rest until I bury the box. I slither out the front door into a frosty night with the cat close behind. I run beneath the streetlights that guide the way to Lakefront Cemetery and I pant. The icy air burns my throat and lungs with every intake. I know I am doing this for her. She will see that I keep my promises. She will.

The entry gates are chained shut. "Damn it!" I slam my fists against the hard metal.

The cat bumps my shin with his head and leads me to the service gate, the one the hearses use. It is lower, and I climb the cold iron easily, snagging my pajama pants on a rusty tip. I fall onto the ground and scramble up again, the box safe in my arms.

"You're doing good, Josie," she whispers to me. I smile so hard it hurts and run to the hill that holds her bones. As I near the cedar, the sound of a thousand crows rings in my ears. I hold a hand to my head, but the noise doubles. They shriek at me from the tree branches and make it hard to think. I have to do this for her. I can.

As I approach her grave, I kiss the angel on her stony cheek. I touch a finger to the feathers on her wings and pull away my finger. It throbs with pain. Must have cut it on a sharp edge. Shadow purrs, rolling across my mother's grave. He twists and turns to show off his soft tummy and I join him on the ground. I set down the box gingerly and realize I forgot a shovel. The crows laugh at me from the tree and take turns diving down from their perch, zipping past my head like feathered flyswatters.

"They're trying to stop me, aren't they Mom?" I ask the wind.

The cold works its way into my toes and up my legs and I shiver. I crouch over the rocks and roots and dig into the earth, determined to keep my end of the bargain. The stingy dirt takes my nails and the skin at the ends of my fingers, but doesn't yield an inch. I scratch and scrape with all I have and begin to see the tops of the roots and rocks.

The cat pounces on the roots and yanks at the shortest one, pulling it free with his sharp teeth and a rock springs free. I grab up the rock and chisel at the earth, finally making progress.

"Woo hoo!" I cheer, pumping a victory fist at the noisy birds.

Wham! A bird strikes my head. I rub the side of my face until the stars go away. And then, wham! Another bird hits me. And another. I clutch the box to my chest as I fall to the ground.

I wake up safe and snug in my own bed to the infernal beep of my alarm clock. Shadow is curled above my head and when he rises and stretches, I see the puzzle box he used as a pillow. I pull it to me and remember the dream. I touch the shiny lid and notice the black under my fingernails. My hand shakes as I dig under the nail and a clump of grit falls free.

The dream seemed so vivid, so real. But, it couldn't have happened. I look to the comforter settled over my legs and fling it away and stare at my filthy legs and feet.

I cradle my blood-crusted feet and shake. "I am such a freak."

CASEY AND
GIRLS' NIGHT

IT HAS BEEN FIVE DAYS since our tumultuous Valentine's Day. Josie made the executive decision to plan a girls' night. She brought her mother's puzzle box, and the three of us, Grace, Josie and me, plan to bury it tonight. Josie seems calm now that the plan is set, and that makes me happy. Maybe she'll be back to her old self after we bury the box, because this moody Josie is getting old.

"So, Casey. What'd the boys decide to do tonight?" Josie asks. Her feet are propped up on a fluffy ottoman in Grace's living room, cotton stuck between her toes. The air is ripe with nail polish fumes, littered with chick magazines, and dotted with bowls of half-priced Valentine's candy. Grace is busy whipping up something amazing in the kitchen as we chat, a chick flick droning in the background.

"The boys are playing mini golf," I answer. "Sounds pretty boring, but they were excited."

"Sounds miserable, especially if it rains tonight," Josie says. She unzips the miniature backpack that has become her constant companion the last two months and peeks inside, no doubt to check on the puzzle box. She glances at me and then zips the pack shut.

"Are you sure you want to bury the box tonight?" I slip a bottle of purple nail polish from the bag of supplies, but the cap won't come off, so I switch it for a shade of blue.

Josie pulls the purple bottle back out and turns the cap off with ease. "I have to. My nightmares have gotten so much worse lately. I'm hoping once I do this for Mom, the bad dreams will finally stop."

She dabs the dark polish on her perfect toes and hums, stealing glances at the pack that holds the puzzle box.

I wipe off a muddled paint job on my thumb. It's nice to have Josie at the cottage with us. It makes me miss home less. "Hey! Did I tell you that Blaze went to my house yesterday to drop off a thank you card? He is so funny." I try to sound light and carefree, but this news means everything to me. "He went to make sure they didn't convert my room into an office or something. He pretended to need the bathroom as an excuse to check out my room. As of yesterday, all my stuff is still there." I catch myself chewing my lip and I stop, then laugh to convey how silly the situation is.

"God, Casey. Of course your stuff is still there. I'm sure they want you back, but they must expect an apology. You need to suck it up and apologize."

"Apologize? Whose side are you on anyway? I'm the one that deserves an apology." I fume.

She caps the polish and checks her phone screen. "I'm on your side, as always. But, I can tell you miss your family. Would it kill you to give a little on this? Just say you're sorry and be done with it."

"I do miss home." I catch myself chewing my lip again. "Every once in a while I get a text from Dad. But he says my mother would kill him if she knew. She expects him to shun me; it's the family policy." I use a tissue to wipe away a smear of blue polish from the top of my big toe. "Dang."

Josie slips the bottle of polish out from my fingers and finishes my toes. "Oh, Casey. You're working so hard to act like this doesn't matter to you, but it hurts. I wish I could fix the situation, make your family change, get you back home. But, it's up to you. I'm sorry." And I know she is, as she tenderly paints my toes.

"Subject change!" I command and we laugh.

Josie says, "So, thank goodness Seth and Blaze are back to normal, right? What was up with them? Did they dare each other to do something stupid on Valentine's Day?" Does this mean Josie doesn't have feelings for Seth? I thought for sure she did. I wonder if I should bite my tongue about my fuzzy feelings for Blaze?

"It was temporary insanity. Cupid-induced insanity!" I grab another tissue and wipe blue polish from a smeared finger. "Man alive! I'm doing an especially bad job tonight."

Grace enters the room with a tray of food and hits the 'pause' button on the remote and our chick flick freezes; the mouth of a hunky, unnaturally tan man gapes wide open on the screen. "Spill the beans!"

Josie stops painting my toes and jumps in. "Seth and Blaze made some moves, you know, tried to woo Casey and me on Valentine's Day. Epic fail!"

"Details!" Grace demands.

"I thought it was sweet." I say. "Blaze made me these delicious chocolaty truffles, and Seth left a flower and a poem on Josie's windowsill. It was sweet, that's all."

The tray of nachos Grace set on the table look yummy. She wears a black apron that says Kiss the Cook, a Christmas gift from Blaze no doubt, who owns the twin of it.

"Teenage boys, even good ones like those two, have an excess of hormones. It'd be best to keep it on the friend level for now, not that anyone asked my opinion. But, if it were me, I'd let those boys season up a bit."

We all laugh. Everyone dives for the snacks and Grace hits 'play' on the remote, animating the beach hunk once again.

After the movie ends, we channel surf through a handful of goofy reality shows. We push the furniture to the side and toss pillows and sleeping bags across the rug. By the fourth episode of *Ghost Seekers*, my brain starts to numb. Grace has built a crackling fire and if it wasn't for the excess of caffeine I drank earlier, I would be dead asleep.

Just as the hottie ghost hunter digs into the backstory of another abandoned mental hospital, Grace hits mute. "Anyone want to hunt for a real ghost? I know a place." We laugh. "Really! We can grab flashlights and take a little walkabout, unless you're too damn scared! Then maybe we can get your mother's box buried, Josie."

I hand Josie a glow stick and crack mine, watching as the gray stick glows green.

We put on coats, and then gather on the porch to root out our shoes from the pile on the welcome mat. In a matter of minutes, we're parading down the steps into the cemetery grounds.

"Only one grave in Lakefront Cemetery scares me. And that's where we're heading, girls. You sure you're up to this?" Grace asks.

I follow close behind Grace's beam of bright light and Josie follows behind me. A thick fog is coming in from the lake, laying a white cotton blanket over Lakefront. I shiver.

Grace's voice comes out in a muffled hush that sends a ripple of fear down my spine. I clutch my glow stick, but it casts a feeble glow, so I creep closer to the mighty Mag. Everything outside the flashlight's beam is inky black, and I don't want to get lost. I check behind me and Josie lags behind.

"Hey, Josie! Over here!" I wave my glow stick and she hurries to catch up.

"Thanks, Casey. I thought I heard something," she says. She checks the straps on her backpack to make sure the box is safe. "Is the zipper closed?"

I reach behind her and confirm that the zipper is fastened. "Yep."

Grace says, "This-a-way girls." She points her beam toward a distant corner, but all we see in front of us is a wall of white mist. She aims the light to the grass and we start toward the mystery grave again.

"If there's one thing I can't stand, it's a body that won't stay dead. Now, ghosts, they're another thing altogether. They got trapped here somehow. Didn't finish their stories in the living time. But this one has a different sort of tale. You might not have the stomach for it."

We are passing the grave of Josie's mom. I reach out to squeeze her hand, but she's not there. "Josie, come on." I see a flash of her glow stick and wave mine in the air again. All I can see is her green light bobbing toward me, closer and closer.

"God. You didn't just hear that?" Josie asks.

"Hear what?"

Grace stops walking and waits for us to catch up. Josie whispers in my ear, "I thought I heard my mother's voice. She was calling for me." She tightens the straps to her backpack.

"That's freaky. Are you sure it was her voice?"

She clutches the sleeve of my jacket. "Casey! The one thing I miss most about her is her voice and when I heard it back there, I knew it was her. She was calling my name, I swear!"

Grace comes up on the two of us. "Girls? Is there a problem?"

I look to Josie to guide our answer, but between the fog and darkness I can't read her expression.

"Sorry, Grace. Please go on. The fog is freaking me out. I need a distraction."

"Yeah, story please," I whisper.

"Well, then here it goes." We follow behind Grace as she leads us to the mysterious family crypt. "The Toymaker was the only child of a furniture maker and his wife. His father made furniture for their little village and drank the town dry. One night, drunk as usual, his father was tending the fire that steamed and shaped his wood when the embers got out of control and destroyed his shop.

"The fire wiped out their home above the shop where his wife and infant son lay sleeping. At first, the old furniture maker was too drunk to rush into the raging fire. Townspeople raced to the burning shop and watched as the furniture maker pulled his infant son out alive, but his wife had perished in the flames."

I look behind me and Josie is there, walking behind me just steps away. The fog is thicker here as we near the edge of the lake.

Grace's words continue. "The baby was horribly burned, melted like wax by the fire. His arms, legs, face, and hands were grossly scarred and deformed. The old woodworker buried his wife and fled to America with his son.

"He opened a new furniture shop where nobody knew his sad history, but his son bore the scars and could never go outside to play, attend school, or make friends. The little boy grew up behind a pane of glass, alone and friendless, watching children play outside his window...

"He fell in love with a young girl from behind the glass, and she became his obsession. One day, he decided to carve a wooden doll for her and leave it on the park bench where she came to sit each day and read. Instead of loving him for his gift, she showed the doll to her friends, who made fun of her and tormented the boy by standing outside his window and tearing the head and arms off of his doll and throwing the pieces into the street.

"A few days later, the girl was found on the park bench, lifeless. Drawn across her hacked flesh was the crude face of a doll etched in thick strokes of color: wide black lashes, a clown-red smile, and rosy cheeks. In her lifeless hand was the doll, fully restored. Her parents and friends knew who did this awful thing, but the police didn't have a scrap of proof."

It feels like I have cotton in my ears; Grace's voice sounds far away. I step toward her beam of light and something scratches my cheek. I hold my hand over my mouth to keep my scream inside. I swallow down my fear and realize it is a twig, not a spectral finger that did the scratching. A nervous laugh burbles from my lips. I can hardly make out Grace's words now. *How did I fall so far behind?* I hurry to catch up.

"One night, seeking retribution, the townspeople set fire to the wood shop, burning it to the ground, and killing the boy and his elderly father. They're buried in a crypt, this one here."

Grace shines her light across the white marble and lingers on the stained glass fragments that cling to the edges of the window. The black iron bars that were supposed to keep people from breaking into the crypt are bent outward toward us.

I know it's my imagination, but I think I feel the evil that pulses inside this crypt. It has a heartbeat and I hear it in my ears, a high-pitched whine. I recoil from the massive crypt. I take a step backward, but the squeezing feeling inside my ribs won't loosen.

Grace's voice sounds like a whisper now. "Weeks later, one by one, each of her friends found a small wooden toy buried in a pocket, under a pillow, in a lunch pail, and in a school desk... And within a few days, each child was found maimed and dead with a small wooden doll tucked in their hand."

I take another step away from the Toymaker's crypt and trip over a headstone, and crash to the grass. As I stand, I realize I don't see Josie anywhere.

My knee sears with pain and when I touch a finger to it, I feel sticky, hot blood through the rip in my pajama pants. "Josie!" I cry out.

Grace reaches a hand out to me. She pulls me to my feet and points the beam at my torn pajama pants. "Oh, my goodness. You're hurt. Can you walk on it?" She glances around us. "Where's Josie? Josie!" she yells.

But only silence answers. Grace holds my hand as we zigzag through headstones calling for our lost friend. My leg hurts, but I push away the pain to search for Josie. Panic rises in my chest. I gasp for air. "Where'd she go, Grace? How'd I lose her? She was right behind me."

We wander into the far corner of Lakefront, not far from the children's cemetery, calling for Josie. I wave the green glow stick above my head and listen between cries. All I hear are the caws of a distant crow echo through the fog. I stumble toward the sound of the crow and Grace takes my lead. Then like a whisper, we hear it. Josie's voice, faint, but unmistakable.

"Grace! Casey! Anyone?"

Grace flashes the beam of her flashlight onto a white marble crypt, not unlike that of the Toymaker's, except on this one the door gapes wide open. "What the hell?" Grace says. She moves to swing the iron door closed and we hear it again, Josie's voice, but closer now.

She shines her light into the dark crypt, and there tucked into a corner, holding her knees sits Josie, shaking and her eyes wide with panic. I dive into the crypt behind Grace's light and we pull her outside. We clutch her to us, a group hug and I feel her tremble from head to toe.

Grace touches her face. "You okay? Gave us a helluva scare. What were you doing in there?" she asks.

Josie stays between us and I realize she is holding her backpack to her heart. "I thought I heard my mom. I was following her voice. She was calling for me and I ended up in here."

She drops her head and sobs. I rub a hand against her back and Grace breaks free to swing the crypt door shut. She flicks her beam of light to the handle of the door.

"Now that is the strangest thing. Where'd the lock go? The padlock on the door is missing. Come on girls, we need to get back to the cottage; someone's been messing around on the grounds." Grace links elbows with us and leads us to the cottage, her light cutting a path through the darkness.

We thunder up the front steps, eager to get inside the cottage and away from crypts and ghost stories. I swivel the knob to the front door and kick my shoes to the side. I turn to Josie, who clutches the puzzle box to her middle, her boots still laced to her feet. I unlace them and she leans against the doorjamb as I pull the boots off one at a time.

"Thanks," she says. "I don't know what happened out there, but this box saved me from something bad out there."

We step inside the kitchen and Grace stops us. "Nope, not yet. I've got one more thing I need to do."

She reaches a hand above the doorjamb, in search of something. Her fingers land on a tiny amber bottle and she pulls it to her chest, mumbling under her breath. She unscrews the shiny lid and a spicy, earthy scent ushers forth. Grace puts her finger over the top and tips the bottle upside-down. She dabs the pad of her finger to Josie's forehead then mine as she continues to mumble. "Amen."

"Were you praying over us, Grace?" I ask. The fragrant oil smells of cedar and makes me feel clean and sleepy.

"Yup! This here is anointing oil. Like the rusty shovel and the red wheelbarrow, I inherited the oil from my uncle when I took over Lakefront. Can't be too careful, if you know what I mean." She reaches up and replaces the tiny bottle on the thin wooden ledge.

Blessed and shoeless, we push inside the little cottage. Grace bolts the door and then slumps against the doorjamb. "We need some hot chocolate, girls."

As Grace sets a teakettle on the stovetop and scoops hot chocolate mix into mugs, I sneak into the living room and find Josie sound asleep on the sofa by the fire, her body curled around the puzzle box. I stretch a blanket across her and kiss her head, as if she were a small child in my care and tiptoe back to the kitchen.

Over cups of hot chocolate, Grace and I whisper about Josie. "That girl has such a heavy load on her shoulders. She won't rest soundly until she buries that puzzle box, Casey."

"I told her the same thing, but I think she wants to hold onto it for herself. She said something tonight about it protecting her. What if she has it in her head that the box is like a lucky charm that's keeping her from danger?"

Grace adds a handful of marshmallows to my second mug of hot chocolate. "She's desperate to find a reason to keep that box. I guess 'lucky talisman' is the latest excuse. But, the right thing to do is bury the box. Should we wake her and get on with it?"

I try shaking Josie awake, but she's out. I pull the comforter off my bed and fall asleep on the sofa opposite her. Deep asleep, dreaming about nice things, someone shakes me awake.

"Casey, wake up," Josie commands.

"What do you want?" I grumble half asleep. I remember something we were supposed to do, but it slips away from me before I can catch hold. The box.

"I had another dream, Casey." Josie holds the box to her chest. "My mom came to me. She said she doesn't want me to bury her box anymore. She said it will keep the evil from getting to me."

"Josie, you're not making sense. What evil?"

"I don't know. There's something evil that will try to kill me, and as long as I have my mom's box, the evil thing can't hurt me."

I rub the sleep from my eyes and watch the dying flames in the hearth. I think about what Grace said, that she is looking for a reason not to bury the box. I yawn. I'm too tired to convince her otherwise tonight. "So, I take it we aren't going through with the burial then?"

"Of course not. I can't now. Don't you see?"

I don't see, but I need sleep, so I agree and let my eyes flutter shut.

JOSIE AND THE
SKI TRIP

IT IS PRESIDENT'S DAY and Mr. Starbaugh is the man at the helm, threading through Snoqualmie Pass to reach the ski slopes by eight o'clock sharp. He has gone rogue by agreeing to chaperone our ski day, disowned daughter and all. Mrs. Starbaugh knows he's snowboarding today, but is unaware that he has an SUV of teens along with him.

The sun rises over the tips of the Cascades in a glorious display of pinks and purples bright enough I wish I'd packed sunglasses, not that we could fit another thing into this overstuffed SUV. It took Seth's Tetris skills to accommodate ski bags, snacks, snowboards, skis, and poles for the five of us. I check to make sure my mother's puzzle box is stowed safely underneath my feet and then rest my face against the cold glass of the window, listening as to the others chatter. With every mile on the road, the stress of midterms falls away.

"Thanks, Mr. Starbaugh," I say to the back of his head. He turns down his eighties music and cranes his neck.

"No problem, Josie. I've been meaning to get up to the mountains all year. Just make sure not to say anything to the missus, okay?" He hits the radio knob and thrums his fingers across the steering wheel. Mr. Starbaugh has been Casey's lifeline during the last two months. They text back and forth, so she still has some connection to her family during her days at Grace's cottage. The least I can do is keep my mouth shut for him if I happen to see his wife.

"All right, *Monk* or *Castle*?" Casey asks holding up DVD cases with a broad grin.

"Which season?" Seth asks.

"Two of *Monk* and Three of *Castle*."

"My vote's for *Castle* then; Beckett's hot!" says Blaze. For some reason the guys knuckle-bump.

"Guys! We've only got about fifteen more minutes. Save it for the trip home," Mr. Starbaugh announces.

I was half-asleep when they came to pick me up this morning. I do a mental inventory of my ski bag and hope I remembered everything. I've got my mom's box, that's the most important thing. "Are you skiing with me or snowboarding with the guys, Casey?"

"I'm going to try out skiing. Maybe today I'll graduate from the bunny hill." Casey digs through a paper bag on the floor mat and something drops out of her jeans pocket. She unearths a bag of cookies.

"Casey, something dropped out of your pocket," I point to the shiny red stone on the carpet between us. I stretch a foot to scoot it her way. She looks at me with raised eyebrows and big eyes.

"Share!" Blaze barks from the back seat reaching his big mitt to grab the cookie bag. Casey pulls the bag out of reach, and then dishes out a cookie, her stare never leaving the round object.

Seth takes a cookie. "Man, you didn't even ask what kind they were, Blaze. You just went for it." Taking a bite, he says, "Chocolate chip. There's no going wrong with the classics!"

I raise a hand to pass on the cookies, although Casey forgets to offer; the red shiny stone on the car mat has all her attention. She reaches for the object with her foot and picks it off the ground. The object shines red in the cabin light.

"What is that? Can I see it?" I ask.

She stuffs it into a front pocket and mumbles, "No." Her arms cross her chest defensively. She seems mad.

"What's up with the red stone? It's pretty." I say. She glowers out the window and chews her lip. "You seem upset. Is this about the red stone?"

"I'm not upset. You're imagining things with that wild imagination of yours again, Josie," she says with attitude.

Her words come out of nowhere and feel like a slap. "Wild imagination? What are you talking about?" My mind traces back the last few days in search of something I might've said to offend her. I always tell her about my nightmares; is that what she means?

I whisper so Mr. Starbaugh won't overhear. "I can't help having nightmares. God. And how dare you hold that against me. It's mean, Casey." I've always shared my nightmares with her because that's what friends do. We trust each other with everything, the good stuff and the not so fabulous.

"I'm just saying, you have a record for having a big imagination. Give it a rest today, alright?" She reaches a hand in to her front pocket, and I suspect it is to touch the red stone. Was the whole imagination comment meant to distract me from the red stone?

"Casey, out with it. Where did the stone come from? And I'm not letting you change the subject again." I watch her face color.

She pulls her hand from her pocket and hands me the round piece of red glass. I rub the warm object with my thumb. "It's no big deal. It's just something I found at the cemetery." She's lying; I can tell by the way she avoids my eyes. She holds out her hand and I give her back the red stone. Her mouth turns up in a sneer. "It's just like I said before, your imagination made a mountain out of a molehill." She giggles and it comes across as mean and patronizing. I fume.

"Do you think it's fun to have awful dreams? Do you? When I go to bed, the last thought I have before falling asleep is what kind of horrible story will my brain make up tonight. I don't want to be this way, but I am. And as my friend you should care!" I grab the puzzle box off the floor and hold it to me. "Maybe you're not my friend after all."

Casey glares at me, then swivels to face out her window.

Mr. Starbaugh pulls into the ice-crusted parking lot and slides into a space by the crosswalk. I spring out of the vehicle, wanting to make a quick getaway from Casey, and strap the backpack with the puzzle box over my ski coat. I have to loosen the straps to make it fit. I reach for my skis locked in the roof rack, but I'm not tall enough. Blaze comes to my side of the car and clicks the magic red button. I take my skis, sling my ski bag over a shoulder, and run across the street. Car horns blare as they skid to a stop at the crosswalk. I don't look back.

Ten minutes later, as I ride the lift to a black diamond trail I know Casey can't do, I see Blaze and Seth swoosh down the mountain on their snowboards.

I don't understand. Casey's my best friend. Why would she hold my nightmares against me? "That's not what friends do!" I don't even realize I've said the words out loud until I notice the man next to me shift a couple inches toward the other side of the chair.

I glide off the chairlift and shush through the fresh powder. I draw in a deep breath and process as I ribbon down the trail. As I near the bottom, I see Casey struggling to stay upright on the bunny hill. She falls off the magic carpet and tumbles into a group of little kids, beginners like her. I feel sorry for her and want to make a rescue. It takes everything I have not to ski over and lift her up, but I turn left instead and queue for the lift. The guys spot me on the chair and wave. I wave back, but have no heart for sweet gestures.

I glide the last part of the run to the chairlift. There is no joy in skiing today. The day has gotten complicated, messy, and ugly. Regardless, I ride the lift again, deciding to attack a mogul run. Maybe the bumps will loosen up my tight legs.

As I bounce and glide between the round snow mounds, a thought whispers in the back of my mind and takes shape. When Casey reached down to grab the red stone off the car floor, maybe she noticed my mother's puzzle box at my feet. Is that what got her so uptight?

That's it! This is about the puzzle box. The night we were going to bury it, I thought I heard my mom's voice and I ended up inside a crypt. The air inside smelled like rotten eggs. I listened to hear my mom call me again, but all I heard was my own breathing. And then, I felt like I was being watched. I pointed that stupid glow stick into the corners of the crypt, but found only dirt and dead leaves. It felt like something bad was inside the crypt with me, watching me, and I held my mom's box to my chest for protection. I sunk into a corner and held her box to fight against the evil thing I couldn't see. And then, just like that, the scary feeling lifted.

The others expect me to bury the box like I promised, but I can't now. Not ever, because it keeps me safe, like a lucky charm. I can't be without it. And I wonder if Casey has figured out my intentions. She asked me last night if we could bury it this coming week, and I answered her too quickly. "Of course not."

She doesn't understand, and that may partly be my fault for not explaining better. But that doesn't excuse her meanness, I forget to focus on what I'm doing and lose control of my skis. Before I get my edges into the icepack, the skis slip out from under me and I roll forward. My poles fly free and one ski pops off, but the other lands under me as I come to a stop against one of the giant metal columns that support the chair lift. I try to pop off the ski manually. Jammed with clumps of snow, the mechanism stays clamped. My ankle throbs and I can do nothing.

Within ten minutes, a red snowmobile zips up the slopes. "Oh, my God. No." I wrap my scarf around my head in hopes no one will recognize me on the descent. How mortifying to be scraped off the mountain by the Ski Patrol.

I ride to the hospital in an ambulance, and EMTs give me a pain reliever to make the throbbing in my ankle stop. As the EMTs slip off my ski coat, I search the space for my backpack. I do a visual search and don't see the small pink pack. I need to hold my mom's puzzle box. The pain ceases and I grow tired, then fall asleep. When I wake, I am in a hospital room. Dad, Owen, and Grace sit next to my bed. I ask about the backpack and my dad slips it down from the coat hook. A nurse comes in and wraps my ankle, administers more pain medicine, and checks me out of the hospital.

Owen rides home in the front seat because I have to keep my foot raised across the back seat. My ankle isn't broken, just badly sprained, so the doctors expect it to heal over the next four weeks. A surge of pain jolts up my leg. For a distraction, I turn on my phone and find a slew of unanswered texts from the Baby Group all asking what happened and how I'm doing.

I delete Casey's handful after noting there is no texted apology from her and send a quick summary to the guys. I hit 'Send' and the phone vibrates. On the screen, a close-up of Casey with her football player grease paint running across her face stares at me. I click 'Ignore Call' and power down.

Seth Gets Real

THERE BETTER NOT BE a power outage, because I'm starving, I think as I stand waiting on the Jamesons' porch for someone to answer the door. It is Saturday, March 3rd, and we are here to celebrate my parents' birthday. I vow to celebrate along with the others, but I'm still irked at my dad about his executive decision to 'ruminate' on what to do about Mel Akaka and his letter to the sergeant. All the while, as I waited for my dad's big trial to wrap up, I found out he was working on the sergeant quest in secret. God, in order to make it through the night, I need to push the thing I found out into a dark corner in my mind.

I ball my hand into a fist and pound the door a second time. As I wait, a storm swirls around me. I wonder what the newscasters have named this latest burst of weather. Snow OMG? Snow-tastraphe? Snow-mageddeon? No wonder the East Coast mocks us! Though, in our defense, we have way more tall trees in the Northwest, so add a little snow, a dab of fierce wind, a lack of salt on the roads, and weather around here can get serious real quick!

We modified our plans for the night so Josie wouldn't have to navigate a restaurant on crutches. When she twisted her ankle, Grant and Grace stepped up, offering to host a birthday party for my parents at the Jameson's home. Yep, that's right. My parents share the same birthday, except that my dad has been around to celebrate four more of them. It is a little too saccharine, but there it is.

My mom seems blissfully happy tonight and I want her to stay that way. I'll keep my mouth shut about the sergeant and Mel, for the sake of peace. My parents hold hands and whisper back and forth, oblivious to the wild wind that whistles through the tall pines above Josie's house. If it weren't for the distraction of my mom, Dad would be rattling off grisly statistics about the annual deaths due to falling tree limbs. Instead, I'm forced to run them down in my head as I wait for some merciful human being to answer the door. Before I can get too comfortable, or uncomfortable with my thoughts, the door swings open.

"Hi, Josie. You look great." I smile and bite my tongue so I don't gush on and on about her overwhelming attractiveness. After the Valentine's debacle, I promised to rein in my outward expressions of like.

But she does look great, in spite of the flesh-colored crutches stuffed under her arms. She wears a sweet blue-and-white gingham dress that brings out the copper in her hair. I stuff my hands in my pockets so I'm not tempted to reach out and touch a curl. I wish I'd thought to bring her flowers or a get-well card or something. No, that would've broken my post-Valentine promise.

"Hi. Come on in! Honored birthday guests first, please!" Josie says, as she blocks me out with a swift crutch. My parents kiss Josie's cheeks, then head into the kitchen after shedding their outerwear. I stumble inside behind them and Josie smiles as she slips her crutch back under an arm.

"Where's Owen tonight?" I ask.

"It does seem quiet, doesn't it? Owen's at a sleepover tonight," Josie explains. Damn! That little man was going to be my saving grace, the one to keep me from being all into Josie this evening. I was going to teach him the wonders of Wii mini-games, too.

"You let him go to a sleepover, Mama Josie?" I say, giving her a wink. God. Where'd that come from? There's something about her with those crutches, she's cute and vulnerable all at once. I'll try to ignore her cuteness and focus instead on the place where the top of her crutches smash into her armpit. Smooshy flesh. So. Not. Cute.

"Ha, ha! Very funny, Seth, but Owen's seven. I think that's plenty old for a sleepover. Didn't the Baby Group have sleepovers at the ripe old age of two?" she asks. We did have sleepovers. I wore pajamas and slept in a sleeping bag next to her.

"Mmmhmm. What a waste, though; I wasn't old enough to appreciate them then," I wink again, and Josie squinches her face, smashing her little freckles into a tan blob across the bridge of her nose.

She laughs. "Honestly, Seth! Do you have something in your eye? Or are you trying to be charming?" Her cheeks flush pink. Hmm.

"Boy, that leg isn't slowing you down one bit. You can smack me around, wounded or not."

"Yep, and don't you forget it," she giggles. I hang my coat and follow Josie into the living room.

"What smells so good?" I ask. "I didn't miss the main event, did I?"

"Yeah well, the lights flickered a couple of times, which made the chefs panic. They started cooking two hours early. But the good news is that if Mother Nature knocks out the power, we will still eat like kings…and queens."

Josie hobbles through the living room and makes a slow descent onto the sofa with a throaty grumble. She struggles to prop her foot on the stack of pillows at the end, so I step in and gently lift her wrapped ankle onto the soft pile. "Anything else, Miss? Do you need a blanket? Or something to drink?" I ask. I stand at her side like a butler awaiting a command.

"No thanks, Seth. Sit! I hate not being able to help them in there, so maybe if you keep me company, I won't be tempted." Oh, yes. I'll sit next to you. It's for the greater good. I smile.

The birthday couple enters the living room with two platters of finger food and sets them across the coffee table.

"Hey! Who put you to work? It's your birthday!" Josie says. I pat her sore foot and she stays down, even though I know every muscle is ready to spring into action.

"Don't worry, Josie. We were only thinking of our stomachs. Have one of these spinach puffs! They are amazing," my dad says. He smiles and I notice flecks of green across his white teeth. I don't know if it's because I'm sitting next to Josie, but I don't feel the raw irritation toward my dad right now. I laugh into my hand and he squints across the room at me.

"Honey, is there something stuck in my teeth?" Dad smiles at my mom and she bursts into giggles.

"Don't worry. Now we're a matched set!" She grimaces to flash a green-speckled smile.

Josie leans into my ear and whispers, "They are so cute together. Remind me to marry someone that makes me laugh." Her words tickle my ear. I like whispering.

I whisper back, "Yeah, but you're forgetting that they aren't married anymore." I don't know why I just said that. It sounded different in my mind. Different as in, "I'll make you laugh." Duh.

Josie elbows me in the ribs hard enough to make me groan. "God! What is wrong with you, Seth? Who killed your inner rainbow?" She gives me a fierce stare and my ears burn. Damn, she's cute when she's mad.

Where's Owen when I need him? Oh, right. He's gone. That's a shame, because he always has a way of keeping things light. I reach for a spinach puff and wolf one down before Josie can ask me anything else.

"Suppertime!" Grace announces from the dining room.

She leads us to our seats and Grant serves up slices of the most amazing Beef Wellington I have ever seen. Okay, it is also the first one I have ever seen. The mushroom and beef-stuffed pastry smells like savory goodness. The mashed potatoes look more than edible. There's a bowl of green vegetables, too– creamed spinach? If it weren't for my parents' twin green grins, I would heap some of that on my plate. Not now.

I drape a napkin across my lap to muffle the growls coming from my hungry belly. "Wow! What a spread. We should do this more often," I say as I take up my fork and knife.

"Well, I am glad you approve, Seth," Mr. Jameson says. "But, before we eat, let's have a toast to the birthday couple. May the next year of your lives be full of joy. Cheers!"

He raises a glass of champagne and we join in the toast. I drink sparkling water out of a crystal flute, and Dad bumps my arm as he struggles to turn his chair sideways.

He clears his throat. "It feels like the perfect time to do this, if I may." He kneels next to my mom's chair and cracks open a blue velvet box. "Tabitha, you have taught me so much. But, the most important lesson you've taught me, is how to forgive. Thank you for seeing past my mistakes to the person who tries every day to be a better man. I love you. Will you marry me? Again?"

Josie, Grace, and even Grant use their napkins to dab the corners of their eyes. Mine remain bone dry even as I stare at them as they kiss. I take it her answer is yes. It's like I am watching the scene from outside my body. To see my mom's face look so content as my dad slips the ring onto her finger should make me feel something, but all I feel is a big, empty nothing. I should be happy for them, especially my mom. This is what she wants, clearly. But, as I think about it more, the most prominent emotion I have right now is skepticism. What if he cheats all over again? A headache starts to pulse across my temples. It's like my face is in a vice grip, and someone keeps turning the crank tighter and tighter. I stare down at the plate in front of me, and find my appetite is gone.

"Another toast!" Mr. Jameson refills the champagne flutes and holds his glass over the table. "A toast to love. Here's to your future. Cheers!" I watch my mom's face, flush with happiness.

Everyone clinks their glasses and I join in, although a beat behind the others. I clink my glass and close my eyes, wishing I could make myself disappear because I don't want to watch this scene.

A soft ding comes from where Josie is sitting. She reaches into the pocket of her dress and reads the phone screen. Her dad frowns. "Josie. What's the rule about cell phones at the table?"

"Sorry, Dad. I forgot to turn it off."

"Who was that?" I ask. I peek into her lap and see her tap, 'Reject Call' on the screen.

"Nobody important." She stuffs her phone out of sight. 'Nobody important' is Josie's new code for Casey. It's been two weeks since their falling out, and Josie shows no sign of forgiving her.

"Are you going to be mad at Casey forever?" Josie shrugs me off.

"Hey. Don't ignore my question. She's been your friend your whole life. Let her make a mistake and be forgiven. She'd do as much for you."

Josie stuffs her mouth with an oversized bite of beef. She probably did that to shut me up. I know how many people die each year from choking. On beef. I can't stand that she is ignoring me. I am sick about my dad's impromptu proposal. I would like to slink into the night, but can't think of a smooth way to exit.

People chatter and celebrate with such ferocity during dinner that no one seems to notice I'm not a part of the lively party. I manage to get my appetite back and clean my plate; after all, it *is* Grace's cooking. I make a note to try this meal again someday, but next time I'll pass on the side dish of bitter.

When Grace comes into the dining room with a pot of hot coffee, I gather dirty dishes. I need something to do with my hands. Josie scowls across the table and points at my chair, mouthing, "Sit!" I plunk back down.

Josie hands me a refilled champagne flute and commands me to drink. I slug the water and set down the glass a mite too firmly.

My mom turns to me. She reaches across my dad to pat my arm. "Seth, are you all right? If you grip that glass any tighter, it's going to shatter."

I push her hand away and watch her expression change from mild concern to miffed. Closing my eyes, I rub my eyelids until little white stars erupt. When Josie reaches under the table to pat my knee, the last of my self-control evaporates. I lose it.

"It comes down to trust!" I stand up and my chair slams into the wall. "Don't you understand that?" I point a finger at my dad. "Why do you guys have to jump back into being married again so fast? How come neither of you asked me? Do you think I'm some stupid baby that can't process complicated, serious things? Because I can!"

My dad reaches a hand out to me. His face matches the red tablecloth and looks like he is about to explode, but his voice comes out smooth and controlled. "This is not the place for this conversation, son," he says. "If you were old enough to process complicated things, you would also be mature enough to know what discretion is and use it." His voice stays at a level timbre, and somehow, that makes me madder than ever. All the anger I felt toward him about the letter and his selfish reasons for putting things on hold come boiling to the surface.

"You're a selfish pig, Dad! You only think about you, what's best for you, what would make you happy. It's disgusting!"

"Are you kidding me? If I was a selfish S.O.B., would I have stuck around to take your abuse for four years? You've done everything you could think up to make my life a living hell and I've continued to reach out to you. That's not selfish, Seth."

Slowly, quietly the table empties as everyone but us exits to the kitchen.

I stew. "Yeah, well. What about all the times you've butted into my sergeant quest?" I shout.

"What do you mean? I only made the one suggestion that we wait awhile before we contact Mel Akaka." He says.

"Like you haven't totally taken over? I know about the letter you got from Mel Akaka. I called your office and your secretary told me about it. I've been waiting to hear it from your lips, but somehow it has slipped your mind, for what? A week? Last I knew, we were 'ruminating' on what to do next. We weren't going to do anything rash, remember? Then, you go and write Mel a letter? Did you even think to clear it with me? I rubbed the sergeant's grave in the first place! You totally left me in the dark on this." I pace back and forth across the dining room.

Dad crosses his arms across his chest. "I don't think this is a discussion for a birthday gathering. But since you've gone there, here's the deal. I intended to ask for your help writing the letter to Mel. But, then the words just came to me. I jotted them down. It was meant to be a draft and then I got a bit too eager. I had my secretary type it up and send it off to Hawaii. By then, I knew it was too late. God. I knew I'd messed up. So I kept my fingers crossed that I'd get a response and have something great to share with you, and you wouldn't be angry. I blew it." He rises from the table.

"Yep. You blew it alright." He reaches out to me and I back away.

He rubs the back of his neck and paces. "And there was the hold I put on Sergeant Paxton's medical records," he mumbles.

"You what?" I bark.

Sweat breaks out across his forehead. "Yeah, I did that so long ago, I almost forgot about it. I contacted Fort Lewis awhile back, right after our trip to Hawaii. It was a long shot, but I inquired, and it seems that Sergeant Paxton still went to the military hospital to have his annual medical exam. They still had blood draw results from 2011 on him. I did some legal paperwork, to assure they'd hold his medical records for the next year. I figured if a potential heir was found, we'd have some way to check his or her blood against the Fort Lewis records." He takes a seat at the table and puts his head down in his arms. "Crap, Seth. I meant to tell you and I forgot. It was during the rush before the trial."

I can't stand to look at him anymore. I storm out the front door into the howling wind, and let the air and rain smack me from all sides as I sprint into the dark.

Somehow, I find my way into the backyard. The art shack draws me like a magnet and I push the door open, glad to escape the terrible weather. The rocker in the corner beckons and I sit, pulling a blanket over my lower half. I click on the space heater and wait to feel something besides cold air push out the vent.

Right before I fall asleep, I make a secret wish that my dad will panic. I want him to think something awful has happened to me. I hope he worries that I might be lying dead somewhere, crushed by the fallen tree limb he forgot to warn me about. Ha!

I wake to the sound of soft voices and the smell of something lemony. I open my eyes and watch Josie and Grace. They visit with one another in hushed voices and sip something warm, maybe tea. When they notice I am awake, they stand. Josie hobbles toward me without her crutches, and then she drops into the stool at my side.

"How are you doing?" Grace asks from her seat on the area rug.

"I'm fine. Did my parents go home?"

"Yep. As soon as they knew you were safe, they left. I watched you head this way when you left. I figured you needed some time to yourself, what with the big proposal and all."

I sink back into the rocking chair. "She shouldn't marry him. He'll just hurt her all over again."

Grace purses her lips together then says, "Now, that is none of your damn business. You don't have a dog in that fight, you hear?"

Josie bursts out laughing. "Oh man! How'd I ever get along without you Grace? Your sayings are the best."

I sit up straight and push the blanket to the floor. "I don't understand, Grace. This *is* about me. I'm the one who listened to her cry herself to sleep every night after she kicked him out. I'm the one they tasked with being the man of the house when he disappeared. I'm the one that helped her after he crushed her perfect little world. Me. I do have a dog in this fight, Grace. And it's a big scary Rottweiler, itching to bite someone." I knead my hands together.

Grace rests her face in her hands. "Seth, it was their marriage. It was his affair. And it is their future. They don't need to consult you to make a move, you understand? I am sorry for what happened to your family and I am especially sorry you had to carry so much on your shoulders. But, it was never your burden to bear. You never really had to watch over your mama. She managed things fine on her own. The problem is, you still hold a grudge against your dad for all that.

"But, take a look at him. He's paid for his mistakes and I would say he's more than made up for them. How many times have you brought up those mistakes and rubbed them in his face? Seems like you made it awfully hard for him to forgive himself, and make something better of his life. But, he got the job done anyhow." She stands and folds the blanket into a tidy rectangle, then drapes it over the easel.

I say, "I hadn't thought about it that way before. But, what about the way he's taken over my quest? What about that?"

Josie stops sketching in her journal and looks at me. "I think he just got too excited, that's all. Your mystery is the first thing the two of you have shared in a long time. Do you remember when you told me that I had to forgive myself before I could move forward with my own adventure? I really thought you had forgiven your dad because you guys were working together like a team."

She scrunches up her nose and scribbles something in her journal. "Yes! He should have gotten your blessing before sending that letter to Mel, but things were at a standstill. Weren't they? Your dad was simply letting Mel know that Sergeant Paxton had died." She looks at me with her big green eyes and starts scratching in her sketchbook again.

"You're not drawing me, are you?" She tucks the book behind her back and laughs.

In an instant, all the anger I'd been holding onto all these years starts to crumble away. I stand up and grab the sketchbook from her and examine the black-and-white sketch of my face. She made me look better than I really am.

Josie watches me as I appraise the sketch. Her green eyes sparkle. "Hey! That's not your business. Give that back to me! Come on, I'm injured here."

She struggles to her feet and, even with Grace there, I stand up and reach around her neck, pull her to me, and kiss those sweet lips of hers. I kiss her until Grace clears her throat. And when I open my eyes, everyone is smiling.

BLAZE GATHERS UP THE PIECES

"WHAT'S THAT OLD SAYING about too many cooks in the kitchen, Mom? Is it, 'the pot won't boil?'" I ask over my shoulder as I chop ingredients for a salad to go with supper.

My mom laughs as she stirs a pot of chicken gumbo. "Blaze, honey. It's, 'too many cooks spoil the broth.'"

My dad, so focused on wrapping prawns with bacon strips, steps on my foot. At long last, he tucks the final morsel onto the cookie sheet, so the broiler can perform its magic.

It is Sunday evening and we are in the midst of what has become a new tradition over the month or so, cooking supper together. With three of us at work, the counter space is tight, but it is a nice kind of crowded. I think about the poem Father James left for me at Kujala's grave. My favorite line echoes through my mind: *This day is all that is good and fair.*

I stop chopping long enough to take a mental picture. In it, my parents stand elbow to elbow in matching aprons. No one has to point out how sweet this moment is in time. We are healthy. We are a family.

"Husband?" my mom says. I cringe, used to old arguments that began with that same innocent word. "Maybe it's time to put in that kitchen island you've wanted for so long. We need more work space, if we're all going to be in here at the same time. What do you think?"

"Well, dear. I've got an island dog-eared in a catalog. Can you take a look at it to see if it's what you have in mind? After I get your approval, I'll order it." He pulls the fragrant, smoky prawns from the oven and they sizzle on the pan. Prawns Dad can't eat now, to keep his ticker in good shape.

My mom comes to his side and picks up a prawn with her long nails. She kisses him behind the ear and says, "Nah, I don't need to see it. I'm sure it will be perfect. I didn't marry a slouch, you know?" She nibbles the smoky morsel and smiles.

I keep my head down and chop radishes. How long will it be until I don't cringe when my parents talk about things? Respect is the new norm, but I still worry that things will switch back to how they used to be. What if my mom returns to her bossy, bullying ways? That's when things could get tricky.

I like the new norm. It's just weird, that's all. I scatter radishes into a wooden bowl and search the fridge for a piece of fruit to dice into the salad. I pick a Roma apple and set it on the counter when the doorbell rings, and rings, and rings.

"Yeah! I'm coming!" I shout as I zip to the front door.

"Don't run. It's probably just a solicitor," Dad calls from the kitchen.

When I open the door, I stare into the face of a wet rat that sort of looks like Casey. Her soaked hood hangs over her face, so I can't be sure.

"Casey? What are you doing here? Why are you all wet?" I pull her into the entryway by the arm and water drips onto the stone floor. "Come on! Get inside."

I shepherd Casey to the front room and set her on the best seat in the house, the window seat that overlooks the yard. When she finally speaks, her voice comes out shaky and weak. "I love the sound of rain on a metal roof."

She stares up at the living room ceiling and I worry. She is mentally shot. I think about texting Seth, but I drop the idea because I'm not sure how to spell hypothur.. hyperthermia? Instead, I grab a blanket off the couch and fling it over the top of her, then rush down the hall. I yank a clean sweatshirt from my dresser and race back. As I pass the kitchen, Dad pokes his head out the door.

"So, who was it, Blaze?"

"Casey. She's drenched. I think she rode over on her bike."

"What the heck? It's pouring out there. What was she thinking? I wonder if it's her mother again," Dad says, his voice thick with disgust. "I'll put on some hot water; you get her something dry to wear."

"I'm already on it."

When I reach the front room, Casey is curled up in a ball and the blanket lies crumpled on the ground. She is sound asleep. As I tuck the blanket around her, I notice the shivers that ripple her cold skin.

I switch on the gas fireplace and pile another thick blanket across her legs. Dad sets a steaming cup of tea onto the end table and hands me a bowl of gumbo.

He whispers, "Go ahead and eat here. Let me know when she wakes up, and I'll bring her some supper, too."

Sometime after my second bowl of gumbo and my third Sudoku puzzle, Miso rumbles into the front room with sad, brown eyes. I check the clock. "Did your tummy alarm go off, boy?"

I rub the top of his head and stand to feed him, when he spots Casey and goes ape. He yips, barks, and stuffs his wet muzzle into her face. She wakes with a start and her blank eyes dart around the room until she remembers where she is. I know she's back in the land of the living when she roots a hand out of the blankets and strokes the side of Miso's face. She rubs his ears and he licks her cheek.

"How long was I out?"

"A good hour or so. I need to feed this guy and then I'll bring you supper. After, if you're up to it, we can talk," I say as I stand and stretch my legs.

Casey says, "What makes you think there's anything to talk about?"

"Oh, I don't know. Maybe the fact that you showed up unannounced at my house drenched to the bone. There's a story here somewhere." Miso whimpers and I lead him to the kitchen.

It takes everything I have not to pepper Casey with questions as she eats. My mom tiptoes into the living room and refills Casey's teacup. She sets down a plate of pink mochi and I give her a frown. Smiling, she slips out of the room, leaving us in peace again.

Casey takes a square of the sugar-laced strawberry mochi from the plate and whispers, "Grace threw me out."

I choke. "She what?" Powdered sugar flies from my lips. Nice. Real suave.

"Yep. She packed my stuff in her truck and drove me home. End of story," Casey sobs into her wet sweatshirt sleeve.

I remember the dry clothes I brought earlier from my room, currently stashed under my leg. "Hold that thought," I say, and hand her the clothes. "Here. You should change into these."

Casey wanders down the hall to the bathroom and shuts the door. As if on cue, my parents scuttle into the room and ask, "So, what's the scoop?"

"Grace kicked her out; that's all she's said so far."

When the bathroom door opens, my parents disappear once more. I picture them crouched around the corner ears to the open doorway, listening.

Casey emerges from the bathroom. "Thanks for the clothes, Blaze. I feel better now." She looks better, too. She has color in her cheeks and her eyes look bright and sharp once more. "So, I'm the world's worst person. I deserved to be kicked out. I'm awful."

"Hardly. If you're awful, what am I?" My cell phone vibrates in my pocket and I check the screen. "It's Josie. Should I take it?" I ask.

Casey nods and I answer. "Hey, Josie. What's up?" I whisper in Casey's ear, "She's been looking for you. I guess her dad told her what happened and she's worried."

She whispers back, "Yeah, right. She hasn't spoken to me in two weeks." New tears roll down her cheeks.

"She called though, so she must still care a little…." I say.

Casey rolls up the ends of the too-long sleeves of my sweatshirt. "Can you put this on speakerphone? I don't want to explain more than once."

I nod. "Follow me."

We walk down the hall to the office and I set my phone in the charger. "Josie, she's actually here, at my house. She wants me to put her on speakerphone. Just a second." I click a button and say, "Are you there?"

Josie answers back, "Yes, now what is going on? By the way, Seth is here, too. He's over at my house to help me on my history paper."

Casey clears her throat. "So, I don't know what all Grace told your dad, but basically she finally found out what a terrible person I am. Took her long enough, if you ask me. Then she gave me the boot. That's it."

Snot sputters down Casey's lip. I hand her a tissue and whisk my dad's laptop from the desk. Can you ruin a keyboard with tears and snot?

"What?" Josie asks. "She didn't say a word about this to dad, and they were out last night. In fact, all she said was what she's said all along, that she loves having you at the cottage. I'm lost."

All that comes out of Casey is a sob, a long, low, juicy sob. "Casey, do you need us to come over?" Seth asks.

"No, it's all right. I've got Blaze." Then she surprises us all and giggles. Her voice breaks into pieces and then the sobs start again. "I'm an emotional wreck. Sorry, guys."

There is silence, except for the sound of Casey crying, and then she huffs in a breath and says, "It was the stones, the red stones I've been taking off Ettore's grave."

"I knew it!" Josie's voice says over the speaker. "You went all psycho on me when that one fell out of your pocket, remember? I thought you hated me because of my mom's box. It was the red stone. That's what did it." She sounds relieved.

She laughs into the receiver and the speaker crackles.

Casey says, "Glad we took two weeks to clear that up. You could've just asked." Her voice drips with bitterness.

"I did ask, but then you went off about what a 'wild imagination' I have. You basically called me a freak!" Josie says.

"I never called you a freak. You're exaggerating! Listen, can we just let that go?" Casey pleads.

"All right," interrupts Seth. "Virtual group hug. Better? Now, tell us about the stones, Casey."

"It's something I've been doing since Halloween night. Every time I visited Ettore's grave, I'd find these red glass stones, one or two of them lying along the base of his grave. I liked them. I liked the idea that someone came to visit and left them for Ettore. I don't know why I stole the stones, but I did. I kept most of them in my jewelry box, except the one I'd carry with me. I thought it was no big deal, like a lucky rabbit's foot or something. Anyways, Grace found out about the stones. Actually, I left them in my pocket and one fell out in a load of laundry. She asked me about them and I told her. I knew I shouldn't have stolen them. But Grace went ballistic, acted like I'd killed someone. I've never seen her so angry."

I shake my head. "Grace, angry? I can't picture it," I say.

Casey grabs another tissue from the box and continues. "Yeah, so she went on this rant about how Ettore is someone's child and those stones mark time, something like that. Maybe it was that they mark a visit. Those stones let Ettore know that someone missed him and stopped by for a visit. I don't know. It didn't make sense."

Seth's voice cuts over the line. "Taking stones from a grave is terrible. Leaving a stone on a grave is a really old custom. I think it started as a Jewish custom. When we visited Arlington National Cemetery last summer, I noticed stones on the tops of some of the graves and I asked the tour guide about it. He said it started as a Jewish tradition, but now people of all cultures have adopted the practice. Visitors lay a stone on the grave to tell the deceased they are still loved and remembered. The custom has ancient origins, too. In the olden days, before we had tombstones, a cairn was built on top of a person's body to protect their remains from scavenging animals. Stones were also placed on the grave to signify the memories visitors left behind."

Josie cuts in. "Why didn't I do my history paper on burial rituals? Dang!"

"He was someone's son, Casey," I say. Grace lost a son and a husband. She shared her painful story with me. I imagine someone hurting their graves and what it would do to Grace and my blood boils.

"Yeah, I know," Casey whispers. "I couldn't help it. I'm sorry."

I try to understand the void in Casey's own family life that drove her to commit such a heartless act. I force my voice to come out kinder than I feel, because she is my friend. "Man, Casey. That's some bad karma, taking away that little boy's protection and love. That is not the Casey I know."

Casey bawls and I put an arm around her. I hear Josie whisper to Seth, "Maybe next time, keep the details to yourself." I don't need a visual to know Josie's giving Seth a searing scowl right about now.

Seth whispers across the line, "I'm sorry. I always say too much."

Casey cuts in. "It's fine. That explains things." She wipes her nose with my sweatshirt sleeve. "Even without knowing all that, I think I knew that already. I took something good away from Ettore and kept it for myself. It felt good to steal the stones. I guess it felt good and awful all at once. I was greedy for what he had and wanted to keep it for myself."

"Did you put his stones back?" I ask.

"No, Blaze. I didn't have the chance. Everything happened so fast. Grace found the stones and told me to go to my room and pack my stuff. When I came out with my garbage bag of possessions, she was already in the truck. Oh man, and the look on my mother's face when I showed up at the house? I've hit a new low."

"So, this happened when?" Seth asks. "I'm just trying to get the timeline straight."

"I guess it was a little after lunch." Casey takes a deep breath. "I dumped my stuff at home and then wandered around, and ended up at Blaze's."

She takes a deep breath and I'm worried she's going to start crying all over again. "I screwed things up good, and after Grace was so nice to me. I loved staying at the cottage with her. She made me feel necessary, important. She made me forget I was invisible for awhile, and now that's gone, all because I was jealous of a dead boy.

"It just ate at me, the difference between his family and mine. I wanted to change places. I even had this fantasy that his parents would come visit his grave and see me. They'd be touched that I was visiting their son and they would fall in love with me, maybe make me their own.

"It was crazy. I'm crazy, that's the truth of it. Grace did the right thing by throwing me out. I'm not safe to be around."

Her sobs are soft and muffled by the sweatshirt that she uses to cover her mouth. My fingers tingle because all I can do is sit here and listen. I can't fix this. I keep my arm around her and watch her melt into my best sweatshirt.

Softly I say, "You're not crazy, Casey. You shouldn't have stolen the stones, but that doesn't make you a bad person. You're human, a really strong one, too. The truth is, I couldn't survive in your family."

I hold back my words because I'm afraid I might make her cry again. Her face looks calm and intense so I say, "Sometimes I wonder about your mother. I've never seen her be nice to you, not once."

Seth jumps in. "It's true! She's nice to other people, strangers even, but not you. All she's ever cared about are achievements: good grades, an award, a scholarship, not the things that really count in life, like you."

"She doesn't get your jokes, she doesn't bother to read your amazing stories, she doesn't see you step in and help smooth over difficult situations," Josie says over the speaker.

"Exactly!" Seth says. "She doesn't value any of those things because they don't bring her kudos. It's weird, Casey. And to your credit, you have never let your largely absent mother drag you down."

Casey clenches her jaw, as if she's resolved to do something hard. "Did I ever tell you guys about the orange chair?" She pulls my arm off her shoulder and grabs my hand, and squeezes it.

Silence comes across the speaker. I nod.

"I was maybe five, and my parents got into this fight, a knock-down, drag-out fight. They were screaming at each other about I don't know what all. But, at some point I remember my mother saying, 'Well, if you leave me, I get Drew!'

"And my dad started screaming that *he* got to keep Drew. Whatever the fight had been about in the first place was forgotten, because they were fisticuffs over who got to keep Drew. And the whole time, no one mentioned me. I wasn't even a consolation prize.

"Anyway, after the fight, I hid behind this ugly orange chair that sat in the corner of our living room, just to see if anyone would miss me. I sat behind that thing all day. I fell asleep at some point and when I woke up the sky was pitch dark. No one noticed I was gone. No one bothered to look for me. I crawled out from behind the orange chair and knew I didn't matter to those people. They'd never see me."

I feel hot tears prick my eyes. "God, that's awful," I say. I wipe my eyes with my sleeve.

Josie's voice breaks the silence. "I'm not defending your mother, Casey. But, maybe they never mentioned who would take you because it was assumed that you would go with your mother. Isn't that the natural thing to do? Let the mother have custody of the youngest kid?"

Casey rubs her cheek and says, "Maybe. I hadn't thought about it that way. But my point is, I deserved to be thrown out. Grace did the right thing. I'm a bad apple."

"You're not a bad apple!" Josie barks. "I know for a fact that Grace loves you. You're like the daughter she never had. She told my dad that she's reached out to your mother every day. She's kept her up to date on your life, how much you've pitched in around Lakefront Cemetery, how well you've done in school. She's tried in her own way to heal your family."

Casey slumps into my side. "I didn't know. Oh man, now I feel even worse. Now I'm an ingrate, too!"

I can hear Seth pacing across the floor and rubbing his hands, even across the phone line. "Grace is more than the caretaker of Lakefront. She's a living history book. She honors the people buried at Lakefront by telling and retelling their stories. No wonder she flipped when she found out you'd been stealing from Ettore. But, she's sensible, too. She'll forgive you, Casey. You need to apologize. I'm not saying she'll let you move back, but she will forgive you."

"It was time for you to move back home anyway, Casey." I add the obvious. "You can't hide from your problems. You need to make peace with them. I tell you all the time, but it's their loss. Your family is missing out on knowing you. It's time to get over it and move on. But, you do owe Grace an apology. Seth's right."

"Yep, I know. I'll call her tonight. And maybe I can think of it as a fresh start in the ole' Starbaugh household. Who knows?" Casey sounds unconvinced, but a little upbeat for the first time tonight. "Maybe I'll ask my mother about that fight, and if she was always going to keep me..." She settles in my arms, not content, but calm at least.

"Casey, I think you should apologize in person," I say. "It's tough. Man, I almost couldn't go through with it when I apologized to Father James. Believe me, crow does not taste good. But, it'll end well. I promise."

"All right, I'll do it. Thanks guys." Casey tosses her crumpled tissues into the wastebasket. "Subject change?" she asks.

I smile, "I got this one! So, Josie. Seth is over, huh?" I laugh.

"Yeah, well. He's the research paper god." Josie giggles over the line.

Seth says, "Yeah, and it didn't escape my notice that you ran to Blaze's house when all hell broke loose, Casey. Hmmm."

Casey grins. I'm hoping that means she has some feelings for me. Feelings, with a capital 'F.'

After we click off the phone, Casey and I head to the living room.

"What we need is a bowl full of popcorn and a bad movie!" We fire up the air-popper and grab the big, red and white striped bowl from the cabinet while the kernels pop.

"Thanks, Blaze. I don't know what I'd do without you."

She kisses me on the cheek, and it is easy to forget the crust of dried snot on her upper lip because her touch is soft and warm. The smell of burnt kernels shakes me out of the moment.

Casey laughs. "Perfect. You know I love popcorn a little burnt."

CASEY AND THE STORY OF THE DEATHBED

ON THE WALK TO LAKEFRONT CEMETERY, I pick at my hangnail until it bleeds. I stick the wounded finger into my mouth and suck away the salty blood like Dracula. Which is appropriate, considering I manage to suck all the good energy from people, leaving them weak and empty, like a psychic vampire.

Sweeping the grounds, I find Grace immediately. She's not far from the entry gates, and it looks like she's in the midst of a whopper of a project. There is a pile of dirt five feet high near the black fence. She doesn't look like her normal self as she bends over her rusty shovel, ankle-deep in a pile of dirt, hair sticking out around her face, and ranting about something I can't hear; all Grace needs is a crusty pipe hanging off her lip to be frightening extra in a horror film. If it was nighttime, she'd scare the you-know-what out of me.

For a moment, she freezes and peers into the distance. I think she's seen me, but then she jumps down into the dirt. She must be digging a hole for one humongous tree, because all I can see of her is the top of those crazy black curls. *Funny place for a tree.* That close to the fence the tree will grow into the iron bars in no time; Grace knows better than that!

Fifteen steps away from her and the butterflies in my stomach take flight. I try to channel my big, brave inner vampire, but he shrinks away in the sunshine and all my resolve melts right along with him. It's time for desperate measures. I give myself a pep talk. "I can do this. It's a simple apology. 'I'm sorry.' I can go through with this."

As I near the rim of the massive hole, I hear Grace mutter, but the voice that comes from below doesn't sound like her at all. I'm reminded of that episode of *Ghost Seekers* we watched a few weeks ago. Zane was possessed by a demon and when he spoke his voice wasn't his. I make out gruff, gravelly bits from the depths. She's saying, "Damned worthless fool; that's all you are, Grace. Should've left the fairy tales in the children's section, girl. You're a damned fool."

When I peek over the rim of the hole, I see she has the shovel raised over her head, and I recoil as she strikes the ground with a bang. *Put that thing down!* Grace grabs at the ground and chucks a large round rock out of the hole. I dodge before it can smack me in the head. A newly revised pep talk runs through my mind. *Let's get this over with, the sooner the better.*

I spit out a shaky, "Hi, Grace."

When she jerks around, her eyes drink me in like a hungry wolf looking at a plump rabbit. I take a step backward and trip over the massive pile of dirt. As I dust off, Grace climbs out of the five-foot hole and her face looks softer. She smiles and a crust of mud on her cheek cracks and crumbles onto the front of her overalls.

"We're twins now," she says as she wipes at my cheek with a hand. I catch a glimpse of red and grab her hand, twisting it around to see her palm. "Grace, you're hurt! Your poor hands are a bloody mess." She doesn't back away as I touch the wounds, and I take that as a sign that I haven't completely ruined our friendship.

"I don't mind the blisters. A person *should* bleed when they dig an angel's grave, don't you think? It should hurt to bury a person this perfect." Such a tragedy, and it seems to be tearing Grace apart, but I can't help but feel grateful that she's talking to me.

She squints and I follow her gaze to the shiny black tombstone next to this hole. "Barely sixteen and killed by a drunk driver. Imagine that! My only comfort is knowing her mama is waiting for her up in heaven. She's buried here." Grace points a finger to the black tombstone. She shakes her head and rubs her bloody hands onto her denim overalls.

"God, Grace. Shouldn't you let the maintenance guy dig this grave with the John Deere?" She has a couple guys that dig the graves for her, the same men that mow and do general handiwork.

"Some things you can't give to other people to do. The children? I always bury the children by hand, every last one of them." She mumbles something I don't quite catch. "... I'm so tired of digging graves for babies...." Like the mud across her cheek, Grace looks like her emotions are breaking apart and falling away. I see glimpses of the Grace I've come to know in the patches of brown skin that the mud doesn't cover and her alert, golden eyes. But, even her eyes look strange, sunken into her face somehow, sad and broken.

I hesitate to ask, but I want to know what she's saying under her breath. "What was that, Grace?"

She yanks a yellow bandana from her overall pocket and swabs down her face. She wraps her blistered hand with the cloth and plunks down onto the pile of dirt. "Did you know I've dug nearly a hundred baby graves since coming to Lakefront? A hundred people that should still be alive and I am weary of it; I am damned sick of digging graves for little coffins. The first one I dug was for my own child."

The sun ducks behind a cloud and a chill settles over me. I shiver. Grace had a child? What else don't I know?

"It's the first time the old Deathbed had any draw for me, Casey. It is a strong temptation right about now." Grace shakes her head and stands. She stabs her shovel into the middle of the pile of dirt and walks off.

I hurry to catch up, speaking to the back of her head. "Grace, what are you talking about? I don't understand."

We amble past Father Kujala's plot into the furthest corner of Lakefront. I didn't realize that the graves reached so close to the water's edge. We stand in a place where the pine trees crowd out the view entirely. I know if I wait any longer to apologize I will lose my nerve.

"I wanted to talk to you about something, Grace. I've got something I need to say." My voice comes out in a raspy huff because I am so scared. Is this a panic attack?

Grace turns and scowls. "It can wait," she grumbles, as she tugs back a thick branch that sags near the ground. She snaps it off with her boots and bloody hands. She tosses the branch into the lake and exposes the grave hidden below.

This is the strangest grave I've ever seen. As best I can tell, it's a gray stone bed, an honest to goodness bed. In front of me is the headboard of an old-fashioned four-poster bed, but the entire thing is carved out of gray stone. Moss has claimed the right side of the sculpture and a plush carpet of green spans the stony mattress.

"What is this?" I want to get away from this strange grave. It unsettles me to see a bed carved out of stone. Eternal sleep and all that.

"This here is the most talked about grave in Lakefront. It's the Deathbed." Grace sits down on the mossy mattress and I take a step toward her, and she scowls.

"Move away from here! You've no idea what you're getting into. Go on, get!" She dismisses me with a flick of her hand.

I think my inner-vampire likes the shade of these trees, because I get my fierce on quick!

"Excuse me?" I bark at her. "I am not a cat you can just shoo away. I'm not exactly sure what is going on, but I've seen enough to know that you're not right in the head at the moment. What is all this crap about a deathbed?" I sit on a pile of rubble at the end of the weird grave, and pain shoots up my spine as a sharp stone pokes into my tailbone.

"This here is a quick ticket to peace, that's what it is." Her sentence comes out like she's making a wish and it creeps me out.

Grace strokes the stone headboard with her hands like she's petting a cat. She clears away dead pine needles from the words etched into the gray face and traces her finger over the name Joseph Eaton. Underneath are the words:

Be you in pain my friend?
Say my name, lie down, and know your end.

"This grave is beyond creepy, Grace. Get up!" I hold my hand out to her but she looks past it to the headboard.

"There have always been dark rumors about this grave as far back as I can remember. I let the trees take it over most times to keep the curious from stumbling across it."

She snaps off another low branch with a crack and keeps talking. "Rumor has it, you lie across the grave, say his name three times, and he'll pull you down into hell. When I was in high school, some kid took the dare. He and a group of his buddies broke into Lakefront. He rested on the Deathbed and called for the man buried underneath. That boy was a hero around the school for six days. Then on the seventh day, his heart gave out in the middle of a pep assembly. So the thing you have to understand is, most rumors have a grain of truth to them."

She caresses the stone with her hand and hums a haunting tune. She's got her crazy on big-time and it is scaring me. Any other day, this woman could herd cats if she put her mind to it, but right before my eyes she's falling apart. She's longing to lie on some cursed grave. Would the real Grace please stand up?

"What's that song you're humming, Grace? It sounds familiar," I ask, mostly to distract her for a moment and draw her out of the madness.

"Something I remember from a dream last night. Do you like it?" Grace smiles crookedly and hums louder, and then stops. The hair rises on my arms. "Casey, would you hate me if I stretched out on the Deathbed and called it quits? I'm about done with this life."

"Are you kidding? Yes! Yes, I would hate you for that. You? I don't know anyone as full of life as you." I want to shake her by the shoulders and rattle her back to her old self. "I don't know anyone as important to the world as you! Stop talking like this! What is wrong with you?" I shout.

I kneel down and grab hold of her overalls and shake. I shake her and shake her until she sits up. When she looks at me then, she seems to actually see me. I let go of her overalls and wipe the sweat off my face.

As she stands up, she brushes a hand over her wild curls, dusts off her overalls, and takes a long, deep breath. "You know what your biggest problem is, Ms. Starbaugh? Not your family, no. You only see what you want to see in people. You need to grow a spine and look at folks for who they really are.

"I'm gonna let you in on a little known fact. I'm not some wonderful, caring, nurturing person. In fact, I'm the opposite. I cause things to die." She stares at her hands and I hold my breath. I don't know if I should say something. I try, but I am so stunned by her opinion of herself I find my tongue won't work. She goes on, "Most cultures leave cemetery work to the lowest class of people. That's me, Casey. I'm just a lowly, good-for-nothing gravedigger. Society picked me to do the dirty work. That's all I am. Sorry if that comes as a disappointment."

Her face looks like a droopy basset hound from cartoons, and if those words came out of anyone else's mouth, I'd feel sorry for them, but coming from Grace, I feel altogether different. Her words make me angry, and I have to admit I am disappointed in her.

Finally my tongue loosens. "No, Grace. My biggest problem is that I see people for what they really are underneath it all. Cut the pity party, will you? Where is this coming from?" I think about the hurt I might've caused her by stealing from that boy's grave. Maybe the answer lies with me. A whisper in my ear tells me I need to get on with what I came here to do. It feels urgent now, because somehow I've made someone I love despise herself.

"Grace, I came to say I'm sorry!" I bark. She needs to hear this!

"Sorry for what?" she asks, staring into me with haunted eyes. Or not haunted so much as hungry, like she is looking for a reason not to lie down on that awful grave.

I reach inside my pocket and draw out a thin, muslin marble bag, hoping beyond hope that what she is about to receive feeds her. Maybe vampires can change. And when she grabs it, something does change in those eyes; they glow gold again, and I know I'm doing the right thing. Bolder now, I continue. "I'm sorry for taking the stones off Ettore's grave. It felt wrong but I did it anyway. I'm so sorry."

She opens the black drawstring and pours the red stones into her wounded palm with a rattle. Soon her tiny hand fills and stones overflow onto the ground. She stares down at them and her body shakes. I scramble to pick up the fallen stones. "Grace, are you okay?" As she silently weeps, she gathers up the stones and returns them to the bag, cinching the top closed.

"Casey, walk with me," she commands. Her dirty boots cut across the cemetery grounds toward the stone lambs and miniature apple tree I've come to know so intimately.

My feet know the way, so I rack my brain to try and figure out what cruel punishment she may have in store for me. Maybe she'll make me prune blackberry bushes without gloves. Or I'll be forced to clear out the yellow jacket nest from the maps bin.

The ideas are starting to flow when Grace stops at a grave I've never noticed before. Confusion wrinkles my forehead because we're a good thirty-feet from the children's cemetery.

The grave we stand by is a sterile black slab. The words chiseled in white have no flowery epitaph or fancy decoration, only this:

Renaldo S. Versino
(b. 1964 – d. 2002)

Grace says something under her breath and when she quiets she reaches into her palm and extracts one of the small red stones I just returned to her. She sets it on top of the austere tombstone, and then looks up to the heavens. She seems surprised to see me at her elbow, but recovers in a heartbeat and smiles.

"You think you know people, Casey? See if you could've guessed this. Renaldo Versino was my husband and I'm the reason he's dead," she says as she zips her sweatshirt up to her neck, and then unzips it again as if her nervous hands don't quite know what to do with themselves. She tucks a ghost curl into an absent ponytail, forgetting for a moment that she cut off her hair months ago.

"We were the odd couple if there ever was one: His olive skin, silky straight black hair, and thick Italian accent, and me, an educated black woman, stubborn and plain. Oh, it was love at first sight, but soon life did to us what it does best; we were handed a slew of trouble, one thing after the next. And I don't know which road bump did it, but what drew us together shook loose and fell away. Pretty soon it was only our son that kept us together."

I want to dive in with a million questions, but I don't want her to stop talking. I've watched enough cop shows to know better, so I bite my tongue. A husband? A son? How? Where's the boy now?

"Looking back, I ignored the obvious."

"Yeah, that's called 'Monday morning quarterbacking," I say.

"Perfect name for it. Renaldo never wanted a ring on his left hand. Nope. Felt like a dog collar to him, I imagine. But, that didn't keep me from wanting to change him." Grace turns her face away from his grave and stares at me.

"Don't ever set out to change a person, you got that, Casey? It's wrong. A long time ago, I heard someone say, 'Show me who you are and I'll believe you.' Damn good advice, if you ask me. Take the time to get to know a person. Don't see them for what they could be, but let them show you who they are. Then decide whether or not you want to spend time with them, see?" She digs into the pocket of her overalls and hands me a small knot of something.

I look at the lump in my hand and ask, "Is this coal?"

"That's right. Look at that and see coal, not the diamond it could be. Got that?" Grace says.

For some reason my mind flits to my family, my unfeeling mother, mostly absent father, and over-achieving brother. I stuff the coal into my pocket.

Grace reaches out a hand and touches my sleeve. "You all right?"

"Mhmm." I do see people for what they could be and so many times I end up disappointed when they fall short. I'm no different than my mother, am I?

"I guess you're wondering why I am going on about this, huh?" Grace says.

It unnerves me to listen to her. I've heard enough. I don't know if I can handle more revelations. I suck in my breath too fast and my head feels light and tingly. I try to slow down my breathing, using one of those yoga techniques Josie swears by, but I'm on the verge of hyperventilating. I sit on the wet grass and Grace squats down beside me. She grabs my hand and strokes it, staring into my face with wide, worried eyes.

"I'm trying to show you who I really am. I'm not doing this to lay my burden on you, Casey. But, you need to know this story, I promise. When my life unraveled a decade ago, I made a vow not to speak of it again, but then on Halloween night, when you made a beeline for the children's cemetery, I knew it needed to be told.

"And then you rubbed that grave, Ettore's grave, and that was the moment my faith in God was restored. There had been a plan all along. Maybe I should have told you sooner, I don't know." Grace's eyes drift over the cemetery, lost in thought.

She looks at me. "I wanted to be patient. I was afraid if I jumped in with my big mouth and big feelings I'd chase you off. I needed to see His plan revealed in His time."

I scratch my head and try to see what she is getting to, but the pieces don't fit together yet. "I am so confused. You're talking in riddles, Grace. You don't owe me anything. I was a brat. You gave me safe haven from my family. You've shown me a different way of looking at myself, as a friend, a daughter, and a sister. I owe you thanks. You don't have to tell me any of this if you don't want."

"I do, Casey. I do, because you see, Ettore is mine. He is my son." She looks at me with giant owl eyes. She's scared of me. Tears fall onto her cheeks and leave dark tracks through the dried mud.

My hands shake. I should've seen this coming, but I feel blind-sided by what Grace has confessed. Angry blood pulses in my veins. "He's what?"

"Ettore's my son. When you rubbed his grave, I... oh, I don't know." Grace hides her face in her hands and weeps. "I thought Ettore was working some kind of magic. Maybe he wanted me to step in and be a better mother for you than your own kin had been. I miss being a mother, Casey. I miss it something awful. But then when you moved into the cottage, I realized I was doing it again, being selfish.

"I wasn't helping you. I was trying to take you away from your own mother. It's terrible. Awful. After New Year's when you pulled that stunt and ran away, I sided with you. I let you go on and on about what a terrible person your mother was. But the truth was, I saw she cared about you. I saw through her tough lady act and knew she loved you. But did I stick up for her? No. I wanted to keep you for myself for a time, so I kept quiet. Then, every day you stayed at the cottage and your mother neglected to call and beg you to come home, I watched you get sadder and that's when I tried to make amends. Everyday, I called your mother and told her what a helpful person you are. Funny. Smart. Kind. I tried to build bridges, but I knew as long as you were under my roof, your relationship with your mother would never get better. So when I found the stones, Ettore's stones, it was easy to toss you out."

Grace shakes her head and stares into her blistered palms. "You were my second chance to do right and I bungled it." She wipes down her face with a sleeve and digs at the ground with the heel of her boot. "The truth is, I'm no good with living folks. It's best if I keep to myself."

Part of me wants to reach out and hug this precious woman who carries the weight of the world on her shoulders. But another part of me feels angry and betrayed. She watched me obsess about Ettore, his grave, and his ever-loving parents. She knew I pined for that kind of love. I never wanted anything more than that in my life, loving parents like Ettore's.

I didn't know what I was missing, what was so wrong with my own life until I looked at that grave week after week and saw the raw devotion his parents, well Grace, had for him, even after he was no longer alive. And then it was all I could think about. Dammit. "I was doing fine before you came along, Grace! Just fine! Then I rubbed that grave and everything went south."

"I know, and it is all my fault. I should have told you Halloween night. I'm sorry. It's probably best to get the hell away from me." She looks meek and shrunken somehow. The strap of her dirty overalls slips off her shoulder as she hugs her knees to her chest. She rocks back and forth and mutters so inaudibly that I cannot hear what she says. She doesn't seem to notice I am still here, just feet away. I shake my head. Maybe I don't read people as well as I thought. She's not right in the head. Didn't she say something about putting her husband in that grave? Living among the dead all these years has led her to madness.

Josie Helps Grace Move On

IT IS THE LAST DAY of March in the great Northwest. Know that old saying, "March comes in like a lion and out like a lamb?" Well, around here it is more like, "March comes in like a lion and out like a lion." Actually, this year feels more like a wet dog than a lion.

In the last few weeks, I have watched my life crumble to pieces. I can't sleep. I refuse to bury the puzzle box. Seth still isn't speaking to his father. And probably the worst thing is that Grace broke up with my dad, out of the blue. It was the day after the funeral for the teen girl that was killed by the drunk driver.

Grace is moving, too. This morning she texted me to ask if I could help her pack. The message came in at 5:00 a.m. The second text, an apology for texting so early, came in at 5:01. Ha! You have to be asleep to get woken up! These days, I try not to sleep. Thank heavens for caffeinated drinks. I can't have any more God-awful dreams if I stay awake.

Giant cardboard liquor boxes are strewn across her once-sweet living room. We've gotten through the kitchen and most of the living room, but with a guest room, her bedroom, and the basement left, I text Casey and Blaze for backup. I can't bring myself to reach out to Seth because it feels complicated. I want him here as a friend, but I can't deal with the other feelings I have for him right now.

I bring a fresh box to Grace's room and find her sitting on the end of the bed, her head in her hands. She looks like *The Thinker* by Rodin, except she's black and lithe and pretty without trying. Oh, and she's not naked. A manic laugh spews from me. It must be the lack of sleep. I can't quite control myself these days.

Grace startles from her frozen pose and glances sideways at me. "What's gotten into you, Josie?"

"I've got the tired jollies. You ever had those?"

"Not recently, no." She rakes the room and her eyes come to rest on the nightstand. I wonder what she's thinking about. Maybe she's having second thoughts about moving.

"How are you holding up?" I ask.

I step to the nightstand and peek inside the open drawer, finding a funny assortment of items: cough drops, lip balm, notepad, pens, reading glasses, and a hoop of gold. A ring? I dig in the drawer and pluck out a gold ring and slide it onto my pinkie finger, or "finkie" as Owen used to call it. Grace cranes her neck and stares back at me.

"You can keep it if you like. Of course, it didn't bring me anything but bad luck."

"Oh, well. I'm already knee-deep in bad luck, Grace. Was this your wedding ring?"

"Mhmm. I forgot where I put it until I started digging out this room. I should've left everything right where it was, bought new stuff for the apartment. Stupid!"

"How'd you find someone so fast to take your place here? Craigslist?"

"Craig's what? Nah, I expect my cousin's been waiting to hear from me for a long time. It was his turn. I wasn't supposed to last more than a year or two. This place isn't good for anyone over time." She rises, pulls the drawer free of the nightstand and dumps the contents into a cardboard box.

"Think I'll leave the furniture." She slides the drawer back in place and pulls pictures off the wall, setting them across the bed. She stares into a faded wedding photo. It is of a young and gorgeous Grace and her husband, Renaldo. "What were you talking about when you said you had enough bad luck? What's got you down, Josie?"

I spin the ring around on my finger and stare into the shimmering diamond. "I think I'm bringing bad luck on myself for not burying the puzzle box. I'm having bad dreams. I mean, I've always had bad dreams, but these are like bad dreams on steroids." An involuntary shiver erupts up my neck and down my arms. I rub my arms and stare at the cozy bed. "Maybe if I slept here, I wouldn't have them."

"Would you mind telling me about the dreams? I don't mean to pry," Grace says. She wraps the pictures in old newspapers.

"I accidentally fell asleep last night for maybe half an hour and had the worst dream yet. In the dream, I walked to my mom's grave and when I got there, it was different. The grass above her grave was missing; the dirt was gone, too.

"In the moonlight, I saw the outline of her vault. I could barely see the white porcelain through the tree roots knotted around it. I wanted to crawl inside that hole. I wanted it so much that it made my heart hurt. Does that make sense? Maybe it felt like a heart attack, I don't know.

"So, anyway, I sat on the edge of the hole and lowered my legs down. I couldn't reach her vault, but I knew it was there, so I jumped. My feet slipped and got caught in the roots. Actually, now that I'm thinking about it, the roots sort of grabbed my feet and pulled." I look at Grace to make sure I'm not freaking her out. She pauses from her work and watches me.

"Go on," she says.

"I found my mom's puzzle box there, on top of her coffin. I wrapped my arms around it and stretched across the top of her vault. It felt peaceful. I remember thinking how tired I was and how I wanted to close my eyes for a minute before climbing back out of her grave. I closed my eyes and fell asleep. Can you do that, Grace? Fall asleep in a dream when you are already asleep?"

She shrugs her shoulders, "Anything can happen in dreams, honey."

And I continue. "I was so content, and then I heard it, the caws of a thousand birds. They were swooping past the grave, diving lower and lower. One at a time they flew into the grave and held me down until I was covered with them. They pressed my whole body down. I couldn't breathe and tried to raise my hands to my face to push them off, but I couldn't budge my arms. That's when my head started hurting and my lungs, oh, they burned from the lack of air. I knew I had to get out of that grave! I clutched the puzzle box and climbed out.

"The next thing I knew, I was standing on the rim of the grave looking down at the crows, black crows. They spread out their wings, blocking me from my mother's vault. And all I could do is stand there and watch. I tried to lay her puzzle box inside the grave, but the birds flapped and shrieked. And then I woke up."

I stuff my hands under my legs to hide their trembling.

"Thank God for Shadow, that's all I can say. He is my saving grace. It never scares him away when I wake up screaming. He stays there on my chest with this determination written across his face. I don't know, Grace. He's like a guardian angel. Sometimes I wonder if he's sort of like part of my mother's spirit, protecting me from all the bad stuff. Do you believe in things like that?"

Grace sets the last of the pictures inside the box and sits next to me. She reaches for my hand and holds it in hers. "You are some kind of special, Josie. Do you realize you were Owen's age when your mother passed? You were a baby, really. After Sarah died, you put your focus on making your family whole again.

"You took over the responsibilities of that house. Owen, Grant, everything. Somehow you decided it was your job to take her place. I don't think she ever would have wished that burden on you, never in a million years. Yet, you tried.

"It's no wonder you are having such a hard time these days. What with all this stuff about a stone heart, all those mysterious clues, that puzzle box. It's a miracle you're able to function at all."

"You don't believe it, do you, that a piece of my mother's heart is inside that box?" I ask. I grip her hand tighter.

"What I believe is that she was very ill as a child. The tribe did something to keep her alive and she liked thinking there was something special about her, something magical. Don't we all wish for that?

"After she died, it was too much for Grant. He went into that autopsy and looked at the woman he loved all cut up and bared to the world, and it was too much. He wanted to see something there, a stone where a heart should be, because that meant he could hate her for being different rather than mourn her for what she really was–his wife, mother of his children, his best friend. No, I don't believe it."

"What about the bad dreams? Is that her? Is she mad at me for keeping the box so long?"

"Josie, I think you're mad at you for keeping that box so long. That's what I think. If it was my life to live, I would have a funeral for Sarah, do it properly, and put that box in the ground next to her. I think that's what you need to do."

My phone dings in my jacket and I read the screen, "Answer the door!"

"Our relief team is here–Blaze and Casey." I lumber to the front of the house to let them in, my legs feel heavy and tired. I feel so tired.

They rush inside, full of fresh energy and raw concern. They take in the boxes, stacked, marked, and ready to be brought to a new home. The sight of them rejuvenates me.

Grace comes at Casey and gives her an awkward hug. Then Casey wraps her arms around the woman and they stay like that for a moment. Grace whispers something I can't hear into Casey's ear and Casey nods, then they break apart. "Why are you leaving, Grace?" asks Casey.

"It's time, honey. That's all. I've been surrounded by the dead too long. Time to do a little mingling with the living."

Blaze fiddles with an ear and asks, "Then why'd you have to break things off with Mr. Jameson?"

"Now that would be none of your business. I will say this, something snapped in me. We were lowering that girl into the ground, the little sixteen-year-old killed by that drunk driver, and something broke in here." She holds a hand against her heart. "I've buried enough people. It's brought me down. I don't want to pull anyone else down with me. Time to do something new."

I understand about pulling people down. Poor Seth. He has all these big feelings for me. I knew it was wrong to cross that line between friends and something else when we kissed in the art shack. I didn't have the energy to hold back at the time. And part of me loved the kiss. Now though, I stay mostly to myself to avoid infecting Seth or anyone else with all the darkness in me.

"How's your father taking it, Josie?" Casey asks. She flicks a look at Grace.

I think about what Grace said about never letting myself mourn. Actually, what I've done is just to keep everything inside. I'm sick and tired of it. Even though it may hurt Grace to hear, I decide to speak the truth.

"Not good. Poor Owen. My dad's gone back to his old habits. He sends us to school on the shuttle bus. He forgets Owen's baseball games. He doesn't remember to buy groceries. He goes to bed at eight."

"That's a damn shame. I'm not worth all that," Grace says.

I shake my head. "It's like your break up triggered something, and he went back to his old ways. It would have been so much better if he had never changed at all. Then Owen wouldn't have realized what he was missing all those years." Grace and the others look sad to hear about my dad.

The old familiar guilt, my steady companion, tries to grab my hand, but I shake it loose. This feels good. I don't have the energy to make this better for my dad or Owen or Grace or the Baby Group. It is my father's life. He has to decide to start living it.

I feel tired suddenly, so tired. My eyelids droop and I stumble down the hall, ready to rest my head on a pillow.

Josie Shops for Funeral Wear

IT IS DAY THREE of possibly the worst spring break in recorded history.

Casey and I are at the mall to shop for new clothes, not for prom, but to wear to my mother's second funeral. I hate shopping, but I couldn't bring myself to call my Aunt Karen to save me this time. The least I can do to honor my mother's memory is to find something black and appropriate on my own–well, sort of on my own.

Casey's mom has taken an uncharacteristically active role in our outing today. She picked us up, treated us to lunch, and then volunteered to shuttle us home after we finish shopping. I almost passed out when she handed Casey her credit card, instructed her to pay for everything, and then hugged her goodbye.

"Well, things have sure changed between you and your mom."

Casey smiles. She tucks the credit card into her shiny blue patent leather wallet. "Yeah, I have to pinch myself sometimes to believe we are actually getting along."

I hug her. "I'm happy for you." She giggles.

"So, where should we head?" Casey asks.

We study the map of the mall and Casey closes her eyes, spins around three times, and points a finger to the glass. "Looks like this is it!" She smiles. I grab her hand and pull her to the teen section of the mall.

Somehow we make it past the teashop, despite the overly aggressive saleswoman that juts into our path to force a sample of white jasmine down our throats, and then we ride the escalator to the main level of the mall. I smell french fries, and know we're nearing our destination.

This part of the mall is swarming with activity. All I can figure is there must be a new video game out, because we are swimming upstream in a creek of teen boys. What would normally drive me to distraction, I find downright annoying today.

"Here it is." The clothing racks in the department store brim with the bright, cheery colors of spring. With everything that is going on in our lives, I had forgotten we are in the throes of spring fashion week. The bold hues strike me as garish, considering our somber purpose. A quick search indicates that the nearest shade to black anywhere in here is light tan.

"I don't think we're going to have much success."

"Yeah, I agree, Josie. If we want to show up looking like extras in an old eighties music video, we're in the perfect store. What about that place that sells black and white clothing? Should we try that one?" Casey asks.

"It's worth a try, I suppose. Or maybe what we need is a warm cookie?" I suggest. "Or a cinnamon roll?"

Casey puts her hands on her hips. "Huh? I thought you liked to shop?"

"Not really," I laugh. "I never told you, but my Aunt Karen does all my shopping."

"I should've known." She smiles. "You have a personal stylist. No wonder you always look perfect. What do I have to do to get her to do the same thing for me?" She looks down at her mini-skirt and leggings and adjusts her denim coat.

"You don't need her, Casey. You always look cute." And it's true. She mixes textures, colors, and patterns in ways I would never dream up, giving her a look that is all her own. I've never thought about it before, but she really is a fashionista. I giggle.

"What's so funny?"

"Nothing really." I shrug. And when Casey frowns at me I say, "It's not funny. I was just wondering how much worse this month could get. See? Not funny."

"Technically, all the bad stuff happened in March. This is April. Nothing bad has happened yet."

"Well, Grace moved. She remains broken up with my dad. There's the weirdness between me and Seth because of the kiss."

"Yeah, that's all kinds of bad. I miss Grace. She lives all the way downtown now. Do you think she made up all that stuff about Ettore to get me back for taking the stones?" she asks.

"Are you kidding? She wouldn't make that up!" I say. "What makes you think she made it up?"

"I don't know. It doesn't make sense. That day I found her digging the grave she said she killed them, Ettore and Renaldo. Come on! Grace wouldn't hurt a fly."

"But, it's true. Blaze told me. I mean not literally true, but she blames herself for their deaths." I say. Surprised, Casey looks at me with hurt written all over her face.

"He wasn't supposed to repeat it," I add quickly, "but she told him some story about answered prayers and how they can be a curse. She wanted her husband to die, but she hadn't foreseen that her prayer would actually be answered, much less that it would put her son in harm's way. I don't know why Blaze told me and not you."

Casey slumps onto the metal bench across from the black and white store. "It's no big deal. He didn't realize she was talking about Ettore. It's fine." But, I can see that it's anything but fine with her. I shouldn't have said anything. I reach out to her and she grabs my hand and gives it a squeeze.

"Owen misses Grace so much. I don't know. It seemed like Grace and my dad were really happy together. Who pushes happiness away?"

"She's pushing everyone away." Casey jumps to her feet. "She's punishing herself. Oh my gosh. That's exactly what she's doing! She doesn't think she deserves him and she's pushing him away. I almost feel sorry for her. Almost. She should have told me about Ettore a long time ago. I feel like I was the butt of some sick and private joke of hers every time she watched me visit his grave and report back what I found. It was cruel. I thought she was better than that." She paces across the marble floor.

"She must've had a good reason, Casey. Look at you! Why are you so quick to judge her after all the nice things she did for us? Actually, I think it's high time that we did something for her. If she *is* pushing people away on purpose, I think we should push right back.

We could get you, me, Blaze, Seth, Father James, Owen, maybe even my dad to come with us to her new apartment and tell her what she means to us."

"She's going to be at the cottage tomorrow. I overheard her on the phone with her cousin when we were helping her pack. She's turning the keys over to him."

"Perfect. I can invite the others, but do you mind texting Seth?" I ask.

"No way! You do it! You've known him your whole life, and you're going to let one stupid kiss get in the way of that bond? Nope. I am definitely not texting him."

Her phone trills and she says, "Well, black clothes will have to wait. My mom is picking us up in ten minutes. She scheduled a mani-pedi for the three of us in a half an hour."

"Did you ever in a million years think you'd be saying that? It's mind-boggling. You two are actually a mother and daughter. Not bad. Not bad at all."

SETH ROCKS
THE BOAT

THE SUN SHINES in all its glory above the great Northwest. It is a picture-perfect Sunday morning and Mom is driving us to the Mercer Slough so I can meet my dad for a day of kayaking. It's been a month since my parents got engaged, and exactly that long since I've spoken to my dad. My grudge is dragging down Mom's wedding hype, so I decided to organize this little boat trip to clear the air. Mom actually did all the legwork, proving how determined she is to see me speaking to my dad again. I thought the Mercer Slough would be the perfect place to have it out with Dad, because this land has a history of hosting fights.

A vast 370-acre wetland playground, the Mercer Slough has everything a native Seattleite needs to make the most of this glorious day. From hiking trails to blueberry fields, the park winds from the shores of Lake Washington to the hills. Even with the buzz of traffic from the I-90 highway overhead, it is hard to remember you are a stone's throw away from a bustling downtown core alive with dotcoms and retail giants when you visit the park. On any other day, I would be settled and content, ready for a day on the lake. But today, I am pumped up for a one-sided conversation with Dad, so the beauty and tranquility mean nada to me.

Our kayaks are strapped to the top of Mom's station wagon, and as she drives us through the retail hub of Bellevue to the launch site, she bubbles over with wedding news. She shares her plan to bring the family to Australia in June for the big event. Why Australia? My sister Sadie has an internship at the Australia Zoo, so it was a natural choice for the nuptials.

I catch every other word as I mentally rehearse what I'm going to say to my dad when we are out on the water. I'm trying my best to grin and nod at the right times, but when she gawks at me across the seat with the hint of a smile, I know she's onto me. "Seth, honey. I'm sorry all this came as such a shock. We should've handled it differently, done something less public I suppose. Your father was going to propose after dinner at the Jamesons', but he got caught up in the moment," she says.

She holds her left hand out and the sunshine illuminates her diamond ring, casting prisms of color across the roof of the car. "All you need to know is that I'm happy, really happy, for the first time in a long time. I was hoping you could share in it?"

Her voice is gentle and sweet, with not a trace of sarcasm. She slides the car into one of the few open parking spaces left in the lot and kills the engine. I roll down my window and check the parking lot for my dad's car. I don't see it yet. I'm anxious to get out there in the water with him and give him a piece of my mind. The feeling makes me giddy.

A laugh gurgles out. "I'm sorry," I say.

Mom drops her ringed hand in her lap and frowns. "What is so funny, Seth?"

Thinking fast I say, "Did you know that the Mercer Slough was the site of the original Battle of Seattle back in 1856 when Native Americans and European-American settlers fought with one another over land ownership?"

"And that's funny, because?" she asks.

I smile and say, "I guess it's funny because people flock here on nice days to hike and boat; you know, participate in peaceful activities. I'll bet most people have no clue about this land's bloody past, that's all. It's not really "ha-ha funny," just interesting." Serendipitous really, considering my plans for today: Battle with the Paddle.

My mom slides her sunglasses on and shrugs, "Well, one thing we know how to do in the Northwest is enjoy a nice day, at least from the looks of this parking lot. I hope your dad's able to find a space." She pulls her phone out of her purse and checks the time. "Oh! There he is."

Before my mom can reach the door handle and jump out of the car, I pat her arm. "I'm sorry I seem indifferent about the wedding, Mom. I'm happy for you. Josie calls it being guardedly optimistic." I shake my head and grumble. "There I go again, making this about me. I'm sorry. You, of all people, deserve happiness. I love you, Mom." I kiss her on the cheek and pop out of the car.

My parents say their hellos as I fumble with the black straps that hold the orange and blue kayaks to the roof. Dad rounds the car and frees the other side. We lift the boats to the pavement and I try to summon a dose of rage for him, but it has evaporated somehow. Cursed sunshine.

"I'm going to hike the trails while you fellas are out on the water. Do you want to have a late lunch together after your kayaking?" she asks.

"It's your call, Seth. What do you think?" My dad bothered to ask me? Hmm.

I shrug a shoulder, trying to look indifferent. Dad doesn't take well to indifferent. "Whatever. Sounds fine, I guess."

The lake is perfect today. There's barely a ripple as we row through the cattails and reeds on the watery path. Blue herons dart across the sky, and when we stop to eat a snack after an hour of rowing, the Canadian geese land next to our boat and beg with their black beady eyes for a morsel. My boat rocks gently side to side and as the sun ducks behind a cloud Dad hands me an ice-cold bottle of root beer.

He fastens the latch on his kayak compartment and says, "Your favorite! I went to three stores to find this brand. Maybe we should stockpile it, huh?" he asks. I twist the cap off the bottle and try not to show how excited I am. As I gulp down the soda, he continues. "So, I wanted to clear the air, Seth." He takes his baseball cap off and combs down his hat hair. He looks nervous.

"I owe you an apology. For the last year, your mom and I have worked really hard to process the past. We've learned a lot about each other, the most important being that we don't want to spend another day apart. She's my best friend, son. I blew it once, but she helped me forgive myself and move forward. But, there's a big part of the past that's been left unsaid."

He takes a swig of his root beer and wipes his mouth. "I remember the day I moved the last of my stuff out of our house. I pulled you aside and told you, 'You're the man of the house now.' Do you remember that?" His hand reaches to my boat and grips mine. I feel it tremble.

Do I remember? I've repeated it to myself a million times since then, and tried to live up to the statement ever since. "Yeah, I remember." Gross understatement.

"Well, I don't know why I said that. It was something to say at the time, but I didn't realize how badly those words would hurt you. It was stupid. In one sentence, I transferred my burden to your shoulders. After that, I watched you change. You felt it was your job to guard your mom and Sadie. There went your childhood, right?"

He takes his hand away from mine and presses his fingers into his eyes underneath his mirrored sunglasses. "That was about the time you started doing everything you could to make my life a living hell: the grades, the Goth looks, the messy room, everything. And I deserved it, believe me." He shakes his head. "God, I hated the black dyed hair, Seth. At least you didn't get a tattoo."

I finish off the last of the root beer and toss a goldfish cracker to the goose at the nose of my boat. My dad's words knock the fight out of me. I didn't think he understood what their divorce did to me. But he gets it. "If it's any consolation, the black dye was torture. It stained my pillowcase and ruined a perfectly good hat. I paid for the black dye like tenfold."

"Yeah, well. It wasn't as bad as when you stood me up on my visitations. That was way worse than hair dye and messy rooms." He rubs his chin with a hand and I look at his face. Etched into the sides of his mouth are deep wrinkles, carved by years of sadness and worry. All the emotions I tried so hard to evoke in him.

"I'm sorry about all that, Dad. I was an idiot. I was too young to realize that every story has complications, with black, white, and in-betweens. Instead, I cast you as the villain and Mom played the damsel in distress. It was lame."

"No, no. It was my fault." He slouches and the sun makes the white in his salt-and-pepper hair shimmer. When did he get so old? I guess I sped that process along, too.

The Seth that planned our kayak excursion today would've said something snarky to his 'It was my fault,' comment. But, that Seth is back on the banks of the slough. This Seth, the one I am right now would look like the portrait Josie drew two months ago, kinder, wiser and apologetic. "No, it was my fault, Dad."

"Maybe it was both our faults, son." And I nod. "But, the more recent mistakes were all mine," he says.

"Yeah, I'll let you take credit for those," I say.

"Man, Seth. When you started including me in your search about Sergeant Paxton and the whole question of property rights and all that, well, I got excited, too excited, really. We were going on a journey together, for the first time in a long time." His face is flush with color.

"And when you found that journal and we decided to visit the Big Island, I thought we had turned a corner. I guess I thought you were giving me another chance. And I got greedy. I wanted to help you by unlocking this thing. I got us more time with the state for taking down that sign. I was able to keep Fort Lewis from destroying the sergeant's medical files. And I wrote that letter to Mel Akaka. I knew I was doing too much, but I just wanted to see that look on your face again." His forehead wrinkles in pain.

My voice sputters. "What look?"

"The one you used to give me when I'd come home from court after the jury found the bad guy guilty and put him away for a long time. You'd look at me with such pride. Back then you were proud to be my son. I wanted you to be proud again." He pushes his sunglasses up the bridge of his nose, like I don't see the wet tracks the tears leave down his cheeks.

"What I've realized in the last month is that I never earned a second chance with you like I did with your mom. I never took the time to tell you how sorry I am for what I put you through. Seth, I'm sorry I forced you to grow up before you were ready. I'm sorry." He rubs his hands across his oars and takes a bite of his nutrition bar, and then offers the last crumbs to the waiting geese.

I can hardly remember why I was angry with him. What words was I going to use against him today to cut him into pieces? All I see is the man that I might be someday, a man asking for another chance. "Thanks for thinking about what all this did to me. The truth is, whether or not you'd said those words all those years ago, I would've felt it was my job to protect Mom. You didn't see it, but she changed into this sad person overnight. And when I couldn't fix her, I got spiteful. And you were the easy target. Pretty soon, hating you became a habit, no different than biting my nails.

"But, then you got me out of that pinch with the police after I broke into the sergeant's house. You broke the rules for me! After that I knew you were there for me, even after everything I'd done. Of course you deserve a second chance, Dad."

And this time, it's me that breaks down. It is a snotty, messy, ugly scene because I haven't let myself do this since I don't know when. And when I dare to raise my head, I see a ray of sunshine cut through a lone cloud and a clear beam shines across the lake.

"Dad, look at that. It's beautiful."

"Yep." He says.

"What do you think the sergeant would think of us? I rubbed his grave and it brought a father and son back together. And if we can prove Mel's his, the sergeant will have brought together two fathers with two sons."

"I think he'd like that."

"So, how soon can we fly Mel out here for the blood draw so we can compare it to the sergeant's sample at Fort Lewis?"

"If I have your permission, I'll get my assistant to make the arrangements tomorrow. How's that sound?" he asks.

"Sounds perfect."

As we row back to the boat landing, I think about that battle fought here long ago. Aren't we living proof that sometimes things have to get messy before they can get better?

They battled for two days, but in the end this land is all of ours. Our blood flows through each other's veins. Our dreams for freedom are the same. We are Americans, every one of us. And the fight made us better.

JOSIE AT THE POTLUCK

EVERYONE IS GATHERED at the Starbaughs' for Potluck Night, a tradition that began sometime after my mother's death almost seven years ago. Typically, the Makis' host the event, but Casey's family stepped in to host this year in light of Mr. Maki's heart attack, which everyone thought was nice. Dress code? Casual. But the food is made to impress because the person voted Best Chef gets to crow about the honor for the next 364 days.

Owen takes our masterpiece, buttermilk fried chicken, into the kitchen as the rest of us gather in the entryway and exchange hellos. Greetings take all of a minute, and then the teens split from the adults, sequestering ourselves in the game room. You'd be hard-pressed to separate eggs faster!

The air in the basement is chilly and slightly dank, but for me it is the smell of nostalgia. Before this was a game room, it was the site of every play date we had at Casey's. In reality, the big transition from playroom to game room required a few thin coats of blue paint, fresh wool carpet, and the removal of a stair gate.

The video games, Ping-Pong table, and Pachinko have always been here. I grab a red paddle off the green table and challenge Blaze to an epic match. As reigning champion, I plan to keep the title tonight. He rolls up his sleeves and spins a green paddle in his palm and taps a fiery-orange ball to the table, his eyes glued to the low net.

"Man, Josie, your dad looks downright lost without Grace," Blaze says.

He serves the ball with a backspin that makes the ball impossible to follow. I swat at the air and he says, "1-0," under his breath with a quick wink.

Did he bring up Grace to mess with my head? I curse under my breath. Refocusing, I stare down the middle of the table with steely eyes. I tap the ball to the table and say, "Yeah, he's depressed, that's for sure. But I don't know who feels worse about the break up, him or Owen."

I serve and the ball skims the net and taps the edge of the table. This time it's Blaze scrambling to make contact with the blur of orange. He catches the ball with the edge of his red paddle and it bounces off the ceiling and falls dead on the carpet.

"1-1," I say a mite too loudly.

He serves and we volley back and forth with an easy rhythm.

I say, "I was hoping it was a little lover's quarrel and they'd make up, but it's not looking that way. She hasn't returned Dad's calls." The ball clicks and bounces across the table until my backhand flounders and Blaze scores another point.

Across the room, Casey fires up the vintage Galaga game and the machine chimes out a chipper little ditty. As she peppers alien spaceships with digital lasers, she says, "It goes with our theory that Grace is punishing herself! She's pushing everyone away. We've got to do something. If the tables were turned, Grace would find a way to help us!" She smacks the fire button and squints into the dark screen. "Game Over" glows yellow across the middle and she smacks her palm on the console.

"So, what do you suggest we do?" Seth asks.

The face of his Pachinko machine dances like liquid mercury as thousands of silver balls slide down the glass between metal pegs. Between that and the zippy Galaga music, I start to get a low-grade headache. I set my paddle down in defeat and Blaze gives me a funny look as I go lay down on the couch.

"We don't even know why she's punishing herself. How do you help someone when you don't know what's wrong?" Seth asks.

Casey smacks the start button again on the Galaga machine and aliens drop across the black screen in yellow bursts. "It's gotta be about Ettore and Renaldo. Somehow we stirred up the past when we walked into her life. Let's face it; before we showed up, Grace spent more time with the dead than the living. In fact, she said as much."

"We forced her out of her comfort zone, that's for sure," I add.

As I rub my head, now throbbing, I try to recall the last time I ate. Dinner last night? I vaguely recall pork chops and applesauce. No wonder my head hurts. Casey abandons her game and stretches across the fluffy gray couch next to me. I squeeze my stocking feet under my knees to make more room. "You comfortable, Casey?"

"As comfortable as one can get when they are about to consume a meal called a 'potluck,'" she giggles. "I mean really."

"Huh?"

"It's just plain wrong to eat something with the word luck in it," Casey laughs. "It's like saying, I'll eat this, but in a few short hours I could be hunched over a toilet. Or not."

"Gross! Thanks for the visual!" Blaze says.

Laughter ripples across the basement and, as we collect ourselves, Mrs. Starbaugh shouts down the stairs, "Guys! Ten minutes until supper!" And the laughter erupts again.

Blaze rubs his belly and says, "Oh boy! Supper!"

I dab happy tears from the corners of my eyes and realize my headache is gone. Seth scoops up a paddle from the Ping-Pong table and takes up a vigorous game with Blaze.

As we shuffle up the stairs to dinner, Seth says, "Mmm! I feel lucky tonight." I smack him, meaning to slap his back, but I hit his booty instead. He turns backward and smiles. I can feel my cheeks burn red. So much for my secret vow not to cross lines.

As I hit the landing, I notice that everyone inside the kitchen is engaged in warm conversation, sipping glasses of wine and smiling. Everyone except my dad; he looks like a deflated balloon in the middle of a birthday party.

I break away from my friends and go to him. "Hey, Dad."

I reach my arms around him and squeeze. "Hey, Josie. How were the games? I tried to send Owen your way, but he's been face first in his Pokémon cards." He smiles, but the crinkles around his eyes look tired, not happy.

Then his face brightens, "Oh! I have something for you. God! I almost forgot." He pushes past the lineup of casserole dishes and slow cookers that dot the countertop and returns with a manila bubble-mailer. "I hope you don't mind me bringing it here. You were at Blaze's after school working on your project, and I didn't think you'd want to wait until late tonight to open it."

I see the airmail stamps across the envelope and squeak, "It's from Ireland!"

And this time his smile seems genuine. I try to grab the envelope from him, but he holds it above his head and laughs.

"You know that won't work much longer, Mr. Jameson!" Casey says, watching us.

She tries to lift me up and I grab at the mailer before I drop to the ground again. I snatch it out of Dad's fingers and shake it in his face.

"Should I open it now?"

I give the black arrow a gentle tug and the strip at the top of the mailer rips open an inch. My heart races. But, like everything else to do with Bain McLaren, nothing goes as planned. I'm interrupted by a heated conversation at the front of the house.

I catch snippets like, "Is this good for Owen?"

"What puzzle box?"

I hear enough to know they're talking about my mom's funeral, her second funeral that we plan to hold on Mother's Day. They're debating the need for it. From the voices, I predict Mrs. Starbaugh won't be attending. While the others wander to the dining room, I linger and think about the day when we will say goodbye to Sarah Jameson at last. Will that make the bad dreams finally end?

I touch a finger to the unopened mailer and hope. I hope the mailer holds some answer. I hope the funeral brings me a little peace. I hope. I finger the mailer again and decide to wait, savor the hope and possibility in my hands a little longer, maybe until after dessert.

I join the others, squeezing into a seat between Casey and Seth. My hands itch to open the envelope, so I stuff them under my legs and try to focus on the conversation that has shifted away from the funeral and turned to the topic of summer vacations.

Seth's parents share details about their upcoming nuptials in Australia, from the site to the photographer to the catering. It is a nice change to see Seth involved in the conversation, his grudge against his dad forgiven at last. Talk of wedding food gets people hungry and we queue for the potluck line.

Seth asks me something that I don't catch and I whisper, "I want to open that mailer! Come with me." We slip past the others into the kitchen and I grab the envelope from the counter.

"Open it!" he says. I tear the black strip at the top another inch and then pause.

"But then I'll know. This might be great or it might be a dead end. Let's keep it a mystery for a little longer." I tuck the envelope under my arm and line up at the buffet behind the others.

"Ugh! You're killing me," Seth says. He queues behind me in line and gives the envelope a gentle tug. I turn around and scowl and he taps a finger to my nose.

After at least one helping of everything and two of some dishes, I roll into the living room and sink into a giant gray beanbag. Seth tosses the manila mailer onto my bulging stomach. "Forget something?" he asks.

"Oh my gosh. Give it here."

"You ready now?" he asks.

"Let's do this."

When he nods, I rip free the strip at the top of the mailer and shake the envelope upside down. A white letter flutters out and behind it slides out a small black leather journal. My heart beats like a rabbit's as I unfold the letter and read the words.

Seth reads over my shoulder and soon I find myself surrounded on all sides by people trying to make out the contents of the exotic letter. I read aloud:

Dear Ms. Jameson:

Thank you for your recent inquiry into the genealogy of Bain McLaren. I was forwarded your inquiry from the Genealogical Society of Ireland after the name and timeline was confirmed to coincide with our lost daughter of Blarney. If it is confirmed that you have found the remains of Bain McLaren, formerly Bain McCarthy, then you have indeed solved a centuries-old mystery for our family and deserve the highest praise and most sincere gratitude.

As the resident expert in McCarthy genealogy, I thought you might enjoy learning more about Bain McLaren. Here is a brief overview of what the documents tell us.

The only surviving child of Donogh McCarthy, Bain was brought up within the rubble of a once-great family. As the original builders of Blarney Castle and regular holders of the office of Governor of Cork, the McCarthy family was near ruins by the time of Bain's birth. What remained of the glorious castle after the tragic fire of 1820, the McCarthy clan was forced to sell to Sir Jeffreys, along with the structures and expansive land that surrounded the once great castle. This included the famous Blarney Stone, thought to be a piece of the original Stone of Scone.

On the cusp of poverty, Donogh was brought on as groundskeeper by Sir Jeffreys, and raised his daughter as best he could after the death of his wife during childbirth. Bain was known for her curiosity and unquenchable thirst to learn. The girl spent most days at the heels of some worker or another on the expansive estate, but our records note she took a keen interest in the resident doctor, Dr.McLaren.

In an age when education was not readily available to girls, Bain stood apart. Her father taught her to read and write at an early age and encouraged her to spend time with the most educated citizens of Cork. Sir Jeffreys and his wife, unable to sire children of their own, indulged the child as well, opening their expansive library to young Bain. She loved the library in the great castle and was known to read everything from works of fiction to books on the emerging sciences. Most often it was Bain that cracked the bindings of every new book that entered the great library.

As I mentioned prior, the resident doctor held Bain's attention the longest. Dr. McLaren, it was noted in more than one diary kept by staff and family at the time, indulged Bain. She spent the bulk of her waking hours at his side tending to the infirmed of Cork. When the doctor's son, Jacob, returned from university, Bain was merely thirteen years of age. Jacob completed his medical training under the watchful eye of his father but proved to have no stomach for the profession. Though, Jacob developed a fondness for Bain over the course of the next year. When Bain turned fifteen, Jacob turned his attention to becoming a farmer and set his sights on the New World. When he departed for America to claim his piece of a new land, Bain joined him as his young bride. Her father was left behind and, heartbroken, he disowned the girl in a burst of cruelty at the ship's casting off.

From that point, our history of Bain is largely lost. We know her husband Jacob returned to Ireland from America ten years later with their daughter Regan in tow. He would never speak of what happened in the Americas or what fate met his young bride. All that is known is that he returned to Cork as a minister of the church and devoted the rest of his days to the service of God and care of their daughter, Regan.

As for the nature of Bain's death and the crimes that she was accused of, we have found no records to confirm these outlandish claims. Like the women executed during the witch trials two centuries prior, Bain's only crime was being a strong, educated woman at a time when society expected the opposite. No more. No less.

If what your paperwork reveals is true, then we would do well to exhume our precious lost daughter and re-inter her remains in Ireland. I have begun the legal process of claiming her remains for the McCarthy family so she can return home, and I send to you the warmest regards for solving this great mystery. As a token of our gratitude, please find enclosed the journal of Bain and Jacob's daughter, Regan McLaren. You have, undoubtedly, earned it. We will be in close touch as the day of Bain's reburial nears.

Warmest regards,

Madam Blythe McCarthy

As I finish reading, we give a collective sigh. Hands reach out to hold the letter and I pass it around.

Seth is the first to speak. "Well, that's very enlightening!"

I grope inside my purse and extract the stone heart fetish I found in the secret drawer along with the paperwork that led me to Bain's dark history. Clutching it in my fist, the strange object warms easily and I say, "I think Bain is happy I rubbed her grave."

Seth reaches for the fetish and the object is passed from person to person around the living room. My dad holds up a hand to say a silent, "No, thank you," and pulls Owen away from it before he can touch the strange object.

"I've always been convinced I made a mistake that night. I watched the rest of you unravel your mysteries in such an easy and natural way. Mine? I don't know. Every time I tried to dive in, I felt unwanted, like an awkward imposition on Bain.

"Sometimes, and I know it'll sound strange, but as we found things out about her, like the paperwork, or finding this," I hold up the fetish that is passed back to me, "I've felt physically overcome, either zapped of all my energy or literally sick."

I hold up the fetish and turn it over in my hands. "Now I understand why it all felt so repulsive and wrong. Her death was clouded by ignorance and hate. She was killed in a barbaric way, all for being clever and opinionated. Women weren't supposed to have a strong voice back then, so her voice must've sounded like a scream. Then, worst of all, her husband deserted her when he should've stood by her side. And he took their child with him! No wonder all this felt so horrible.

"But, now it's changing. I'm holding her fetish, and all I feel is peace and a calm resolution. Maybe rubbing her grave was the right thing to do after all."

The Baby Group surrounds me in a hug, and I'm shocked at the tears that run down my face.

When a cell phone jangles and shatters the moment, I take advantage of the distraction to wipe my face. Mr. Anthony speaks into his cell in a low voice and mouths "I'm sorry," to me. I hold up a hand to say everything's fine.

He clicks off the phone and says, "Son, that was Mel Akaka. His plane from Honolulu just landed. I'm off to the airport. Are you coming?"

Seth looks at me with puppy-dog eyes and I nod my consent. I'm so glad I opened the letter with him. "Definitely!" he says.

They gather their things, say a hurried goodbye, and scoot out the door. After they leave, the party winds down. Mrs. Starbaugh puts on a pot of coffee and starts a quiet movie in the family room, but all of us watch through a fog made up of our own personal thoughts. We hardly say a word as the black and white opening credits scroll across the flat screen.

Someone's phone rings again. My dad pulls his out of his pocket. When I see the relieved look on his face as he checks the number, I know it must be Grace, at last. He leaves the room to find a quiet place to talk, and Owen snuggles up to me in his absence.

I stroke his red hair and it dawns on me how little quality time I've spent with my baby brother since Halloween night. I make a silent vow to reconnect with him in the days to come. I kiss the top of his head, take in the smell of his strawberry-scented shampoo, and hold him as he drifts off to sleep.

CASEY PUSHES PAST THE GHOSTS

TOMORROW, MOTHER'S DAY, we will meet at Lakefront Cemetery to say goodbye to Mrs. Jameson. But, this day my friends and I will come together to offer tokens of our affection to Grace. I rest on the curb outside the gates and wait for the others and yawn. I stayed up way too late last night.

After the house cleared last night, I helped my mom tidy the remains of the potluck party. Exhausted from gathering garbage, scrubbing dishes, and vacuuming floors, we collapsed onto the couch and ended up having our longest conversation to date. Beating a five-minute talk is not hard to do, but for us it is a big deal. We chatted about the evening, our friends, and somewhere in the mix my mom apologized. I wish I had thought to commit the conversation to memory, because it's one of those moments I would love to replay when I need a quick lift.

She explained what it was like to grow up in southeast China. At the ripe old age of ten, she was sent to an English boarding school, alone! Her family expected her to make high marks and earn a scholarship if she wished to stay enrolled at the school. At an age when children tend to be more interested in comic books and cartoons, she ate a heavy diet of pressure, all while learning to blend into an English-speaking foreign country without a friend in the world. Me? I would've cried myself to sleep every night, but not my mom. She got tough.

She sought help from the older students. She didn't have any money to pay for tutoring, so she did laundry and other grunt errands in return for their services, which left my mom with very little time to study and even less time to sleep.

Her sacrifices paid off, though. Soon, she achieved top marks and a full-ride scholarship, all without a word of congratulations from her family. In fact, except for the occasional red envelope that came around the New Year, she had no contact with her family at all. Phone calls were too expensive and airplane tickets were unaffordable.

My mom continued to work her way through high school and college, eventually earning a scholarship to a prestigious graduate program in the United States, where she met my dad. She explained that as an adult, she can see the sacrifice her family made to part with her in an effort to give her a better life, but as a child, she only knew affection from them when she achieved something substantial: high marks in school, continued scholarship, college degrees. And once my mom was able to afford her own airplane ticket to China, she realized she didn't know her Chinese family anymore.

By the time she was a wife and mom, the scared little girl from China was buried deep within her marrow. She explained to me that when she became a parent she realized she didn't know how to be a mom. She did the best she could, but her stunted childhood had left many holes in her parental education. She ended up mothering us the way she was raised, which meant giving affection for achievements.

Her story made sense. I felt bad for the little girl that was sent alone to a foreign country. I told her she was brave and strong. And she agreed with me. But she said that I have all the traits she wished she had. I can express myself in words and art. I share my feelings with people. I listen. I am a good friend. I am patient and forgiving. She always saw these traits in me and envied them. *She envied me.* And at some point we hugged, which feels awkward still, but somehow we're getting better at it.

I asked her why she was telling me this now. She said something about old dogs learning new tricks, and how her conversations with Grace after I ran away opened her eyes to all that she'd missed out on as a mom. She also said that saying goodbye again to Sarah Jameson was a reminder to her that all our days are fleeting. We only have so much time left to live differently, better. She didn't want to wait any longer to try and be a better parent.

Both of us were already yawning from our busy day, and I remember being torn between heading to bed and telling my mom about Grace and how she'd pushed us all away. When my mom grabbed my hand and held it in hers, which felt awkward, I admit, I knew she wanted to hear me.

It was after midnight by the time we said goodnight. Before falling asleep, I texted the Baby Group and confirmed we would meet at Lakefront to try and break Grace out of her funk. She's not expecting us at the cottage, only her cousin, Erik, who is taking over as caretaker. It seemed like such a good plan then, but now in the light of day, with a huge balloon bouquet tangled around my arm, I wonder if my plan will make a difference. Still, as I picture my friends gathering at the cottage, arms full of offerings, I feel hope grow inside me like a snowball rolling down a hill.

We are exactly what Grace needs right now. After a decade of hiding away in a cemetery and keeping the company of ghosts, she needs to know she is more than a widow, a sonless mother, and a gravedigger. She didn't cause the deaths of Renaldo and Ettore. She needs to listen to her own advice and make peace with the past, once and for all.

By turning the mirror, we're going to show her the strong, funny, capable, caring, beautiful woman we see. We are going to introduce her to a woman who makes everything she touches better. Our Grace.

Brimming with nervous energy, I arrive half an hour early with nothing to do. I sit on the curb outside the gates of the cemetery and wait for the others to arrive, holding a ridiculously large balloon bouquet. I shrug off the strange looks I get from passersby. One bold artsy fellow jumps out of a beat-up import to snap a picture of me for some class at the university. After going off about "visual irony" or some nonsense, I let him take a couple shots, but I make it a point to glare into the lens. Come to think of it, my frown made the shots better: "Dour Girl Clutches Happy Balloons." Damn! I should've smiled.

Caught in a cloud of anger, I don't notice the gang come up the sidewalk until they stop at my feet and tug me off the curb.

"Hey, Casey! Great balloons. She'll love them," Blaze says.

He readjusts his grip on an oversized casserole dish, and I smell something spicy through the foil that makes my stomach rumble.

"What'd you make?" Blaze always cooks for an occasion because food equals love in his family. Lucky us.

"It's a new recipe I found online, Casey. I call it Seven Layers of Sunshine, but that's a fancy name for enchilada casserole. I hope Grace invites us to lunch!"

"Yeah, me too," Seth chimes in. "So, as you know I'm not much for cooking and flowers. This is my contribution." He shakes a pile of papers in the air. "I did some hasty research this morning and found all the articles that ran after Grace's family died. Here's the longest article about the accident, and I found two short follow-ups. The first details Renaldo's blood-alcohol content, and the second covers the memorial plaque Grace had installed at the crash site."

Josie tucks the bunch of flowers she carries under her arm and flips through the printout. "I'm not sure we should bring this up, you know?" she says, scrunching her perfect freckle-dotted nose at Seth like a modern-day Tinker Bell.

"Yeah, but on the off chance we can't get it through her stubborn head, maybe cold, hard facts will drive the point home."

He takes the paperwork from Josie and tucks it deep inside a manila folder, and then slips it into a weatherworn leather attaché I haven't seen since forever.

"Well," I say, "let's get going."

I walk into the grounds and then stop with a jerk when one of the balloons wraps itself around a spire. I untangle it and jog to catch up with the group.

A big orange rental truck is parked in front of the cottage. The roll-up door gapes open and a shiny aluminum ramp yawns to the grass. The back of the truck is stuffed to the gills with cardboard boxes and furniture covered up with shabby blue blankets. My chest tightens and acid bubbles up my throat like I've already partaken in Seven Layers of Sunshine. I knew she was gone, but to watch someone else move into her cottage is harder than I thought. We reach the front yard in time to see two beefy men stuff a plaid sofa through Grace's front door.

Blaze asks, "Casey? Do you have any clue what's going on?"

"It's her cousin. The only reason she's coming today is to turn over the keys."

Josie scoffs. "Red plaid furniture? Her cousin must be a lumberjack!" I swat away her hand and the balloons pound the side of my head.

We climb the makeshift ramp slumped over the porch steps and rap on the jamb of the open front door. A burly man approaches, his hairy arms locked across his expansive chest.

Looking like a photo from a Norwegian tourist brochure, the man watches us with bright blue eyes. And lily-white skin. This is Grace's cousin?

"Excuse me? May I help you?" he asks.

I step to the front and say, "We're looking for our friend, Grace. Is she here?"

Blaze makes for the kitchen to set down his cumbersome baking dish and we follow him

His bushy blonde eyebrows furrow as he takes in the balloons, the flowers, and the food, and then his face softens around the edges. "Well, she doesn't live here anymore."

"Yeah, we know that. She was supposed to be around today to give her cousin the keys. I'm guessing you're the cousin," I say, a question mark in my voice. I scratch my head, confused.

Seth jumps in. "So, Grace is your cousin? But you're..." Seth sputters.

"White. Yes. Yes, I am," he says. "I'm a cousin from her mother's side of the family. Erik," he says, holding out a hand. "Come on in." As we pass, Blaze offers the man the casserole dish. Erik peels back a corner of the foil and takes a sniff. "Thanks."

As we enter the cottage, I inventory the collection of dark wood and heavy furniture that has replaced all the lightness and femininity that was here just days ago. As I sweep the room, my gaze locks with the dead glassy eyes of a stuffed moose head mounted above the fireplace. The blood in my veins turns to ice, and I force air down my throat with a dry gulp and stare at the burly man.

"Listen, she's gone," Erik says. "She put the keys under the mat. She doesn't want to spend any more time here. You have to understand, this is how Grace does things. She decides to make a change and BAM!" He slaps his hands together and I jump an inch in my boots. He extracts some paper from his pocket, scribbles down an address, and gives it to Blaze. "The best advice I can give you is to take Grace's new address and track her down! I'm sure she'd be happy to see you. But, I have to get moving; got two funerals in as many days, you know." He tucks the foil back over the steaming corner and walks us to the door.

As we exit the cottage grounds, we stand, unsure about what to do now. "Let's see the address," Josie says. She reads the slip of paper and passes it around the group. "Hmmm. I think that's in Georgetown. Maybe we should try to go tomorrow after school."

Seth taps the address into his phone. "Yep, Georgetown. Should we try to get a ride from my dad after the funeral tomorrow?"

We all mumble answers and make our way back to the entry gates in sad silence.

"I sure hope Erik knows how to take care of this place, or he's going to get an earful!" Seth says.

"He's got big shoes to fill," I add, thinking of the way Grace knows the stories of the people buried at Lakefront so intimately. "Really big shoes."

I let go of my balloon bouquet and we turn our heads to the sky and watch them float into the white clouds until they become a speck of black and disappear completely. We say casual goodbyes since we will reconvene at Lakefront tomorrow for Mrs. Jameson's funeral. I reach my bus stop when a car horn blasts at my back.

My mom's car pulls to the curb and she shouts out the open window, "Do you want a ride?"

As I settle into the front seat, I glance out the window at the cemetery. I smile and vow to try again to reach our friend Grace. Seth's right. We will go visit her soon. It's the least we can do.

JOSIE SAYS GOODBYE TO SARAH JAMESON

FROM UNDERNEATH MY COMFORTER, I whisper into the phone's dial sounds. "Please answer, Seth." It is 3:16 a.m.

When he answers, he responds with a groggy, "What's up, Josie?"

"I had another bad dream. I don't know. Something's got to be wrong with me that my brain can make up such awful things." I hold the phone against my face and wish he was here to hug me.

"Do you want to tell me about it?" His voice is already comfort enough.

"I was in this dark house. I think it was our house but I couldn't tell because there wasn't any light. I heard my mom's voice, the same gentle voice she used to read me bedtime stories. She was calling my name. I stumbled in the dark toward her voice and kept my hands stretched out before me so I wouldn't run into the walls.

"It was so dark and cold, really cold. 'Josie!' she called, the tones got stronger with every step. There was a flicker of light and I ran to it, reaching the end of the hallway where I found a mirror hanging from the wall. I looked into it and could see myself, only the outline of me, and I smiled. She whispered in my ear. 'Josie, you've become so beautiful and strong. I am proud of you.'

"I looked to the right and found her. It was like she had never been sick. My heart was filled with all this love and peace." I sniff. "Sorry. I haven't felt peaceful since I don't know when. She reached out for me but I couldn't touch her. When I tried to touch her, my fingers hit a wall of soft feathers; thousands of soft feathers rustled under my fingertips. I clawed at them to get to her.

"I remember feeling so angry that even in a dream I couldn't have what I wanted, a perfect moment with her. I screamed out, 'Let me touch her!' Then all the feathers fell away. I clutched her hand and it was warm in mine. She knitted my fingers into hers and the room around us brightened, like someone was raising a dimmer switch. I searched her face, that beautiful face I've missed looking at for so long." I sob and the phone falls from my grip.

"Josie, where are you?" I hear him shout. "Josie!" I grope in the darkness under the blankets and find the phone.

"I'm here. It was more than a dream, Seth. She was so real. I touched her face, and I saw her freckles; we stood eye to eye, and she gazed at me like she'd never seen something so good."

"Anyway, I knew she was there and I had all these questions. Does dying hurt? Does she watch over us? Can she ever forgive me for holding onto the box for so long? I found my voice and asked her that, 'Mom, can you ever forgive me for keeping the box to myself this long?'

"Her eyes shimmered with tears. She opened her mouth to answer and black feathers flew out of her mouth! Millions of black feathers, and she coughed like she was choking on them. Oh, God! It was horrible. She coughed and coughed, and finally her voice came back, but it wasn't sweet anymore; it was gritty and hoarse.

"She said, 'Don't bury the box, Josie. Keep it with you. Don't bury it with me!'" And then she screamed. And then I woke up. Which is when I called you." I weep into my pillow and clutch the phone to my cheek.

"I'm here. I'm not going anywhere," Seth whispers. I cry until there isn't another drop left and he stays on the line. His breathing steadies me and calms me.

"Seth, am I a freak?"

"No. You're not."

"Are you sure?"

He huffs over the phone, "Look, do you trust me? Am I pretty much the most rational person you know?"

I nod, which I realize he can't see over the phone and I say, "Well, yeah."

"Right! So, I'm not going to fall in love with a freak, am I?"

Did he say "love?" My hands tingle, and I wish he was sitting next to me. How could I be so lucky?

"You are falling or fell?" I whisper.

"Girl! I fell like fourteen years ago. I just didn't know what it was then."

I smile. "Me, too. I fell, too." I hug myself and smile.

"So, let's take an objective look at these dreams. Did you sleep walk this time?"

"I don't think so," I raise the comforter up and see feet that are clean and dry. "No, I didn't sleepwalk."

"Okay, so that's a major improvement. And your fingers obviously aren't coated in dirt."

"True. Clean." I've calmed enough that a small giggle escapes.

"All that is really positive. Also, you had the good sense to call me; that has to count for something!"

"Yes. Excellent point. I'm not keeping all this inside, right? That's an improvement."

"Exactly. I believe this will all end as soon as the funeral is over. You've put so much pressure on yourself, as usual! You have every right to be torn between burying the box and keeping it, but today you finally decide.

"Sometimes making a decision and following through is the quickest path to peace. Haven't you ever noticed that? Someone says, 'What do you want for dinner?' They give you two choices, pizza or subs, and you pick one. Done. My advice, take it easy on yourself for the next twenty-four hours. Don't go checking into a padded room. Not yet. Sound good?"

"Sounds really good. I'll see you soon." I look at the clock and do the mental math, "Eleven hours, thirty minutes." Realizing the funeral is that close comes as a relief.

"See you soon." He makes a smooching sound into the phone before the line goes dead. I curl under the covers and blessedly sleep without dreams until the alarm rings.

At three, loved ones gather under the shelter of the cedar to say goodbye to my mom. I can't shake an icky feeling deep in my gut that tells me I am about to make a mistake. This is not a day to dwell on dark things. It is Mother's Day, the perfect time to rejoice in the life of Sarah Jameson and lay her to rest at last.

As people stream through the front gates of Lakefront Cemetery on this sunny afternoon, I hold my nose against the pungent scent coming from the roses scattered around her gravesite. I am shocked at the massive outpouring. I expected the three Jamesons and a handful of others, but the art community has come out in full force, as well as her fellow gardeners, customers from Aunt Karen's clothing store, and others not familiar to me. After all these years, family and friends still care; proof of a life well-spent, I suppose.

Many of them whisper that I look just like her. It's nice. I touch the garnet through my dress and know my mom is looking down on us and on this spectacle her life set in motion.

The puzzle box feels heavy in a way I don't understand. It could be the tug-of-war in my heart between doing the right thing and doing the greedy thing that makes the box seem like such a burden. Seth said that making a decision would bring me peace. I think I'm ready.

My dad leans close to my ear and says, "I was worried the new caretaker, Erik, wouldn't know how to pull off a perfect funeral service, but it looks pretty good." The grass is lush, the hedges are trimmed razor sharp, and the flowerbeds are filled to bursting with fresh perennials.

Father James joins our family behind the pearly white podium.

Dad says, "Thank you for being here." Father James grins. He pulls a thin stack of index cards from his blazer.

I search the crowd for the Baby Group and find them standing in a cluster a row away. Blaze gives me a feeble wave, Casey smiles, and Seth blows a kiss. My legs might as well be rubber bands. Then, soft as a butterfly, Shadow rubs against my legs. His purr vibrates against my skin, warming me from the inside out.

"What the heck?" I ask my dad. I feel the stress slough off my shoulders like wet snow off a sloped roof, and I breathe.

My dad shrugs his shoulders, "Shadow came here on his own," he answers. "Strange."

I lift the cat in my arms feeling grateful. "You're always there for me, aren't you?"

He rubs against my cheek and his whiskers tickle my nose. Suddenly, he hisses, vaulting out of my arms. Then I hear them. Crows perch above us in the branches of my mom's cedar. They shriek at Shadow, who answers with a low growl. He digs his claws into the tree trunk and climbs the bark in pursuit. He slips and tumbles to the ground and the crows seem to laugh from above. He tries again with the same result and finally slinks off into the crowd. Why is it always crows?

Father James clears his throat into the microphone and his deep, smooth voice announces, "Please, friends, take one big step forward. I promise not to bite."

Laughter echoes across the crowd and Dad gives my hand a reassuring squeeze.

"A few people are still trying to park, so we'll wait another minute before we get started." "Good turnout, isn't it?" Dad asks, and I nod.

We stand together in silence and I search the ground for Shadow. Where did he go? My emotional pendulum swings to sad. I am not strong enough to let go of her. I grab the puzzle box and clutch it to my heart. As I draw in a ragged breath, Father James begins.

"We come together today to honor the life of Sarah Jameson. We gather to celebrate a wonderful life. As I look across the sea of faces, I can't help but smile. You see, the ripples of her life are still at play!

"Gone from this world for many years, Sarah Jameson still moves others to action. Her life and our love for her brought us together today. Go ahead! Take a moment to say hello to your neighbor and bear witness to the fellowship Sarah has created."

And most unexpectedly, a stranger near me offers his hand and shakes mine. We exchange hellos and he whispers, "You look just like her, you know." I return his smile. He introduces himself and says, "She and I were friends in college, and then I became the first person to commission a sculpture from her. It is still the most striking piece in my collection. She carved three crows on a bench, our favorite bird."

"I had no idea," I say.

"In fact, we became friends in college because of the crows. She fed them outside the cafeteria every day. So did I. Anyway, she was a special woman."

I trip on my tongue, sputtering a lame thank you as he walks back into the crowd. Her favorite bird was a crow? I set the box onto the podium, because I can't think straight when I hold it.

Father James's words interrupt my thoughts, "Sarah Jameson did much with the days she had on earth. She was a sculptor, a mother, a wife, a sister, and a friend. I got to spend some time with the Jameson family to prepare her eulogy, and what stood out to me was her boldness. Yes, boldness. She carried out God's work on earth with boldness.

"I heard from her husband, Grant, and her sister, Karen, that everything Sarah touched was made better. I've seen her artwork in parks, homes, galleries, and museums, and recently I've gotten to know her greatest works, Owen and Josie. Sarah made good things. Her life calls to mind a few passages from the Bible."

He opens a leather-bound book and reads, "From Colossians 3:23-24: Whatever you do, work at it with all your heart, as working for the Lord, not for human masters, since you know that you will receive an inheritance from the Lord as a reward. It is the Lord Christ you are serving. And from Ephesians 6:10, "Finally, be strong in the Lord and in his mighty power.

"If we are doing the work of the Lord, we can walk boldly. Sarah walked boldly. God was right there with her. He was her sword and her shield, cutting a path for all her endeavors. His hand will make our work in His name endure forever, as it did for Sarah Jameson. I encourage each and every one of you to walk boldly in life; make a difference as your living tribute to Sarah! Please join me in reciting the 23rd Psalm. "The Lord is my shepherd..." As Father James recites the psalm, I think about how my mom asked me to be her shepherd when she left the puzzle box for me to bury. I'm a lousy shepherd; my flock's lost and hungry, even now as I fight to carry through with her last request.

After the service, as the crowd slowly disperses, Grace steps forward. I am surprised to see her here, happy and relieved as well. She wraps her strong, thin arms around me and squeezes. Owen grabs her around the waist and my dad wraps around the group of us. We break apart and Grace hands me a silver trowel. I kneel onto the soft mat near my mom's headstone and dig.

I ignore my shaking hands and chip away at the stubborn roots. I am going to walk boldly. I can do this. My dad places a hand on my shoulder. This is my job. I need to see this through. The roots give way to soft dirt and the trowel cuts through with ease. *Be bold. Be bold,* I chant in my head. What about the crows? As if summoned by my thoughts, I watch the birds alight from the tree branches and dance in the sky above. They caw and circle.

Owen hands me the puzzle box and I clutch it with white knuckles. What about the dream? She told me not to bury the box. I count ten sets of eyes, eleven, watching me. I can't walk away. Be bold.

"Owen, do you want to say anything now?" Dad asks. I clutch the box.

The boy nods and reaches into his pocket to pull out a pearly pink button and a miniature action figure. "Mommy, I miss you. I think you lost this, so I wanted to give it back." He drops the pink button into the shallow hole. "And, this is my favorite super hero. I call him Captain Gummy because he feels like gum. I want you to have him so you don't feel so lonely down there. Thanks for leaving Josie with us. She takes care of me and Dad and makes sure my hair always looks nice for school. I love you." He crouches down and places Captain Gummy into the hole, and then retreats to our father's side. I set the puzzle box by the shallow hole and give my brother a hug.

There's a soft rustle of movement as Shadow slips through my legs to get to Owen.

"Shadow? Why can't you be a normal cat and sleep on the couch all day long?" Owen asks. He reaches out a hand and Shadow walks under it, getting a long, gentle stroke down his back. The cat purrs and rubs against Owen's legs, leaving tufts of fur across his good pants. He rolls on the ground and bumps at the puzzle box, knocking it into the little hole. He jumps into the dirt after it and scratches the sides, crumbling earth onto himself, and then he leaps out and shakes off his coat. I stare down at the dirty cat that has essentially made the decision to bury the box for me. Part of me wants to reach inside the hole and extract the box, but there's no way I can do it with all these eyes on me.

With Owen plastered to one leg, my dad steps to the grave. He reaches inside his blazer pocket and pulls a piece of yellow paper free. "I want you to know how sorry I am for disregarding your last wishes, Sarah. I was a–Owen, cover your ears–a thoughtless a-hole. I wrote this apology, which is much more eloquently stated." He tosses the folded yellow paper into the shallow grave and clears his throat. "I'm sorry I ever doubted who you were." He wipes his eyes and continues, "Thank you for all the magic you left behind on earth. Thank you for our beautiful children, Sarah. They kept me in the land of the living after you died. I love you."

He digs one more time into his pocket and pulls out a ring of gold. "I will always love you," he says, and he tosses his wedding ring into the hole. Grace links an arm through his and he kisses her cheek.

My hands itch to take back the box. Be bold. Be bold. I look to the sky to ask for a little shield and sword from the Big Guy, and I see the crows. Three crows sit in the branches above. They watch me and caw. My mom's favorite birds were crows. Did she send them to cheer me on? One by one, they dive off the branch and swoop at my head. They whiz by my ears and feathers fall free from their sleek bodies. I cover my ears against the noise, and then I swat the silver trowel at them.

"Let us do this in peace!" I bark. I shovel dirt onto the top of the box until it is buried entirely. I tamp down the soil and rise. "Are you happy now?" I ask. The birds fly away, no longer interested.

I feel worn out, tired, and empty like I do after having a cathartic cry. We buried the box. I hope I feel normal again soon.

"You did good, girl! I'm so proud," Grace says. She wraps me up in a hug and the scent of gardenias engulfs me. I step back and take in our long, lost Grace, and she looks better than ever. I hold my hand to her soft, brown cheek.

"You look like you just got home from a tropical vacation. You look refreshed somehow," I comment. "Where can I get some of that?" I ask.

The Baby Group clusters around us.

A deep, thunderous laugh erupts from Grace and, for no reason at all, we join in until her cousin Erik steps forward.

"Hey, cousin. You all right?" he asks, taking in the crowd of crazies we are. The skin around his blue eyes crinkles, and I know he's fighting a smile.

"Here's the hero of the hour, Erik! How are you settling in? Got all those stuffed heads mounted across my cottage walls yet?" Grace asks.

"You know it! Wish you'd taken those girly curtains down in the bedroom though. They don't match the "Alaska Survivalist" vibe I've got going."

Grace brings her head in close to his and whispers, "Thank you for saving me from myself."

He whispers back, "It was time, Grace. You'd held down the fort long enough. Can't say I'll be around much more than a year. Ben's already calling to ask why you didn't reach out to him first. Did you know that he and Patty just had a baby?"

And as the two cousins catch up, we step away to give them privacy.

I search the cemetery for Shadow, needing to hold something in my arms now that the box is gone. Where'd he go? My friends move about me like a cloud of gnats as I make my way toward the Ghost Forest where the cat ran. I must look like a storm cloud as I race across the grounds in this gray chiffon dress. Seth holds the gate to the Ghost Forest open and we enter.

I see Shadow staring back at me from the mound above Bain's grave. His eyes look wild and I stumble back, tripping on a chunk of tombstone. Seth catches me before I fall. Today, the Ghost Forest makes me feel anxious. I feel scared and vulnerable without the puzzle box and clutch Seth's hand to feel safe. I search the tree branches for the crows. Where are they now?

Shadow rises and stretches, clawing at Bain's grave. He rubs against the tombstone and leaves fur on the edges. He bats at the strange grave and licks his paw, all the time watching me.

The troubling thoughts I hoped to quiet today whisper. I buried my mom's box, with all the last vestiges of her earthly magic, as she called it in her letter. So, why is Shadow still here? If he was part of her magic, he should've disappeared. Maybe my mom didn't send the cat. Then who?

We buried the box and the crows disappeared. The crows! A crow was waiting for me at my mom's grave on Halloween. And the truth clicks into place. Her magic was the crows, like the ones that circled as we buried the puzzle box. Like the crows that blocked me from the black smoke figure in New Market. They were protecting me all along. They were protecting me from Bain McLaren, the stone witch. I shudder.

"Josie, are you okay? You look like you've seen a ghost." I'd forgotten Seth was with me. I unclasp his hand and stare in horror at the red marks I left across his palm from gripping it so hard.

My voice comes out in a scratchy croak, "Seth, I had it all wrong." I tremble as the pieces of the puzzle slip into place.

"Josie, explain." He grabs my hand and I suddenly feel like there are unseen eyes watching us from the shadows of the Ghost Forest.

"Oh, God." I can't talk about this here. I pull Seth through the gate away from this place. As I walk to my mom's grave, I try to explain. "I thought the crows were encouraging me to bury her box.

They were there, cheering me on." He listens and a crease forms between his eyebrows.

"I saw the crows, Josie, but they were just doing what birds do when a cat is around."

"No, they were trying to block me from burying the box. The cat," I shiver, "he pushed the box in the ground, remember?"

"Yeah, but that wasn't on purpose. He's a cat for God's sake."

"Seth, he's the same cat that led me away from my mom's grave on Halloween. The same cat that led me to discover Bain's grave."

I continue. "I had it all wrong. I wasn't supposed to bury my mom's box. Don't you see? Everything changed when the cat led me away from her grave to Bain. My mom tried to use the crows to tell me to keep the box. Her magic was protecting me!" I scream as we reach her grave.

I fall to my knees and claw at the fresh dirt I tamped down just minutes ago. As I claw at the dirt above the puzzle box, I get nowhere. The ground has sealed up somehow, coated over and hardened, and I can't do a thing to free the puzzle box. It is gone to me forever. She is gone for good, after she begged me not to let her go. I fold into a ball and weep until there are no more tears to shed. Seth, poor forgotten Seth, sits on the grass behind me waiting. He offers a clean white handkerchief and helps me to my feet.

JOSIE ON
MEMORIAL DAY

IT IS MEMORIAL DAY; roughly two weeks have passed since my mom's funeral. The Baby Group is gathering at Lakefront Cemetery to visit the graves we rubbed on Halloween. Everything is the same and everything is different. In the days since her funeral, I have become a part of the living again. No more worries about phantom cats and ghost crows. Casey was right. I wanted to be different and special, but I really didn't know anything. Chalk it up to an overactive imagination.

"Sorry, Josie!" Owen squeaks after hitting me with the plastic-wrapped bouquet for the third time, the one soon to adorn our mom's grave.

I grit my teeth. I readjust my grip on the planter I carry and try to muster a little patience. "It's fine. But can you stop whacking the fence with them? We won't have any flowers left by the time we get to Mom's grave!" I bark this last part, watching my resolve to be patient crumble around my feet.

My dad lopes ten feet ahead of us holding hands with Grace, oblivious to everything but her. Thanks for nothing, lovebirds. I slow my pace to create distance between this skipping, overactive boy and me.

The sky above matches my surly demeanor. Stormy, swirling clouds thunder across the sky at a dizzying pace and I have to look at the sidewalk to keep from getting ill. In spite of the thick cloud cover, the air is hot and sticky. I wish I'd picked old shoes over these new ones that are already working a blister into the back of my heel. Sometimes old is better than new.

Why does everything have to change anyway? I liked things the way they were.

In two weeks, we graduate from middle school. In four years, I go off to college. Maybe I'm not ready for all this growing up and moving on! A pigeon coos from the top of the iron fence.

"Shoo! Go away!" I shout, and Owen turns back to look at me, a strange expression across his freckled face, as if I've grown a second head. "What are you looking at?" I snip.

"Josie, you lost your smile. Want me to help you find it?" He reaches at me with tickly fingers, jabbing at my ribs. It is an old joke between us and I muster a fake giggle and spin out of his reach, nearly crashing into Blaze, who's crept up behind us with his gigantic cardboard box. I keep the fake smile plastered on my face.

"Hey, Blaze. What'd you bring for Father Kujala?" I ask.

The box is filled with leafy plants and something wrapped in tissue. "I've got some sage, lamb's ear, white licorice, and this is golden thyme." He breaks off a citron-colored leaf and rubs it between his fingers, and then holds it at nose-level. I take a whiff.

"Doesn't that make you hungry for pork chops?" he asks.

I nod and the fake smile falls away, making room for something better. "But, what's in the tissue?" I poke a finger inside the purple paper.

"It's a cross. I know Father Kujala already has one on his grave, but this one was carved out of soapstone by an Alaskan artist." He unwraps the tissue and the stone shimmers copper, gold, and green in the muted daylight. I reach out and stroke the carving. It is so smooth under my fingers, smooth and cool.

"Beautiful! He's going to love it," I say.

Owen approaches with a wide, toothy grin. "Hey, little dude. What've you got there?" Blaze asks. Owen holds the remnants of our bouquet up for Blaze's inspection and we burst into laughter.

"It's the thought that counts, right?" Blaze asks. And my brother is speechless.

None of the flowers has a top. The plastic wraps around green stems and stray petals. It looks like we plucked the bouquet out of a garbage can on the way here. I realize only Blaze and me are laughing as I take in Owen's bright red face. Fat tears shimmer in his eyes.

I grab the boy and hug him. "Hey, Mom's going to love them. I'm sure she's been watching you sprinkle them all the way here and has been smiling up in heaven."

He wriggles free and says, "Yeah, it's like they do before a wedding, you know? Sprinkle the flowers down the aisle. Do you think Dad and Grace will let me do that at their wedding?"

Not willing to break his heart again by telling him Grace's nieces were already asked to do that job, I say, "Yeah, maybe. Or you could do the most important job of all."

"What's that?"

"You could be the ring bearer. You have to keep the rings safe until they say their vows. It's really important."

"And I might have to bring my squirt gun. You know, in case robbers try to steal the rings, right?"

"Yep, that's a great idea."

We gather inside the gates of Lakefront and the rest of the Baby Group, Mr. Anthony, a man I don't recognize, and Erik join the group. Seth introduces us to Mel Akaka, fresh off the plane from Hawaii, his second trip to Seattle in a month. He thanks Mr. Anthony for his legal petition to Fort Lewis to retain Sergeant Paxton's medical files, without which Madigan Army Medical Center couldn't have confirmed the DNA match between the two men. And in the midst of the conversation, Grace scampers off toward the cottage. She returns with a wooden case the shape of a triangle and whispers something to Seth. He nods and Grace steps forward.

"Mr. Akaka, I meant to give you this on your first trip out here for the blood draw, but somehow it got lost in the shuffle. This was presented to your father at his funeral. He was given a full military service because of his sacrifices for our country during World War II, and I wanted you to have this," she says, handing the case to him.

Mel smiles into the sky and the bright blue eyes that set him apart from his Hawaiian family shimmer. "Thank you for keeping it safe, Grace."

"You are very welcome."

Mr. Anthony steps closer to look inside the glass case at the folded American flag. "Grace, it means so much that you kept this safe. What is this place going to do without you?" he asks.

"Erik's got it covered. Besides, I'm glad to be back at the library. I'm a librarian at the University of Washington now. No more hiding behind tombstones for me," she smiles.

"You are too special to hide behind anything ever again," my dad says. And the two share a quiet moment.

Erik steps onto the road where we stand, and herds us onto the grass. "Watch out folks, I've got a crew coming through."

He gives me a knowing glance and waves the hearse and construction vehicle past us.

Exhaust billows out of the yellow machinery and Seth bends over and whispers, "Mini-excavator, in case you're wondering."

"Thanks, Seth."

Chills run up my legs because I know the two vehicles are for Bain McLaren. They will dig up her remains and transport them to the airport. I grew purple shamrocks for her in a wire-mesh container and added Irish moss across the top so she would have something beautiful with her while she traveled. I hope things go smoothly today, but I'm too nervous to watch as they exhume her remains. We silently look on as the vehicles crawl down the road toward the furthest reaches of the cemetery.

"Since everyone's together, I have something I want to share," Grace announces.

She shifts her weight from one foot to the other. As she fumbles with the strings on her dress, I realize she's nervous, nothing more.

"On Halloween, when I saw you all gathering, I assumed you'd come to vandalize the cemetery. And then Josie pulled art supplies out of that little bag of hers, and I felt awful that I ever thought you were here to do harm. I felt so bad that I did something I hadn't done in a decade. I got down on my knees and prayed. I asked God to send you all on a journey. But, more came of that prayer than I could've ever predicted.

"I don't know if it was Ettore, or angels, or the good Lord himself, but I went on my own journey.

"You included me in your searches, your lives and it felt good. Every night, I went to bed bone-tired, but filled up and content. Then, I dug up my own past and my own mistakes, and things broke apart. I felt guilt and sadness and longing I hadn't felt since my Ettore was taken from me, and I knew I had to get out of Lakefront. That's when I called Erik and begged him to take over.

"And in the quiet of my new apartment, amidst the stacks of books in the graduate library, I searched my heart. Why was I running away from all the good that was brought to my doorstep? What was wrong with me?

"Casey, girl. I'm sorry especially for falling apart on you." Her voice chokes off and on as she struggles to continue. "After you ran away, I thought God was giving me a second chance to take care of someone, so I took you in. But, somehow I ruined that chance. Instead of working to bring you and your family together, I wedged you further apart. I judged your mother. I criticized her to your face, and that was absolutely wrong."

Casey interrupts, "But, that's not true, Grace. You called my mom every day. She told me. I know what you tried to do."

Grace shakes her head and my dad puts a steady hand across her shoulder, and she continues.

"It's true. I tried to make amends. You understand I had to throw you out so you could face your problems? Make peace with your mother."

Casey nods. Grace says, "As far as I can tell, that's just what you've done. I couldn't be any prouder."

"But, you made all that possible." Casey pauses and glances around the group. She looks confident and strong. "You made me believe that I was worth loving, Grace. That wasn't a bad thing."

The two come together and hug, and when they break apart, Grace wipes a tear off Casey's cheek.

"Well, taking you in was never the problem, Casey. I worked through all that pretty quick, and then I was left staring into the mirror. I had poured myself a glass of Merlot, and it hit me like a ton of bricks. I circled it around the glass like you taught me, Grant, and took a whiff. Something about that smoky, fruity odor made me miss all of you so much. I poured the wine into the sink and as I rinsed the glass it hit me.

"At first, I came to Lakefront to watch over Ettore, but sometime between then and now vigilance turned into penance. I gave myself these years as punishment for my hand in Renaldo's death. Something about all of you making me live again broke me from that weight. I couldn't carry it anymore.

"So, that's why I got the heck out of here. I'm sorry if I upset any of you by up and leaving like that, but I've never been one to sit around after I've made up my mind about something." And it is my dad that erupts in laughter.

He pulls her into a kiss and laughs. "That is the truth!"

I take a moment to soak in the faces of my loved ones, the people that would lay down their lives for me, and something cold around my heart melts. My hands tingle and I reach out for Seth. I decide to be bold and see my journey through to the end.

We walk to the Ghost Forest, to stand guard over Bain as they exhume her remains to deliver her back to Ireland. Numb from the cold that has descended in the last two hours, I double-wrap Seth's scarf around my neck as we escort the hearse to the gates of Lakefront. The car slows to a complete stop and we move around to the side to find out why.

That's when we see him. Shadow. I wrote him off to being nothing but a bad dream. He rubs against my leg, but I know what he is now, and I shoo him away. I hope he disappears for good after Bain is off to Ireland. I remember what I have in my purse and I rap on a window as the hearse slips past. The driver lowers his glass.

I shout, "Hey! I've got something of Bain's. Open the back, please."

The driver hits a button that swings the tailgate free; inside sits a dirt-encrusted coffin. I lay the stone fetish on top and swing the door closed. I tap the roof like I've seen in countless cop shows on television and the hearse pulls forward.

No more phantom cats or angry crows. As the sky cuts in two, rain pours down on us until Seth pulls me into the shelter of a mighty oak. While we wait for the squall to subside, he kisses me.

JOSIE AND THE JOURNAL SKETCH

TEN HOURS LATER, I collapse onto my bed, not even bothering with pajamas because I am so tired. I shake off my shoes and rub the bloody wound on my heel, but it doesn't sting like it should.

I miss my mom tonight. But, I know she's up in heaven watching over us, because I feel her like sunshine on my face when I choose to pay attention. I fall asleep without brushing my teeth, and when I wake, the sky out my window is black. For some reason, I remember the journal, the one I was given as a thank you for reuniting Bain with her family.

I slip it off the bookshelf and crack the weathered, black leather binding. The parchment is creamy yellow and the handwriting is in faded, sepia-toned ink. "Private diary of Regan McLaren," it says in careful cursive writing.

I thumb through the pages until my eyes get too heavy to read any longer. I set the book onto the nightstand, and a page flutters free, falling to the ground. I pick it up and squint into the crude black and white drawing scrawled across the page.

A sinister woman stoops under a wide tree trunk. Long black hair falls over her thin form. She holds a knife above her head and chisels at the roots of a tree to make a hole. She stares into me with black eyes. Her torso drips with blood, blood that falls onto the soil soaking into the tree roots.

I drop the paper as if it might bite my fingers if I hold it a moment longer, and I remember the picture I took so many months ago behind the Pioneer Cabin, a picture of a flock of crows that broke a malevolent spirit into a thousand pieces. *The birds were protecting me.* And as the horror sinks in, something bangs against my window and I jump. This wasn't only about my mom; it was about Bain. It was always about Bain.

I rush to the window and stare into the foggy darkness. I clutch my ears to block out the chirps and twitters that come through the glass. They are the cries of a dying animal. As I squint into the pane, I see a flurry of feathers.

A dead bird lies on the windowsill. I stumble backward and tell myself not to look again, but my eyes flick back to the window. The cat I invited to live in our house not long ago, sits on the window ledge, teeth buried deep inside the bird's throat. He stares at me through the glass as he rips into the poor bird.

My mom was trying to save me from Bain and I had no idea. The cat feasts on the dead bird, eyeing me as if to say I am next. My legs crumple and I hit the hard wooden ledge on the way to the floor.

Everything goes dark.

The End

Coming soon:

The Stone Witch Society

The next installment of
The Stone Witch series.

MORE GREAT READS FROM BOOKTROPE

The Collection by **T.K. Lasser** (Paranormal Romance) A human lie detector and an immortal art thief are thrust together in a ruthless plot of high stakes acquisition and murder by a black market art buyer.

The Water Sign by **C.S. Samulski** (Science Fiction) In the post-diluvian world of the future many children find themselves lost in the fog of war.

No Shelter from Darkness by **Mark D. Evans** (Paranormal) In the post-Blitz East End of London, orphaned teenager Beth Wade is bullied for looking different. But it goes far deeper than looks. With a growing thirst for blood and the arrival of a man who could kill her just as easily as help her, Beth must fight for control of her life . . . and of herself.

Dead of Knight by **Nicole J. Persun** (Fantasy) King Orson and King Odell are power-stricken, grieving, and mad. As they wage war against a rebel army led by Elise des Eresther, it appears as though they're merely in it for the glory. But their struggles are deeper and darker.

Demon Weather (Da Silva Tales, #1) by **Chico Kidd** (Fantasy) The adventures of Captain Da Silva, who has lost an eye and gained the power to see ghosts. A rollicking, rip-roaring read.

Discover more books and learn about our
new approach to publishing at **booktrope.com**.

CPSIA information can be obtained at www.ICGtesting.com
Printed in the USA
LVOW06s1237090913

351538LV00003B/23/P